WARPAINT

A Cadence Drake Novel

HOLLY LISLE

Cool, fun, and instantly available to everyone

Over the years, I've built some cool extras for this world... and I don't require an email sign-up for you to get them.

I have downloadable full-sized walk-through models of Cady's spaceships and space stations, a full-sized walk-through model of the *Longview,* a full-sized walk-through model of the City of Furies, and a just-for-fun model I built to demonstrate story generators in one of my classes:

https://hollylisle.com/spaceships-and-worlds/

These are in Minecraft, and I update them when I have the time, and I do NOT offer support on them. They're just there for folks who are familiar with Minecraft (or who have a friend or kid who is) and who want to walk around inside the worlds and read the signs where I've asked myself questions.

I do have a mailing list for folks who like my Settled Space stories:

https://hollyswritingclasses.com/fiction/settled-space-readers.html

I'm emailing the pieces of an extra story to folks who

join. Something to keep in mind if you like Cady, or the Longview folks.

Holly

Content Editor: Matthew Turano

Cover Design © 2019 by Holly Lisle

Book Design, Holly Lisle

Cover Art: © iordani from BigStockPhoto.com

Photo Work: Rebecca Galardo

PUBLISHER'S NOTICE
This is a work of fiction. Seriously. Resemblances to real characters, real
solar systems, real spaceships, and real faster-than-light travel are entirely
coincidental. Names, characters, places, and tech are products of the
author's imagination, and any brilliant guy who appears halfway through the
story is not your cousin Bob, no matter how much he insists otherwise.

The cookies, however, SHOULD be real.

ISBNs
PRINT: 978-1-62456-069-9
EPUB: 978-1-62456-007-1
MOBI: 978-1-62456-006-4
SMASHWORDS: 978-1-62456-070-5

For Matt

DARKOUT

Chapter 1

Crazed, starved, they clung all over my shuttle's hull, bashing at it with anything they'd been able to grab. Those crammed up against the molei-bond forward viewport were trying to bite me, unable to understand why they could see me, but couldn't reach me. The screeching and clicking of their teeth and claws on the hull made my skin crawl.

Insane, all of them. Staring, mindless monsters — Legends, they called themselves when they were func-tioning normally, or vampires, though in truth they were neither. They were humans who'd changed themselves into horrors.

They'd bled dry the little moon I was trapped on, and without fresh human blood to drink, hadn't been able to hang onto their sanity long enough to escape. Starvation had stripped them of their pretense of humanity, revealing their pure essence. It didn't kill them, though. It would *eventually* kill them... probably. I knew they could exist in this nightmare state for months. Maybe they could go on this way for years. I'd never seen one dead of starvation.

But they had to starve to death sometime, didn't they?

I would have destroyed them, had there been fewer of them, had there been more of me, had I had a way to shoot them with the one weapon that would have destroyed them — my blood. Only by my best guess, there were a couple thousand of them on and around my shuttle, swarming over it and me like ants on sugar. Like rats on a corpse. Like... name your own nightmare.

They blocked my sky.

My shuttle hull was moleibond. Best stuff in the universe, moleibond: light, impervious to radiation, tough as hell. You can subject it to massive gravities, hit it with fire or light of any composition or in any concentration, slam it with projectiles of any composition, and you won't scratch it. You can shoot massive shock waves through a moleibond hull and turn the entire contents into pudding, and a cleanup crew can come along with a big hose and a pressure sprayer and have the flawless hull ready for resale in the time it takes to wash out the goo.

Moleibond is indestructible unless you have an Anabond drill or Anabond cutters — but even a little resort moon will have a few Anabond tools on it, because you do have to fix the stuff that breaks inside.

So my theoretical outside survival time was limited to the arrival on the moon of a fresh meat shipment — a transport full of live tourists. The second one of the Legends got fresh blood, his mind would start working, he'd realize that my survival was their destruction, because I had seen what they were, and he'd go get the damned Anabond cutter and come after me. All he had to do was cut a hole in my hull. One hole, and I could not leave the atmosphere.

My *real* survival time was under a week, though, because I'd failed to fully stock the emergency rations.

Carelessness on my part, or exhaustion, maybe. I had three days worth of water, and almost no food. It would have been enough had I been hoping for quick rescue from my home ship, in orbit around the moon.

Only problem there was that my home ship belonged to me, I flew alone, and at the moment, I was on the damn shuttle.

And I couldn't call out via comlink for help from anyone else, because once I landed, I discovered that all live com to and from Tropica Petite had been cut. Tropica Petite was running a stream of programmed fake chatter through its com, making the resort seem like someplace real people would still want to go, and someone had set its autodrone to handle shuttle landings.

No rescue would be coming.

Meanwhile, I was — judging from the appearance of my attackers — the last source of living blood on the verdant, terraformed moon, and at least two thousand mindless monsters were determined to have me for lunch.

In my favor, I had myself, my shuttle, my wits and my rage.

So things weren't looking too good for my long-term prospects.

And this had started with a job I took just because I had to keep my ship in space, had to pay my docking fees and refueling, had to pursue the monsters I hunted. This was not supposed to have anything to do with the damned Legends. This was supposed to have been a milk run, a simple job of locating two women who'd extended their vacation without notice and getting them back home to their worried, waiting husband.

LESS THAN TWENTY-FOUR HOURS EARLIER, I was sitting in the Hammergirl Lounge in the bleak, windowless core of the Hammerfield Mining Station, a space station that spun just outside the farthest edge of the Hammerfield asteroid belt. The miners were indies. They owned their own rigs, and mined and processed the rare ores civilization craved. The indies had a nice setup going. They owned their own means of production, they were partners in their methods of distribution, and between hard work, intelligence, and skill, they'd made a name for themselves as a station full of winners. Hammerfield Station's biggest *byproduct* was billionaires.

However...

The Hammergirl Lounge was a strip club, and not, as I had requested, a quiet, comfortable restaurant.

Worse, my client was late. This annoyed me, because I had better things to do with my time than fend off scantily clad women who wanted me to buy them drinks, or drunk drill jockeys who wanted to buy them for me.

In all fairness, a woman sitting alone at a table in a strip club is going to cause that club's denizens to make certain assumptions.

I had the long blonde hair and blue eyes of Candibelle on the stage at that moment, the coffee-with-a-touch-of-cream skin of Torch — who looked anatomically impossible to me — and the Old Earth Asian cast to my features, including the almond eyes and epicanthic fold, of the drink girl who'd just asked me if I wanted to buy a lap dance from any of the girls on stage. All of that courtesy of three biological fathers, and the psychotic mother who'd bought their genes and paid some illegal gene-hack to rearrange them to make me. On the other side of the equation, I had my mother's height, and the solid muscle I'd earned living at two Gs aboard my ship and working all those muscles through daily combat routines. And I was wearing a ship suit, which fit like skin because it was designed to stay out of the way.

While I doubt I was anyone's particular fantasy, I apparently looked like someone who intended to be on one end or the other of a financial transaction that included the removing of clothes.

My name is Cadence Drake, but I was officially dead, so I was using a deep-cover alias created by a friend of mine named Storm Rat.

My client had contacted me as my alias, JT Loggins. The real JT Loggins had been murdered by space pirates, and one of Storm Rat's minions had identified the body during a salvage sweep, and had grabbed all details of her identity, which Storm Rat had cleaned for resale — JT had been from some low-tech world with abysmal document security, so Storm Rat had been able to alter the few records that described her short, miserable arc through existence to make her look like me. Not having to have melanin lifts or bone restructuring or any of the other things I'd had to live through to get the job done in the past was a surprising benefit to being officially dead. It was, as far as I could tell, the *only* benefit.

My client's name was Nat Phangar. We hadn't met, we hadn't spoken, and billionaires can buy excellent security, so I was having no luck worming my way through Hammer-field Station's comlinks into the station data. All I knew about my prospective client was that he was rich, and that he paid a lot of money to keep his personal life and details completely off the datastream.

And that he was late, and getting later.

I don't work for people I don't know, so I hadn't yet accepted the job. I wanted it, though. A two-hundred-fifty-thousand-rucet retainer was sitting in escrow, verified and validated, to be dropped into my — well, JT Loggins' — credit account the instant I greenlit the contract.

But I didn't get a dime of the money if I didn't agree to the contract, and fuel and supplies for a Trans-Fold Navigation, or TFN, ship are expensive. First, there's the fuel for the two sublight drives. Rare-earth-stabilized bismuth trioxide isn't cheap. But the fuel for the TFN unit, which takes the ship through the folds of hyperspace from origami point to origami point, is incredibly expensive, and I was getting low. So I kept my ass in the chair, ignored the naked bump-and-grind up on the stage, cringed at the loud music, and nursed my non-alcoholic drink.

Then a short, blonde woman dressed in a miner's jumpsuit, her hair mussed and her skin flushed, pushed her way into the club like someone in the middle of having a very bad day. She looked around, studied me, frowned, and walked toward me, her steps hesitant.

"Red and black ship suit," she said as she reached my table. "You're JT Loggins?"

"You are...?"

"Nat Phangar," she said, and held out her hand.

I stood, took her hand, and tightened the muscles in my right palm just enough to shoot the microfilament nanoviral needle into her palm as our hands touched. She didn't even flinch. "JT Loggins," I said. "With the first name you gave, and you referring to yourself as the husband of the two women named in the contract, I assumed you'd be male."

The corner of her mouth twitched. "Knowing Cherry Korvitch, from whom I bought the recommendation, I assumed you'd be a petite, curvaceous, green-eyed red-head. Life is full of surprises." She studied me for a moment, assessing, then added, "She raved about you."

"It wasn't because of anything personal, I assure you," I told her, sitting back down. "I did a job for her, she liked the results. I don't get involved with my clients."

"That had to have been a first for Cherry. Not that you're her type, but I could see where she would have made an exception. As for me and my situation, though..." She sat carefully in the seat opposite me, and her eyes narrowed. "I'd figured when Cherry recommended you, you'd be..." She paused.

You can see people working their way through the thicket of gender politeness and prejudice. I could have jumped in, but generally it's better to let them get where they're going in their own way.

She sighed and shrugged, "I assumed you'd be *lor*. Not *hinter*."

"You lost me. *Lor*?"

"Women who prefer women and who want multiple permanent relationships. *Hinter* is anyone who isn't *lor*. I figured you for *lor* because Cherry was so pleased with you, and thought it meant you wouldn't have a problem with my arrangement with my wives."

I shrugged. "With a few exceptions, I have no interest in my clients' personal lives. I won't work for slavers, thugs, pedos, or killers, and before I sign off on your contract, you're going to give me proof that you're none of those, and you're also going to convince me the women you want me to find are not hiding from you." I took a sip of my drink and continued.

"And you must understand that while I *will* find your wives, if they refuse to come with me, I will not use force to bring them to you against their will. I'll record their statement, present it to you as my evidence, and you'll still owe me costs and follow-through for having found them. As for who you choose to be with, I don't care. If you're all adults and all there because you want to be, I have no problem helping you."

She studied me, and sighed. "But you don't go my way, do you?"

"No. I don't go *any* way anymore. The man I loved was murdered, and the part of me that could love anyone, or desire anything, died with him."

"Then I apologize. From my assumption, I figured this place would appeal to you. And I like it, and the food's good. Speaking of which." She waved one of the barely dressed drink girls over and said, "Pepper, two Surface Specials."

The girl left, and Nat turned back to me. "The work out here is hell, but when you own your rig and can run processed ore straight through the station system, the money's amazing. So I can afford you. And my wives love me. I take good care of them, I make them happy, I make sure they get to live the lives they want." She grinned. "And I get to live the life *I* want." Her eyebrows furrowed and her eyes unfocused. She didn't say anything else.

"But..." I prompted.

"I'm not sure why they're running through so much money at the resort. It isn't like them. And neither is the fact that they haven't sent me any personal coms since they got there."

I nodded, getting a feel for the real issue. "You realize people change," I said. "You think you know them, and then you discover they've met someone, they've been seduced by some other sort of life..."

"Not Nicci, and not Sugar. They're the two best wives I have."

I sipped my drink to keep from saying anything stupid.

"Seven," she told me with a little smile, so apparently my eyes asked what I'd managed to keep my mouth from blurting out. "I have seven wives. Most of them I met here."

The food came, brought to us by a woman introduced to me as Summer. The food was all real. Fresh fruit, fresh meat, fresh vegetables, all surface-grown, all flavored by a real sun in a real sky. I ate everything my client put in front of me.

And I watched her. She ate the food, too, but I've discovered *they* are capable of eating food. They simply can't digest it. They chew, they swallow, the food sits unchanged through their atrophied gastrointestinal system until — best guess here — they regurgitate it.

I was looking for a sign that she was one of them. My recent past is a nightmare of up-close-and-personal encounters with bloodsuckers, and I'd given myself every advantage I could to survive these encounters. The microfilament I'd injected into the palm of her hand carries only a few dozen copies of the nanovirus that lives in my bloodstream. That nanovirus, injected into the bloodstream of a Legend in large numbers, reacts with the nanovirus that changed the normal human being the Legend had been into a blood-drinking, nearly immortal, almost unkillable, superhuman nightmare. Within minutes of a full dose of the nanovirus, the nanovampire would swell up and explode.

All it did to humans was turn their blood into a substance poisonous to vampires.

To my way of thinking, *win-win*.

Sitting across the table from someone who suddenly swells up and explodes, scattering bits of flesh and blood across a large room, however, causes unwelcome attention.

So I have a microfilament injector implanted in the palm of my right hand. When I tighten my palm in contact with human skin, the injector delivers a tiny dose of AntiLegend nanovirus that allows me to make sure my client is not a vampire already, and to guarantee that my client will not become one between the time I take the job and the time I return to get paid.

I found from my one experience working — unknowingly — for a Legend that you can't count on collecting your money. They think they don't actually owe you for services rendered, you being what they consider lunch.

In half an hour, the virus would reach a level in my client's bloodstream that would, if she were a vampire, cause her skin to develop a fine sheen of sweat. It would have no physical effect on an unmodified human.

If I saw the sheen, I would publicly, verbally, and somewhat loudly accept the job instantly — because any time you eat someplace public, someone somewhere is recording everything you say. I would then tell my prospective client I would require the upfront portion of my fee two days from that date, sign the contract, and leave. She would accept that I was in her employ, and return to her plans. I would put as much space as I could between myself and her, because within twenty-four hours, the nanovirus with which she'd been injected would reach critical mass, and overrun the nanovirus she'd put into her own bloodstream when she decided to become a monster, and she would come to a horrible, messy, permanent end. And I'd have an alibi. I was someplace else when it happened, and with my client dead, I wouldn't get paid.

Only she didn't develop that sheen of sweat.

So we ate good food, and she watched women take off their clothes and told me which ones she was considering as possible future wives, and I took her contract because she sounded very much like she liked the wives she had, and like she was afraid someone might be taking advantage of them because they were beautiful and young and rich and trusting, and because they were staying at a pricey, elegant resort likely to be full of people who wanted to be friends with women like that for less-than-honorable reasons.

It all made perfect sense, it all seemed so clean and clear and obvious, and I thought the thought you *never, ever* permit yourself to think if you want to survive, which is, *"I need the money, and how tough could it be?"*

Chapter 2

So there I was with my view through all my shuttle's viewports comprised of my personal nightmare made real — gaunt, crazed, fanged faces and starved, clawing bodies layered on top of each other so deeply midday was nothing but more night to me.

For them, things could only stay the same. They would stay where they were until food arrived, and some of them would kill, eat, and get smart, and then come after me.

For me, the situation could only get worse. Every second I lost came off a clock numbered in days.

I started digging through my supplies, inventorying.

I had very little in the way of weaponry. Two sticky pies — deep-space concussion weapons that latch onto the hulls of ships and use the rigidity of the hulls to blast amplified shockwaves through the contents of those ships. Doesn't damage the hulls. Purees all contents — including people — within the blast radius.

Sticky pies are next to useless in any open space. They can destroy something attached to them, but they have no way to compress soft tissue if they don't have a rigid surface against which to compress it.

I had my two neatly hidden, illegal ship-to-ship guns. These were loaded with hole-punchers, twenty-five rounds apiece.

The guns, if found in most star systems, were worth a sentence of from five to fifty years in local prisons. Survival is worth *more* than five to fifty years in local prisons, so I had them. They were useless against anything that could go through hyperspace, but there are lots of in-system criminals, too. In-system criminals own in-system ships.

From a shuttle's perspective, the great thing about in-system-only ships is they're *not* moleibonded, and they're not moleibonded for two reasons. The first is this: there are no natural in-system forces that duplicate the nightmarish twisting, folding pressures of hyperspace, so all things being equal, moleibonding is a useless extravagance.

And the second reason is this: a moleibond hull makes a ship approximately ten thousand times more expensive. Interceptors, whether owned by governments or criminals (and if you can always find a difference between those two, you're better at this than I am) are faster than shuttles, and a hell of a lot more maneuverable in tight spaces. All the pilot of a TFN shuttle needs to do if attacked by a non-TFN craft is punch a hole or ten in its hull. The atmosphere in-ship either leaks slowly into space, or decompresses rapidly, depending on the size of the holes. Either way, the folks in the ship lose their will to fight.

Hole-punchers work well against humans, too.

They are useless against nanovampires. Nanovampires are not supernatural, not undead. They have nothing to do with those disgusting Old Earth legends of magically animated corpses who seduced women, drank blood, and only came out at night — except for their origin in someone's screwed-up desire to control people.

Nanovampires are the products of science, of an engineered nanovirus that adapts users at a cellular level to be stronger, faster, blood-drinking living people capable of going out in daylight, of crossing water, of tap-dancing on silver crosses and looking at themselves in mirrors, seducing and controlling men and women against their will... and of auto-regeneration. When you punch a hole in a nanovampire, the hole closes over, heals up, and stops being a problem for the vampire before he's even aware that he's been hit. The monsters were designed to withstand anything but being burned at tremendous temperatures, or having their heads separated from their bodies. And the nanovirus in their bloodstream is hellishly efficient in patching them up on the fly.

Fifty rounds of hole-punchers wouldn't even distract the bastards.

And that was it. The shuttle weapons were supposed to be a stopgap to get me safely back to my ship.

And all of that meant this: I had nothing else to throw at the vampires but me.

It was in the despair of realizing this that my idea formed. It was a pretty little idea. Dangerous, but if it worked the payoff would be lovely. And if it didn't, I was dead anyway.

I had a RexSurvyve emergency med-kit aboard, which is what you have to make do with when you don't have a Medix handy.

Folks on technologically regressive planets don't have Medixes. Neither do folks whose worlds are controlled by religious or political demagogues. But rejuvenation technology, which started on my home world of Cantata, has spread through settled space, and in civilized places (including on my ship), you can throw your badly damaged self — or friend — into a Medix, and it will fix everything that's broken, cut, crunched, skinned, poisoned, or otherwise damaged.

You can't reju a corpse. Dead is dead. But anything else? The Medix has you covered.

My kit contained two bags of sterile artificial plasma expander with tubing and vein-taps, wound spray ("Fills and Pressurizes a One Meter Wound in Two Seconds!"), four press-on heart restarters, five skinjects of non-addictive painkiller, instant splint wrap, and the Emergency Cookie. The Emergency Cookie is RexSurvyve's gimmick, and it's the reason I've never had a med-kit made by anyone else. The Emergency Cookie is a big cookie, about the size of your hand with fingers outstretched. It's vacuum-sealed, guaranteed to last forever if the pull-tab is untouched, and you can get refills of the Cookie for free any time you have to purchase refills of any of the other items. The med-kit company claims to have thirty different flavors of Emergency Cookie, all guaranteed delicious and reconsta-free, but there is no way of knowing which one you'll receive. Every Cookie is a surprise.

I — and I'm sure a lot of other space travelers — have "lost" items from my med-kit on numerous occasions, and paid to have those items refilled, just so I could get more Cookies. You can't get them anywhere else, or in any other way, and they really are delicious.

That's why my shuttle med-kit has four press-on heart restarters and two plasma expanders, instead of one of each. But just one Cookie, because I always ate the new ones as they came in.

On my ship, the *Corrigan's Blood*, I have twelve Emergency Cookies tucked away in their RexSurvyve kits... and that is down from an all-time-best level of twenty-three.

Where the exquisite Emergency Cookie is concerned, I have no willpower.

I sighed, took out both one-liter plasma expander bags and the wound spray. I punched holes in the top of one of the two bags with my knife — so much for sterile — and poured the fluid into the trash receptacle. I then sprayed wound spray lightly over the hole. The wound spray expanded quickly and dried within seconds, and made a tight, if ugly, seal.

The average human body has about five liters of blood in it. You can go down a quarter of a liter and only be slightly woozy. You go down half a liter, you're going to be less than functional. I was going down a full liter — roughly twenty percent of my body's volume, which is enough to make your heart race, your breathing speed up, your skin sweat, and to cause you to get dizzy or faint. But I needed a lot of fresh, warm, tasty blood, and because there was only one of me, and at least a couple thousand of them, and I was only going to get one shot to save my own life, I had to make my one shot count. I needed as much blood as I could get into the bag.

I hung the full bag of plasma expander from the side-light next to my cockpit seat, and lay the other bag on the floor beside me. I ripped the membrane covers off the vein taps, and pressed them against the skin on the insides of my arms just below the crooks of my elbows. I felt the icy cold of the antiseptic numbing agent, and then nothing else. Both taps glowed green. I set the line of blood flowing out of me into the empty bag on the floor to half-speed, and set the line of plasma expander flowing into me to quarter speed.

I'd empty faster than I'd fill, but I wanted the blood bag

on the floor to be as pure and free of fluid expander as I dared. And I wasn't sure how much I dared, so I was a little conservative.

Then I opened the cookie pack, and ate the cookie. Golden-Flake Chocolate Chip.

I made the cookie last as long as I could. While I had it, I didn't have to think about the warmth of my blood in the tubing against my skin as it flowed out of my body. I didn't have to think about how strangely heavy and personal that tube felt. I didn't have to think about how I was getting dizzy, or about the way I was having to work to breathe.

I nibbled the cookie.

Good cookie.

And then there was no more cookie, and I felt oddly bereft, but also warm and fuzzy and very far away from myself.

I closed my eyes.

When I opened them, my sky was still nothing but monsters. I didn't remember the one in the red sunsuit being there before, but I did remember the one in the blue-and-white resort uniform, so the Legends were jockeying for positions nearer to me. I wasn't looking at the same crazed eyes and peeled-back lips and razor fangs I'd had before. I was getting to see those belonging to the truly *motivated* nightmares.

The bag on the floor was full of my blood. The bag hanging from my sidelight was empty.

I'd either passed out or slept, but either way, I didn't feel too badly. My fluid volume running through me was the five-ish liters it should have been, and the plasma expander carried red blood cells around just as well as my regular plasma. Not as many of them, unfortunately, so I still felt light-headed.

But I was ready for the next step.

I pulled off one vein tap at a time, and sprayed the skin with wound spray. Felt the skin pucker and tighten.

If I stood up, I knew I'd be dizzy, but I didn't need to stand up. My launcher for the sticky pies was on the right side of my control console, hidden under the shuttle's in-flight entertainment system. Which worked, by the way. Sporcs and cops and regulators all check that sort of thing when they're searching your ship for illegal weapons, and Storm Rat's weapons guy had done an amazing job of making the entertainment system elegant, sophisticated, and entertaining.

I did the careful keypress-plus-faceplate-press combination that opened the launch chute. I removed both sticky pies, and used a combination of wrapping the blood-bag tubing around one of them, then spraying it into place with wound spray to make sure it would stay put.

I dropped the modified sticky pie into the chute, put the unmodified pie in after it, and closed the panel. A quick swipe of the right controls brought up my weapons HUD. I aimed the sticky pie at a building with a flat, solid surface the sticky pie could adhere to, which was a good two-hundred meters from my position, and launched.

My modified sticky pie exploded on impact, the air two-hundred meters away from me filled with a mist of warm, fresh, living human blood, and the vampires clinging all over my craft vanished, thudding and scrabbling and clawing through the writhing mass of each other, launching toward that smell — mindless, uncaring about traps, incapable of suspicion or reason or any sort of thought.

They were the incarnation of hunger and horror fighting to drink their own death.

The instant the last sound of scrabbling against my hull

vanished, the weight of a couple thousand nightmares all trying to claw their way into my shuttle designed for a maximum load of five people vanished, and I pounded the launch sequence into the controls and lifted free of what remained of Tropica Petite.

There would be fewer vampires on the resort moon the next time someone visited it. My poisoned blood would ensure that.

I hoped *all* those monsters would get a good taste.

ALL FREQUENCIES ARE MONITORED.

You can't know by whom or for what purpose; you can't know how often or how intently, but outside whatever tiny shell of privacy you manage to build for yourself and those you love, someone somewhere is listening.

This is the universe we live in. You say nothing without acknowledging that someone else might hear it, and if you have something to say that you know people who want to kill you are listening for, you don't say it anywhere it can be overheard. You don't even hint about it.

What I'd found on Tropica Petite was deep inside the hell I'd lived in for the past year, deep inside the warzone where I'd been fighting and losing ground against the nanovampires who'd gained nearly every advantage by tossing aside their humanity. And the sane, well-fed versions of the monsters I'd left behind, the ones who had used the advantages they'd bought to sidle into positions of power and prestige and fame — with the goal of turning settled space into their own private feeding ground — were listening for any sign that someone had recognized them for what they were.

They knew I'd known what they were. That I'd found a way to kill them. Word spreads through the corridors of power.

But they thought I was dead.

And I knew they weren't.

These two facts were my advantage.

It was not enough of an advantage, and I was losing ground.

So I sent a simple, clear-text transmission to Nat, with the following words. "As you suspected, your wife found religion. Will meet as agreed for further instructions."

I hoped that Nat would be a smart woman, would figure out from the numerous errors I'd hidden within the plain text that I'd run into a big problem that I couldn't discuss — and that she would keep her mouth shut and show up at our agreed-upon rendezvous point, her favorite strip club.

The whole job had been in-system, which meant no origami points for me to negotiate, and no high-level tracking I'd have to elude — but it also meant the vampires had established themselves in the system, and could be anywhere.

I didn't get a call-back. That either meant Nat was being smart, or that Nat was in trouble.

I showed up at the club with enough disguised weapons on me to take out the entire station. And Nat wasn't there.

Trouble, then.

I asked around, casually. Said Nat had asked me out on a date the next time I was on the station, and I'd called and left a message, and she hadn't showed up.

And one of the dancers said she'd been killed a couple days earlier in a freak explosion out where she was mining.

I nodded, and thanked the dancer, and went back to my ship. Hit the telltales I'd set up to let me know if anyone had tried to tamper with the ship while I was gone. Everything came back clean.

Nat could have died in an accident. Only I didn't believe that.

I felt the pull of people in power making things happen.

And I got the sudden, overwhelming urge to get the hell out of the entire star system before some of those things happened to me.

Chapter 3

I set a course that jumped my ship through four origami points in quick succession, and I came out the other side of the last one shaking, vomiting, paranoid, and barely hanging on to my memory of who I was or why I cared.

Hyperspace twists you. While you're in it, you become everyone you are in every alternate reality, everywhere and everywhen, and you become the overself from which all those otherselves emanate, and for a while that is both an instant and an eternity, you are immortal, infinite, omniscient, deific, divine.

And then hyperspace spits you out and rips away everything but the one thin, frail, mortal self that belongs to you, and if you're weak you go mad, and if you're strong you roll up in a ball and weep over everything you are not and can never be, and if you're a tough bastard you drink some coffee — or occasionally throw up and *then* drink some coffee — and you pretend it doesn't get to you.

My ship AI has been trained to have coffee waiting for

me the instant we're through, and after rough passages, to have an autobot at my feet to take care of the mess.

And sometimes my pretense of toughness is almost convincing.

But after two origami point insertions in two days, and mid-point course changes on both of them, I wasn't fooling anyone — had there been anyone around to fool.

I knew in advance what a wreck I was going to be, though, so before I jumped, I'd set up a list of steps I needed to take, and fed them into the AI.

The AI prepared vitamin-laced food and told me to eat. I ate. The AI told me to sleep. I slept. The AI woke me and told me to shower. I showered. Finally, the AI led me to my Medix and instructed me to do a full reju.

So I stripped and lay down in the box, let it seal me in, felt the various tubes and connectors snaking across me, and then felt the gentle flow of life and health running into me.

Twenty-four hours later, I emerged from reju a complete human being. Self-controlled. Focused. Sane.

Sane-ish. I still had my mission, and my mission was crazy, so I couldn't lay claim to sanity.

But I was going for help, so from my perspective, I was at least looking for real sanity in the right direction.

I'd intentionally burned my past life in order to keep breathing, and to protect people who had known and helped me — if I was known to be dead, none of the evil in the universe would go after those folks to twist information concerning my whereabouts out of them by any means necessary — and the means my enemies would use were unthinkably horrible.

Better my friends thought I was dead. Better everyone thought I was dead.

I had one place left in the settled space where people knew I was alive. Where I could run when I was in trouble.

Where I might be able to buy myself some help.

Tegosshu. And on Tegosshu, Storm Rat.

Using protocols we'd established years ago, I sent a message to my old friend Storm Rat, letting him know I needed clearance to visit Tegosshu, the harsh, ugly little private world he owned and ran.

This time, though, I got to send it via the datastream.

The datastream is new.

Until about a year ago, settled space communicated at the speed of light — which, when over two thousand solar systems in a galaxy are involved, is damnably slow. Urgent communication traveled by courier through origami points, or by comships that made weekly rounds through origami points to update the data in Spybees.

The thing you have to remember about this system is that human operators controlled what was updated.

Along came a man named Peter Crane, who financed the research and creation of interstellar ships that could do two things such ships had never been able to do before. They could change their destinations while in hyperspace, and they could, while in hyperspace, locate uncharted origami points.

There were only twenty-seven of these ships, and through my unfortunate interaction with Peter Crane — now dead — I have one of them.

But those twenty-seven ships, nicknamed *sidewinders* for their ability to evade the rigid folds of an origami point, and what they could do, pushed law enforcement to create their own technology to track these new ships through space.

Law enforcement needed instant updating of the

Spybees in every system to keep track of the movements of sidewinders. It needed the Spybees to all keep the same time, so it would be possible to know when sidewinders left, and when they arrived, so that clear lines of movement could be built. And it needed a constantly updated stream of data that covered every known destination point in settled space that would tell it when and where ships it was searching for appeared.

Law enforcement hasn't yet built a perfect system — for which I'm deeply grateful — but it has built a better one. The new system depends on tiny, light, inexpensive communication orbs that copy all current system info from one Spybee, pop through the origami point to another, download the updated information to that Spybee, upload its new information, and pop back through the point to repeat the process.

The balls have a long technical name, but some history drib called them pingballs, apparently after an Old Earth game, and they've been pingballs ever since.

Billions of them flow through settled space from every known point to every other known point, constantly, and every time a new origami point is discovered and a Spybee is placed, every other Spybee in settled space gets notice of its existence and sends its own pingball to start communicating.

There are two lovely things about this, especially if your job is to find people or their treasures that have gone missing. The first is that it's now possible to sit beside any up-to-date Spybee and send and receive information from any other human-settled location.

The second is that the information you receive is no longer filtered through a human censor. Everything goes everywhere.

Almost everywhere. Some systems are resisting the placement of modern pingball-transfer Spybees.

So I was in a completely different solar system when I sent my message to Storm Rat.

It took me less than five minutes to get my all-clear, along with coded navigation points through a new minefield.

I set my course through the origami point to Cantata with a programmed midpoint change to come out in the Tegosshu system. The Tegosshu system Spybee had been programmed to mangle all ship-passage related data. No one who visits Storm Rat has a trail.

Tegosshu. Not quite home. But I liked the place.

However, Storm Rat's world is a world in the same way your best friend's ugly baby is cute. You call the baby cute because you don't want to offend your best friend, and you call Storm Rat's big floating rock circling its distant, weak yellow dwarf sun a world because Storm Rat is the purveyor of the universe's best illegal technical expertise, and you love his tech, and he loves his ugly rock.

The damn thing is too small to have an atmosphere, or gravity worth mentioning, so your ship docks on one of a dozen disklocks attached to a moleibond gravdrop spindle that runs from what he calls space to what he calls surface. While you're there, you breathe generated atmosphere and walk around in generated gravity, but you eat almost-real food and you drink wonderful water because when Storm Rat bought the place, the rich guy who discovered that pale, distant dwarf suns make lousy sunsets had already drilled out the center of the rock and filled it with fresh water and a cycler to keep it that way, and had installed Krawitz RealSun genfarms. Pour reconsta in one end, and the processors subjected it to sunlight and fed it to clone cells and from the other harvested meats and vegetables and fruits and grains that looked and tasted almost like they'd been grown under real sunlight on Old Earth.

Badger — my murdered best friend, partner, and on-again, off-again lover — and I had done business through Storm Rat's paranoid empire of services barely legal and deeply illegal for almost six years. I guarantee before the two of us ever got within shooting distance of Tegosshu that first time, Storm Rat knew more about the two of us than we knew about each other, and we'd been best friends since childhood.

Tegosshu had been where I ran after Badger died.

If anyone in the universe was still my friend, it was Storm Rat.

He was a short, quick, nervous man with pointed features, a stringy physique, and a mind that comprehended destruction and survival and how to accomplish both with unequalled brilliance. You could see the road he'd taken through hell when you looked into his eyes. He did not talk about his past. Badger, who had been a master at uncovering other people's secrets, had been unable to find anything about Storm Rat beyond the facts that he had purchased Tegosshu legally, for about the price of the equipment that had already been installed on it, and that he had done so for cash, and under the name Storm Rat. He had then paid an ungodly sum of money, also in physical rucets, to have Tegosshu's designation changed from Class J40K Resort World, to Class W97T Independent Home-world, Non-Allied, and had declared himself its first citizen and entire government. If he travelled, he would have to do so under Tegosshu documents — Badger had been unable to find records of him elsewhere in known space. Because we'd both preferred to know who we were dealing with, we'd looked. Hard.

So. Storm Rat was smart. Talented. Probably rich. Invisible in the universe under any name but that one, and lacking a past before he bought Tegosshu.

And when I came through the gravdrop, he was standing on the landing, waiting for me personally, alone as I'd requested. He gave me a long, questioning look and a quick hug. I hugged him back, hard.

He said, "You look like shit."

"Which is twice as good as I feel. I ran into trouble I can't talk about over open air. I'll give you the details, but it needs to be just you and me, and we need to be in the most secure spot you have here."

The landing was in a moleibond bubble, with a view of the craggy, dead surface and Tegosshu's pale dot of a sun. We didn't take the usual surface route to the tech center, though. Instead, he led me into a palm-locked gravdrop. We dropped a good sixty meters, past three separate ID checkpoints, each of which used a different input method, and stopped at the bottom, where another security door opened into a small, round room with a round table and a dozen chairs in the center. We didn't stop there, though. Storm Rat walked to a blank curve of wall on the opposite side of the room, and stood very still in front of it, with his face only a few centimeters from the wall.

After a moment, the wall showed a seam and slid open, revealing a split corridor of ten meters of moleibond blast shield on deep, grooved slider tracks.

"How the hell did you do that?"

He grinned over his shoulder as we walked through the corridor. "Breath analysis."

"Damn."

"One of my guys made it for me. No one opens that door but me, and if I'm dead, no one will ever get in here again. The door scans my whole body, and reads my core temperature, carbon dioxide content, oxygen content, moisture ratios, and DNA content, and makes sure my veins are full of moving blood, my heart is pumping, and my lungs are cycling air."

"Damn," I said again. I thought *I* was paranoid.

"This is my safe room," he said as we reached the end of the corridor. He tapped a panel on the wall, and the massive sliding block of moleibond moved shut.

Storm Rat's idea of "safe," I realized, was an archaic cell block built to withstand anything a universe could throw against it.

I tried to imagine what it would take to get through ten meters of solid moleibond, and could not come up with anything. Cutters? Ha. Cutters will go through the fifteen molecular layers of a standard moleibond hull in about ten minutes, and the thirty molecular layers of a warship in about half an hour, because of the geometric curve of layer density to strength characteristic of moleibonded materials.

If you hold a cross-section of standard moleibond hull, you can just barely see it. A cross-section of warship hull is about the thickness of a human hair. Sundippers are built with hulls about triple that.

Ten meters.

The walls had the gloss and translucence of tinted moleibond, too. "Ten meters all around?" I asked.

"It's a sphere extruded into bedrock," he said. "Ten meters at the corners of the cube we're in is the thinnest point."

I'm not entirely sure, but I think a fifty-meter sphere of

moleibond with a twenty-meter cube carved out of its core might withstand the implosion of the universe.

To my right, an ancient spaceship air recycler hissed softly. Across the ceiling, a grid of embedded strellitas gave off the sort of eternal twilight I'd known on Cantata. Storm Rat said "Light five," and other lights came on, filling the room with comfortable daylight.

Everything was self-contained, self-sustaining, built for the long haul. Nothing had a connection that went outside or through the walls. He held up his portable com and switched it off in front of me. "Turn yours off, too, and we're alone in the universe."

I held the comlink on my shipsuit until it blinked red, then went black. Switched off my wrist compac.

"What kind of trouble can't you talk about in front of my people?" Storm Rat asked.

He pointed to a table in the corner, and I took a chair. He got us both drinks, and sat across from me.

"You know about the Legends."

He gave me the look people give you when you've said something so far beyond stupid that they're suddenly not sure they want to talk with you anymore.

"Don't," I told him. "Just don't. How many people work for you?"

"Eighty-nine." He shook his head and grinned a little. "Ninety as of yesterday."

"How many of them do you know personally?"

"Ninety."

"How many of them—"

He waved a hand to stop that line of questioning. "Every person who works for me is an ex-slave, and a Tegosshu rescue from slaver colonies, from the holds of pirate ships, or from deep space after a pirate attack. Every

31

single person who works for me, I have risked my own resources and in many cases my own life to free.

"There are no exceptions to this, Cady. Not one. Each person on this world, including me, was a slave or was captured for sale, or left for dead by slavers. I discovered most of my people by tracking slaver networks and reading buy-and-sell classifieds from slaver feeds concerning people with skills I needed. When I found them, my people and I went in and wiped out every pirate or slaver who stood between me and them. I cut loose all the slaves within my reach, and the ones I had come for, I offered jobs that would let them use their skills to get back at the people who'd tried to destroy them."

His glance in my direction was defiant.

"And I make sure the people I hire make spectacular amounts of money doing what they love, and that they get to see the fruits of their labor out in the real world. They're loyal to me. I'm loyal to them. We're all in this together."

I waited, saying nothing.

He waved a hand to encompass his safe room. "We are all warriors together, my people and me. The worst people in the universe want us dead for what we do," he said.

"No," I told him. "They don't. If you're very, very lucky, the *worst* people in the universe don't yet know you exist."

"You're saying the Legends are worse than slavers."

I nodded. "How many of your people have traveled anywhere since they joined you here?"

He frowned. "They're loyal, Cady. I trust every one of them with my life, and they're the same way about me."

"Not my question. How many?"

He glared at me, his shoulders stiff and squared, his hands pressed flat to the table. "All of them at one time or another. They make good money. It'd be a hell of a life if they couldn't go anywhere to spend it."

"It *is* a hell of a life." I sat across from him, sipping the drink he'd brought me, watching him. More than anything, watching his skin, looking for that first sheen of sweat, waiting to find out if, when I'd hugged him, when I'd injected him with the serum in my blood that kills vampires, I'd killed a monster or assaulted a friend.

A touch of the door panel would open it, but I wasn't sure if it had to be his touch. If he'd been infected — if he'd joined the other side — the odds were pretty good that I was going to die in this self-contained twenty-meter cube of his. He had four beds in the place, a reconsta generator, four Medix units. Food dispensers, drink fabricators, recreation in the form of readers with massive libraries, music libraries, viewer libraries. I would live as long as I chose. Alone. Would die when I chose. Alone.

But I would be helpless to affect what was happening outside the moleibond walls of this terrifying best prison in the universe he'd built for himself.

So I willed him to not break a sweat. I willed him to still be the real Storm Rat, and not a monster wearing a Storm Rat skin.

"What are you staring at?"

"A man who has ninety vectors to hell living with him, and who thinks trust means something where the Legends are involved."

I felt like a traitor and a villain for injecting him. For not trusting him. But I knew Legends.

I hadn't felt any unreasonable attraction to him. But I had felt comfort, and warmth, and joy at seeing his gaunt face, and as much as I wanted to believe all of that was real, I knew how convincing the seduction of a Legend was, and how carefully it could be manipulated to enhance what you were already inclined to feel.

But he didn't break a sweat, and I rested my head on my arms so he couldn't see the tears that were dripping from my eyes and running down my nose.

"Cady?"

Crying sucks. Even if people don't see you doing it, they can hear you sniffling like an idiot.

I sighed, and lifted my head, and wiped my eyes, and blamed my tears not on their real cause — my betrayal of him — but on my ugly, unpaid, failed last job. "I hired out for a nice, well-paid little retrieval mission — finding and extracting a few ex-strippers married to a very rich woman with a thing for lots of pretty girls at once. Instead, I ended up on Tropica Petite in the Caulder-Burdash system with my shuttle pinned under — best estimate — two thousand starving Legends who had devoured or converted every tourist on the moon, and who had gone so stupid with starvation they couldn't escape. I left my calling card and got away, and if I was lucky, all of them are dead now. If I wasn't, there are a few survivors who will feed off the next batch of tourists that lands there. But when I returned to give my client the news, she'd suffered a convenient accident, and wasn't around to spread the word about Tropica Petite and her missing wives."

He was studying me, frowning. "I've never seen you cry."

"I don't," I told him. "Crying slows me down. But something is wrong, Storm Rat. Big-time wrong. Things are going down-chute in ways that feel bigger than they look, and being JT Loggins is keeping me from hooking into my old network. No one knows JT Loggins. She has no rep, she has no history, she has no backstory. As JT Loggins, I'm barely getting by, finding an occasional job, rebuilding pieces of the network Badger and I created together and that right now I can't touch. I can barely keep my ship flying, and when I can't fly, I can't hunt them. I can't fight them." I shuddered. "And you know there's never any news about them, but I have this gut feeling I'm losing ground. Badly."

I told him how I dealt with the vampires on Tropica Petite, and while he laughed at me when I told him about the Emergency Cookie, the rest of the time his face just got grimmer and grimmer.

When I finished, he sat there for a long time, staring at his hands, thinking. I kept quiet.

When he looked up, I could see he'd come to a decision. "Let me make sure I understand all the points before we work out how we're going to do this. You need to get your own identity back, because that's the only way you can afford to go after the Legends, and the only way you can use your old contacts. You need a clear, legitimate title to the *Corrigan's Blood*, because without it, you're going to end up in prison on the first world that does a background check. You need to make sure no one can charge you for the murder of Peter Crane or Haskell Corrigan. You need to have your record cleared in that business with your mother trying to kill you back on Cantata, so you don't have criminal charges showing up in those same background checks."

I hadn't even thought about my mother. "I don't think I have any outstanding charges relating to my mother's death," I told him. "But I do have a problem that goes back to when I was a kid." I told him how my mother had framed me after she murdered my brothers and sisters and my stepfather.

He shook his head. "I'd forgotten that. You are more of a challenge every minute, Cady."

"Sorry."

He grinned. "Lucky for you I like challenges." He studied his fingers. "You need to have people you can trust to back you up, so you don't get stuck someplace in a shuttle again with no one knowing you're missing. You need a better way to kill Legends than one at a time with your blood darts. And at the moment you're essentially broke, so you need all of this on credit."

I hadn't actually thought that far ahead. But he was right. That was what I needed. "Hell, Storm Rat..." I said, but again he cut me off.

"I can do that," he said.

Chapter 4

I lay in my bunk on my ship. Everything was sealed off, closed down. My personal compac was off, my ship-suit com was off, and shipcom was holding all contact. I was alone. Storm Rat told me he needed some time to get his weapons guy, his stats girl, and his nano expert working the Legend problem, and he wanted to put his money guy and his lawyer to work clearing up my backtrail so I could become myself in the universe again, albeit with the real worst people in the universe once again alerted to my survival, and once again after me.

He was keeping the team to the barest minimum at my request, and had his people working sealed off from everything else. He called me paranoid.

The man who owned a fifty-meter moleibond-sphere hidey-hole called me paranoid.

I guess it took one to know one.

In any case, he needed his time, and I needed mine.

I got out the doppler chip I'd recorded when Badger and I were alone for the last time, going up the gravdrop in the *Hope's Reward* together.

I put it into the player.

Lay down on my bunk.

Tapped the button that started the recorder on playback.

I felt the lump in my throat at the sight of the old *Hope's Reward* as I walked up to the airlock, Badger half a step behind me and to my left in the umbilical, taller than me, broad-shouldered, tense.

I wanted to touch him, to feel the warmth and the weight of him next to me, to run my fingers over the furred skin of his forearm and the back of his hand.

I wanted.

But the two of us were shadows from an earlier time, from a single year before when the universe still had light and hope in it, because it still held Badger.

Three-dimensional gray, a bit translucent, the two of us hung just off the right side of my bunk, and I rotated the image so I could see Badger's face again.

It was, in its gray-on-gray way, perfect. Doppler recorders capture everything going on within their radius simultaneously, by bouncing waves with different penetrations through objects and recording the info those waves brought back, along with any sounds that hit the recorder sensors directly. Thanks to Storm Rat's folks, I had a mostly illegal doppler recorder embedded in my right thigh, under a fleshtab only I knew existed. The recorder was indistinguishable from the bone to which it had been fused, and the fleshtab that allowed me to insert doppler chips only opened when I touched the skin along the line of it with a specific pressure and in a specific direction.

Like Storm Rat's door, it wouldn't open for anyone else. And like Storm Rat's door, both the bone-graft doppler recorder and the flesh-tab access had been created by his people. As far I know, I'm the only person in the universe who has either.

"Welcome back," the *Hope's Reward* said as I put my palm on the access panel.

The airlock slid open and Badger and I stepped into the gravdrop holding hands. We reoriented ourselves to ship down, which was at a ninety degree angle from station down, and dropped to the first level. The rotation of everything around us was disorienting to watch.

We rode up the drop in silence. "Medichamber for you, too?" I asked as I stepped out.

Badger stepped out of the drop behind me, and said. "In a minute." He caught me from behind and pulled me against his chest. He wrapped both arms around me and pressed his face into the back of my hair.

I kept my eyes open, because when I could see it, I could remember it. I could feel his touch, his warmth, the hard muscles of his chest pressed against my back, the fierce strength of his arms pulling me tight against him.

"I love you, Cady," he told me. "I will always love you."

"I love you, too." I could see myself struggling with the question I had to ask him, watched my discomfort and fear, saw in my expression the knowledge that the three times he'd asked me the same question, I'd told him no, and the third time, told him to never ask me again. I watched myself come to resolution, and turn within his embrace to look up into his face. I watched his face as that earlier me asked him, "This is old-fashioned and corny and I don't care. Will you marry me, Badger? Will you have children with me and grow old with me?"

I saw his arms tighten around me, and felt them in memory, and remembered the stubble of his beard, less than a day grown, as he pressed his cheek against mine. "If we get out of this alive," he told me, "that will be the first thing I do."

I had the player set to stop there automatically. I didn't allow myself to watch that scene often, but when I did, it was the only part of the scene I could bear to see. Minutes later, he would be dead, I would fight desperately to save him, and I would fail. I relived *those* moments in my nightmares. Nothing would make me see them reenacted while I was awake.

I only wanted to see Badger alive. I only wanted to see him when he told me that he would marry me, that he loved me, that we would be together. I told myself he was still out there somewhere, that in some other universe the two of us had gotten out of the final confrontation with my mother alive, and that in some other reality, we were safe, had a little home some place, maybe had a kid together, were happy and in love in a million realities that were free of the nightmares living in mine.

But I still wanted him now, in *my reality*, with *me*.

I WOKE WITH A START, from a dream in which I had not locked access to the ship, and as always when I woke in that fashion, I was already swinging my feet to the floor, and I had the blood-dart gun in my hand.

And as always, I'd locked the ship down tight, I was the only living creature aboard, and my dry mouth and racing heart were the products not of real danger, but of paranoia.

Paranoia will save your life if you let it, though, so I didn't berate myself for being silly. I simply ran through an all-systems check from top to bottom, skipping nothing, then turned personal com back on and reconnected to shipcom.

And was instantly bombarded by pending messages from Storm Rat.

Message one: He needed anything I had on my agreement with Peter Crane, the deceased owner of my ship, the *Corrigan's Blood*, and any proof I had that Crane had reneged on the terms of our deal.

Message two: He needed any information I had on the Legends, on my dealings with them on Tropica Petite, and anything I could give him and his researchers who were going to find out the scope of the problem I faced going up against the nanovampires.

Message three: He needed access to my financial records.

Message four: What was taking me so long getting him his information?

Message five: What the *hell* was taking me so long getting him his information?

Messages six, seven, eight, nine, ten, and eleven: Are you dead in there?

Message eleven had come in six seconds before I turned com back on, and I opened the channel to Storm Rat, who started shouting at me, and I cut him off. "It was personal time, Storm Rat. I needed to be alone, and I needed quiet. I'm better now, I'm fine, and I'll walk everything you need into the station. Take me to a conference room, and bring everyone who is going to be touching this data with you."

I started gathering data. I had a lot of it. I pulled my entire bank of doppler chips and duplicated them. Chips are awkward, they're primitive, they're slow. Physical data is subject to loss, destruction, or decay. I know this.

Info streaming is convenient, and storing info in your

stream safe is reliable and generally secure enough, but no stream safe is proof against a sufficiently talented, highly motivated data hacker.

What isn't in the stream can't be hacked out of it.

I kept all my growing bank of Legends data out of the stream. I did not want anyone looking for that sort of information to know what I knew, or to know that I was the one who knew it. Humans died around Legends like cattle died around butchers, and for much less reason.

I had duplicates of all my doppler chips in three separate off-ship locations. I had a small credit account set to pay each location monthly, and I kept six months' worth of payments in the account at all times, topping it off by a manual payment more or less monthly. If I stopped filling the account, the first missed payment to each location would trigger the contents to be broadcast through the stream. The broadcasts would trigger a week apart, and would go out from three different major hubs in settled space, and they would reveal the Legends to anyone hooked into the stream who was tracing that particular band.

Paranoia, again. I didn't want the Legends to benefit by killing me off. I wanted to hurt them from beyond death. That was the only way I'd been able to think of to do it.

When I'd copied all my doppler chips and put the originals back in their hiding place, I duplicated my financial accesses, my contract with Crane, and the worm codes to a handful of stream feeds I watched that I knew carried vampire traffic. I did another full scan of the ship, just to make sure I hadn't missed anything the first time, announced my readiness to Storm Rat, and locked the ship down behind me.

Storm Rat and I met in a conference room in Tech Research. Unlike the conference room that fronted his private safe room, this one was plugged into every conceivable point on his planet. A wall of infoscreens could connect in an instant to offer either one-way observation or two-way communication with any section of the compound, or all sections at once, plus to clients hanging overhead from one of the spindles, and with a few gestures, Storm Rat could drop a client onto a screen with one of his techs, and the two could have a private or observed conversation with each other.

At the moment, all the screens were black, which was odd because generally when such screens are off, they're transparent. It took me a moment to realize they were all viewing the dark side of Tegosshu.

"Sit next to me." Storm Rat took a seat, and I took the chair on his right. "You're going to meet my lawyer first, so separate out anything you have that could be used to give you a claim to legal ownership of the *Corrigan's Blood*.

"Already done," I said, and handed him the first packet, which included duplicates of my contract with Peter Crane and the doppler chip that recorded his attempt at defaulting on payment by murdering me. I had not received the rest of my money for that job.

The lawyer arrived.

"Cady, this is Books. Books, Cadence Drake. She's a friend."

Books and I shook hands, and I studied him. His skin was about twice as dark as mine, with blue rather than brown undertones. He was short, wide, and muscular, with a shaved head and eyes dark as space.

"A pleasure," he said, and turned to Storm Rat. "She one of your rescues, too?"

Storm Rat shook his head. "She's a free agent. Grim

past, lunatic mission, skills I'd buy if I could — but she prefers her own company."

I grinned at Storm Rat. "I dread your ugly baby — that's all."

He raised an eyebrow at me, and I waved it off. I'd never told him my ugly baby analogy for his world.

I thought if I got to know Books, I'd like him — but then, he was one of Storm Rat's people, and he had the intensity of folks who work with a purpose, and value their purpose. I watched Storm Rat give him my documentation, and I quickly explained what was on it.

I kept it short. Every lawyer I've ever known has guarded his time jealously. I respect that.

When Books left, Storm Rat said, "Now you'll meet my financial manager. He's going to have to dig pretty deeply into your finances to put money into places where you legally won't have to pay taxes on it, and then connect those into your regular accounts. If you have anything you need to keep him out of, let me know and I'll tell him where to stay."

I laughed. "I'm damn near broke. I have my JT Loggins accounts through Stellar—"

Storm Rat groaned when I said the name, and muttered, "Those asses?" under his breath.

"—and three monthly payments I make that are a virtual dead-man's switch. And there's my Cadence Drake account, which I have not touched because if I had, monsters would have looked up from their kills to start sniffing around for me again. Where money is concerned, I have no secrets."

"We'll fix that," he said with a grin, and I met Tarko Armbruster, the first dwarf I'd ever seen outside of holos.

I had to bend down to shake his hand. His eyes actually went above my cleavage when I did.

I have made an art of not staring at people; being someone others stare at has ingrained in me that courtesy.

Tarko didn't share it. He gave me a long, full-spotlight up-and-down stare, shook his head, and asked, "Who screwed around with your genes, darlin'?"

"My mother, the psychopath." And then, meeting his direct stare and deciding I could play his game, I said, "What's your excuse?"

He chuckled. "Low-tech home world, no genetic engineering capabilities, no pre-natal diagnostics. I had things rough, but they could have been a lot rougher." He gave me that long, thoughtful stare again. Then, as if he'd decided to chance something he didn't usually say, added, "I discovered if you give folks something odd to look at on the outside, they don't look any deeper."

I considered that, and chuckled. "Actually, I've discovered the same damn thing. Which is why I wear the face my mother gave me."

He grinned at me as if I'd passed some sort of test, and I realized I liked him a lot.

And instantly became suspicious of him — people I liked without knowing them had shown a tendency to grow fangs and try to kill me when I relaxed.

Storm Rat said, "Tarko is a criminal mastermind, a financial wizard, a genius whose depth is impossible to calculate."

To my raised eyebrow, he added, "He's the best man in the universe for the work you need done."

I nodded, keeping to myself my opinion on handing over my financial details to a criminal mastermind. It made a certain odd sense when I allowed myself to get past my dismay. If Tarko was that good, he could commit his crimes against people who actually had something worth stealing. He'd know I was of no interest.

Tarko had been watching my face. "My genius is more in creating original wealth than in liberating it from others. I only steal from slavers, and the worlds that support them," he said.

"I have some new folks you'll be able to add to your list with a clear conscience," I told him.

He gave a noncommittal shrug, took my financial packet, and left.

When he was gone, Storm Rat told me, "So far, no one on your team knows that anyone else is on your team. However, I'm bringing in my statistician, my chief nano-engineer, and my top weapons guy together, because to accomplish what you need, they're going to have to work together."

"You're firewalling everyone?"

"Yes. I haven't seen what you have yet, so I can't assess the need for myself. But I know you're competent, so I'm trusting your judgement. I'll be with them while they go through the data; I'll learn what you've faced and what settled space is facing as they do. My hope is that we can get back to you inside of three days, let you see the bigger picture so you'll know what you're fighting and give you our assessment on the tools you'll need and the strategy you'll use to fight more effectively."

"Perfect," I said.

I focused on the introductions. The statistician was Bluejay, a curvaceous redhead with bright green eyes and an impish grin — not the person I would have thought of when I thought "plays with numbers." She was enthusiastic about what she called "your project" and interested in the "phenomenon" I'd faced. I found myself curious to see what she thought once she'd seen the doppler images from Tropica Petite.

The nanoengineer was Sky, who reminded me of a younger, female version of Isas Yamamoto, the man who invented the origami drive, who died long before I was born, and who I considered my spiritual father. Her eyes were the same shape as mine, but golden-brown. She'd pulled her hair back in a tight knot. She looked... distant.

Finally I met Wire, Storm Rat's declared top weapons guy.

"Storm Rat told me he wasn't the one who invented the gravity shear. Were you?"

"You're *that* Cady?" he said in response. "I was so happy to hear it worked."

"*I* was so happy it worked. Half a dozen vampires were cutting their way through the umbilical to get us, and we hit the panic button on the gravity shear — it tanked our power, but there was nothing left of them but goo. Your experiment saved us. I've always wanted to say thank you." I hugged him. "And thank you for working on this for me."

If Wire was any indication, Storm Rat was devoting the very best people he had to my problem.

I gave the four of them all my other info: the comlink data; copies of every doppler chip recording that included any dealings with one of the Legends, starting with Peter Crane and my first test of the doppler recorder, and ending with the one on Tropica Petite; my blood samples; a couple of vials of pure AntiLegend serum; and, all the other documentation Badger and I had accumulated since my first run-in with a Legend.

We all shook hands again.

And then I went back to my ship to wait.

In my meetings, I had shaken hands with every single

member of "my" team, and if Storm Rat was as thorough as I'd asked him to be, had injected every person who would come in contact with my data. If there were vampires among them, Storm Rat would find out before I would. If he discovered one of his trusted employees had exploded, he would know Tegosshu was compromised.

And then he would come looking for me.

The possibility existed that I had killed one or more of Storm Rat's trusted people, his best associates, and from all appearances, his friends.

Worse, I'd liked all of them. Once upon a time, liking someone was a good thing, something you wanted to have happen.

Once upon a time, people were all people, and making you like them was not the way they got close to you so they could kill you.

Maybe all of Storm Rat's people were still people, not monsters. If nobody exploded, I could put my paranoia behind me.

Chapter 5

I'd had time to have Stewleen and Corned-Beefarole Hash out of the ReconCuisine. The ReconCuisine was better than the old Berliner Reconsta-Chef equipped on my first ship, the *Hope's Reward*.

But reconsta is rarely great, and this wasn't either.

I'd had time to get comfortable in my bunk with my reader and the newest Sabo Talagarvy mystery.

I'd had time to let my body sink into that blissful state of relaxation where the world and all the horror in it melted away.

So the warning blat of my ship alarm as Storm Rat's face appeared on the infoscreen above my bunk scared the wooly furbits out of me. Storm Rat stared down at me, looking like death. "Need you in Tech now," he said by way of greeting. And then cut com.

I dropped my reader, rolled to my feet, and started running. Storm Rat could be abrupt, but this reeked of the sinister.

"How long since I've been aboard?" I asked the ship as I ran.

"One hour, thirty-seven minutes, twenty-eight seconds at my mark. Mark."

"Shit."

That wasn't long enough for anyone to have exploded.

It was long enough for one vampire planted on the team to see what I'd been dealing with, to realize I was the enemy, and to take Storm Rat hostage to bring me in.

How many, I wondered? How many monsters had I shaken hands with this time?

Was Storm Rat about to discover he'd been betrayed by not just one but a multitude of people whose lives he'd saved?

It wouldn't surprise me. Nothing surprised me.

I dove into the gravdrop, rolled out on the bottom level of the ship, and palm-lapped the bio-keyed emergency panel I'd had installed by the exit hatch. The moleibond door slid up to reveal weapons. I strapped on my gun belt and made sure the clips in both serum shooters were full. I also grabbed two full wrist recharges and slipped them on, and as I palmed the hatch, shouted instructions to the ship. "Security One lockdown on my exit, no conditions. Repeat, NO conditions!"

"Confirmed Security One, no condi—"

The closing hatch cut off the rest.

No one was on the dock. I expected it to be locked, expected to have to find an external path to Storm Rat.

But it wasn't locked.

Right. They were smart.

They were going to let me walk into their trap, going to let me reach whatever position they'd staked out, where they would surround me.

They were doing what I would have done. Let the enemy do all the work, let my prey come to me.

If it weren't for Storm Rat, I would have run — but Storm Rat was more than a useful contact. He was a friend.

So I'd go to them.

I engaged oxygen and pressure on my shipsuit, and switched on the fabric armor. Doing this would slow me down a little, but the only way I could save Storm Rat was if I was alive to reach him.

If the Legends had control of his world, Storm Rat was in trouble. If he needed my help in a hurry, he wasn't in his safe room.

He looked like he'd been in Tech. I'd only caught a glimpse of the backdrop during his brief cry for help, but the layout looked like what I'd remembered, and the screens in the background had been alive and busy.

I didn't go for clever side-routes. I ran straight in.

I knew as I was doing it that I was going against the ancient Sun-Tzu dictum to always be where the enemy did not expect you.

However, I was doing a great job with another of his dictums, that of appearing weak where I was strong, and strong where I was weak. Storm Rat had sounded frantic, so I'd take what I could get.

My deception, such as it was, came in the form of my shipsuit, some settings I'd changed in my personal Medix reju unit... and my weapons.

My shipsuits sported not just flexible fabric impact armor with inbound missile/energy sensing, but shaped, pressurized atmosphere shields that made traditional helmets unnecessary. These suits were good for thirty hours of high-capacity oxygen use each before a recharge.

My suit was fully charged.

Better yet, it didn't look like a commercial-issue shipsuit.

I'd programmed the ship's central autofabricator to make me suits that looked like the work of several popular designers who'd costumed shipsuits for actresses who wanted to look stunning in their roles as captains of space-craft. Or the mistresses of space captains.

The designer ship styles had caught on in the real world, and tourists bought and wore them for luxury cruises.

There were whole lines of ship wear — *not* actual space-worthy shipsuits — that now looked like what I had on. Professional crew made snide comments about them. Professional captains would never be caught dead in them.

I looked like I'd been caught off guard, as if I were prepared for nothing.

As for my body style...

Tarko Armbruster chose to wear a dwarf's body rather than have a medichamber rebuild him without the genetic defect — because it caused people to focus on his appear-ance rather that him.

He'd looked at me — really looked at me — and somehow had realized I was doing the same thing. The shipsuit was part of it, but there was more. Since Badger's death I have manipulated my own appearance to look softer. Rounder. More femininely helpless. I dump that look when meeting with clients, because I need to have them see me as competent from the instant I walk through the door.

But... let me be blunt. The rest of the time, I've reset my medichamber to give me bigger tits, a smaller waist, and a rounder ass. I've discovered that when the eyes of the enemy rarely make it above your chest, the enemy is a helluva lot easier to take by surprise.

Moreover, in keeping with the "Hi, I'm blonde and

chocolate and yummy all over" look, my blood-needle guns are built into the cases of standard Karvoti Safe-T-Stun short-range personal protection devices. And because they're bio-keyed to me, customs agents testing them find that they truly are stun-guns, and set to a stun level that might give mice a headache, but wouldn't stop a man.

A number of (male) customs officers since my little makeover have gently explained to me that for my personal protection devices to do me any good, I'm going to have to be willing to power them up high enough to hurt an attacker.

And I nod, and smile, and thank them very kindly.

And shake their hands.

Just in case.

So whoever was monitoring the corridors as I ran toward Tech Research saw a woman with useless weapons and useless clothing stepping defenseless into their trap.

Which is what I needed them to see.

Unhampered by anyone, I burst through the doors of the Tech Research conference room, dropped, rolled and grabbed both guns, and came to my feet to the sound of screaming, to find what looked like the whole team I'd met hours before trying to crawl under the conference table, or frozen to their seats in fear.

Even Storm Rat, who *knew* me, looked shaken.

"Cady," he said, his voice wavering, "what are you doing?"

"Rescuing you," I said, looking at the people who were failing to act in the least like the fast, lethal monsters I'd been hunting and killing for the past year.

"From what?"

I looked at him, flatly annoyed. "You didn't tell me what. You just said 'Get down here now,' and from the terror in your eyes and the color of your skin, I had to assume that someone offscreen had a gun pointed to your head and was forcing you to give me a message you didn't want to give." I still thought that, and kept my weapons up and my back to the wall and scanned the room for the threat I couldn't see.

He was staring at my weapons, still leveled at his people. "Why would you *think* that?"

"Because if I don't act based on the worst case at all times, people I love end up dead."

His gaze flicked to the blood-needle guns. "Those aren't stun guns?"

"Of course not."

"No. No. Of course not. Can you put them away, then?"

I kept them aimed at the people who were hiding, and kept my voice as level as possible. "You're scared to death, Storm Rat. Your people are on a hair trigger. Something big is wrong. What?"

He cleared his throat. "Bluejay just finished running the number simulations on the data you gave her, and called in my mathematician to double-check her numbers, and I've called your whole team in here to figure out how to deal with what we're facing. We needed to show you the projections."

I stared at him. His skin was the same shade of pasty gray I'd seen on the shipcom. He still looked terrified. But his gaze met mine directly, and there was no lie in his voice. No shift in his eyes. No one had a gun to his head. He was telling me the truth.

My arms dropped to my sides. The fighting tension that had coursed through my body, the dread that I was going to be facing off against an unknown number of nanovampires

armed with nothing but my blood darts against their terrifying speed and strength and mesmerizingly lethal powers
of seduction — all of that had been reduced to facing off
against a now-less-than-perky redhead who wanted to show
me graphs.

If my knees hadn't turned to jelly from relief, I would
have hurt Storm Rat right then.

"Life or death, Storm Rat," I growled. "Before you send
out a panicked com, consider whether the issue is life or
death. If no one is going to die right NOW, you do not have
an emergency, and you do not blurt out a scared-shitless
message and *then cut com*. You say, 'When can you come
down here so we can show you the special little ***holomath***
presentation we have put together for you?' Emphasize the
word MATH when you do this. And *then* you give me time
to answer. You do not make it sound like someone has a gun
to your head and his finger on the trigger."

Storm Rat looked unrepentant. He said, "This is worse
than a gun, Cady. It's the end of humanity. Darkout is
coming. And I think we're already too late to stop it."

I STARED at the holochart in front of me. It was a classic
exponential growth curve limned in glowing blood red. The
line starting at the left was almost flat, then began to arc
upward. The initial slope was gentle, almost imperceptible,
until at the midpoint of the curve, where it rapidly steep-
ened to an almost vertical line.

Bluejay was explaining her chart. She was all earnest-
ness and sincerity, and I was transported back to Meileone
and my tutor and his angry insistence that my learning the
deeper meaning of upward curves and downward curves

and long lists of numbers unattached to anything were essential to my having value as a human being.

"...and from a population of just two at my estimated start date of five years ago — because of factors I am categorizing as Sexual Derivatives, Power Derivatives, Compulsion Derivatives, and Delusional Derivatives — this nanovirus is replicating itself into new hosts at a rate that is currently doubling every six months, but as you can see the rate is accelerating along with the numbers of infected. While I am unable to validate cases of total host saturation beyond your one doppler chip from Tropica Petite, I am extrapolating total population saturation on all worlds where the nanovirus exists within six months..."

Her words washed over me.

I couldn't look away from the graph. On the curve of the holochart, at a point just before the line shot straight upward, she had placed a dot, a little arrow... and the words "You are here."

Then my ears caught and processed the phrases "total population saturation" and "six months," and I tasted bile at the back of my throat.

"Stop," I said.

She stopped, and I saw a flash of fear in her eyes. Clearly the effects of my dramatic entrance had not yet worn off.

"This is what you're calling Darkout? The point where the only living sapients in the universe are the vampires?"

She nodded. "Only they won't be sapient anymore. Without any remaining source of fresh human blood, they'll be mindless, starving monsters, so in essence all knowledge, all humanity, all civilization, all thought will be gone for good. Settled space will swarm with the creatures of Tropica Petite, for as long as it takes for them to die."

"In *our* reality," the woman sitting between Bluejay and Wire said. I realized I hadn't met her. I looked at Storm Rat. "Who's she?"

"Marta Tay, our new mathematician."

"Ours is the reality that matters to *us*," I told her. "We can't escape to any of the others."

"It's God's judgement," she said. "I've run the numbers with Bluejay, and there is nothing we can do. These creatures' populations are right at the tipping point. We can accept gracefully, and end our lives with some measure of serenity, or we can thrash and flail, but in the end, we'll still die."

"You haven't seen them," I snarled. "There is nothing of serenity in the way they slaughter their prey."

"She has seen them," Storm Rat said, and his tone of voice was protective toward her, and hostile toward me. "She saved herself and a handful of fellow slaves from vampire slavers just days ago. My privateers liberated her and the rest of the survivors on their wrecked ship when they got the emergency call. Her companions are in our refugee quarters now, trying to locate loved ones."

I raised an eyebrow. "But she's not?"

"She's staying here as an employee and one of my colleagues. She's the one I hired yesterday. She survived them, Cady. Just as you did. If anyone can understand the importance of what you've been doing, and if anyone can be motivated to bring her best to this, it's Marta."

I looked at her, and she looked at me, and suddenly I understood. I remembered the ordeals on the Legends ships. I remembered the horror, the visions of depravity. Looking at her, I could feel everything again, as fresh as when it was happening.

I closed my eyes and made myself to breathe regularly. I

forced my hands to relax, forced my muscles to unclench. I said, "I'm so sorry for what you've seen, and what you've been through. I know what those monsters do. What happens to the people they take." I rose and walked around the oval table to crouch beside her, and rested a hand on her arm. I could feel the pain pouring off her, could feel my heart breaking at the suffering she had undergone. I wanted with everything in me to help her. To save her.

I fought through the thickets of emotion for the right words. "You have to understand that nothing that happened there was your fault, and that the people who hurt you and everyone with you were monsters by choice," I said. "I know you want to help us. I understand. You think hiding with others will make you feel safe, but you won't *feel* safe if you're with *anyone,* and you won't feel safe for a long time. It's part of their effect on us. You need to be alone for a while, *to know that nothing and no one can touch you,*" I told her. I patted her arm, her shoulder, stroked her hair with the palm of my hand. "Because right now, all you're able to think is that they can be anyone, anywhere, and they'll come after you."

She nodded slowly, looking a bit puzzled, as if this was not quite the reaction she'd expected. "I'm... holding myself together."

"You think you are, but you can't see yourself from the outside. You're trapped in your head. You're trapped in your memories," I told her. "Everyone who goes through this goes through exactly the same thing. All you have is nightmares, and you can't find your way out."

She hesitated, then nodded again. "Everyone... feels like this?"

I was emphatic. "Everyone. It's part of the proof you have that this really happened to you."

"Yes," she said. "I can understand that."

I turned to Storm Rat, "You can't do this to her right now. You cannot ask her to try to work so soon after what she's been through. She's suffering. I know how she's suffering. You don't. So I'm going to walk with her to a room where no one can go in unless she lets them in. And where no one can make her let them in. Where she knows nothing can hurt her. Where she has food and water and entertainment, and communication with us, and perfect, secure walls. You can't understand what she's been through, or what she needs," I told him. "But I do."

He frowned, then said, "You want a... safe room... for her? But..."

"It's an emergency, Storm Rat. She *needs* this. Now."

Something in my voice got through to him. He keyed into his compac, and an instant later, the four largest men I had ever seen squeezed through the doors. They had to be heavyworlders, I thought, with bodies adapted to a baseline three or four Gs, and height and bulk massively increased for protection from hostile terrain or hostile fauna or hostile weather — the heavy worlds are rich in resources, but require a lot of body modification to inhabit.

"Please take our guest to a safe room on three," he told them. "Cady is going to go with Marta to make sure she is not frightened during the trip."

Marta was studying me warily. "This is more than I deserve."

I stroked her arm, patted her shoulder. "No," I told her. "I promise you, it's not."

Our trip down to the secure room Storm Rat had chosen was quick. Quicker than Marta had hoped, I think.

It was not like *his* safe room. The moleibond walls were only half an inch thick, and the infoscreen on the wall next to her bunk would let her call us, and let us communicate with her.

She wanted to talk, to delay things, to invite me in with her.

I wanted desperately to go in with her, but I gave her a hard hug and said, "Marta, I'll be back as soon as the meeting is over, and you and I will talk for as long as you'd like. I know what you've been through. I know how to make it better."

She looked deep into my eyes, and I felt the stirrings of desire. "I'd like that," she told me, and her eyes gleamed.

"Yes," I whispered into her ear, feeling the warmth of her skin, feeling my own quickening breath brushing against her cheek. "Yes. I'll like it, too."

She wiped little beads of sweat from her forehead and stepped into the safe room. "As quickly as you can, then, dearest," she whispered. "And don't tell anyone about...us."

The door to the safe room slid shut, and all my desperately held control over my body fell apart, and my knees gave out. I collapsed to the floor, shaking, queasy, feeling the pull of her even through half an inch of solid moleibond wall.

Three guards helped me to my feet, while the fourth called back to Storm Rat, his voice too low for me to hear.

"Tell him to make a hole for us, but to put the rest of the compound on silent lockdown *now*," I said. "We're in trouble."

He relayed my words.

I held the hand of one of the guards, and the five of us ran back the way we'd come. My feet barely touched the ground. Had I not been a tall woman, I would have dangled and flapped at my guard's side.

Behind us, I could hear doors snicking shut, could hear

moleibond bolts clicking and compartment atmosphere seals hissing.

Lockdown. No sirens, no announcements.

Good. There are damn few people who can hear trouble, can take an order to set up walls against its spread, and who won't delay the process with a hundred stupid, deadly questions about *why*. Storm Rat had seen enough plain and fancy hell to know that *now* is the difference between live friends and dead ones.

So with Storm Rat's world locked tight, the five of us careened around the corner and I told my four companions, "Stop anything that moves out here. It's life or death."

"We'll hold," the one who'd dragged me to my destination at such tremendous speed told me.

I made a second dramatic entrance into the meeting room, and the door sealed itself tight behind me.

"What the hell, Cady?" Storm Rat asked.

"Marta's a Legend," I told him. "A fairly strong one, so my guess is she's been playing this 'survivors' game with her friends for a while now. And if she's a Legend, so is everyone who came in with her."

"Oh, shit," Storm Rat whispered.

Chapter 6

The presence of Legends in Storm Rat's world changed the people around me.

They'd been analytical before. Distant from the problem. They'd been worried, and grim, but their worry held the coolness of the theoretical.

Now, suddenly, they were scared, and scared, they were harder to deal with.

They were, I realized, looking at each other, veiled fear in their eyes when they thought no one was looking.

For a moment, I couldn't understand the source of the fear.

And then I knew.

"People, calm down," I said. "It's unlikely anyone in this room is a vampire, or infected."

They stopped glancing surreptitiously at each other, and stared at me.

Storm Rat walked over to face me, and I didn't much like the expression on his face. "Why is it unlikely?"

"Because none of you is sweating or pale around the eyelids. I hit every one of you with multiple injections of the serum extracted from my bloodstream when Storm Rat introduced us and we shook hands." I held up the palm of my right hand. "I had a palm injector fabricated by a tech out in the Borland Quad," and looked Storm Rat straight in the eyes. "I hit *you* with about twenty doses when you met me on the dock."

His expression went from cold and suspicious to enraged in a nanosecond.

I cut him off before he could speak.

"No!" I said. "You don't get to be pissed off at me for preserving my own life. *You* let the vampires in. *You* gave one access to the information I've spent the last year accumulating — information that could cost me my life if she managed to leak it to any of her people. *You* brought her past the safeguards I set up when I got here, brought her right into this room with your people, your friends, your trusted colleagues..."

"I didn't know—," he said, and again I cut him off.

"You didn't know this time. And maybe there was a last time, and you didn't know then, either."

"I trust my people," he told me.

I remembered trust. Pure trust, unverified. It had almost gotten me killed several times. "When you deal with Legends, you cannot permit yourself the luxury of trust. You cannot count on faith in the goodness of humanity, nor can you believe in the sanctity of friendship or love without first proving that it has not been corrupted so that it can be used against you." I took a deep breath, and looked at the people around the room, all staring at me, all with expressions that ranged from dismay to betrayal to fear to suspicion.

"You handled Marta easily enough," Storm Rat said. "You recognized what she was, you pretended to be her friend, you manipulated her. I don't understand why, when you knew what she was, you didn't just shoot her with your dart gun and save us all that drama."

In that instant, I wanted to hurt him. But I took a deep breath. He didn't know. He didn't understand.

"First, I didn't handle her. I didn't manipulate her. Everything I said to her was the absolute truth. I was on her side, I was under her control, I wanted to help her and save her and it was only because I managed to hang on to the tiniest bit of my rational self while she was forcing me to like her and pity her and desire her that I was able to inject her over and over with my palm injector. It was only that single thread of *me* she hadn't grabbed that allowed me to use her force to move her away from all of you. She *owned* me, Storm Rat. If she had told me to do anything and put her will into it, I would have done it. But that would have given her away. She went with me because she knew she owned me so she could make me do whatever she wanted me to — once no one was looking — and because what I told her about vampire victims is true, and she needed all of you to believe she was one. Your belief would give her access to and control of every person on Tegosshu. She could have lived a long time on eighty-nine human slaves, plus your children and grandchildren.

"Second, assuming I could have drawn one of the dart-guns and shot her when she knew what my weapons contained and understood who and what I was — and I'm not stupid enough to assume that — she would have had time to kill all of you before the serum could kill her. In large doses, the serum is fast. But not fast enough to have kept you all alive. *That* was the reason for the drama."

I started pacing. Close calls left me with enormous

energy I needed to work off. If I didn't pace, I'd start shaking again.

What they didn't understand, and what I didn't tell them — what I couldn't tell them — was that I was still under her control. Her command that I return to her soon was eating at me. Her command that I not tell anyone about us kept me silent on the fact that I was her slave even while I was with them. As long as she was alive, she would have hooks into me, and my need to go to her would get stronger and stronger until it consumed me, and I would go. I said, "Storm Rat, turn on the infoscreen to her room. One-way viewing if you have it. We need to see how she's doing."

I needed to see how she was doing. I didn't say that, either.

He gave me a look, then spoke into his compac, and one of the screens in front of us showed Marta. Like me, she was pacing. Unlike me, she was sweating, her clothing was soaked, and her hair stuck to her scalp, dripping. "You can't do this to me," she said. "I own you. Come back here and get me and save me. You loved me. I felt it. Get back here now."

My salvation was that they could only command physically. I'd been in the room with her, breathing her air, feeling her energy, when she made me love her and made me want to return to her side. And I still felt all of that. I felt *nothing* from her spoken demand, transmitted via com, that I join her.

So I stood, barely hanging on, needing to be with her, and simultaneously congratulating myself that I'd managed to get enough of my AntiLegend serum into her while I was comforting her to kill her quickly. "She's minutes from dying," I told them. "You've seen this in the gray-on-gray of the doppler recordings, but now you're going to see it live. She's going to stop moving, then swell up, and then she's going to explode. It's horrible. But you have to understand that the same serum that is going to make her explode is — right now — making each of you a quick and deadly poison to any of her kind who drink your blood."

They watched her. Rapt. Frozen. Listening to her increasingly frantic demands that someone let her out, that someone come help her.

She started to swell. I'd seen them swell a lot faster when I'd managed to inject them with full doses. But her change was quick enough that each of my companions in the room could see it.

We waited in silence. The screaming got bad, and I saw Bluejay flinch. But she didn't look away. Tarko sat, rocklike and grim. Wire had gone white as a sheet and was wiping anxiously at his brow, which had started to perspire. I gave him a second look. He didn't have the pallor, his features weren't changing — so the perspiration was just fear. Books alternately watched and wrote with a stylus on a pad. Sky wrapped her arms around herself and nervously nibbled her lower lip, shivering with every scream.

When Marta exploded, bits of her hit the infoscreen, and everyone who hadn't been prepared for it jerked backward.

I knew it was coming. I felt the snap of release. Marta no longer owned me.

I turned away from the screen and said, "And now I'm free. I didn't tell you that I was still under her control, because I couldn't. Fortunately, she didn't tell me to kill all of you. I would have fought that, the same way I was fighting her command to come back to her. But this close to her, sooner or later she would have overcome my resistance, and I would have done what she wanted."

I took a slow, steadying breath. "The Legend nanovirus

is a poison for the soul — it offers immortality, the seduction of power, and the power of seduction, but it does so at the price of blood. Literal blood. Its creator designed the nanovirus to change the digestive system of the infectee to derive one hundred percent of its nourishment from living human blood.

"In exchange for becoming blood-drinkers, Legends become physically stronger, develop more acute hearing, sight, and smell, acquire what I *think* is pheromone control that allows them to become incredibly alluring to their chosen victims, gives them control over the actions of people they choose to own... and their body tissues regenerate with incredible speed. They are almost unkillable by any sort of weapon — though cutting their heads off quickly and cleanly does work, and if the flame is hot enough and they can't get away from it, they can be burned to death. Aside from that, I suspect the same tissue regeneration makes them nearly, if not truly, immortal. I know that was its intent."

Sky asked, "Why the blood drinking? Most of the characteristics you describe in this nanovirus are ongoing goals being researched in a number of private laboratories, but blood-drinking seems to me to be a dreadful nutritional compromise, and a serious flaw in the design. Unless it was some inescapable side effect?"

"No," I said. "Blood-drinking was the *point*." I looked at them. Storm Rat. Sky. Books. Bluejay. Wire. Tarko. They were all scared. They needed to be. "Vampires — immortal blood drinkers — were a legend from some cultures of Old Earth. The legend had admirers, and a couple of those admirers happened to be an incredibly rich, power-hungry businessman — Peter Crane of Monoceros Starcraft Ltd. — and his brilliant friend, renowned nano-augmentation designer Haskell Corrigan. They decided they wanted to live the legend."

None of them reacted to Crane's name, but I saw Sky's eyes widen when I mentioned Corrigan. "Corrigan led the team that developed the neuro-repair nanovirus," she whispered. "Reversed spine and brain injuries."

"He started his career on the cancer-reversal nanovirus," Books added. "I knew him. His family... owned mine. Before Herog wiped them out and rescued us. Pity that little shit Haskell wasn't home when he hit."

"When were you rescued?"

"Seven years ago."

"That is a pity, then," I said, and shook my head. "We wouldn't be in this situation if Haskell had been home. Because between Crane and Corrigan, they had nearly unlimited resources, unbelievable brilliance, and a shared obsession with becoming the monsters of their own favorite fantasy — creatures who could drink blood, live forever, make anyone they wanted desire them, and do anything they wanted to their human toys with the toys' passionate, self-destructive consent.

"And because once they had the working virus, they couldn't resist creating a few slaves with it, they created the situation in which the Legend nanovirus started spreading. Legend I — their first production vampire nanovirus — offers those who desire it the opportunity to live out every evil fantasy they can imagine, to act out every desire for revenge and spite and to be rewarded for their acts, to turn into slaves those whom they desire and into corpses those whom they despise... and to pay no price for their evil. Instead, they gain power with every slave they make and with every victim they drink to death.

"You want to think," I told them, "that you would withstand the temptation this virus offers, and I want to think so, too. But I've stood face to face against these creatures, and have had them inside my mind, making me do things I did not want to do. And while they were controlling me, I wanted them to keep going. I felt the pain, I felt them killing me, and I... I wanted them to *keep going*.

"I didn't want to die." I looked at the five of them. "But I wanted them to keep killing me."

I was looking into blank faces. Faces of people who couldn't understand. Who, had they been luckier, would never have the opportunity to understand.

None of us were lucky. Storm Rat's tiny world had Legends in it, locked down at least temporarily, but we were going to have to deal with them. And we were weaker, slower, more fragile. Mortal.

And we were food. Prey for the creatures who moved unidentified among us. Who looked like us. Who acted like us. Who could make us want them, love them, need them.

"The AntiLegend serum I injected in each of you was originally designed by a vampire to kill her makers. She hadn't chosen to be a vampire, had been forcibly converted by one of Peter Crane's escaped vampire-slaves, Danniz Oe, to become *his* slave. She wanted to die, but she wanted to kill her makers first."

There was more to that story. A lot more, but I didn't tell it. I had no way of knowing which parts of the story I'd lived were still true — or which parts had ever been true. So I'd told them the version I'd believed to be true when I'd been living it. That was the best I had to offer.

I said, "The serum injected into your blood is now being produced by your bone marrow, right along with your red blood cells. It doesn't make you stronger or faster. It doesn't make you immune to the seduction of Legends. It will not necessarily save your life — not if you're careless, not if you think you're immune to them." I took a deep breath. "But it does kill the virus on contact if it enters your bloodstream, so you cannot be made into a vampire."

I looked at them. "And if one of them drinks your blood, he or she will die. Quickly, horribly."

"Not one of you is showing symptoms — so you can trust each other. *From now on*, you can trust each other. Always. *You're now immune* to the Legend nanovirus, and your blood is poison to any vampire who tries to drink it. And if you have the AntiLegend nanovirus in your blood, you can never be infected with Legend."

"How did you know to inject us?" Storm Rat asked me.

I shook my head. "I inject everyone I meet. Always. Because I always have to consider the worst thing that could happen if I didn't," I told him. "Since Badger died, the only operating order I have is, 'Act to prevent the worst thing that could happen if you don't act.'"

WE WERE STILL IN LOCKDOWN, but my tiny team was past the shock of what I'd done to them, and we were back to facing the fact that humanity was right on the edge of blinking out of existence.

We picked up with the exponential curve chart where Bluejay predicted Legends were about to overrun their human food supply, wiping out humans and destroying themselves in the process.

"Where are your estimates coming from?" I asked. "The Legends weren't posting recruitment numbers to the datastream last time I checked."

Bluejay said, "I did population studies of reported

missing people, pulling from any worlds which fed their comprehensive data into the stream. I used ten years ago as my start point for averaging across worlds, since that was well before my estimated date of creation of the Legend I nanovirus."

She waved a hand, and a new holochart appeared. "Missing Persons Reported" it said in pale blue lightlines across the top. The chart itself was a long, fuzzy line made up of the thousands of pale blue dots that comprised world averages across settled space, and for about seven years, the line, though thick, was essentially flat.

Then it took an arc upward, and that arc mirrored the exponential growth curve of the first chart. Bluejay flicked a finger, and the two charts merged — the fuzzy blue dots now had a glowing red line right through their center. The match was nearly perfect. A few scattered dots along the bottom suggested worlds that had not yet been infected by vampires, but the match otherwise was hard to deny.

The red line of predicted vampire population growth shot upward into the future, suggesting that those missing persons numbers were going to go higher until there was no one left to report loved ones missing.

She continued. "I also ran the numbers of people presumed missing after pirate attacks."

A third holograph appeared. It held the same scattered dispersal pattern, the same massed average, and the same overall sharp rise at the end of the line.

"Correlation doesn't prove causation," I said carefully after a moment. "But your numbers combined with my first-hand experience suggest vampires are behind the rise."

"And the inevitable outcome of exponential spread of the vampires is Darkout," she said. "Sky's term. In every world where they exist, the vampires, unchecked, will completely overrun the human population, all humans will die, all but a few vampires will deteriorate into starvation mode... but shortly before this happens, a few vampires will escape to spread the infection in another location."

"How sure are you that six months is our outside limit?"

She cocked her head to one side and looked at me. "I have no proof. I can look at the increasing numbers of deaths, missing persons, and presumed pirated spaceships with presumed captured or dead passengers and posit that as my number, but without sure knowledge of the worlds already in Darkout, I can't prove anything."

My gut flipped, and the contents of my most recent meal tried to make a hasty reverse exit. I planted both hands flat on the table in front of me and breathed through my mouth until I was sure I wasn't going to throw up. "Worlds *already* in Darkout?"

"I estimate half of one percent of all worlds, stations, settled moons, and other human outposts in settled space are now in Darkout."

Sitting in that damn room, I could hear the scrabbling of blood-starved monsters' hands and feet on the hull of my shuttle, could see their crazed faces pressed against the glass — skeletal, fanged, madly hungry.

Whole worlds.

Half of one percent of settled space. That might not seem like a lot, but there are roughly twenty-five hundred solar systems in settled space, about that many full-sized planets inhabited by people, and endless space stations, terraformed moons, fused asteroids, and who knows what else that people have turned into home.

The little worlds would go first — the satellites, the resort moons, the religious settlements. Places where the population was already small, or where it was voluntarily isolated. Places where tiny populations made people more vulnerable, places not that many people traveled to. Or left.

Space stations would, I thought, hold out longer. Maybe until the end. They had small resident populations, but even if the residents all became vampires, the food would just keep coming, until there were no more worlds capable of sending it.

But places like Storm Rat's world would vanish early.

"What kind of proof are you looking for?"

"It'll be like searching for black holes. Places where something should be, but isn't." She shrugged. "We don't have time to travel. We don't have time to build software. I don't know what it would take to find those places."

I thought of my ship, of Badger's worms. "I do," I said.

Chapter 7

The entire team Storm Rat had assembled for me settled into the seats on my ship's bridge with me, and amazingly all of them avoided the helm chair — the captain's by right and only ever used by the officer in charge.

I took my place and opened up the lines into Badger's worms.

"This is how we knew things," I said. "Badger programmed loops to read public and non-encrypted data out of Spybees, comsats, world feeds... anything anywhere that wouldn't raise flags. His worms will ask questions in Open, because no one pays that much attention to Open, at least as long as you don't get greedy and stupid and start asking high-level security types of questions. I've had a lot of practice asking not-stupid questions, and not getting caught. So tell me what behaviors will characterize Darkout worlds, and I'll work out the questions to ask, and send out a few little threads."

Bluejay was sitting backwards on her armless seat. She said, "Right." Took a deep breath and closed her eyes, rested her head on her arms, and sat there, silent, while two minutes passed. The rest of us kept quiet and waited. "Reporting has stopped on a Darkout world. Messages go in. Nothing directly relevant to a sent message is going to come back. Ships go in, but no ships come back out."

"Wait," I said. "That isn't going to be true in the beginning. If ships with live humans go in, there may be a few ships that come back out, because vampires who get fresh blood shake off their mindlessness. They revert to intelligent, aware states — and if only a few of them have access to a sufficient food supply, there's a small chance they'll be able to get the ship off planet and make it to a world where enough live humans exist that they'll be able to resume their hunting."

"No." She shook her head. "You were swarmed. Characteristic of the Darkout world is that *all* the vampires will have regressed to mindless states. Extrapolating from what we've seen and from what you've said, if the Tropica Petite vampires had reached you, the first ones would have ripped you apart, but the wave behind them would have ripped the ones who fed on you apart because they would have smelled like fresh blood. The slaughter would have continued until the fresh blood was gone. There would have been fewer vampires, but all who remained would still be starving and crazed.

"So when living humans with a working ship drop onto a Darkout world, if the vampires gain access, the attackers won't know to save the captain, to preserve the crew, or to only feed off the passengers. If they get in, they'll rip every living creature to shreds, and then each other. The only ships that get out will be those that never open hatches, that realize they're in trouble when they hit dirt and escape before they're pinned down. Or who manage a clever diversion as you did."

I considered. "There may be a few survivors with horror stories, then."

"Yes."

I started putting the questions together in my mind, started figuring out innocuous ways to bury the critical words and concepts I needed into innocent, Open search phrases.

It took me a good ten minutes to figure out how to get what I needed into one query.

I activated the shipcom, and said, "Misdirect private message to all available access points, forward everywhere, from ID Piki, female, age nine, no registration, bounce apparent destination status LOST: CAN'T LOCATE RECIPIENT from origin Wilson space station, query wording in Open code, language Standard, follows:

"GRANDMA, my cat escaped and hasn't come back, and mama has no reply. We had swarms of bees attacking the gardener, Papa said they were hungry. I had to do a report on missing heroes in history. I got bad marks, but I'll redo it. I'm getting good marks in numbers. Love, Piki.

"END MESSAGE. Match exact and similar following terms from all available datastreams. Term one: Swarms attacking. Term two: Hasn't come back. Term three: Missing report history. Term four: No reply. Term five: Escaped. Nonspecific markers: hungry, bad, numbers. Compile data from all information with two or more hits, any language, any source. Build map based on point of message or source origin, notify when you've located statistically significant matches."

I turned to the folks on my deck and said, "The worms will start collating the old data Badger and I scooped from every feed the *Hope's Reward* read — I have about four years of data, transferred to the *Corrigan's Blood* before I scuttled the *Reward*. We'll also have everything the worms have pulled into this ship since I brought them over.

"I've been a lot of places in the past five years; we'll be able to build a good baseline map from all the old data. The query is going out now to live feeds. If there's much out there, we'll get the first of it back in minutes. Nothing comes back directly. If it did, my searches would start calling attention to themselves. So there's a necessary delay. And the query will spread out through the transfers for a couple of weeks before it saturates settled space, so we won't have everything in time to do us any good. We might have enough, though, to show you proof of Darkout somewhere. If things have gone that far."

Storm Rat said, "That seems like an awfully fuzzy search."

I nodded. "Badger and I worked like this for years. People won't all use the same words in their reports and communications; won't all have the same concerns; will dump their information into databases in all the languages out there; will not see the actual problem facing them and so will be asking all the wrong questions. To find the information you need, you have to come up with fuzzy terms, and search broadly for anything that might match. You get a *lot* of garbage—"

The shipcom said, "Initial map ready. How shall I present it?"

That was quick. *Quick* suggested there'd been something to find. *Quick* was not good. My earlier queasiness returned.

I considered what I wanted to see and how I wanted to see it, and told shipcom, "Time lapse data one year to one minute, all available data oldest to newest, standard settled space map in bluelight, vertical holograph, place map eyes forward compressed to holo size five, redline all hits, connect any concurrent hits in-system or from contiguous systems. Loop data times three, then freeze at five."

I wasn't sure if we were going to see anything, so I wanted the data to go slowly enough that we could spot anything that did show up, and at least get an idea if it was meaningful or not.

The map appeared across the forward viewports, suspended in the air, glimmering. Every known point in settled space was a glowing pale blue dot, and new blue dots kept blinking into existence, filling in black areas, spreading the map outward.

The map was a beautiful thing. It reminded me of dropping into the atmosphere above a big surface city at twilight, watching the lights blink on beneath me, knowing that those lights were the proof of human existence, of civilization, of the countless joys and comforts, both large and small, that made life not just tolerable but good. Little red dots winked in and out across all of settled space, but in the first minute, two minutes, three minutes, nothing stuck.

At minute four-point-five-eight-eight, though, something changed. A red ring appeared around one pinpoint out near the dark edge of the map. And stayed. The map drew lines to connect the dots.

It was joined by another, also out along the rim, this time a semicircle because nothing lay beyond the point of light. Shipcom connected the dots on this one, too.

And then a third.

By minute five, twenty-two clear circles hung out along the periphery, limned out by multiple simultaneous connected hits, and I could see the sketchy shapes of red circles building around other settled areas closer to the civilized core.

The last full circle to go red was the Hammerfield system. Hammerfield Station, where I'd been, just days earlier, and Tropica Petite, and the asteroid belts, and the little settlement world of Hammer Home. My skin-crawling sensation to get out of there fast had been justified.

I stared at the map. *Hammerfield Station.* The miners, the strippers, the cooks and drink girls, the shopkeepers, the dockhands, the families who had lived and loved and worked there had been reduced to shredded corpses or to the scrabbling, insane, starving monsters who'd slaughtered them. Monsters still waiting for fresh blood.

And the horror was that they'd keep finding fresh blood, because those critical ores were going to keep luring in the agents of customers who sent them to find out what had happened to their missing shipments, as well as new miners hoping to buy stakes, and parasites hoping to steal them.

Darkout was no longer a word for me. It wore real faces. Nat's. Nicci's. Sugar's. Candibelle's. Torch's. Those of the two heavyworld bouncers by the bar. The cold-eyed manager's.

Darkout was not distant. Darkout was a couple days in my past, and it was people I'd touched, talked to, listened to, watched. It had almost been me.

Around me, I heard indrawn breath. From my own throat, a tiny whimper.

The map looped, and once again space was clean,

marked by tiny flashes of red that that were coincidental. Or were related, but not yet definitive.

"Don't make me watch it again," Bluejay said. Her voice was ragged. She was crying. "Please."

I understood. We had our proof that everything we loved had been invaded by a disease that was killing it. We were watching the death of not just one world, but proof of the danger to every pinpoint filled with human life, everywhere.

"Shipcom, stop loop, move map to final second of minute five and freeze."

We stared at the end of everything.

Eventually I found my voice and asked Bluejay. "How does that match your numbers?"

"I was too conservative. Those are whole systems, not just worlds or outposts. Those systems represent .009% percent of settled space. I think we're done. If someone had understood what this was the second it was invented, if someone had created countermeasures, I think maybe..." She stared at the map and shivered, and wrapped her arms around herself. "You want a timeframe?"

"We have to know."

"Please have the shipcom split out the final year-four frame, and the final year-five frame, and overlay them, and have the year-four redlines changed to green."

The ship said, "Captain, do you approve the request?" Everyone jumped.

"Yes," I said, and to Storm Rat and his team members, "This ship came with the best AI available. As long as we're in emergency lockdown, it won't even get you a glass of water without my approval... but it will understand your requests, catalogue them, and run them past me. And I have it set to listen to and record everything everywhere aboard.

Please understand that, with the current settings in place, you have no privacy here."

I'd had bad experiences born from assuming I knew who was on my ship, from assuming my security was sufficient. I didn't make assumptions anymore.

The split maps overlay each other. The contrast from year four to year five was terrifying.

Bluejay waved a hand over the map, muttering. I realized she was scanning the data points manually, which made sense since I had direct data access locked down.

She tapped her compac, and whispered into it, and after a moment said, "Figuring for geometric growth without anything that pushes additional acceleration, we have four months, three days, twenty-one hours, forty-two minutes, eleven seconds Standard to total Darkout."

I turned to my future colleagues in saving humanity, and said, "This looks bad. But we're standing here looking at each other, still aware and breathing — we are living, thinking human beings. We're not dead yet. And as long as we're human and thinking and capable of taking action — any action — we're going to act on the assumption that we still have time to turn this around. Until the instant in which we lose, we fight like we can win it all."

They looked at me. At each other. No one said anything, but they were nodding.

Finally, Storm Rat said, "We don't have a lot of time. So let's get back to the labs and get to work."

WE SAT IN THE LAB, in the middle of station lockdown, surrounded by screens to all the locked-down areas of Storm

Rat's tiny world. Storm Rat was giving his stationcom commands.

The rest of us watched the screens.

We could see the humans. We could see the vampires. And we could see the few bodies of the humans who had been with vampires when the lockdown started. The vampires trapped with each other — which were most of them, fortunately, had gone from demonstrating feats of inhuman strength in their attempts to escape, to simply waiting. In their stillness, in their open-eyed patience, lay a naked, ugly threat. That threat was, "We have all the time in the world. And the longer you hold us in here, the more dangerous we'll become."

The humans who had been trapped either alone or with other humans were pulling food out of emergency reconsta units, playing cards, watching shows, reading, talking. Those in groups were mostly laughing. They'd come to the conclusion that whatever was the cause of the lockdown didn't involve them.

Where vampires and humans had been trapped together...

Storm Rat had lost friends.

What was worse, he had lost two of them *to* a friend. Not only were his most recent rescues vampires... but one of his long-time employees had, at some point, gone over. And in the twenty-eight hours we'd been working, had killed both women he was with.

The three of them had been together, had been getting friendly. Talking, undressing. In deference to their privacy, Storm Rat had blacked out the screen. When he brought it back up an hour later, both women were dead and their killer lay on the floor, staring up at the ceiling. Waiting.

We were surrounded by the inescapable images of what we were fighting, and what we were fighting to save.

Sky said, "I've decided on a two-pronged approach, spreading Cady's AntiLegend serum by droplet contact for the short term, and by viral droplet nuclei transmission longterm. With sneeze transmission hooked to a highly contagious but generally harmless virus, we can immunize about eighty to ninety percent of most populations quickly, and by doing so remove the majority of the vampires' available food — and wipe out those vampires who attempt to get their food from those populations. My hope is that when nanovampires inhale the droplets, most of them will also contract the nanovirus, and be killed by it.

"By also including a mechanism for long-term contagion in the form of airborne virons, I can ensure that surviving populations will continue to spread the immunization laterally, so we don't have to explore the much riskier approach of vertical transmission."

I sighed. I was trying to keep up, but disease science was not one of my strong suits. I was with her on viruses and droplets and got lost on virons, but the vertical transmission is a small but important part of an origami drive. I was betting that wasn't what *she* meant, though. "Vertical transmission? Can you say that in Standard?"

She glanced at me, cool and distant, the expression on her face suggesting I had somehow failed her. "If I design even a carefully engineered immuno-agent to cross the placental barrier — that is, to go from mothers to their unborn infants — I run the risk of creating something that can wipe out humanity. We don't have the time to test this in a vertical transmission scenario, and it is entirely possible, however unlikely, that a disease harmless to adult humans is going to kill fetuses. And since the bare minimum valid vertical test would be ten months, and we have four..." She shrugged.

So now I understood. Wiping out humanity was the thing we were trying to prevent. No vertical transmission. Got it.

Wire was shaking his head, though. He said, "We need to have one hundred percent of the Legends' food supply immunized. Otherwise, we cannot completely eliminate the Legends."

"I agree," Sky said, "but it won't happen. Natural human genetic biodiversity will leave some portion of the human population immune to whatever comes floating past. This is an essential part of why humans are still a going concern in the universe, and I am not going to manipulate that."

Sky shed her cool, distant exterior for a moment, obviously passionate about this, ferociously engaged in what we were doing. In that instant I saw how much this mattered to her — not just that we do this, but that we do it right. She said, "If it were possible to wipe humanity out with a disease, some disease would have already wiped us out."

"What about nanovampirisim?" Wire asked.

Sky winced. "You're right. That virus was designed to be fully transmissable. Consider we've gone from no vampires somewhere between six and ten years ago to human extinction in four months and a bit. I'm *not* going to engineer a second disease that can achieve complete transmission, because over time and with mutations, that disease — like our current problem — would wipe us out."

Storm Rat said, "Good point. Do the best you can."

Books was shaking his head. "There's a problem."

Storm Rat looked over at him. "You mean aside from the extinction of humanity?"

Books sighed. "I'm working from the point of view that we're going to survive this. If you do this — spread this Anti-Legend disease throughout settled space — there is no legitimate legal system in existence that will ever see it as anything less than genocide. You are attempting to wipe out an entire... race? Sub-species? The Legends are all human, no matter how much they've modified themselves."

I fought my battle with this issue every day of my life. I knew not all vampires had chosen to be what they were. I believed some of them had to be living off of blood repositories, tissue cloners set to manufacture human blood separate from human beings — that even among the vampires there still had to be innocents somewhere. Books saw it too, and suddenly I didn't feel so unutterably alone.

"If we succeed in saving humanity," Books continued, "this will be your ugly and inescapable reality, and you are going to have to figure out how you will deal with that reality. The law — and this is true for every legal system that recognizes the rights of the individual as the basis of all law — cannot take sides and favor one individual over another. The law must value each individual equally at the starting point, then look at existing statutes, at precedent in interpreting those statutes, at facts, at actions, at outcomes, at harm done.

"I've been mentally building a test case against you since I watched Marta die, and I can confidently state that wherever you are charged and tried, you'll lose. An *idiot* lawyer could win this case."

Storm Rat said, "Humanity is going to be wiped out in four months and change, and you're telling me if we can stop that, *we're going to be the bad guys.*"

Books said, "Yes. Because it's not going to be that simple and clean to the survivors. Consider this. Humans, except for those enslaved by the Legends, have no clue the Legends exist. And consider who the Legends are, who they have become in society. The Legends were humans who became what they are because they *needed* and *hungered for* power over others, because they yearned to enslave others, to force others to love them and worship them, and because they wanted to cause pain and suffering to anyone they hated.

"You already know they've used their abilities to move into leadership positions in politics in worlds they inhabit. And in religions. And in social groups.

"But think of who else will be drawn to immortality, sex, seduction, and endless power." Books studied us, waiting for just a moment. Then he smiled, but it was not a warm smile. It was the icy smile of irony. "In the aftermath of this, the human survivors are *only going to know* that people they worked with, people they worked for, people they voted into office, people who entertained them, performed their favorite music, acted in their favorite shows, and in a multitude of other ways mattered to them died horribly. They will have *seen* many of them die horribly, while awake and aware, after someone near them sneezed. They will have watched what we saw — they will have seen the bodies of people they adore, admire, lust after, even worship, explode with that horrible ripping sound. Perhaps they will have been spattered by their blood.

"And then, because not all the vampires will die, one of them somewhere is going to bring a lawsuit against the creators of this manufactured disease, *in absentia* if necessary. Or the human survivors, many of whom will be doctors, lab techs, nanovirologists, bioengineers, communicable disease researchers, and others capable of looking at the results of what you have done and reverse engineering it, and they will backtrack the deaths, trace the organism, analyze it, and discover its nature. And then they will file suit. Either way, all of humanity is going to start hunting for you. When they find you, they will destroy you."

Books was right. There was no way in hell to make the viral inoculation voluntary, because doing so would have to go through channels, and somewhere in all those channels there would be Legends with veto power... and even if that weren't true, we didn't have time for bureaucracy world by world to decide there was a need.

"So we'll be criminals," Storm Rat said already. "We'll be criminals who saved the bastards who are hunting us. I'm not going to die so I can preserve the niceties of legal technicalities."

I discovered that at some point in the conversation, I had come out of my seat, and I was pacing beside the table. I couldn't sit still. *The answer was in the problem.*

The answer is always in the problem. In this case, it lay in the nature of the Legends, in what they needed, in what they wanted. I could feel it, somewhere in the recesses of my mind.

We had to inoculate humanity against their demise. We had to stop this.

But we needed... something.

Something.

We needed humans to know that the vampires existed, that they were real.

We needed some proof of that. In writing.

I almost laughed, thinking about it. How the hell could we get the vampires throughout settled space to stand up and say, *I'm a vampire, and I'll sign my name to it, or better yet give you a sample of my blood that proves it?*

What would draw them out into public? Or if not that, what would convince them to send something in writing and a blood sample or tissue sample that would *prove* they were what they were...

We needed the vampires' *consent*.

Getting the consent of victims is easy. Promise them safety, security, and that they'll have as much of whatever they lust after as everyone else, and when they sign, deliver slavery and oppression. Governments and religions have been doing this since the dawn of time.

Getting the consent of the oppressors — the predators — that was not so simple. To do it, you had to promise them more and bigger victims, more power, more adulation — and you had to be able to offer proof that you could deliver....

Holy shit.

I stopped pacing.

I breathed slowly, running the whole thing through my head, checking for holes, finding none.

And when I'd run through the whole thing in my head, I shivered, knowing that this was our answer.

"We have to recreate Legend II," I said. "We have to recreate the upgrade to the Legend nanovirus that allowed the Legends who had it to control those who didn't. And we have to leak not just its availability, but proof of what it can do."

Chapter 8

Silence surrounded me. Five people stared at me with expressions of sheer horror.

They'd all seen my doppler recordings of Danniz Oe presenting his invention, Legend II, to a mob of admiring vampires. They'd seen him demonstrating the power Legend II offered by transforming himself into a grotesque, gigantic bat that was able to fly once around the room, land at his takeoff point, and transform himself back into a man. They'd seen the effects of his tremendous grace and power. They had seen the way he'd been able to control other vampires. He had been their master, unquestioned.

They had seen, too, what a nightmare it had been for Badger and me to kill him.

Storm Rat voiced the thought I could see clearly in each pair of eyes. "Are you *insane?*"

But I was bouncing on the balls of my feet, grinning. "I'm not. I'm not. I'm not. Hear me out. We have a whole list of problems, right?" I started pacing again, counting off on my fingers. "*One.* Nanovampires control positions of power in all the places that need the AntiLegend serum most.

"*Two.* The majority of humanity has no clue it's being ruled by murdering monsters.

"*Three.* Nanovampires look and act like everyone else, and there's no way to identify the bastards or prove that they are what they are unless they sprout fangs and bite someone in front of witnesses.

"*Four.* Many of them have made themselves beloved by billions, and killing them directly would turn billions against those who killed them.

"*Five.* Targeting them because they're vampires and destroying them as a class, or sub-species, or whatever they'd be designated by judges, would be called genocide." I took a deep breath. "Have I missed anything?"

"No," Bluejay said. "But you've done a wonderful job of pointing out how hopeless all of this is."

"No," I said, and my smile got bigger. "No. It *isn't* hopeless. What we need is a way to alert humanity to the true nature of vampires, to get the vampires themselves to prove that they exist, that they are are in positions of power over people, and that they are nightmarish killers, and to do this in writing... and then we need to have each of them step forward and tell *us* 'I'm a vampire' so we can kill them with their knowledge and consent."

"And while we're at it, we need a way to turn hyper-space into chocolate *bisote*," Sky muttered.

"Nah. Emergency Cookies," I said automatically, and then wished I hadn't.

The "you're a lunatic" looks were deepening. Except on Tarko's face.

He'd leaned forward in his seat, resting hands on thighs, and his expression was rapt. Until this point, he'd been utterly silent, listening. Now, though, he said, "Go on."

"The monsters in that auditorium in Meileone wanted Legend II the way droppers want their next fix. They would have killed to get it. They died *trying* to get it. Legend II is the thing they won't be able to say no to. Oh, you should have seen them. They would have done anything for him — anything — if he would have simply made them like he was. Because Legend II would have given them absolute control over their appearance, intensified their already amazing powers of regeneration, made them more seductive, faster, stronger, heightened their senses even further — in every way it would have made them bigger, better monsters.

"So we present proof that we've re-created Legend II. We present it to the vampires... and we leak their responses to humans. And then we sell Legend II to them, and get them to sign consent forms when they buy it.

"And hammer the nail in humanity's coffin ourselves," Storm Rat said.

"We don't make or sell them *real* Legend II," I said. "We sell them AntiLegend in Legend II packages, so when they take it, they explode. I'm not talking about creating real Legend II."

"If you don't sell them what you say you're selling them, you're back to genocide," Books said, but he wasn't looking at me like I was crazy anymore. "You'd have to come through with the real thing."

"If they're signing consent forms..."

"Are you planning on having the consent form spell out the fact by taking your nanoviral augmentation, they will die instantly and horribly?"

"Ah... no."

"Then it's still genocide."

"Even if they acknowledge that they're killers and are getting Legend II so they can be worse killers?"

"That would give officers of the law in possession of their consent forms reason to take legal action against *them*," he said. "In most systems, legal action would not include killing the accused without benefit of trial."

"You're impossible," I said.

"Not at all. Every loophole you close now is one that won't become your noose later." And then he closed his eyes, and a blissful smile spread across his face. "You must make a working version of Legend II," he said slowly. "But you won't have time to do full tests on this nanovirus, assuming you can make it at all. Correct?"

"Time is what we have least of," Sky told him.

Books opened his eyes. "Good. Then I've closed one loophole for you. Include a disclaimer: 'Legend II is in first-run testing and may have unanticipated side effects, including headaches, mood swings, personality changes, and others not listed but still covered under this disclaimer, which could lead to serious damage or death. If you use this nanoviral augmentation, you agree that you do so at your own risk and bear full responsibility for the consequences.'"

I looked at him, and laughed. "*Damn*. If I'm ever in trouble, I want you on my side."

He smiled at me, and bowed his head in acknowledgement. "You are. And I am."

But then Wire said, "Wait. We're not good yet. So you're going to make some version of Legend II, and it's going to be real Legend II as a legal cover-your-ass, but it's going to kill any vampire who takes it. So how are you going to prove it exists, and make vampires want it?"

"Dummy up doppler recordings and holos and leak them through the datastream."

"And your nanovampires will look at them, and say, 'Those are doppler recordings and holos that have been dummied up and leaked through the datastream.' Everyone knows anything in the datastream could have been faked. These monsters aren't stupid."

I sighed. "Do you have a better idea?"

Wire said, "No. My idea is terrible. But it would work."

He didn't say anything else, though.

All of us looked at him, waiting, until finally Storm Rat snapped, "Well...?"

Wire looked at Storm Rat with a sick expression on his face. "We have to present them with a real Legend II vampire. One who can show them the transformation in person. Who can control them, prove he can be their master, that he can do everything they desire, that he is everything they want to be."

"That *is* a terrible idea," I muttered. "A real Legend II vampire would wipe us all out."

His voice was small, and he was staring at me with a fixed, unblinking expression of scared determination. "It has to be one of us. Someone who has sought them out, who has fought them, who knows first-hand who they are and what they can do, who has been able to resist them and survive when under their control. Someone who knows why what we're doing matters, and who can resist the temptation of immortality and power and everything else this stuff will offer, and will stay on our side, fighting for us."

By the time he finished, they were all looking at me.

The silence in that room hung like death. I stared at them, they stared at me.

The datastream is filled with garbage, and idiots love it

and the intelligent ignore it. And when Danniz Oe wanted to present Legend II, he stood live before his admirers and proved to them just how amazing the augmentation he'd created was.

Wire was right.

About everything.

"It has to be you," Storm Rat said.

"Yes," Tarko said. "You've been up against them in every imaginable situation. You never lie down. You never quit. If anyone can do this, you can do this."

"But then I'd be a vampire," I said. "I don't want to be a vampire. And besides, my bloodstream is loaded with Anti-Legend. Injecting me with the Legend II nanovirus would just destroy your nanovirus."

Sky said, "I can work around the AntiLegend serum in your bloodstream. Adapt the Legend II nanovirus so it uses AntiLegend as part of its structure."

"That would be bad. If we hope to kill vampires with AntiLegend, we cannot give them an augmentation which will make them *immune* to AntiLegend. That *would* be the final nail in humanity's coffin."

She shook her head. "You're misunderstanding me. I'll need to have tissue samples from vampires we have in lockdown to see how the nanovirus is structured, but I can build the Legend II augment so that it works with your AntiLegend, and is fatally incompatible with Legend I."

So.

All the objections could be answered, all the legal issues worked out, all problems would be solved. Except that, to make everything work...

I shuddered.

This had been my idea, and the idea, worked out, debugged, could still save humanity. It was still beautiful.

Except for the part where I would have to spend the rest of my life as a blood-drinking monster.

Storm Rat said, "If you're going to have to meet with them in person, Cady, you aren't going to be able to do this alone. You're going to need my best people backing you up. You already have these," he said, with the wave that encompassed the team he'd created for me, "but you need someone to go with you. To be your first officer. Your backup. I'm bringing Herog into this."

I nodded dully.

I couldn't think anymore. Was not ready to meet anyone else. Was suddenly too exhausted to stand straight on my own feet. I was terrified. I needed to be alone. "I'm not thinking straight," I said. "I need some sleep, and once I have that, I'll be able to come back here and we can talk about this."

Blood, I thought. If I accepted the task they'd put before me, I would have to live out the rest of my life drinking blood.

I went back to my ship, unable to get past the awfulness of that.

I SLEPT. Woke. Slept. Woke. Alternately sweated and froze, thrashed, kicked and twisted and flailed. I was suddenly made of too many angles, so that no position was comfortable.

I had a nightmare of being trapped on a Legend ship with bodies stacked in frozen lines along endless icy corridors, all of them with their throats ripped out, torn apart the way I'd seen so many times. Weapon in hand, I was searching for the killers, and then I was somehow up on the bridge, and it was the bridge of *my* ship, and when I saw my reflection, I had fangs, and my face was covered with blood.

I woke after that and stayed awake.

I paced my ship's corridors. I talked to myself. Argued with myself. Played both sides of the discussion, *For* and *Against*, and realized what I already knew: *Against* had a shit position and lousy arguments and if I wanted to live to see tomorrow, I was going to have to side with *For*.

No matter how much I loathed *For*.

I drank coffee and I ate one of the Emergency Cookies I had stashed away in different spots on my ship (and dropped my mental count of those remaining to eleven), because if ever I'd needed comfort, it was in that moment.

Someone has to do this.

Someone had to become the living proof of Legend II. Assuming Sky could figure out how to recreate what Danniz Oe and his people had done before, someone was going to have to walk in front of rooms packed with those bastards and prove to them that they could become even more nightmarish than they already were.

And who else in all the universe had dealt with them as I had? Perhaps there were other people like me out there, hunting the bloodsuckers, killing them when they found them... but I didn't know those people. And I didn't have time to find them.

And of all the people I did know, who could do this terrible thing better than I could?

I would have given anything to come up with a name, but there was none. I could not figure who would be better, or more capable, or more knowledgeable, or more prepared to deal with the monsters I had been hunting for the last year; I could not think of anyone else to offer up in my stead.

I would have, had I been able to honestly recommend someone who could do the job better.

But in the end, I wanted to live.

I wanted to live, and keep on living — to keep on thinking and knowing and discovering, and I wanted to do it with people I cared about around me. If I did not do this one thing, this one terrible, terrifying thing, then the people I valued — the ones who gave me shelter and friendship and a certain knowledge that settled space contained goodness and wonder and great worth, the ones who created, the ones who built, the ones who invented, the ones who dared to dream and dared to reshape their lives to fit their dreams — would die. And so would I.

I had a chance to save humanity. It was a shit chance. The universe held, by Bluejay's best estimate, billions of them, and there was only one of me.

But *I* had the chance. Right here, right now, no one else could do what I could do.

In every life there comes a moment when you must run toward the fire, or run away.

I could run away. If I did, one of Storm Rat's people would go in my place, and would try to do the thing I had been training for since Badger's death. I could run away. But I wouldn't.

This was *my* moment.

I put on my favorite shipsuit, one of the ones I'd fabricated on the ship. It was a deep, rich purple with black panels and gold piping. It was pure, ridiculous fantasy stuff, as silly and over-the-top as anything you'd see in an episode of *Captain Danger*, the show most mocked by real captains and real crews for its ability to get absolutely everything wrong all the time.

But my suit was real, and good for thirty straight hours

of deep space work in any conditions, just as it was. And wearing it made me laugh.

Well, usually.

This time, wearing it just took a little of the edge off the screaming going on inside my skull.

I looked at myself in the mirror in my quarters, rotated the hologram to make sure I looked good all the way around. Wriggled the neckline around to improve my cleavage. Took a deep breath. Smiled.

Not a convincing smile, but I'd work on it.

STORM RAT'S only comment on my change of apparel was a raised eyebrow. The team he'd put together for me clustered around one table, all of them working on and arguing about a three-dimensional flowchart.

Except, I realized, for one man I hadn't yet met.

When I caught sight of him, sitting utterly still, facing away from everyone else, wearing an immersion headset, I returned Storm Rat's raised eyebrow.

"Herog," he said.

"He needs to be... inoculated to be in here."

"Done," Storm Rat said. "We've already extracted Anti-Legend serum from our own blood, and Sky has analyzed it. Herog injected himself, and now he's going over your doppler recordings. Far as I can tell, he's already seen most of the violent parts of your previous year."

I sighed. Once you've seen one of those recordings, you've watched them all. I identify a vampire. I shoot the vampire with a dart gun. The vampire, or his allies, attack me. I fight to survive, and then I leave the site before I'm identified.

I'd watched each recording after I returned to my ship to see if I could figure out any ways to improve my odds of surviving my next encounter. And I saved them as proof of the existence of the vampires, in case I ended up dead and another human found my ship, or my body, or both, and wondered why.

Storm Rat had walked over to Herog, clearly planning to tap him on the shoulder and let him know I'd arrived. But before he'd crossed the room, Herog had removed the immersion headset, risen from his seat, and turned to face Storm Rat.

A little shiver ran down my spine. Immersion headsets block out everything. They put you fully inside the world you're viewing, removing all contact with reality. So how had he known Storm Rat was there?

Storm Rat said something to him, and he looked over at me.

He was big. Not heavyworlder big. But taller than me, with bulky, heavy muscles, a broad solid body stripped of all fat. His skin was swarthy, as if it had been burned by an unforgiving sun. His hair was black, shaved to a stubble on his head and face. My gaze locked on his, and he walked over to me, and neither of us blinked.

Or said a word.

If you fight much, if you have been in life or death situations, you start learning to size people up, to know from a glance who is harmless and who is deadly — and as he crossed the room, I knew I had come face to face with the deadliest human I had ever met.

He didn't pause, he didn't blink, and neither did I, and suddenly I knew a fist was going to come for my head, and in the split second before it did, I put my head where his fist wasn't and jumped away from him. He came at me, then, and, oh God, was he fast.

His eyes held no emotion, his movements suggested no weakness, his focus was fully on me, and his intent was to kill me. Bare-handed.

As if they were a million kilometers away, I was vaguely aware that Storm Rat's people had jumped out of their seats and were screaming, but I knew it in the same way I knew where the fixed objects were in the room that might trip me up, and where the loose objects were that might become weapons for me. I knew because if you find yourself fighting for your own survival very often, your mind notes these things for you constantly, and if you suddenly need them, presents the information to you as you pass near something dangerous or useful.

Herog was human, not vampire — he wasn't as fast as a vampire, and he wasn't playing with my mind, which is the first thing those bastards do when they realize you know what they are. But he was trying to kill me.

There was some sort of solid metal rod lying on one of the worktables. I fled to it at a flat-out run, grabbed it, did an imperfect roll-and-drop across the table, and came up facing him, punching for his throat with both hands gripping the rod...

...And too quickly for me to see or even comprehend, both my wrists were in one of his hands, I'd been spun around and was clamped against his chest with the rod that had been my weapon now held against my throat, I couldn't move, I could barely breathe, and in my ear, a low rumble of distant thunder murmured, "And now you're dead."

And he released me.

I turned, shaking, my heart pounding in my throat and

my pulse hammering in my eardrums, and braced myself for a second attack.

"Your best chance to survive was to drop and roll toward me as I was coming at you, to move under my fist and come up behind me, and grab the spanner lying on the table I'd just walked past and smash it into the back of my skull," he said. "Then you could have used my momentum in the other direction against me."

I'd seen the spanner, I realized. In the fraction of a second I'd had to act, though, going through him to get it had seemed like suicide.

"I didn't see that as an option."

"I know. I've watched you fight. You're brave. But if ever one of your monsters is a professional like me, you're dead."

"What do you mean?"

"Your monsters are amateurs. They were bakers and politicians and *musicians* before they became monsters. They count on superior speed and strength because that's all they have. They don't know tactics."

"They don't *need* tactics."

"So they think. I could beat them."

"So *you* think. They cheat. They play with your mind."

He shrugged. "We'll see."

He was wrong about them. But he was right about me. "I wasn't much of a challenge."

No hint of expression crossed his face. "No. You weren't. But a third of the men I killed died with my first move."

I knew I shouldn't have asked, but I did. "How many men have you killed?"

"Professionals? Several hundred. Slavers? Several thousand."

I wanted to know what he meant by *professionals*. I wanted to see from him some sign that he was human. I wanted to ask him why the hell he'd decided to introduce himself by attacking me.

But Storm Rat, pale and shaking, was standing behind him, furious beyond anything I had ever seen before, and Herog turned away to look down at him.

"What in all the hells did you think you were doing attacking her? What if you had hurt her? What if you had *killed* her?! Do you have any—"

"You tell me *she* is your plan to save humanity. Before I put aside my life to guard hers, I want to know how good your plan is."

I had never seen a man who so desperately looked like he wanted to kill another man before who did not then try it. But Storm Rat only clenched his fists and snarled, "And what did you find out?"

His expressionless gaze flicked from Storm Rat to me, and back to Storm Rat. "She'll do."

I had no way of knowing then I'd just been paid the biggest compliment of my life.

———

WE SAT around the main table in the locked-down tech room, and Storm Rat stood before us.

"Are we all committed to do this — to fight for our lives and the lives of humans everywhere, to die if necessary, to die almost certainly — against the impossible odds of billions of them against just those of us who will take this pact today? Understand that once you have committed, there will be no turning back, for once you have committed, if you falter, we will all surely die."

I had already fought this battle alone. I knew my answer. I stood. "I'm in."

Tarko hesitated only a second, then stood on his seat to be at eye and arm level with me. "I'm in."

Sky took a deep breath, and I saw her knuckles go white as she pulled herself to her feet. But she stood. "I'm in."

Wire stood. "I'm in."

Bluejay bit her lip, but she too stood. "I'm in."

Books sat studying us. Then he nodded and stood. "I'm in."

Herog sat with his arms crossed. He showed no inclination to move, and when everyone looked at him, clearly waiting, he looked at Storm Rat. "I already told you I'd guard her with my life, no matter what."

Storm Rat sighed. "For the pact, Herog. Please."

Herog glanced at all of us and stood. It was like having an earthquake notice you. The stillness of stone became for just an instant animate, and for just that instant saw you and knew you, and then movement subsided as quickly to utter immobility. It left you doubting your senses — that he had looked at you, that he had moved.

They all knew him. From what I'd been able to gather, they had known him for years. Yet I glanced at their faces, and they, too, looked wary.

"We pledge our lives to this endeavor," Storm Rat said. "We agree to keep what we do here, who each of us is, and how we plan to fight and win secret for the rest of our lives. We hold each others' lives, now and forevermore, in the same regard as our own lives. What we intend to do will not be forgiven if known. But it must be done."

He held out his hand. We put our hands on top of his.

We were officially a conspiracy.

Chapter 9

I remember the next two weeks only in blurred flashes, painful, exhausting. Our goals were immense, and seemingly impossible to achieve. We had so far to go.

Our tasks were:

To create a working version of Legend II, but to adapt it so that I would be able to drink a blood substitute rather than human blood, one that would work with the primary physiological adaptations hardwired into Corrigan's nanoviral design, and still survive — and *then* to formulate the blood substitute so that it would be indistinguishable from real blood to Legend I vampires (Legend I vampires could only drink live human blood, but they could never suspect that we were drinking something else);

To figure out a way to manufacture Legend II in the volumes necessary to reach every vampire in settled space, including those who would become vampires in the time it took us to get everything done;

To come up with a way to distribute Legend II everywhere in settled space simultaneously, so that no Legend I vampire would discover Legend II was lethal and sound the alarm;

To finance the manufacturing and distribution of the nanovirus, and to do it in a way that could never point back to Tegosshu, to any of Storm Rat's people, or to any of us;

To nail down the legalities so that when it came time, humanity would have clear, inarguable proof both of the monsters in their midst, and the fact that those monsters destroyed themselves on their way to attempting to become more deadly killers;

To come up with my itinerary — the worlds, stations, and other locations in settled space that we were sure harbored large and influential communities of vampires, from whom I would be able to record events and reactions — and to catch faces that could be leaked eventually to alert humans to the danger in their midst. It was going to be my job to sell the wonders of being a Legend II vampire — and I had no idea how I was going to do that. But I knew more about them than anyone else present. And I was counting on the Legend II injection to help me fake enthusiasm for the lifestyle. Or at least to allow me to demonstrate enough power that my customers wouldn't care whether I was enthusiastic or not.

Storm Rat's whole team lived in the locked-down tech room together, but we had our plausible lie in place. We were looking for ways to make AntiLegend faster and more effective, we said, and we were testing it on ourselves, and could not risk contaminating all the survivors should we make a mistake.

What I recall from those days is hazed by exhaustion, fear, and more fear.

From start to finish, the initial setup for my plan took two weeks, and it was a hellish two weeks. All eighty-three remaining humans on Tegosshu worked every hour of every day for seven straight days. We lived on stims and blood cleansers, and better-than-average reconsta prepared by the folks who took on the jobs of feeding us.

A midlevel medtech named Cosh manufactured enough REM3 capsules to make sure every human in the compound got one every twenty-four hours. Without fake sleep, the whole lot of us would have been crazy out of our heads, hallucinating, getting violent, getting scary. REM3 kept down the crazy, but by the end of the week we looked ragged and felt worse.

I was aware that people outside our room were working as hard as we were — everyone was cutting up big tasks into little pieces, and having folks outside our lockdown handle the unrelated pieces. And every single piece had been disguised to look benign, and could only ever be used to prove the residents of Tegosshu had been working on a way to inoculate humans against the Legend nanovirus, as well as on a way to reverse the effects of Legend.

Inside the room, it was a different story.

I remember sitting so close to Bluejay that our foreheads touched, both of us leaning over a map of origami points and systems which she'd overlaid with a heat map of vampire densities, put together with her best estimates.

"The Asler System is thick with them," she said. "You can convert millions there."

And me, pointing to the big band of uninhabitable worlds, asteroids, and other crap outside the inhabited core of planets and saying, "It's three days at top speed from the origami point into the worlds we'd need to reach, and three days back. Six days lost. We can't afford it."

And Wire and I, and my wistful discussion about a handheld gravity shear.

"The gravity plane would rip your arm apart — bare minimum — at the same time it destroyed your targets. There's no way to do a gravity shield that small to protect you from the shear."

"Are you *sure?*" I could hear the plaintive note in my voice, and even in that terrible place and time, the genuine humor in Wire's laugh.

And Wire giving me a contact outside the room who could put together a personal failsafe for me to make sure that if being a vampire turned me into a monster, I would be able to destroy myself. The secret of the failsafe belonged to me, and to the lone tech who'd made it. The tech knew what it did — and warned me about how dangerous it would be — but had no idea why I wanted it.

I clearly recall the loud fight between Sky and Books over the method I'd laid out for safely obtaining the necessary tissue samples from our captive vampires — who'd been in lockdown since we discovered their presence on the station — that would allow us to reverse engineer Legend II.

I'd explained that there was no tranquilizer that would knock them out, no gas that would render them incapable of acting, no trick that would allow a human being to get close to a live vampire safely. And then I'd gone back to Bluejay and our maps, only to hear Sky screaming at Books, "We'll send the heavyworlders. Three can hold them so a fourth can do the cell scrapings."

And Books had said, "No. We'll kill one and get your scrapings that way."

More screaming. "You cannot murder someone to use his body for medical testing. There are laws regarding how captives have to be treated."

Books had looked over at me. "Cady, how do vampires treat their captives?"

"Rape, torture, dismemberment, blood-drinking, murder." And I added, "Any humans put within physical reach of any vampires will be controlled by them, and do whatever they're told. Your four heavyworlders would be made slaves, would be forced to free the vampire, would be forced to free the other vampires, and then would probably become meals."

Sky said, "Doctors cannot murder those under their care to use them for medical testing."

And Books said, "First, they're not under your care, requiring — as they do — no care. Second, they are prisoners of a foreign government who have signed no treaties with Tegosshu regarding the treatment of prisoners. Third, they are a species which regards ours as prey — humans are their only source of food. Fourth, they have demonstrated at every turn both the motive and the means to subjugate and murder any humans for any reason. One does not require the rabbit to preserve the life of the snake, Sky. Nor will we operate on that principle here. We will kill from a safe distance such tissue donors as you need in order for us to preserve the lives and the health of those men who must manually collect the samples."

I had not been surprised by Sky's reaction. I had been surprised by Books'.

And a later flash, with Storm Rat and I, sitting in a corner. "They're going with you as your human servants. As your source of human blood. That will be your cover for having them there."

"They're going to be vulnerable. I'm going to the worst worlds in settled space from a human perspective."

"Herog will be there. They'll be safe on your ship. They have AntiLegend in their blood."

I could only see disaster.

Through it all, Herog was there. Silent, watching me. He had no specific tasks. He helped where he was able, but his skills, like mine, lay elsewhere.

On the final day, I caught Storm Rat and Sky in a heated under-the-breath argument that included Storm Rat using the words "failure of the airborne AntiLegend in live test," and resulted in Sky snarling, "You had no right to run that test."

I could guess who he'd tried the test on, and I figured he'd seen his friends murdered, and it was his world — bought and paid for — so he actually did have the right.

Not long after that, Sky told all of us in the room that the prototype worked perfectly in simulation. And I saw Books and Herog in a corner together with a document and a biometric scanner. Something legal, then.

Books scanned his signature, then Herog did. Then Herog walked to the door that had not been opened since we'd sealed ourselves in, received a weapon I didn't recognize from one of the heavyworlders guarding the door, and left. He returned less than twenty minutes later, expression unchanged, without the weapon. He nodded to Books.

Books sighed.

I studied Herog. Noticed a splash of fresh blood on his right shoulder.

Found a time when he was away from everyone else and said, "You killed them all, didn't you?"

"Yes."

I nodded. I'd wondered how Storm Rat intended to deal with the vampires he held captive. They could not be safely transported. They could not be safely confined. They could not be safely fed.

To preserve the lives of the people on Tegosshu, they needed to die.

"Good," I said at last. I looked at him, hoping to see something I could identify on his face, some emotion.

He was watching my eyes. After a moment, he said, "You're wondering if I enjoyed it. I didn't. I was quick. They had no warning; they suffered no pain. The weapon you saw allowed me to sever their heads from their necks with one shot. They were monsters, and they might have deserved to suffer, but how I kill reflects on *me*. There was no honor in this. No vengeance. No pleasure. It was the extermination of deadly vermin. I treated it as such."

I believed him. And found myself warming to him just a little in that moment. *How I kill reflects on me*, he'd said.

Yes. I understood that.

"You have blood on your shoulder-tab," I told him. "It's how I guessed where you went. If you and Books are hoping to avoid another screaming fit from Sky, you need to get rid of that before she sees it."

He nodded and walked away without another word.

The next time I saw him, his shoulder tabs were both gone.

THE WHOLE TIME we were locked in that room together, a sense of foreboding consumed me.

My plan was as good as I could make it. What I was missing was someone other than me to carry out the ugly end of it.

At the end of two weeks, knowing that nothing we'd done was perfect, but everything was as done as we had time to make it, we found corners or chairs or the tops of tables, and with the room locked down and all monsters on

Tegosshu dead, and the next step ahead of us, everyone slept for eight hours.

Real sleep. It was more wonderful than I'd imagined. I was too tired to dream.

I woke knowing we'd accomplished what we'd set out to do, and had done it in the impossible time frame we'd set for ourselves.

And then I remembered that what came next was all on me.

Storm Rat and his techs did a systems check to make sure there were no surprises, and then he took the station off total lockdown.

He also cleared a corridor so I could get to my ship.

I went back to my ship for the first time in two weeks, and luxuriated in a hot shower, put on one of my flashy, deceptively innocuous ship suits, and went to share a meal with Storm Rat, Tarko, Sky, Bluejay, Wire, Herog, and Books.

Breakfast was in one of Storm Rat's showy surface rooms, domed over with clear moleibond and with a good view of Storm Rat's small yellow sun and big white stars against black sky.

The meal was real food: imported planet-grown grilled steaks and pan-fried fish, eggs, biscuits and rolls, fresh fruit, steamed vegetables, griddle cakes covered in whipped cream.

"Magnificent," I said, enjoying seconds on the steak.

Storm Rat didn't pull any punches. "It could be your last meal. I didn't want it to be reconsta."

"Thanks." I ate, giving each bite my full attention, trying to make it count. I knew it could be my last meal, too.

Thing was, even if everything went as well as it could in our live test, this was going to be my last meal as a human being. That was the part I wasn't letting myself think about. I knew vampires could eat real food — I'd seen them doing it. They couldn't digest it, though. And I wasn't sure how they dealt with the waste. Eating real food might be more trouble than it was worth.

They did not hurry me. Not one of them expressed impatience. And I was grateful.

When I pushed back from the table, however, Wire and Herog excused themselves. Bluejay said she needed to get a few belongings out of her quarters, but she would meet us before we started.

And Sky finally asked me, "Are you ready?"

I wasn't. But while I hesitated, people died. "Yes," I told her.

I added, "Books, if this kills me, Storm Rat inherits the ship. What you do with the plan is up to all of you."

STORM RAT'S station had unused wings in it. He was particular about who he let live there, and who he let visit. He'd built plenty of room for expansion, and after my official last meal, those of us who'd stayed trooped to an unused, locked-down wing that looked like it had been designed to house short-term guests.

In one room, Wire and Herog were putting the finishing touches on a moleibond cage. It had a cot in the center for me to lie down on.

From the amount of moleibond they'd used, it looked like it had been designed by Storm Rat.

Bluejay came in. "Got the last of what I'm taking moved into the transport room, and checked everyone else's gear, too. The room is locked down. We're ready when Cady is."

I stepped inside, stripped down to my underwear, and waited. Dr. Sky brought the injection. "You want to do this, or do you want me to?" she asked.

"You do it," I told her. "I hate sticking myself with needles."

Sky said, "All right, then. Before I inject you, understand that this process is going to hurt. The injection itself will burn like hell, but when the nanovirus runs through your system and starts making adaptations, each of those adaptations will have its own unique variety of pain.

"I don't have a lot useful to offer you here, beyond the basics. Remember to breathe. Think, if you can. Repeat your name, count, recite poetry if you know any. You want to keep yourself centered inside being a person, because the alternative, if you forget who you are, will get very ugly."

She nodded over her shoulder. I saw Storm Rat and Herog standing with their hands on "tank-stunners" — the stun guns heavyworlders used on problem folks — and moleibond-web restraints. I looked at the cot in the center of the cage, built of solid moleibond, with lots of points of attachment for those restraint straps.

"Worst case, they have to have something better than stunners," I said.

She smiled without humor. "They do."

I took a deep breath. "Stalling isn't helping anyone," I said after a moment. "Do this."

I presented my arm to her, and gripped one bar of the cage, and closed my eyes.

The needle went into my shoulder, which is a vile and primitive way of delivering anything, but was necessary. The special version of the nanovirus I was getting was mixed in with a tracking cocktail that would allow Sky to study how the nanovirus spread, at what speed, where it went first, and once it was in me, how I reacted to it. If we were fortunate, she would be able to figure out the 'whys' behind the 'hows.'

If I died, she'd be able to use the data to make necessary adaptations for another run, with another test subject. If there was time.

I trusted her — as one of Storm Rat's best people — to have done her modeling right, to have built this right the first time — because we didn't have *time* to keep trying and failing.

Sometimes you only get one chance.

Midnight bled into my blood, poured down into my fingers and up into my torso, my heart, my lungs, my legs and feet, neck, skull, and time slowed. And slowed.

Cold lay inside me, coiled, terrifying.

One.

I could hear my pulse like drums inside my skull...

Two.

...and the cold in my blood burned like ice daggers into my bones...

Three.

...and I went blind, my eyes frozen, the world white, and I knew I was clawing at my face trying to get them out get them out get them out...

Four.

...and my heart turned to ice, and I fell forward, dying, consumed by a poison that was tearing my flesh off my bones in icy strips, exploding me in slow motion, and I knew that we had failed, and I knew that I was dying, and...

Five.

Hell. With screaming. I was in it.

Forever.

Forever.

THERE WAS NOTHING. And in the midst of nothing, a sudden something. A pinpoint of light, a flicker of warmth, and then a rush of life, sound, smells, sensation.

Pain turned to pleasure, ice to heat, fear and anguish to incredible, calm, centered certainty.

This was how I was supposed to feel. This was perfection. I opened my eyes, and everything lay before me in a flawless detail I had never before imagined possible. Every surface had a crystalline clarity that rendered it beautiful, no matter how mundane its origin or purpose.

The people around me were exquisite, their hair, skin, and features all seemingly crafted out of new materials so much finer and more delicately designed than human flesh had ever seemed to me.

I held out my own hand and stared at it, and discovered that I, too, was extraordinary, the work of a brilliant artist.

I inhaled, and smelled ozone from the air system, real fruits and vegetables, cheeses, meats; plants from someone's private quarters, countless chemicals; hope, rage, lust, curiosity, fear.

Closer, I smelled Sky. Storm Rat. Herog.

They smelled... delicious.

I shivered. The smell went straight to my brain. Direct line, jolt of recognition. All the other smells had been interesting. Rich. Wonderful in their ways. But what I smelled now was *food*. And I discovered I was hungry.

No.

Starving.

I looked at them, standing across the room. Watching me. Especially Herog.

Something funny occurred to me, and I said, "Herog. Come here."

He approached me. Solid. Unafraid. Ready for anything.

I smiled at him, and reached through the bars, and took his hand. Gently. I looked into his eyes.

"And now you're dead," I whispered, and felt his shock run through my skin when he realized he could not move. That I had him.

I wanted the blood beneath his skin. Wanted the feel of his throat against my lips, wanted to sink my teeth into him and tear him apart — and even as the part of me that remained human fought to gain control over the starving monster, I could feel my teeth elongating in my mouth, and feel my bones reshaping subtly to accommodate them.

I was myself. I knew where I was. I knew what humanity faced. I knew that I was the key to saving everything I loved.

Yet in that instant, with the feel of his wrist pulse beneath my thumb, with the scent of his blood rich and metallic and full of unimaginable promise, with his gaze locked to mine and his body, blood, and life mine, I discovered that I loved...nothing.

I heard Storm Rat say, "Cady? Is everything all right?"

I forced the monster's throat and lips to form words. "No. I'm starving. I need the blood substitute. *Now*. As much as you can bring." I took a deep breath. "Get everyone out of the room. I'll be able to let Herog go when you give me the blood. But for God's sake, hurry."

I could lift his hand to my lips, rip open his wrist, drink down his life. Part of me raged that I did not want to do this.

Part of me cheered that I was able to hold myself in check.

But I was losing the battle. And then the door slid open and one of the cleaning bots trundled into the room, three liter bags of blood substitute and a glass balanced on its flat back.

Through the bot's com speaker, Storm Rat said, "Get all three bags and the glass quickly, and I'll send it back with another load."

I couldn't let go of Herog. Couldn't smell the blood substitute — it was still sealed.

I told Herog, "Open one of the bags and pour it in the glass."

He said, "I can't. I can't move my hand."

I realized that my grip had tightened. I loosened it. I could do that much, even though I was fighting my own body like it was a stranger. Like it was my worst enemy. I still controlled him completely. I thought I might be able to peel my own fingers away from his wrist and wrap them around one bar of my cage.

"We're still in trouble," I told him.

"Yes."

"You'll have to be quick."

"Yes."

"Rip the bag. Pour it. Run. You understand?"

"Yes."

I managed at last to let go of his arm. He did what I said, and the overwhelming smell of warm, spilled blood filled my nostrils and my brain.

I dropped to my knees, grabbed the glass, drank the contents in two long, desperate swallows, and with shaking hands drank the next bag. And then the next. When I looked up, Herog was gone. The bot was gone. Everyone was gone.

The blood was gone.

I was alone in a moleibond cage, having just threatened to kill the man who had volunteered to protect me, and I was still starving.

"Cady?" Storm Rat's voice came over the com.

I couldn't touch them over com. Couldn't make them do things they didn't want to do. It was a good thing, because I couldn't trust myself to say hello right then.

"Cady?" That was Sky.

"I'm here. I'm going to need a few more liters of blood."

"What happened?"

"Blood first. I'm in bad shape here."

Three bots rolled in a few minutes later. They carried nine liters of blood substitute between them.

I went through three more liters as quickly as I had the first three. I sipped the next one, though, and was able to look at the remaining five with a possessive pleasure.

Turns out you didn't have to learn to like the stuff. No acting skills necessary.

Sated, in control of myself again, I sat on the cot in the middle of my cage and rested my head in my hands.

"Safe for us to come back now?" Storm Rat asked over com.

"No. Not now. Not ever."

I didn't know how Fedara Contei, the vampire who had created the original AntiLegend nanovirus, had kept from killing me the whole time we'd spent in each other's company. I didn't know how any of them did it.

Was I a worse person than all the vampires who successfully faked being human, who walked around among human beings daily, worked alongside them, lived among them, and managed not to even touch almost all of them?

Or was Legend II stronger than Legend I in its effects on every aspect of the user? If my senses were sharper, if I was stronger, if I could exert more control over humans, did it mean my appetites were also larger and fiercer, and that I paid a price by having less control over myself?

That made a certain depressing sense.

"Talk to me, Cady. Tell me what's going on."

"I can't ever be around humans again," I said. "Legend II works the way it's supposed to, but it makes my appetite for blood as oversized as the power I suddenly have. I drank seven liters of blood, Storm Rat. That's the equivalent of killing two people. In five seconds, I went from normal human to starving monster."

"Five seconds? You were thrashing around in there, screaming and throwing yourself against the cage and climbing its walls for nearly ten hours, Cady."

I stared at him, trying to figure that out. I'd closed my eyes, counted to five, held very still, and then it was over. So I told him that.

"I can show you the playback if you want."

I considered for a moment. "I need to see it."

He said, "Infoscreen key-in, replay Room K-4, last ten hours, fifteen minutes per minute." Around me, screens came to life.

And there I was, not even remotely human, a misshapen lump with arms and legs and fangs, with a tail that appeared and disappeared, with skin that went slick and oily at one point and furry at another, making noises that had never come out of any human throat. Not just screams, but howls and growls. I could see Sky panicking in the background, could see Bluejay hold her hand over her mouth and race from the room, could see Tarko leave, could see Books leave, could see Wire leave. I could read the horror and pity and fear in all their faces. At one point, I developed monstrous muscles and started trying to rip the cage apart — I was going after the people all around me, foaming at the mouth, spraying spittle everywhere. At another point, in my frenzy to get at them, I went over the inside of the cage ceiling, biting the bars, trying to break them.

And inside me, down in the dark, down in the quiet, a little voice that was not mine said, "Yes. That's me. I'm here."

My skin crawled. How had they not shot me, written the experiment off as a failure. How had they held out to let me get from that horror flinging itself against the cage in its desperation to kill them all, to me?

Even Storm Rat had to leave eventually, with his shoulders slumped and his fists knotted.

Only Herog remained through the whole thing. Still. Patient. Emotionless. Waiting.

When I found my way back to human form, when my body fell into its memory of *me*, he was the one who called them back.

When I finished, the question of why I'd been starving was answered.

The question of why he'd been willing to walk into my reach — having seen what he'd seen, and knowing better than anyone else in the room what I was, and what I was capable of — was not. I hadn't made him come to me. I'd made him stay, but he'd walked over of his own free will.

But maybe — if the murderous compulsion to kill him had only been because I was starving — I would be able to be around humans without hurting them. Briefly.

Living with them on my ship was out of the question.

So we were going to have to change the plan into something I could carry out alone.

Chapter 10

We'd argued. We'd talked. We'd fought. We'd gotten nowhere, and now they were sleeping and I lay alone, in the cage, awake.

I wasn't lonely. I had my own company, and I didn't even want that.

I had thirty liters of bagged synthetic blood around my cage, extra fuel I'd asked for before they went to sleep.

The blood substitute we'd manufactured was...edible. I was learning how to use my body, and expending surreal amounts of energy changing myself physically. At first, my experiments in intentional transformation went badly. I bent myself, twisted myself, made myself all manner of deformed and shambling things. There's a trick to getting inside your own skin, to feeling the play of your muscles against each other, the way your bones work together, the way your joints move — and to begin with, I didn't have that trick.

Worst case, I could have had them put the room on lock-down and remotely open the cage so I could use the Medix in the far corner to fix my mistakes. But I needed to be able to transform. It was part of the sales pitch. Part of what had made Legend II something immortal monsters would climb over each other to get.

Also, if any of them needed to get into the room and things turned ugly again, I wanted at least the scant protection of the moleibond cage between me and them. It wouldn't protect them from my voice or my will, but it might keep them out of my reach long enough that someone else could grab them.

So beneath the bright lights, inside my cage, I practiced. And I learned.

Having with my last attempt made myself unrecognizable as a living creature, much less something that might pass for human, I lowered my sights from whole-body transformation to piecework.

I needed a hand. So I focused on giving myself one finger. I visualized the feel of moving one finger on one hand. My right index finger. I concentrated on the way the bones moved, the way the skin felt around the joints as I flexed and extended the digit, my awareness from inside of the presence of the nail over the top of the last segment of the digit.

One finger. I closed my eyes, and saw it, and felt it. And when I opened my eyes, the rudimentary limb of what needed to be my right arm had one human finger.

With one finger in place, I could build out my hand, then my other hand, then my arms.

Then me.

My body had done this automatically when I'd been going through that first change, before I had regained any form of self-awareness.

But even if I'd been able to repeat that automatic change, it would have left me with just... me.

I needed to be able to turn smoothly from myself into at least one other thing, the way Danniz Oe had done. Not the hideous bat he'd turned himself into, though. Because — how disgusting.

I spent hours rebuilding myself. Making mistakes on one piece after another, putting things back together a bit at a time. The nanovirus prevented me from killing myself — I didn't know if it was rebuilding my internal organs automatically, or if, as long as I had the Legend II nanovirus in my system, internal organs were merely decorative. In the future, if I had a future, how the nanovirus kept me alive would matter. For now, it was enough that it did.

I eventually made it all the way back to human. I paused. I walked around for a while inside the cage, getting inside my body in motion, feeling my weight on my feet, the flexing of my hands, the roll of my shoulders, the movement of air into and out of my lungs.

None of this was new to me. Fight training taught being inside your skin, too.

But because the purpose was different, focus had to be different.

I had to be aware of my breathing to train to fight. I had to be aware of the individual sacs inside my lungs filling and deflating with every breath to change the way my lungs worked, and to do so without leaving myself a wreck again.

I worked. I drank my fake red fuel, grateful that we'd done the nanoviral modifications to *not* require living red blood cells. The look and feel and taste and smell of the artificial stuff was indistinguishable from blood. But no one had to bleed for me to live.

I skipped sleep. I skipped rest. I didn't feel much need for either, and the urgings I did feel, I ignored. No time for such luxury.

By the time station daylight came around, I could make myself the burly four-legged creature I'd been when I was changing after the injection, the one that tried to rip the cage apart to get at the people around me. I could, much to my relief, hang onto my own mind while I changed.

I could be tall and slender. Short and fat. I could not change my body mass, I could not alter the number of limbs I had or my gender, and I could not make myself a reptile or a bird, or anything but a mammal. But within those limitations, I could fit myself into the templates of such other mammals as I could recall — though probably imperfectly and definitely at the wrong sizes — and I could change my own human appearance. Eye color. Hair color and texture. Skin color and texture. And every imaginable variation of build.

Hair was the easiest. Those pigments seemed to be the most amenable to suggestion, and required only that I take in enough fuel to sustain the forced growth that let me replace one hair color with another. I grew a stripe of black, a stripe of red, a stripe of brown. Focused on no particular color, and whatever color I'd last chosen was what grew.

This was good. It meant I wouldn't grow blonde stripes into my hair every time I went to sleep, or wake up to find my skin a patchwork of different colors.

Fortunately, some things, like teeth and bone, I could reabsorb and reshape. So the little cage wasn't littered with them, or with tails and ears. But hair and skin changed their nature by having new hair and skin push through to replace old hair and skin — so the only way to change those was to accelerate the speed at which they shed.

I made myself hairless, and the whole striped mess of hair slithered to the floor in big hanks, to join the growing detritus of sloughed-off skin, fur, plates, claws, and nails.

Naked, hairless, generic human female in shape and appearance, I lay on the bed in the center of the cage and stared at the ceiling. The way I set my shape was the way it stayed until I changed it.

I would be able to demonstrate to my customers for Legend II that whatever they wanted, they could become. I could get them talking on the datastream, get them to sell Legend II for me. I could be what I needed to be. Do what I needed to do. I'd be alone, but even alone I could at least give humanity one last chance to survive.

I focused, reshaped myself into myself, grew out my hair just a little, drank a couple liters of fuel, and fell asleep.

I awoke from a dream in which I had been the perfect monster.

The voice down in the darkness rejoiced, hungry for the hunt, for destruction.

I shivered.

STORM RAT'S voice came over the com. "Cady?"

I'd been lying on the cot with my eyes closed. I was frustrated. I'd been in the cage two days while Wire's techs installed the synthetic AntiLegend-laced blood generator, and fit both the *Corrigan's Blood's* shuttles with the same thing, as well as built-in blood-mist sprayers, and while Storm Rat kept talking about "working on alteratives."

The story Wire was giving to the techs was that I'd figured out a way to spray AntiLegend-laced blood substitute on vampires from the air to wipe them out.

As far as it went, it was true. What the folks outside our tiny inner circle didn't know was that the stuff was also going to be my breakfast, lunch, and dinner.

"Yes, Storm Rat. I'm still here."

"I know. There's been a slight change of plans."

The door on the opposite side of the room from the one we used opened. Herog walked in.

"Get him out of here," I shouted. "Storm Rat, do it *now!*"

"Cady, look at me," Herog said. His voice caught me, held me. I stopped shouting and really looked at him — and he looked exactly the same, but he was different. I took a deep breath. He didn't smell delicious. I could look at him and not want to sink my teeth into his throat. I knew what he'd done, and my hands knotted into fists, and I thought of my end game. The kill switch I'd had made for myself when I thought it was just going to be me — for when I knew I'd won — for if I lost, I wouldn't need it. I'd assumed the responsibility of being what I'd become for myself. I knew what would happen to me when I used it.

But now there were two of us. And he hadn't committed to my endgame.

"You don't know what you've done," I said, and my voice was suddenly hoarse.

"I watched you," he said. "The whole night you fought to transform, I saw what you went through. I knew. I told you I was going with you. I gave Storm Rat my word I'd back you up. This is what I had to do to keep my word."

He walked over and unlocked the cage. "You're free."

"There are eighty-four... eighty-*three* people on Tegosshu who need me not to be free," I told him.

"Eighty," he said.

"No," I whispered. My heart raced.

The same door slid open again, and Bluejay walked in, followed by Wire and Tarko.

"You tell her yet?" Bluejay asked Herog.

"Getting to it."

"You're too slow." She grinned at me, and hers was the satisfied grin of a happy human. A smile clear of fear, obsession, compulsion, secret guilt, public hunger. But she was, like me, a monster. I could smell it on her. On Tarko. On Wire. "We worked it all out," she said. "Well, it was Herog's idea. He was going to be the only one, but when the four of us sat down with Sky and Storm Rat, each of the rest of us explained why we had to go, too. We'd all decided separately that we were going to go with you. That you were not going to have to carry this alone."

"So you all knew about the transformations. About..."

"We knew, darlin'," Tarko said. "Herog showed us bits and pieces of what you went through. The worst, I suspect—"

"No," Herog said. "Only I saw the worst."

"I thought we saw everything," Wire said.

"I kept what you needed to see. I destroyed the rest. It was... private."

I looked at him, but he was staring at the three of them, daring them to challenge him. I thought of my struggle to get back to being human, and hoped that was the part they hadn't seen.

"How was it for you," I asked. "Changing?"

"Bad," Bluejay said. "Horrible. When I started transforming myself intentionally, I made an awful mess. I didn't think I was ever going to get back to being human again, but Herog had me start by just shaping one finger, and then the rest of them, working by feel and memory. From there, it got easier — but he talked me all the way through it. It took me almost an hour from start to finish."

"Same with me," Tarko said.

"I was a little quicker," Wire told me, "but I was last

because I couldn't do the change until after we had the ship finished. I think by then Herog had the process of getting us through it worked all the way out."

Herog's gaze flicked to me, then away.

He'd figured out a way to get them through it without exposing me. I was grateful.

"How long did it take you?" I asked.

"About half as long as it took you. Seeing the process is different than doing the process, and I didn't know what it would feel like. I just knew what I saw when you figured it out. Once I'd done it, I knew what to tell them."

The other three looked at me curiously. "How long did it take you?" Bluejay asked.

"Longer than an hour."

"Well, you had a harder time of it. There were no humans present during any of what we did, and Herog made sure we had open containers of the blood substitute within reach — the smell helped a lot."

"Both of those helped," Tarko said. "But so did knowing that, however impossible it seemed, you and Herog had already been through it, and could do everything you needed to do."

The thought that had been nagging at me finally worked its way to the surface. "But you aren't tempted by being around humans?" I asked. "When you go out into the corridors and pass them, you don't have any... urges?"

"We're locked in this wing," Herog said. "The five of us. We will avoid human contact whenever possible, and when we must go near humans, we will do so when we have fed to satiation on synthetic blood, and we will leave at the time we determine based on the one of us with the quickest hunger cycle."

Suddenly I could breathe. I would not be alone. I would

have allies who could watch me, whom I could watch in return. I knew then how Bluejay could smile. How Tarko could be amused. How Wire could laugh.

How Herog... well.

How Bluejay could smile.

I found myself laughing, hugging Bluejay and Wire and Tarko in turn, and pulling up short in front of Herog.

"I'm sorry I tried to kill you," I said.

"You didn't," he told me. "If you'd tried to kill me, I'd be dead. You showed me what I was missing, what I needed to know about vampires. Taught me about my enemy, and taught me about you. And you did it without even bruising my wrist." He paused. "It was an effective lesson."

He held out his hand. I shook it. No palm injection this time. No need for one. In that instant I understood that he and I trusted each other — and more, I began to understand what his presence among us meant. The deadliest man I'd ever met had my back.

Five of us. Uncountable billions of the enemy. And I thought right then we had a real chance to win.

Chapter 11

We drank our fuel. Wire, Tarko, and Bluejay joined me in calling it that, while Herog didn't call it anything.

And then I said, "What are we waiting for?"

"Ships to be ready. Plausible deniability to be firmly established. Money to be finished working its way through the necessary channels to make sure the manufacturing of the Legend II distribution starts up properly, and that manufacturing of AntiLegend does the same.

"I thought AntiLegend distribution would get us executed for committing genocide," I said

Tarko nodded. "Right now, it would."

"We have time," Herog said. "The waiting involved in doing a thing right the first time is hard. But failure to wait is devastating. And while we wait, you need to see something."

The rest of us looked at him. He brought out a handful of doppler chips. "These are the only copies, no one else has seen them, and once all of you have watched them, I'll destroy them."

He popped the first chip into a stand-alone player. "The transformations," he said. "Not edited. We'll go through these quickly."

Gray on gray, a new room shimmered into existence around us, with a moleibond cage in each of the rooms four corners. Herog adjusted the view until the part he wanted us to see was in front of us. I saw stacks of liter bags of what had to be blood substitute, glasses filled with gray liquid, and what looked like feeder tubes snaking along the wall to just one cage.

"Hands-free food for the initial transition?" I asked.

Herog nodded.

"Smart."

"It helped in the later part," Wire said. "I got stuck without hands for quite a while."

Sky was walking from cage to cage, checking setups. "You're sure you want to go through with this?" All four of my allies were with her.

"If we're to have any chance of beating this," Tarko said, "she has to have people with her who can adapt the plan as conditions change — there can be no delay between when she needs something and when she gets it. Even with the datastream, there is always a delay transmitting messages out of system. It isn't much, but it could be enough to be fatal. We're going to be out of system for all of this."

"I want to live with settled space still alive around me," Bluejay said. "That means I go with her and do anything I can to help her stay on best routes to best locations for best chances of success — and that means avoiding any systems that hit Darkout while we're out there, and deciding in the air on targets that are changing rapidly. I have to be there."

Wire said, "Weapons adaptations, ship repairs, unforeseen disasters. Yes. I'm going."

Herog looked at her.

She stared back at him, seemingly trying to force him to speak by saying nothing, but in the end she shrugged. "Right. You already decided. Before I inject any of you, you're going to take a test. It's invasive, it's uncomfortable, and if your results are not good, you're not going."

Herog moved within inches of her, stared down at her, then whispered something in her ear.

"I have to know what kind of monsters I'm sending out there," she said. "*One* like her is too many."

Herog whispered something else, and she froze.

I was seated on the other side of Herog and the player. I hit the stop button and reset the chip to the moment when he first whispered in her ear, focused tightly on his lips and her ear, and brought the volume up.

He glanced at me, but didn't stop me.

The first thing he said was, "Careful, doctor. Stand against us, and you're fighting for the vampires."

The second thing he said was, "Your past can find its way back to your present. If *anything* goes wrong with any of us — or all of us — there is a dead man's switch that will make sure everyone knows what I know. Do your test. Give the results to me. *Everyone goes.*"

I paused the recording and looked at him in disbelief. "What's her secret?"

"Later," he said. "Your ears only, along with the details of the dead man's switch."

I considered that. "All right. What does she mean, one like me? What disagreement does she have with me?"

"She found out," he said, "that you scored an 89 on the Kartach Norgan."

"The *what?*" I'd never heard of the Kartach Norgan.

"In the Hegan Deep Space Academy, it was called the Suitability for Deep Space test."

Oh.

That.

The SDS had been the final screening test taken by all prospective deep-space pilots. No one going into any of the other deep space career fields had to take it. But once the screeners had weeded out everyone with poor decision-making skills, poor emergency response reflexes, sloppy logic, shaky ethics, lousy mechanical aptitude, and no proven ability to quickly adapt to and use technology, they threw the remainder into the SDS.

We knew that we needed better than a forty to ever in our entire careers be eligible to captain a TFN ship. It was make or break, sudden death.

We knew there was no way to study.

We were told that if we passed the SDS, we would be ineligible for public office in all Pact worlds — those are the worlds that agree to prohibit slavery — but if we failed the SDS, someday maybe we could be dirt chancellors. Everyone laughed at that.

We had been told that a low but non-zero percent of those who took the test died taking it. We had to sign a waiver stating that if we died, we did so of our own free will, and no one could sue the school in our names.

No one laughed at that.

It was at that point that a number of promising applicants voluntarily diverted into the In-System Pilot program.

Not me. The universe lay in front of me, and the SDS — or now, apparently, the Kartach Norgan — had been my ticket to it.

The test itself had been an ordeal I'd never wanted to think of again — wires, scanners, actual physical injections, a cot, and full-body restraints, followed by drug-induced hallucinations of being ripped into shreds and waking up to find myself being ripped to shreds again, over and over until my mother showed up and tried to kill me. I came out of that to find that I'd broken my right wrist fighting the restraints.

I don't think anyone in my flight died. I do know about sixty percent of the remaining applicants failed, however. They were involuntarily diverted into the in-system program, and would, for the rest of their careers, have Ineligible for TFN Training stamped on their licenses.

But they could always be dirt chancellors if that didn't work out. Ha. Ha.

Badger had scored a sixty-three, which put him in the top one tenth of one percent of our flight. As long as he passed training, he could have any career he wanted with any TFN line in settled space, and write his own ticket.

Me? I broke the curve. I was the golden girl of that run. One tester referred to my score as 'epic.' Eighty-nine. They told me there was a student who'd graduated two years ahead of me who'd scored a ninety-seven. His was the highest score ever recorded. Mine was the second-highest they were aware of in the TFN licensing records.

Like me, that student had paid for the course himself. Like me, on graduation he'd turned down the unending stream of commercial jobs with astronomical pay that had been thrown at his feet. Like me, he'd found a way to buy his own ship.

Like me, he'd quickly disappeared.

And... like me and every other TFN pilot to hold a legitimate Deep Space Operators License, somewhere on his license he had a little line that said, "Prohibited from holding government office on any Pact world."

As if someone who could grasp the stars in one hand would ever want to spend so much as a day tied to the ground, making a tenuous living appeasing an argumentative rabble, with his livelihood subject to the whim of that rabble.

Give up the ability to sail between the stars and embrace the pure, exquisite silence of space? To have my feet anchored to the ground?

The idea still made me laugh.

"So she had all of you take that? I'm *sorry*."

I turned the recording back on.

Sky was setting up all four cots with the heavy restraints I remembered so well. While she did it, she explained to them that the Kartach Norgan was named after a man who'd once done a decent job of overthrowing most of the governments and worlds in settled space, and turning them into his personal empire. She said, "Back then, that was about fifteen worlds in various stages of development — not including Old Earth, which he'd deemed too crowded, too feisty, and too inconveniently located — and about forty governments. Population-wise, we're talking something maybe triple the size of the ancient Roman Empire. In terms of modern settled space, it would have been a mere drop in the bucket. But still."

She continued, "Those who have Kartach Norgan Syndrome tend to be very good at hiding it — which means the test has to be done with drugs, injectable transponders, and scans.

"I'm qualified to run it and to interpret the results. When I am finished, I'll figure the results and give them to Herog." Even in gray on gray, I could see her glare at Herog.

Herog neither burst into flames or collapsed to the floor. Imagine that.

They all got on their cots. Sky strapped everyone down — forehead, four-point shoulder-and-chest, elbows, wrists, hips, knees, and feet. When she got to Herog, he said, "Remember the dead man's switch."

When they were in their four corners, she said, "The Kartach Norgan test takes roughly fifteen minutes. Those minutes will feel... longer. The experience is awful — I had to take the test once as a medical trainee, and again before my previous owner purchased me." I saw the involuntary jerk of her head toward Herog as she said that, but he didn't respond. "You will not enjoy it."

She picked up a hypogun and started going around the room. "You're each getting the scrubber injection first. The scrubbers will clear the drugs and nanovirals I'll inject next. They're timed to wake up after they've been bathed in the KN cocktail for fifteen minutes. Next you'll get the injectable transponders."

While she talked, she walked between the cots, pressing the hypogun to each person's neck and pulling the trigger. There was a lot of wincing. It would be worse with the transponders. Those, she explained, were delivered in a thick, cold, sludge, and hurt like hell.

"Finally, once I've turned on the scanner and calibrated each of your uplinks, I'll inject you with the KN cocktail, which is a combination of hallucinogens, hormones, neural net stimulators, and vitamins. The test is hard on the body, so I'll also be monitoring your vital signs.

"If you test at thirty-five percent or higher on the Kartach Norgan pre-Legend II, you should not have the injection. Thirty-five percent is borderline KN Syndrome, and the changes made in your body by Legend II seem probable to trigger a full expression of the syndrome."

Full expression, she explained, meant the individual

"expressing" the syndrome would become — if he was not already — pathologically antisocial and egocentric, ferociously ambitious and megalomaniacal, and with a predisposition to seek out positions of power over others.

"I don't recommend the injection for anyone who scores more than twenty percent," she added.

"What's an average score?" Wire asked.

She said, "Two to five percent. High achievers test higher, so I do imagine you will test in the upper ranges of normal."

With that, she calibrated her scanner, then injected each of them with the cocktail.

I watched my prospective crew as their bodies locked up, their spines arced against the straps, and they began to fight and scream. It was the second time I had seen Herog vulnerable. I wondered why he was willing to let me — or any of the others — see that.

Their torture stopped. They lay shivering, and Sky was hurrying from each of them to the next, unstrapping them and giving them drinks and food and as much comfort as she could offer in the few seconds before she ran to the next.

The whole bunch of them was sick.

I watched Sky do another round with the hypogun, giving each of them a combination of vitamins and other things they'd lost in that traumatic fifteen minutes.

The four of them gathered in the center space between the cages.

There was a skip in the chip.

It restarted with the four of them sitting at a table, eating real food. The last meal. In gray on gray, it didn't tempt me the way it would have in full color.

Sky joined them. She looked sicker than any of her patients had post-test.

She sat down in an empty seat at the table and looked at each of them, and shook her head.

"I've never seen anything like it. None of you are suitable for the injection. The lowest score any of you had on the Kartach Norgan was Wire, who scored fifty-four percent. Bluejay scored fifty-eight. Tarko scored eighty-four." She glared at Herog again. "You scored a ninety-seven."

My hand slammed down on the player and the images froze. I turned to Herog. "That was you?"

He didn't say anything.

"The Hegan Deep Space Academy. Highest score ever recorded — you took your license the day you received it, bought a ship with cash, and disappeared. But your name was Wilms Tarbley."

"Wilms Tarbley was the name of my owner's eldest son, who left my cage unlocked after bringing potential buyers in to examine me. When I killed him, I marked my face with his blood, then killed every other slaver in the compound, stole his personal ship and all the slaves in the compound, and escaped with them."

"How did you get past the ship's biometrics?"

"It was an older model. I brought his body with me, and used his."

"Dead-handed it." I nodded, approving. "That still works sometimes."

"I find it unnerving that you know that," Wire said.

"You probably should." I took my hand off pause, and the chip picked up with Herog talking to Sky.

"There's a problem with the test. I want to do what I want, and have governments and other troublemakers leave me alone."

"That may be what you *think* you want—"

He cut her off. "No. It's what I want."

Three other heads nodded. "That's how we all got here," Bluejay said. "We got away from everyone who owned us, who used us — and we came here to build lives where we worked on what we loved, and did what we wanted. Speaking for myself, I have no interest in taking on the responsibility of telling other people how to live their lives. Getting what I want from my own life is difficult enough to manage."

"But the Kartach Norgan—"

Tarko stopped her. "Is the test predictive? Is it a test that tells you who *will* be an evil dictator bent on the overthrow of nations and worlds, darlin'? Or is it a test that simply tells you who'd be really good at it?"

"It's not predictive. But there's a high correlation between politicians who score high on the test and those who become problems while they're in office. Between high-scoring doctors, soldiers, police, sporcs, administrators, board directors, chairmen, and teachers — high scores indicate those who *will* have ethics and control issues later."

And Tarko laughed. "Of course. That's obvious. What those careers all have in common should make it evident why those people become problems."

Sky frowned and thought. "Those careers have nothing in common."

Around that table, three of my four fellow potential dictators smiled. They saw it.

Sitting in the room, watching the chip, I saw it.

"In every single one of those careers," Tarko said, "the person goes into it with the knowledge that sooner or later, he or she will be in charge of other people. That he or she will have power over others. People who want power seek out those careers."

Her eyes widened a little.

Bluejay said, "Not a single one of us sought out such a career. Every one of us, instead, focused on work that we could do alone, and excel at alone. Because Storm Rat recruited only the best from the slaves he rescued—" She dipped her head in Herog's direction. "—or met, he ended up with people highly motivated to succeed. And because his work population came from rescued and escaped slaves, his people prefer to work alone or in the company of those who will not attempt to control them."

"That makes a certain amount of sense," she said.

"Could we take over the universe?" Tarko asked her. I watched him look at the collection of misfits sitting with him, and grin. "Probably. Are we going to? Not a chance. The man on either end of a chain is still chained. We've already been chained, darlin'."

Sky studied them, doubt clear on her face.

Herog spoke. "We'll take the nanovirus now."

I heard in his voice the same threat I'd heard in his whispers.

And I wondered what lay behind it.

AT HEROG'S INSISTENCE, we all watched their transformations, highly accelerated — though he ran the player, and from time to time he slowed it down to emphasize something.

His first slowdown was when, in his four-legged form, he dove under the moleibond cot frame that was anchored to the floor, and became trapped. His body was still twisting and changing, and the space was too small for him. I could see both his shoulders break as he fought to get free, and his screams weren't human, but they were heartrending.

He slowed again when he was attempting his first voluntary transformation, and it went badly wrong. He collapsed as most of his muscles failed, and he lay on the floor. He could, at that point, still speak, though, for he said, "How did you do it, Cady? You found the answer, and I didn't get the chance to ask you."

And then, after he too kept thrashing, seeking a fix, and instead lost form entirely. In that segment, I guessed what I would see. A finger, I thought.

I was wrong.

He used the boneless tissue form to squeeze between the bars of the cage.

He stopped it. Looked at us. Asked, "Do you understand what this means."

I did. Grim and sick, I nodded to him, then studied the other three.

Tarko whooped. "Cages cannot hold us," he said, and laughed. "We will be slaves no more."

But Bluejay was shaking her head. "It means no one is safe from us."

Tarko stopped grinning. Wire paled.

"Yes," Herog said, and moved on.

Outside the cage, he built one finger first, then rebuilt himself.

In each of the other three transformations, he was present, he talked to each crew member before they received the injection, which he gave, and once they returned to rationality and began their test transformation, he talked them through that.

But still, he slowed on certain passages.

Wire, trying to tear himself apart as the first transformation gave him back his mind.

Tarko reshaping his dwarfed limbs into ones of normal length, and discovering when he did so that he could not add mass — so his limbs became thin and spidery and he still didn't look normal.

Bluejay back in human form after her successful transformation, sitting in a corner of her cage, staring at the glass of fake blood in front of her and weeping.

When we finished, no one said anything for a long time. Then Herog turned to me and asked, "Do you know why you needed to see that?"

I'd been considering that very question the whole time I'd watched.

"Because I needed to know that each of you paid a price for giving up your humanity. That we have all suffered the same."

Chapter 12

S torm Rat wanted us to stay long enough to practice
our new vampire skills before we left.

He wanted to have Wire build in triple redundancy for the com system we'd use to communicate with
Tegosshu.

In the end, I think he hoped to find a way to keep his
best people safe.

But time was not our friend, and we had to go. I reassured myself that we'd have time to practice being what we
were once we left Tegosshu.

It was time to tell The Big Lie.

Excluding Storm Rat, Sky, and Books, those who had
worked on implementation but who were not leaving had
only bits and pieces of the truth of what we were doing, and
it was a truth carefully cleaned up, legalized, and firewalled
from the unexpurgated reality of our future. Before we left,
Storm Rat would purge Tegosshu's data of any record of our
real intention, actions — and nature.

The records of my ship's changes were already falsified

— the prep work for the deep changes was all in place, as were the supplies to complete the work in deep space. The records reflected that I'd had work done on the origami drive (true), on forward and aft passive deflectors (true), and improvements made to the cargo loaders to change what was essentially a pleasure yacht into a working craft (false), for which JT Loggins had applied for and received a Tegosshu-certified Multi-Use Vehicle, or MUV, code. (True, if a fictitious person applying for a certificate of use for a fictitious vehicle to which fictitious changes were made can be in any shape, form, or fashion true.)

No one would see the real changes we made to my ship after we sailed , when I and my crew met up at our agreed-upon rendezvous.

Storm Rat's people had *no* knowledge of our overall save-the-universe plan, because everydamnthing we were doing was illegal, and not just "fifty-rucet fine" illegal. We're talking "hang-you-from-the-ceiling, slice-you-into-ribbons, burn-the-pieces-and-piss-on-the-ashes, sell-tickets-to-the-proceedings" illegal. Anyone who was not going with us had only carefully crafted pieces of a benign lie. If someone came along later and starting asking questions — assuming there was a later, which was not an assumption those of us who knew the truth were making — he would have a fight on his hands to put together what Storm Rat's people thought they were hiding. And when he put it together, he would discover that Storm Rat's researchers had uncovered a vaccine against the Legend nanovirus that was eighty percent effective, and caused no casualties, and that they were part of a team trying to get the vaccine legally distributed.

Which was true, as far as it went, and Books and Storm

Rat would drag their feet and reluctantly give out the information if they absolutely had to.

No one who was not part of the crew knew — or could know — what we were *really* doing... or what we *really* were. And nothing of what we were really doing would ever be connected in any way with Tegosshu.

We had two reasons for this. The first was that, if no one knew what we were doing, no one could betray what we were doing, and prevent us from saving humankind.

The second, and much more optimistic reason, was that if humanity survived Darkout and we survived *stopping* Darkout, no one would ever be able to trace our roles in that survival back to us. Humanity has a nasty habit of making martyrs of those who have helped it most. We were willing to skip the publicity, and the almost certainly lethal form "thanks" would take, to try to create lives we'd wanted to live, and to live them quietly.

The third reason was that Storm Rat's people needed a home to go back to — and compromising Tegosshu by allowing it to be connected to Legend II would almost guarantee they didn't.

And even that wasn't as far as it went. Because for the five of us who'd given up our humanity to go to the front lines — assuming you could even call five people surrounded by billions of enemies a "front line" instead of a "middle dot" — what happened to us afterwards didn't necessarily include survival. Not even if we won it all. What we'd done needed to stay with us, and not splash on potential scapegoats elsewhere.

"All personnel assemble in the auditorium. All personnel assemble in the auditorium."

I was already on the *Corrigan's Blood*, because I wasn't

an official part of the Big Lie. As far as anyone needed to know, I was just the last Tegosshu customer to leave.

But I'd brought in sound and a feed from Tegosshu so I could follow along. I sat in the captain's seat on my bridge, the datastream showing on forward screen one, and watched an auditorium empty except for Storm Rat, who stood at a podium, and repeated his announcement.

My feet kept twitching. My stomach knotted. Couldn't eat food, but I could still get indigestion.

It figured.

My crew was part of Storm Rat's show. All four of them wore shipsuits with *Delegate One* mission patches on the right shoulder and their names on the left breast. They looked brave, and ready, and when Storm Rat was almost done, they would play their little part in feeding the Big Lie.

People filed in and walked down the aisle to the front. The auditorium filled from front to back, neatly, as if at some point they'd practiced this.

Hell, maybe they had.

Most of the auditorium was still empty when the last person sat.

The recorder stream I was watching played over the audience. I realized there were multiple streams going, and brought up three more threads from the datastream, then flicked the four views around until Storm Rat stood in front of me, seeming to look at me. I had the crowd views at second left, first left, and first right.

I could hear snatches of conversation as the recorders scanned different parts of the crowd.

"You know what this is about?" a man toward the front asked the person next to him. His seatmate said, "No clue."

The woman to the right of both of them said, "I think it

has something to do with those killers we have locked up in the north wing."

He nodded. "Makes sense."

"Your attention, please," Storm Rat said.

He stood there looking scruffy, disreputable, and tired.

Storm Rat was the face of Tegosshu, and everyone knew him personally, because he had rescued every single one of them from slavery, either personally or by finding the places where they were being kept, and sending in teams to free them. He'd recruited them, had given them homes, freedom, and citizenship. Had greeted them personally, had made it his job to get to know each of them.

They were his people. And he was theirs.

He'd been working insane hours, locked away with a crew working on something no one was talking about, and everyone *did* know that.

They would understand the bone-deep weariness that showed in his stance, his eyes, his voice.

"You know I've been busy, that I've been locked away dealing with trouble, and a lot of you have suspected — correctly — that the trouble stems from the people we had confined in the west end. Now I'm going to tell you the part you don't know."

"They have a self-induced disease — it is transmissible, highly contagious, eventually deadly not just to those who come into contact with them, but to them as well."

"With the help of my scientists and mathematicians, we've discovered that the disease has become a plague, and has already wiped out the entire populations of some worlds. We are calling these events Darkout. The world infected goes silent, and everyone who reaches it after Darkout dies."

He closed his eyes, and rubbed the back of one hand

against his forehead. Took a deep breath. "We've created a vaccine. It's not a cure, so those people already infected are going to die, and they're going to do it soon. We've calculated that, without the vaccine, the best case is that all worlds in settled space will fall into Darkout in four months. *Best* case."

Little susurrations of whispering people erupted into shouts, exclamations, people leaping to their feet and demanding answers.

Storm Rat waved them back into their seats.

"I'm going to show you clips taken by a customer who has been secretly fighting this problem for the past year. This customer, who has requested anonymity, agreed that you could see the view of a Darkout world taken from this customer's shuttle immediately after landing."

And there they were again — the Legends — right in my face, though this time gray on gray. Crawling all over my viewscreen, trying to find a way to get to me. I could hear their nails scrabbling on my hull again, the chill ran down my spine again, and I closed my eyes.

I realized I could also hear screaming coming from the unprepared audience.

My thoughts exactly.

"Now I'm going to show you what happened on Tegosshu that caused me to lock everything down."

And there were the just-rescued Legends, this time fed and human-looking, killing the five Tegosshu citizens who'd been unfortunate enough to be locked in with them when Storm Rat hit the panic button.

More screams.

And then exclamations of anger as they watched their friend and fellow citizen seducing two other citizens, and then saw the recordings when Storm Rat lifted the privacy shield again.

Storm Rat said, "All the killers on Tegosshu have been executed, and all of you have already been exposed to the airborne inoculation we developed to prevent the the disease. But if settled space doesn't survive, our lives will end here, on Tegosshu.

"So Herog, Bluejay, Wire, and Tarko, working with me on this, have undergone special training with our anonymous customer who knew how to fight these blood-drinking nightmares. They have also undergone painful body modifications to improve their chances of survival. They are going to go to critical worlds in settled space to try to convince government officials to make the vaccine we created to inoculate all of you available to their people. Because the carriers of the disease have done an extraordinary job of keeping themselves hidden, and have used the intentional side effects of this nanovirus to infiltrate and corrupt positions of power across settled space, I think our chances of success are going to be slim.

"Those of you who wish to remain on Tegosshu will have to have the injectable version of the inoculation, because the airborne version is only eighty to ninety percent effective. If you refuse the injectable version, you will leave Tegosshu on the last flight out today. You'll receive severance pay and a cashout, and Razor will take you to Threffen Station on the other side of the origami point. Once you leave the ship, you will not be permitted to get back on it for any reason. Razor will not leave it for any reason. This is to prevent any possibility of bringing contamination back here."

I heard murmurs of shock, a few voices sharp with anger, some filled with the pain of betrayal.

Storm Rat raised a hand. "I acted and am acting to preserve the lives of all of those who choose to live on my world. So even if our ambassadors for the vaccine fail, those of us who remain behind will have a chance to survive."

From the back of the room, someone shouted, "How?"

Storm Rat nodded. "Good question. Here's the answer. Everyone who decides to leave Tegosshu will go today. Once they are gone, we'll lock the place down. Both com operators and I will have transmission codes for the crew of the *Delegate One*, and we'll stay in touch with them. We've set up off-site bases for the manufacture of the vaccine, and I'll need as many of you as are willing to help us fight this to run the programs that will keep the lablines producing the vaccine going. These are all mechanical — no people will be onsite on any of the labline stations. We cannot afford mistakes, contamination, or any loss of time. If you decide you're going to stay here and fight this with us, your job until we hear the final outcome from the *Delegate One* crew — or if we get the automated distress beacon from the *Delegate One* letting us know ship and crew were killed — will be to make sure nothing stops production. We need enough product for every human being in settled space. Best guess? Trillions of doses."

He sighed. "And this is going to be expensive, at least initially. So Tarko has..." Storm Rat paused, and his mouth quirked into a tight smile. "...Tarko has set up some clever money funnels for us..."

The auditorium filled with laughter. Apparently Tarko Armbruster's skills with moving money around settled space, including money that didn't actually belong to him, were well known.

Storm Rat arched one eyebrow. "Exactly. So money will funnel in here. Probably a lot of it. If humanity survives and money retains any value in what remains, you will all be financially well rewarded for your part in our fight to save humanity. And make no mistake. What we do, and what our *Delegate One* crew does, is nothing less than a fight to save settled space, and everything in it that we love."

A little ripple of applause.

"If Darkout falls, we'll be covered as long as we can be covered. I've set up — and Tarko has financed — drone runs to funnel good food from the closer automated food manufacturing worlds to make sure we eat well. Real food — clone beef and clone pork, wild-lake-skimmed fish, real-sun vegetables and fruits, and luxuries like real coffee and cocoa beans — will come for as long as the drones keep running. We'll have enough reconsta — as long as the generators run, there will be both food and water of some sort, though over time, quality will degrade."

The laughter was gone, the smiles vanished. Even the sounds of breathing had stilled to such faint movement they seemed not to exist.

"If — and only if — we get word we can verify from the *Delegate One* that they've survived and settled space has not died in Darkout, we'll lift lockdown — after we validate the codes and they pass the tests to prove they're not infected. But until and unless that happens, we'll sterilize every drone that comes in with food — we will make sure nothing living is onboard." I saw him swallow, and saw his hands tighten into fists, the knuckles gone white. "If you stay, know that we will fight to survive, and make the best lives for ourselves that we can."

He was blinking too quickly. "I love you," and it was hard to remember that he was looking at me but talking to them. "You are my friends, my family, my world. We are going to hold this ground against whatever comes, so that we can live, and so that our people who are risking everything have a home to come back to. Understand that you are nothing but a source of food to those infected with this plague, and that our fight may well be as desperate as the one our friends now embark on. But all of us here and on that ship are going to do everything in our power to make sure once this is done humanity will have all of settled space to call home. No matter what happens, we will take care of ourselves and each other, never forget where we came from or why *we* matter... and we will live well and with joy."

He bowed his head for just an instant. Then he said, "The crew is standing by to embark on their mission."

My center screen view changed from Storm Rat to my crew.

They stood, feet apart, hands behind their backs, shoulders back, chins up.

A cheer erupted from the people in the auditorium, and on my other screens, I could see them standing, shouting, raising fists in the air.

I saw Herog giving the other three a count, and I saw as they replied to the cheers on his count with fists in the air. Tarko, who seemed somehow taller in his shipsuit, was a bit off the count.

Through the tears running down my cheeks, I laughed just a little.

Then the screen view shifted back to Storm Rat as he walked off the stand, and the cheers were suddenly for him. They were forming a line — every single one of them. They hugged him as he worked his way down the line, spoke a few words to him, cried a little, patted him on the back, looked him in the eyes and told him they were staying. That they would fight like hell for him, and for the crew of the *Delegate One*.

They were Storm Rat's people, and he was theirs, and in that moment I wished with all my heart that I could be one of them, too. That Tegosshu could be my home, that I could share the bond that brought them all together and allowed them to all be individuals who still had a place to belong. I would fight for a family like that, I thought, until death. Beyond death, could I find the way.

But I was not one of them, and could not be one of them. And I would not pretend I had a place in their world — I had not earned such a place.

So I watched them from my bridge, and waited.

"Tarko's going?" the woman he'd just hugged asked. "He won't be able to fight those things."

Storm Rat said, "He's tougher than you think. And our best hope of getting the vaccine to the people who need it on a lot of the worlds out there is to grease the necessary palms. Tarko *manufactures* palm grease."

She laughed and wiped tears from her cheeks, and hugged him again. He moved down the line, toward the door...

...and the deafening sound of breach klaxons went off in the auditorium.

The containment doors slid shut.

Storm Rat's head snapped left, staring back at the giant display behind the podium.

One of the recorders in the auditorium adjusted to pick up what Storm Rat was looking at, and their images appeared on my left two screens. They'd been leaving the room, but turned and headed back toward the screen, and communication with Storm Rat, when the alarms went off.

"We didn't do that," Tarko said. "And *you* didn't do that. And *they* didn't do that. So who did?"

I put myself into the loop, splitting the screens both

Storm Rat and my crew could see. "Not me. I'm on the bridge of the *Blood* waiting for your stationmaster to get back to give me my passage clearance through the minefield."

"Headcount," Storm Rat shouted.

I could clearly hear his com announcing, "Those not present are Sky and Grinder. I have a recorded message from Sky. Do you wish to hear it?"

Storm Rat broke my record for most profanity in a single exhalation with his reply.

And there was Sky on the screen.

"You killed those people without due process," she said. "What you're doing by vaccinating humanity with AntiLegend is killing other people — even if they are vampires — without due process. I can't be a part of this, or a part of you, or a part of what you're doing. You're wrong. All of you. If this is how humanity has to survive, it doesn't deserve to survive. I've taken the *Delegate One*. None of you will see me, or it, again."

Something was wrong with that. She'd been with us. Fighting right along side us. She knew what we were doing. She'd wanted what we wanted — to save humanity. Until...

Wait. *She knew what we were doing.*

Oh, hell. I was pretty sure I knew what was going on, and it wasn't any desire on her part to see legal justice for Legends.

"I'll be happy to help your folks retrofit your number two cargo ship as the replacement *Delegate One*," I said. "Seeing how you got robbed. It'll give me a chance to say goodbye to a couple of friends."

There was a pause. I saw Storm Rat's left eyebrow go up. He hesitated just an instant, then said, "Come on back. We'll be happy for the help."

BACK IN THE part of the compound still locked down to keep the five of us separate from the humans, I met in a closed session with my four crew members, with Storm Rat sitting in via infoscreen.

"You figured something out, Cady?" he said.

I nodded. "She was with us when we were working on aerosolized AntiLegend. She was fighting as hard as we were to save humanity, because she was humanity, too.

"But it was when we realized that AntiLegend wasn't going to fly legally — when we discovered that we were going to have to create a version of Legend II — that she became unstoppable. She poured heart and soul into her work. Pushed herself, pushed her people, scoured the datastream for any scraps of research she could find on anything related to immortality nanovirals, damn near killed herself making sure everything on the Legend II nanovirus worked in simulation before it came to live-testing it on me."

I took a deep breath. "She wasn't doing all that careful simulator work because she gave a shit about me. She thought I was the only live test subject she was going to get. She wanted to eliminate all possible bugs in simulation to reduce the number of things she'd have to test if it killed me. She wasn't making Legend II for us. She was making it for herself."

Small silence, expressions of dismay and recognition on four faces. On the fifth, the settling stillness of a hunter identifying as prey an object just moving into range.

"That could fit," Herog said slowly. "The story she gave us was that she was one of the Corrigan slaves. She'd been trained to do research, and apparently Haskell had taken her to work in his labs. She did something that made him angry, though, so he sent her back to the Corrigan satellite to be used as a test subject. When I wiped out their compound and grabbed the slaves out of it, she was one of the ones I got."

That confirmed my suspicion that she'd done immortality research before, and introduced the entirely unexpected information that she'd not just known Corrigan. She'd worked for him. But she'd been extraordinary at what she was doing. Brilliant.

Haskell Corrigan would have to have been insane to have sent her away to do... what?

"What were the Corrigans using her for on their satellite?" I asked.

"Medical testing. Torture with the justification of a pretense of knowledge, really. They had more than a hundred test subjects confined in the core of their medical testing unit when we hit. Before we could penetrate that deeply into the compound, a master had run through, scattershot all the test subjects with poison, and tried to set the room on fire to hide the evidence. All of them were poisoned. Sky was the only one who survived."

And my mind clicked over to another scenario. "What if she was the master?"

Herog's eyes narrowed, and his lips thinned. "Go on."

"Is it better to be a dead master or a live slave rescued and on your way to freedom?"

"Rhetorical. Continue."

"She knew it would take a while for you to get deeply into the compound. If she could kill all the witnesses to whatever she was doing, and make herself look like just another victim, and make sure that you spotted her and saved her, she was home free. She could walk away from the descending fury that was going to hunt down and kill every one of her associates."

His eyes got narrower.

I paused. "Describe the scene to me."

"More than a hundred people rounded up into one room, all of them scattershot with iced haptoterzene pellets. Bodies everywhere — draped across cutting tables and stretchers, covering the floor, piled against each other. Some of them were still holding on to each other. But all dead except for her, and she was nearly dead."

"Where was she?"

"On a dissecting table, sprawled against a corpse that had been partially dissected."

"What was she wearing?"

His gaze flicked to connect with mine. "She was naked."

"Attractive naked woman elevated on a raised stand, right up against something terrifying. When you ran into the room, what did you notice first?"

"Her."

"Anyone else naked?"

"The dissected corpse."

"You check to make sure everyone else was dead?"

"Yes. We always rescue with at least two BioViews."

When I raised an eyebrow in question, he said, "Bio-Views are biometric scanners designed to search a one-hundred meter forward half-sphere — they use ultralong frequencies to penetrate the surrounding hardscape. They were created on one of the Periphery planets to scan battle-fields for survivors. So we knew even before we hit the room that she was the only survivor.

"But if you hadn't had a BioView, how long would it have taken you to get around to testing her?"

"Fifteen men bent on saving lives?" He took a deep

breath and looked me straight in the eye again. "She would have had fifteen scans before we even noticed anyone else."

Tarko and Wire both burst out laughing. Storm Rat chuckled. Even I couldn't hide my grin.

Bluejay, however, didn't see the humor. "This is a nightmare," she said. "How can you laugh?"

"I'm sorry," Wire said. "It's just true. You send a pack of raging testosterone into a fight, give it a mission to save what's worth saving, and throw young, naked, and female in front of it, and the testosterone is going to say, 'Yep, *THAT'S* worth saving!'"

"Oh." Bluejay giggled, trying hard not to. And then she laughed. Hard enough to have to wipe tears from her eyes. Stress comes out in many ways, and she was unloading a lot of it at that moment. "All right," she said when she caught her breath. "I get it." She shook her head. "It was also really smart of her."

I nodded. "Sky is not a stupid woman. But now we have a problem."

Storm Rat said, "I've got the big picture. How far do you think she's gotten on the small details?"

I said, "She got Grinder to betray you and steal your ship, Storm Rat. What would it take for her to do that?"

"So Legend II is now out there, live, in someone we know we can't trust," Storm Rat said.

"I think so."

He closed his eyes and rested his head in his hands. "We've made the problem worse."

I said, "I don't think so. She's a problem... but I don't think she's the problem you think she is. The thing that tipped me off to the fact that she'd taken Legend II was what she said in her message to you. Remember, she knows exactly what we're doing. *Exactly.*"

He frowned, "She said something about us using Legend II to kill people without due process."

"No." I shook my head. "Play back the recording of what she said."

He nodded, and Sky's face reappeared on our closed connection.

"You killed those people without due process," she said. "What you're doing by vaccinating humanity with AntiLegend is killing other people — even if they are vampires — without due process. I can't be a part of this, or a part of you, or a part of what you're doing. You're wrong. All of you. If this is how humanity has to survive, it doesn't deserve to survive. I've taken the *Delegate One*. None of you will see me, or it, again."

He shrugged. "Same difference. She's accusing us of genocide..."

I held up a hand and stopped him. "No, she isn't. Remember, she knows about us. She knows we're not going out there to vaccinate anybody. AntiLegend is part of our end game, but she made it sound like we were doing exactly what you told your people we were doing. Going out to vaccinate humans, not going out to destroy vampires. She backed you up, on the record, even as she was stealing your ship and one of your people."

He paused and considered it.

All of them did.

"Why would she do that?" Bluejay asked at last.

I said, "Because she wants us to succeed. Because she wants all the Legend I vampires gone. She wants humanity to survive, because she can only survive if humanity survives. She just doesn't want to *be* humanity. She wants to be a god — but without all the competition of lesser gods. She'll back our story, we'll go out and do her dirty work for her, and if she's lucky, we'll all get killed in the process, and she'll be the only Legend II vampire in the universe."

"Will she?" Herog asked. "Right now, you've taken her word that the nanovirus was designed to prevent vampires from making new vampires by sharing their blood. But do any of us know this to be true?"

I stared at him, horrified. How had I not seen that?

IT TOOK two more days while our clock ran, and bringing Celt, Storm Rat's second-best med tech (after Sky) and a trusted friend from Storm Rat's early days, into our conspiracy. None of us even thought about sleeping while we waited to find out what Sky had really done with Legend II. And to us.

"Sky did exactly what she said she was going to do. And how she did it is remarkably clever," Celt said. "The nanoviral package integrates DNA segments of the original recipient into its structure. It makes the nanoviral package unwieldy, but it also makes it completely unusable by anyone else. In small doses, white blood cells will attack the nanovirus, destroying it. In large doses, the nanovirus will simply kill the recipient."

"Any way around that?" Storm Rat asked.

He shrugged. "No. It is absolutely a one-off design. The stuff in your blood can't even be used to reverse engineer the Legend II design. It destroys some connecting elements in the pure version in order to free up places for DNA segments to attach. Completely alters the structure of the nanoviral package. It's about as perfect a ticket to one-way, one-use godhood as I've ever seen. Except for the blood-drinking, mind-controlling, screw-up-your physiology-forever bits in there." He grinned. "Aside from that, though, it's a neat piece of work."

So we were back in business.

The new *Delegate One* was ready. I was ready.

We split up, my crew in their cargo ship left to cheers and good wishes, and I slunk off in what looked like the opposite direction, as ignored as I could hope to be in a ship as flashy as the *Corrigan's Blood*.

WARPAINT

Chapter 13

I inserted into the origami point out at the periphery of Storm Rat's system with a preset in-hyperspace course change to an unmarked origami point I'd located during my last traverse.

In doing so, I discovered a totally unexpected side effect of being a Legend. It wasn't a good one.

Going through the origami point was incomparably worse as a nanovampire than as a human. All those exquisitely tuned, superior senses I'd gained in my transformation allowed the compression of my awareness as I moved along the folds of spacetime to rip me apart in new and horrible ways. I was infinite — but for the first time I could clearly see beyond my many selves and my overself. I saw Badger, infinitely iterated with other Cadys. I saw him happy. I saw my otherselves happy. I saw them with children and joy and homes in realities where there were no vampires, where there was no Darkout, where there was no horror — and in the moment and the eternity where I was all my otherselves, I had that joy for myself. I had Badger back, and we had girls and we had boys and we had all the time we wanted to be together — while at the same time I knew, I knew, I *knew* that he was dead, murdered, gone forever from *my* life, that for the rest of my existence as my one fragile self in my dying reality, I would never hold his hand or see his face or rest my head against his chest and listen to his heart beating or hear him whisper my name.

Mine was one reality. Shredded in that unending time out of time by the knives of all the selves I wasn't, bleeding from the renewed, reborn, fresh anguish of my loss of the only man I'd ever loved, I leapt at that thought. *Mine was only one reality*. It was a trillion or more lives, but they were lives like mine, lived all across the multiverse, and if I died in this reality, and humanity died because of me — what would it matter?

The pain would stop for me, and perhaps I would be reabsorbed into my overself, or perhaps I would get another chance to find Badger, to be with him again, to get it right the next time.

What would it matter? How could anything I did matter, when everything I saw was worlds where all the horrors in mine didn't even exist. What could it matter, why should I fight, what value did I have if every other choice I could make was already being made somewhere else?

I almost quit. Almost stopped fighting. Almost relaxed my mind and silenced my steady mantra of "I am Cadence Drake, I am Cadence Drake, I am a TFN pilot, I live, I breathe, I *am*."

Almost.

But I had promised Storm Rat that I would fight.

I had promised Bluejay and Wire and Tarko.

I had promised Herog.

Strength returned to me when I thought of him. He would not surrender. He would never lie down and tell nothingness, "Take me." I'd seen that in his eyes. I knew it to be true. When he died, he would die fighting for every last breath.

If I gave up, I would break my word to him that I would fight beside him. Would betray our pact — but more. I would betray everything it had taken him to survive, and I would betray my word. Betray it to a man to whom a promise was a contract. He'd given me his word that he would have my back.

In the middle of that hell, I gave him mine that I would fight to survive long enough that he could.

By that single thread — that I would betray a man who had fought longer and harder for this single chance to save this single reality than I could even begin to imagine — I held on to the part of me that was Cadence Drake through that hellish crossing.

I was supposed to change my ship ID (one of the *real* alterations Wire had put into the *Blood* for me was an on-the-fly ID switcher that even transformed the tail number embedded in the moleibond, and the supposedly hard-coded scan-points so that I could match any of the other twenty-six Stardancer-class TFN yachts in existence. The process was supposed to take fifteen seconds, after which I was supposed to jump again immediately.

I was too sick to move. I lay with my head on the command console, the words "I am Cadence Drake" just exhaled for the last time, while the ship pushed vitamin-laced synth-blood-based coffee at me, and demanded that I go shower, and sleep, and use my Medix, and I and my flayed mind and skinned-bare nerves sobbed.

Even monsters can weep.

THAT FIRST EXPERIENCE WITH THE "NEW" origami traverse cost me a day. It took me that long to shake off my brush with self-immolation. I got my head back together, though, and did the ID change so my ship looked like it had once been the *Fire Eater* — a Stardancer that had gone missing when I was still employed by Peter Crane and that was still listed as "Missing, probably destroyed" in all searchable ship registries. As promised, it took fifteen seconds.

With the ID set, I programmed the ship for a straight run to our rendezvous point, told it, "Autotraverse the point, run one second, ninety degrees left one second, coast to stop. Countdown to point insertion in ten seconds. Initiate count now."

I took a double dose of Oricomatin immediately. Oricomatin is one of a handful of hyperspace meds used by passengers to get them alive and with their psyches intact through point crossings. It induces a state of brainwave inactivity that mimics a coma for anywhere from thirty seconds to a minute. Since crossing the point takes zero seconds in realtime, passengers using it do not experience the trauma of meeting their otherselves in hyperspace. And they have a nice little buffer on either end so if there's a last second delay in the insertion, they'll still be all right going through.

I had never used it before. Not as a passenger when Badger was taking us across, and never as a pilot. It's a brutal process even with less sensitive human senses, but there's something magnificent about standing in eternity and being, for that brief time, immortal and infinite, and until my first crossing as a Legend, I'd managed to appreciate that glory and wonder even in the middle of what had become predictable pain.

If you use any of the comatins as an on-duty pilot and

are caught, you are grounded for life, with no chance of reli-censure.

I wasn't in any danger of losing my license, though.

I discovered it doesn't work on vampires.

My otherselves and my overself pounded through my skull, and the aching presence of Badger in the minds of all the "me"s who were not me, of all of them who were loved and happy when I was in pain and alone in a slice of universe on the brink of wiping out my kind left me weak and shaken on the other side.

But because I knew what was coming, I still managed to wake up the datastream worms and feed our carefully created signal into the com traffic, then set the worms to listen for chatter.

The signal was simple.

"Got it! Legend II lives. Now what do we do with it?" And a modified, enhanced, colorized, flat recording we'd done up from my doppler-chip of me going through the highly edited transformation from nanovampire to other forms and back to nanovampire again.

"YOU'RE VERY LATE," Herog said in greeting.

"Had a very bad first crossing," I told him. I didn't want to risk the second traverse until I knew I could make it. And even then..."

I realized the intensity of his gaze was not even slightly tempered by looking at him on an infoscreen. "How bad was it?" he asked me.

"As bad as it could be with me still here to tell you about it now."

"I found it... unpleasant, too."

I changed the subject. "We're later than we should be getting started. Thanks to Sky, thanks to me... but we still have a lot of work to do to get this up and running. We need to get the *Blood* — oh! Bad slip. We need to get the *Immortal Velvet* upgrades finished, assume our sales identities, and go start pitching product."

Tarko had come up behind Herog while I was speaking, heard my description of our mission, and laughed. "You make it sound so mundane."

I raised an eyebrow. "...Or I could say it's time to turn this ship into a psychopath's fantasy, transform ourselves into vampire gods, and go seduce the most terrifying monsters in settled space."

"Shut up," Tarko said.

I said, "Mundane is not always a bad thing."

EVERYONE HAD MOVED their belongings onto my ship, and had finishing locking up and shutting down the *Delegate One*. We'd attached playboys — disks programmed to bounce misleading data to any scanners that alerted them back to the scanning ship — which would suggest the *Delegate One* was an unexploded percussion mine from a century earlier. Those old mines were unstable as all hell, and because, while they couldn't do anything to moleibond hulls, they effectively pureed the content inside, captains gave them a wide, wide berth.

We'd left the ship in a location far from main transit lines. And the point itself was in a system that didn't have much to offer, so it had low traffic. Odds were good no one would even pass closely enough to set off the playboys, but if they did, they'd back off before they could see it. We'd done what we could to make it unappetizing to anyone who might trip over it.

The *Delegate One* would stay there until we came back. We had plans for the ship — but they didn't include us having to actually travel in or with it.

I watched my crew bringing their belongings from Docking up to their quarters. And I confess I was surprised by the personal nature of some of it. Wire brought an assortment of handmade clothes, each of which displayed brilliant colors, fantastic embroidery, and gorgeous fabrics, none from the same culture, time period, or place. A few of his costumes looked like they had Old Earth origins to me, while some I recognized as having historic ties to various newer worlds in settled space. They were worth fortunes.

Tarko brought dark, polished, frightening wood carvings aboard. All were of different subjects, but in the same style, and I found myself wondering if he was the artist.

Herog lugged in two trunks of antique weapons, which he opened for my inspection. Swords, pistols, machine guns, rifles, droplasers, percussion waves — it was impressive what he'd acquired. He said everything worked like new. I believed him.

Bluejay brought several stringed instruments made of wood. "They're all original Old Earth manufacture," she told me, grinning. So again, I was looking at wealth in an odd form.

I realized after everyone had their belongings aboard that I would be piloting a treasure ship. And for a moment, that worried me.

Then I remembered what we had become, and shook my head. The treasure fit both what we were, and what we had to appear to be.

My new crew claimed quarters and stowed their

belongings, and I went back to the deck to monitor the chatter.

"Legend II..."

"...can we get Legend II?..."

"...Legend II source identified?..."

"...Legend II — any proof?..."

"...can't track Legend II to origin..."

"...can't verify Legend II claims..."

"...can't find evidence of tampering on Legend II doppler recording, but lack of proof is not proof..."

My fuzzy search also nabbed the following "Legend" info out of the datastream.

"...new report of AntiLegend vaccine for meat..."

"...AntiLegend vaccine verified..."

That stopped me.

We'd needed to get that bit of intel out — but while I was the source of the Legend II rumors and conjecture, I had not yet injected our AntiLegend vaccine leaks into the datastream. So wherever this was coming from, it wasn't us.

I started tracking down the source, because if this came from Tegosshu, there was another traitor, and we were dead before we started.

I set up the search to run down each mention along with the time it appeared, and ran the worms upstream to the first appearance of the term "AntiLegend vaccine."

It had hit the datastream in the Caliban system.

I called my crew to the bridge. It was forward from their quarters and on the same level — and marked with a palm-slap biometric panel and a sign that said "Bridge — Authorized Personnel Only" — yet amazingly, it took both Tarko and Bluejay more than five minutes to find it.

New crew, amateur crew members, and our shakedown flight was to save humankind from extinction.

What fun.

Well, neither of them had much experience with the standard ship design principles for crews and bridges, which is that you keep those two critical elements to your survival close.

They'd learn.

So I didn't treat them the way my first captain had treated me on my first crew flight. Instead, I said, "Good news, bad news, and what-the-hell news."

The four of them looked warily at each other, and took seats along the omega-bar — the command console on the bridge. We swiveled to face each other.

"Good news: Chatter is out on both Legend II, in which there is high interest and considerable skepticism, and on AntiLegend, so we can expect that any attempts to distribute AntiLegend legally will be met with extreme prejudice."

"So both plans are now up and running," Tarko said. "Good job."

"Bad news next: We did not leak the AntiLegend information. The *Delegate One* did."

"That's not such bad news," Tarko said. "If she leaked the news, we don't have to worry about the credibility of the rumor, and we don't have to worry about populations looking for the *Delegate One* with open arms."

"It's the next info that makes it "what the hell" news. The *Delegate One* fed the information into the datastream from Spybee 48-D4K-Manganotti in the Caliban system. One day out at sublight speed from Cerberus."

And Tarko yelped. "What the *hell*? Cerberus is the gas giant around which the Corrigan satellite orbits."

"Thought there might be a connection," I said. "Couldn't be sure, but I knew Caliban was a system that lost its Pact status a few years ago when it was discovered to be a haven for slavers."

"So, then..." Tarko's eyebrows had drawn together to form one thick black line. "She's gone back to her old place of employment. Did you leave anyone alive there, Herog?"

"Not that we could find," he said. "We rescued everyone we identified as a slave, along with all children and those men and women identified by slaves as not slavers, and killed everyone slaves identified as a slaver."

"Did Sky ask you to rescue anyone?" I asked.

"She was unconscious when we found her, and in a Medix the whole trip back."

"You have anyone else that spent the ride back to safety out of sight in a Medix?"

"About thirty adults. A few children."

"Then she might have an ally who also survived. Anyone think she announced the existence of AntiLegend, or verified it, to help us?"

"She's getting something out of it," Tarko said.

"Accelerating our time schedule," Wire said.

I nodded.

It wasn't the end of our chance of winning this thing.

But it was a complication. Sky was a wildcard, someone who could at any point turn around and bite us.

But we did have the best hand in the deck. We might be outnumbered, outgunned, and almost out of time, but we had Legend II.

And a hungry, hungry audience waiting to meet us.

WE'D DONE MOST of the prep work on my ship before I left Tegosshu, so putting everything into place once we were out of sight took us only a few hours. Wire, Herog, and Tarko did the external work, with Tarko complaining loudly over com that he was getting all the jobs that offered no elbow room, and Wire stating that he was never doing another install without a dwarf on hand. They were adding flash — gold beadlines, a gem-encrusted nosecone, colored lighting and shimmer effects all over the hull.

They were turning a beautiful ship into a trollop, while Bluejay and I were doing the same thing on the inside. Difference was, we were doing just the bridge and the crew lounge, which we were going to use as backdrops for the recordings we needed to create — and which were also visible through the moleibond hull. During docking and in any close encounters in space, we had to play the part.

The men had to do the whole ship. And it's a big ship.

What had once been the *Corrigan's Blood* had already been the premiere luxury cruiser in settled space. It is one of exactly twenty-seven ships ever built that can disappear in hyperspace between origami points. The value of this, in a universe folded unforgivingly along lines dictated by physics, is that my ship, unlike almost all other ships in settled space, could sail into an origami point at a specific speed and direction, and *not* come out the origami point on the other end at the exact time and headed in the exact direction predicted by its entrance.

It meant that once I disappeared into an origami point, I could *really* disappear.

Since the death of Peter Crane, the inventor of what were now being called "sidewinder" TFNs, authorities in a lot of systems were trying to ban the few existing sidewinder ships because they gave a tremendous advantage to criminals who owned them.

But the authorities fighting sidewinder ships kept

running into unexpected resistance because the criminals who owned the ships were almost exclusively vampires who had been friends of Peter Crane, and as such, were also allies of the vampires who had sidled their way into positions of control in most of the governments in settled space.

I took comfort in the thought that these monsters were making it possible for us to do what we were going to do, and that the technology they owned and controlled was going to play a big part in their destruction.

If, of course, we didn't all die in Darkout first.

"Why red and black velvet?" Bluejay asked me, shaking me out of my reverie. "This ship is gorgeous on the inside. These hangings just make it dark and creepy."

"I know." We'd turned off gravity and were walking around the inside walls using gravboots because it was easier to install the hangings on the decks and overheads at the same time. Her head and my head were about level for a moment, our hair flying around us in haloes of bright red and pale gold. "I've been on a number of Legend-owned ships now. They aren't all decorated this way. This, though, is bright, happy decor compared to the second version."

Bluejay raised an eyebrow. "Which would be?"

"Live humans chained to the walls, human skulls fixed above the doorframes, torture equipment scattered around like sculptures. Which is the *other* favorite of the devotees."

"Who the hell *are* these people?"

"They're people who wanted to hurt other people and get away with it. They've adopted a mythology that romanticizes that. To move among them and do what we need to do, we need to look like we're carrying out the mythos."

"The whole undead, come-out-at-night thing?"

I nodded and crouched on the overhead, spot-bonding black velvet over white non-reflective moleibond. "The orig-

inators of the nanovirus were not devotees of the imagery —
they were very rich men who saw a way to sell a form of
enslavement by hierarchy — but they sold the mythos of
immortality and enormous power in order to gain willing,
devoted slaves. Minions. And that remains the appeal for
the people who choose this life. They may be slaves of the
monster who made them, but they can make their own
slaves and force them to do anything they can imagine."

"Nasty."

"Evil," I said.

"That, too."

"So I've come to being a slaver?" She looked sick when
she said it.

"You've come to passing for one. Remember who you
are and where you came from. I'll do the same. It will help
us hang onto what matters to us in spite of the temptations."

She nodded, looking grim.

Chapter 14

Herog approached me while I was sitting in my chair on the bridge, going over Bluejay's newly revised heat map of vampire locations with her.

"Finished the hull," he said. "We need to talk."

I nodded. "Have a seat."

"Privately," he said. "And now."

He was my first officer, and the only other professional on the ship.

"We'll pick this up later," I told Bluejay. She left.

He sat in the first officer's seat. "You and I may end up switching off through origami points. I need to know what happened that made you a day late getting here."

"Mind if I ask you a question first?"

He waited.

So apparently, when he said we needed to talk, he meant I needed to talk, and he needed to listen. Well enough.

"Was the experience of going through the point any different for you this time?"

He shrugged. "The hallucinations were different."

I found myself tipping my head, looking at him more and more sideways. "Hallucinations?"

"They don't touch me. They don't affect my life. They don't connect with my reality in any way. Whatever someone might eventually prove that they are, as far as I'm concerned, they're hallucinations."

"Interesting approach." It contradicted everything I'd been taught about the multiverse and about hyperspatial physics, but I could see where, if you told yourself none of it was real, it would probably hurt less going through.

I wasn't that good at lying to myself, though. I was surprised he was. I studied him. I couldn't see it. Later, I would do some digging into this odd contradiction with everything else I'd seen of him.

"So... you want to know what happened." I stared out into space, at the infinity spread before me and above me. Sitting on the bridge was like living among the stars. It was glorious, amazing. In that instant, I felt the same pull I'd always felt.

The stars had been my dream since I'd been a kid. I'd fought for them. I'd struggled. I'd given up every other possible kind of life to have just the chance to live among them, and I'd won. I'd won infinity, and it was more wonderful than I'd ever dared to hope.

Only now, settled space was dying, or being murdered, or both simultaneously.

"It's all burning to ashes," I said.

He watched me, and his voice was patient. "You're fighting the fire with everything in you. You found it, you'll put it out, you'll win."

I shook my head. "That moment, coming through the origami point — I almost didn't make it."

Herog almost always gave the impression of stillness,

but now he seemed not even to breathe. He had, I realized, the same qualities as space. Absolute silence, overwhelming presence. One of his eyebrows flicked upward, and I realized I'd been frozen, staring at him. He said, "Oh?"

"This time, going through the point was different. It was clearer. It reached deeper. I know my countless otherselves in countless realities are living out variants of my life — but in most of the realities I saw, they were doing it in a universe not besieged by nanovampires, not facing Darkout. And I knew most of them still had Badger with them — but this time, I could see him. He was happy. Loved. With them. And I'm alone. This time, when I could actually see him, I got caught in the middle of it, and all I could think was that I could simply let go and be with Badger, or fall back into my overself, or whatever it is that would happen to me if I give up. It was like being ripped into infinitely small pieces, seeing the futility of my own existence, knowing the odds against us — and knowing it didn't matter anyway, because somewhere in there, one of my otherselves who still had Badger would stay and fight, and humanity would go on."

Stillness seemed to condense in him, into a well of gravity that caught me and held me. Carefully, he said, "What do you want, Cady?"

"I want to live," I said without hesitation.

"Good. So do I. At the moment, my chances of survival are tied to your will to live. So I'm going to show you two things I have learned that will fix your will to live. If you'll use these two things, you will not suffer mind-drift and go mad. You will not die in hyperspace. Do you understand?"

I nodded slowly.

"Here is how I found the first half of the answer. In order to qualify to take the pilot's examination, I had to learn *everything*. When I killed my owners and escaped, I knew how to survive abuse and torture, and I knew how to kill men. I wanted to stop the people who believed they had the right to own the lives, the production, the existences, of other human beings. I wanted to wipe out those people who were doing to others what they had done to me.

"To do that, I needed to have TFN training and both space and atmosphere aerial ship-to-ship combat training. To get those, I had to know everything most people who weren't slaves take for granted. So I taught myself how to read, I taught myself how to write, I taught myself numbers, and science, and physics. For four years, I disappeared into the public data system on Cantata, turning myself into the man I needed to be to win the life I wanted to live."

I nodded.

"One of the things I learned was hyperspace theory. And one of the first things I discovered about it was that the multiverse theory of hyperspace remains unproven, though it is officially taught as fact."

I said, "That's because it isn't unproven. Isas Yamamoto *proved* the multiverse theory of hyperspace was correct when he invented the origami drive. His otherselves simultaneously invented it in other dimensions at the same time, and like the fingers of two hands folding paper, the origami drives in all the dimensions where it began to exist folded the thin places in space, creating origami points. And now we can travel through them."

"No. Isas Yamamoto proved there was a way to bend space-time in a usable fashion. He never met one of his otherselves. And he never did the math to prove a multiverse. He *believed* in the multiverse, and used his beliefs to build an explanation for why his origami drive worked. But he never proved it."

"The math doesn't matter. The origami drive works. We

can see the multiverse when we travel through the origami points."

"Can you reach those other realities through the points? To the best of your knowledge, has anyone ever traveled from this reality to another reality?"

"No."

"Has anything in other realities reached you, or to the best of your knowledge, anyone else in this reality? Ever?"

"No. But that doesn't mean other realities don't exist."

"It doesn't. But it also doesn't prove that they do."

"I can see them."

His fingers flicked across the console to his right, and suddenly the deck below my feet seemed to vanish. The same space that hung above my head was now visible below my feet. He'd engaged Full-View.

"You can see the stars beneath your feet. Can you reach them?"

"Of course. If I go outside onto the hull, I'll see the same thing."

"If you go onto the hull, you'll see stars. Will you see those stars?"

I studied the constellations spread out beneath my feet. It's entirely possible to display any star field in known space, which is significantly larger than settled space, using Full-View, but the stars I was looking at were the stars currently surrounding our position.

"Yes," I said. "I'll see those stars."

"Touch one," he said.

I raised an eyebrow at him, but reached down to the deck and touched one of the stars displayed there.

"Did you touch a star?"

"Yes. You saw me."

"Did you touch a *star*?"

"The actual star? Of course not. I touched its image, but it is the reflection of something real."

"Is the reflection real?"

I crossed my arms and glared at him.

"Cady," he said, his voice even, "this is your life fighting your death, and you are doing everything you can to hold tight to what's killing you. Is. The reflection. *Real?*"

"No," I said.

"Can you reach one of those stars by touching the deck?"

"No."

"Can you reach the reflections that appear when you traverse the origami point?"

"No."

"Then do the reflections you see when you make the crossing matter to you?"

Yes, I thought. Because Badger is still alive in them. I wanted to give him the answer I knew he wanted to hear — to say *No* — but instead I repeated my thoughts out loud.

He nodded. "Now it becomes a matter of choice. Are you willing to die for a reflection you cannot touch and a theory you cannot prove?"

"I want to live," I said again.

"Not my question. *Are you willing to die for a reflection you cannot touch and a theory you cannot prove?*"

I held out my hands, withholding an answer, wanting the promise of the multiverse, of my overself.

"Physicists now have physical proof that bending space to cross long distances in zero physical time is possible. Yet they still cannot get the numbers to add up to prove the multiverse. It remains a theory. What does that mean?"

"That they need better mathematicians."

He shook his head. "Life and death, Cady. Jokes will

not save your life. Knowing how to strip reality away from speculation is the first of two steps you must grasp to survive."

I nodded and finally shook off my resistance to what he was saying. I quoted Stenhem. *"When there is a contradiction between two variables, one of the variables is wrong."*

"What are your variables?"

"The folding of space-time, and the multiverse theory. But the folding of space-time isn't a variable. We can do it, even if we can't explain how."

"Then which variable is wrong?"

"Multiverse theory. But what is there to replace it?"

"Does it matter?"

I started to say that of course it mattered, but he was right. Beneath my feet, the pretense of infinity spread out before me, beautiful, alluring — as compelling as reality. Untouchable.

False.

Meanwhile, if I went down to the cargo bay and stepped through the airlock, the real thing lay just outside my hull. I could see it. With my ship, I could reach it.

True.

"For a moment, put aside the theory you have been taught all your life, that you are nothing more than one of an infinite number of pieces, that everything you do is essentially meaningless because every choice you make or refuse to make will nevertheless be made or unmade by some other part of yourself, that you are a temporary, throwaway experiment from some vast, immortal overself to whom you are puny and weak and small, and subservient.

"Instead, consider this. What if there aren't realities? What if there is only Reality? What if you are the only you, if your life now is the only life you will ever have, if you have no overself, if there are no alternate realities inhabited by humans who are not endangered by this plague of nanovampires? What if this is everything? If that were true, what would it make you?"

"Terrified," I said, and this time I was dead serious.

"Why?"

"Because then there's no backup plan. Because if I fail, then it's the end of humanity everywhere."

"Yes. Which makes your life..."

I sat there, for the first time in my life looking at the universe without the fallback of all those other selves who, if I got it wrong, would somehow get it right. If this life, this moment, this day, was all I had, how would that change me? How would it change everything?

"It makes my life matter," I whispered. "Really matter. It means that every choice I make counts, that every mistake I make counts. That every time I do it right, that counts, too."

He nodded. "If this were the only reality, what would you do differently?"

"I'd fight harder. I'd never quit." I paused, considering. "It would mean what matters to me is actually important. I love this life. I love what I've built for myself. I love waking up and knowing the day is mine, knowing that I get to soar through space, that I get to find things that matter, that I get to be paid to do that. I love doing what I do, I love that I get to do it with..."

Badger, I almost said. He was always with me in my thoughts. I'd promised myself that he always would be. That somehow, some real part of him was still with me. But if this reality was *the* reality, I'd already lost Badger forever. If this reality was *the* reality, I'd wasted the time we'd had, and I would never get it back.

But it isn't, the little voice inside me whispered. *When you die, you get Badger back.*

I shuddered, hearing that little voice. I suddenly had a name for that voice. It was Death, calling to me, telling me that this life didn't matter, that what I did didn't matter, that *I* didn't matter — because all I had to do was follow the voice, and *die*, and everything would be just fine.

That little voice was the *reflection* of space, the *illusion* of the stars, the *promise* of the overself, telling me that illusion was the same as reality. That wishes were the same as facts. That I was wrong to demand proof.

That voice — the voice of Death — was telling me that the trillions of human beings in *my* settled space didn't matter: that the young woman holding her first child in her arms; that the little girl dreaming of winning the stars; that the young man who'd just beat his pilot's exam; that the old couple holding hands, walking together, enjoying being with each other — *they didn't matter*. That I could die, and they could all die, and it would all be the same.

Only it wouldn't be the same for them.

And it wouldn't be the same for me.

I realized that tears were running down my cheeks. That my hands were knotted into tight fists. That I was choking on my breath.

"You see it, don't you?"

I looked at him. I nodded.

"If you base your life on what you can prove is true, you won't waste it. You'll feel the clock running, you'll know that your choices are your own, and that you and only you are responsible for them. You'll know that if you fail, there won't always be someone else who will come along to succeed — that sometimes you are the only person in the universe who can do what needs to be done in the place where you are, in the moment that you exist. Knowing that, you have a reason to keep fighting, and a reason to succeed."

"And if there is an overself?"

He shrugged. "Then when you die, you are the part of yourself that can step forward and say, 'I lived every minute. I didn't waste the time I was given.'

"Meanwhile, if there isn't... you lived every minute, and you didn't waste the time you had."

Chapter 15

The outside of the ship declared we were the *Immortal Velvet*, and indicated we were people who would have painted the Silver City in black and white checks, while the visible parts of the inside of the ship suggested we were full members of the deadly cult that was about to destroy humanity. All five of us met in the solar.

The solar is the entire top deck of the ship. And it's as awful as it sounds. Nothing stood between us and deep space but a curving layer of transparent moleibond. Automated floating strellitas gave off a light meant to suggest, I'm told, fireflies at twilight. They were part of the default day-night cycle on the top deck — which kept the trees and flowers alive. Since the trees and flowers contributed to the oxygen-carbon cycling on the ship and made the air smell better, I tolerated the decor.

The solar was meant to be the gathering place on the yacht, the place where guests could have parties, dance, and admire the lovely flowers and little trees and manicured grass constantly tended by a discreet armada of gardening bots. It was, in truth, my least favorite place on the ship, because it mimicked the outdoors, and when you grow up in an underground world of enclosed tunnels full of high-quality technology all around you, the exposure of open sky and wilderness, no matter how contained and sanitized and controlled, makes your skin crawl.

But it was the setting in which we were going to create our first Legend II sales recording once we'd done our first planetside surprise visit — and Wire wanted to have everything ready, and lighting and setup checked so we could create the recording as soon as we returned to the ship.

Doing the first recording from the solar had been my idea, but Tarko had loved it. I figured showing ourselves in the midst of the most unmistakable feature of a Monoceros Stardancer — the damned park in a bubble — would automatically give us credibility with the upper echelon of Legend vampires, who knew where they came from. They would be aware of the connection between Monoceros and Peter Crane, who built the Stardancers... and his associate Haskell Corrigan, who created Legend I.

For those nanovampires lower on the food chain — who would have no clue about the identity of their original progenitors — it was simply a demonstration that we were rich enough and powerful enough to own an enormous, fancy, TFN space yacht.

So the five of us gathered at one end of the solar, and studied the setup at the other end: the two portable autofabricators brought up through the gravdrops, five holomirrors, and Wire's array of recorders, and special lighting that he'd set up to emphasize us, our park-like setting, and our deep-space backdrop.

"Legend I vampires have to want to be like us for this to work," I told the four of them. "They have to see us, and in one or the other of us see something they consider ideal. Perfect. Some will want youth, some ferocious strength, some to be terrifying, some to create lust or desire or love in everyone who looks at them. So in one or the other of us, they must see the promise that they can become exactly what they most desire. That they can be their own ideal."

"How do we know what they want?" Wire asked.

"You don't. But you know what *you* want. Or what something deep inside you wants."

"The little voice. The monster voice," Tarko said softly.

I looked at him. "You heard it, too?"

"After I changed. After I got back to human form, and to rationality. Deep in the back of my mind, some part of me that has always been there, but that has never had a way to come up, woke up. It likes the power. It likes the hunger."

I took a deep breath. "I had that moment, too." I looked at the rest of them. "Anyone else?"

They all nodded.

"So... we should consider asking our evil voice what it wants."

Tarko chuckled.

"Be what would make you yearn," I added.

"So a woman, then," Wire said.

Herog actually smiled at that. It was so brief I barely saw it... but it had been there.

I laughed, but said, "If the nanovirus allowed gender changing, maybe. But... ah, never mind. Just come up with something spectacular, because when our prospective customers see the five of us together, they have to see the future of nanovampirism... and themselves in it.

Tarko said, "I'm going to have to go to my quarters, but I'll be back quickly.

We got down to business.

I'd played with transformation while I was in the cage after making the change... but now I considered what I needed to present to those I wanted to seduce. I considered what I wanted to sell.

I needed to be visible. I needed to be the vision vampires had of themselves, heightened and perfected. I needed to be the realization of everything they wanted for themselves, presented to them living and powerful and undeniable — so that I could offer them something I had that they wanted.

There is no human ideal, though. No vampire ideal, either. Individual tastes, individual desires, individual compulsions, all drive to a number of unique "perfect visions" exactly equal to the number of vampires in existence.

I would be able to demonstrate to them that whatever they wanted, they could become. First, though, I had to have their attention.

And an old story came to me — one of those ancient tales people have never managed to shake off. The tale of a girl of perfect goodness born to replace a creature of evil, a girl with hair black as night, lips red as roses, skin white as snow. A girl who was the fairest of them all. She'd been a girl who had displaced aging beauty with eternal youth, a girl who had slept in a coffin, had been mistaken for dead, and who had been awakened with a kiss.

I could do that. I could make myself a girl clearly not quite human, drawn from old human myth, who would resonate with those I needed to impress. She would be both inexplicably familiar, and exquisitely strange.

I kept my height and weight. I like knowing where everything is and how it works, and being at my fighting best requires that I make no changes there.

I made my breasts a little smaller, a little higher and firmer. I was going for the appearance of youth. I wanted to look no older than eighteen to twenty.

I made my waist smaller, my ass a little higher, and worked the extra mass left over after I'd thinned myself into a teenager's form into bone density and a focus on tough, firmly anchored tendons.

I pushed out skin as pure white as I could get, and managed an interesting translucence along with the chalky whiteness. When I was done, I wasn't the albino white Badger had been — he'd had distinct pink undertones. I was the color of porcelain. No human had ever been that color.

I focused next on black hair growing on my scalp, eyelashes, and eyebrows. I needed body hair distribution to be almost nonexistent, because heavy black body hair on snowy skin was not in keeping with my "innocence and youth" look.

I started with straight hair, but changed it to curly when I found out how much younger a halo of waist-length blue-black curls was. I kept my eyebrows tapered and arched, and made my eyelashes ridiculously long and thick.

Tried light blue eyes. Dark blue eyes. Every imaginable shade of green. Brown from pale amber to nearly black. Nothing gave me quite the edge of ethereal strangeness I was hoping for.

Then I tripped across violet blue on my second turn through the spectrum, and that was just right.

I went with a pink-red for my lips. Blood red, which I tried first, was ugly.

My features were delicate. Fragile. Large, luminous eyes, a pert little nose, a small mouth with child-like lips, an oval face, a softly rounded chin.

I made sure my hands, feet, wrists and ankles also gave

the appearance of delicacy, and put serious work into reinforcing my bone structure and musculature with every bit of mass I could move from externals.

When I was done, I looked barely eighteen. Innocent. Fragile. Helpless.

Perfect.

The perfect monster.

I admired myself in the mirrors for a moment longer, then turned to see what my colleagues had come up with.

Perfect, I discovered, comes in many forms.

Bluejay caught my eye first. She'd gone for a look of predatory sexuality, making her body curvier and taller than her regular height. Her skin was a creamy tan, her eyes vibrant green, her hair thick and pale gold and perfectly straight. She'd made hers shorter than mine, just shoulder length. She was stunning in a fully adult, completely finished way, and she radiated a come-on that hit like a gut punch. The men around me kept turning to stare at her, then dragging their gazes away. Even I felt the draw. "I'm going by the name Baby," she purred.

"Sure," I said. "Demon Baby would be closer."

She smiled, and the thought, *That will be the smile that starts a war,* flickered through the back of my mind.

I turned my attention to Wire. Lean and quick and competent, he had reshaped himself into a younger him. He was a bit taller, a bit more muscled, and he was no longer scarred. His face was the face of dreams — square-jawed, rugged, a rich brown, with perfectly proportioned features. His eyes were black, as was his hair, which was sleek, glossy, and long. His hands were big, veined, muscled, well-defined — unchanged except that they, too, were free of scars. I thought he looked like a pirate, but one who could fix anything with those hands. He grinned at me. "I'm Warrior," he said. "You like the look?"

"Absolutely."

Herog's voice of evil had spoken to him of the hells of ancient ancestors. He'd twisted himself into a nightmare, with glossy black horns curling from his forehead, with red eyes and red skin and a mouth full of pointed teeth. He was massively muscled, with claw-tipped hands twice the size of normal hands. He had thick, arched black eyebrows and a neatly pointed black beard, but no other visible hair. By humans, he'd be mistaken for a body modder with disturbing tastes. Among the nanovampires, I suspected he would find a following.

"That's terrifying," I said.

"It's intended to be. I'm the one who takes apart anyone who comes after you, and I'd rather be less busy than more busy." The pointed teeth did odd things to his speech — the fact that he'd lowered his already deep voice to the register of something I could feel at the base of my spine added in a shudder factor that would give anyone intending ill will second thoughts.

"I'll use the name Hell," he added.

I didn't see Tarko, but only had an instant to register the thought before the gravdrop ejected a giant beast-man upward into our midst.

Tarko was only centimeters taller than my height, but was easily three times as wide as me — he was a wall of muscle, white-skinned, black-furred, wild-eyed, with legs too short for his torso, and arms too long, so that he gave the impression of having been stuck in a transformation halfway between simian and human forms. He'd matched the color scheme I'd chosen for myself to perfection, and had brought his own version of deadliness to our party. But where Herog gave the impression of utter stillness, of merciless control, of danger lying beneath a smooth sheet of deep water, Tarko looked like a moving explosion in progress.

"What the *hell* are you?" I asked him.

"I'm the Beast to your Beauty, my dear."

"Not the fairy tale I had in mind," I told him, but he laughed.

"It's the one that will suggest itself when our future customers see us. We'll emphasize the range of what's possible."

"What do we call you?" I asked him.

"Crusher, darlin'. Call me Crusher. I had to use my medichamber to change my body mass," Tarko added. "Without it, I would have looked like your pet."

"What do we call you?" Herog asked.

"Velvet," I said. "Like the ship."

And, as it turned out, like most of the costumes I came up with.

We took turns using the autofabricators, creating costumes to complete our personas. I did everything in black and red, modifying the autofabricator's Ancient Styles selections with fabrics of silk and velvet, lace and brocade. Each of my costumes was elaborate.

Bluejay chose white, pink, and gray for her costumes, drawing from both the Modern and Abstract menus. Everything she ended up with was simple, sleek, form-fitting.

It took the two of us ages to work our way through the menus and get all the pieces and details we needed.

The men?

No.

For both Tarko and Herog, the costume was...

Pants.

Ragged black pants.

Not even pants and shoes.

Neither of them needed more than three minutes.

I could see where Herog's claw-tipped toes would have made shoes a problem. I think Tarko just liked looking at his enormous feet, though.

I heard him tell Bluejay, "You know what they say about the size of a man's feet?"

And she'd laughed. "I certainly do," she told him.

Wire made himself some open-necked silk shirts with what the autofabricator called "swordsman's sleeves." He got them in white. Six of them, all exactly the same. And black pants. Six identical pairs. And black boots the autofabricator called "swordsman's boots." Two pairs.

Men.

We put on our costumes, we stood under Wire's set up of lights, he fiddled around for a bit, deciding to uplight the men and downlight the women.

When we finished, Wire took still images of each of us to use on our IDs.

And we set off to fight fire with neutron missiles.

THE INSERTION into the origami point that would take us to the Blende-Banner system, home of Cantata and twelve other planets equally unfriendly to life was almost the end of me.

Badger came to me. Not with others of my overself. Just to me. Me. He saw *me*, touched *me*, and whispered something to *me*. I could not hear him, could not hold on to him, could not save him to keep him to bring him home he was there, there and I wanted to go with him, be with him, quit fighting.

My beloved Strebban Bede, Dante Beddekar, Badger, with countless lives in countless worlds, went on without me in one, as I went on without him.

Somehow, though — the Badger that was alone found the me that was alone.

And in that moment, in that place, we were no longer alone.

His mouth formed the word, *Come,* and I thought *Yes, this is where I belong, this is where I must stay. I'll let go, I'll release myself from the pain of life, and we'll be together.*

But for just a second, I saw Herog's face, and for just an instant I thought, *He's not real.*

In that instant, spacetime ripped me away from him.

I came out on the other end, on the bridge, shaking, vomiting, to find a massive red demon sitting in the first officer's seat, and I both jumped and yelped before remembering this was the new Herog.

"Coffee," the shipcom said. "Drink coffee. Coffee. Drink coffee. Coffee. Drink..."

It had a smell, and the cup was hot in my hand, and I poured the liquid into me, scalding my mouth — proof that I still lived, however little that meant to me at the moment. Synth-blood coffee plus vitamins and restoratives and whatever else the ship's linked biometric monitor decided I needed poured into me. Reconsta-coffee, which is coffee in the same way that moving your feet and waving your hands without any music is dancing.

Herog was staring at me, and he looked furious. "Why doesn't this ship have a personality?" he asked.

Raw, broken inside, having failed to be as strong as I needed to be, I snarled, "Because I hate this ship," I said, and when the words came out of my mouth, I realized they were true. A truth I'd never admitted to myself. "This ship was the start of Badger's death, the start of the end of everything I loved in the universe. If this ship had a personality, I would hate it, too. This way, I don't have to chat with the damn thing. I give it orders, and it leaves me alone."

"Cady, you were mind-drifting," he said. "I've seen it before. You were already gone. The Medix couldn't have saved you. I was helpless. I don't know how you came back. I've never seen anyone come back."

He actually looked frightened. I'd never seen anything remotely resembling fear on his face before.

"Badger was there. Alone. He told me to come with him. Looked into my eyes. He's hurting, Herog. He's lost, too." I shook my head. "Reflection, maybe — maybe he's a reflection. Not real. But he tried to speak to me, and that didn't look like a reflection. Then I looked at him. "How did you get in here between the time I put us into the origami point, and when we came out the other end?"

"I was already on the bridge, and you lost about two seconds recovering."

And he was fast.

"It's time for the second half of learning how to protect yourself from hyperspace."

"I'll get better with practice."

"No," he said. "You won't. But you'll get better with focus. You need warpaint."

"Warpaint?"

"Putting on warpaint was how I made it through seven years of being a gladiator."

That stopped me. I'd heard the word gladiator before. I knew it had something to do with men fighting each other. But it was an ancient word, and I could not put it into a modern context — I was not sure of its details. "You were a gladiator?"

"My second use as a slave. First, when I was young and relatively weak, I was a toy brought out to amuse visiting slaver women while their men were busy. When I got too strong, too big, and too dangerous, my owners decided to get rid of me. So the old owner took me to the local fighting pit, and entered me against the pit champion. A fight to the death. He'd bet on the other man. He'd intended me to be the other man's warm-up corpse. Instead, he lost money, but still had me."

Herog stared into the darkness before us to the growing pinpoint that was Cantata's red-giant star.

"I'd been a farmer's son, taught from an early age how to deal with dangerous animals. I didn't know how to fight, but I knew how to kill. I had size, I had speed, I had a deep desire to live.

"The bastard put me up against three more slaves that day, betting against me each time, and each time I lived and he lost money, he got angrier. The other owners and the audience were becoming angry, too, because I wasn't fighting the other men. I was simply killing them, quickly, efficiently, in the fewest steps possible. I wasn't making a show of it. So my old owner decided to punish me for winning."

Herog looked straight ahead. I saw his jaw tighten. "Before my owners decided to dispose of me in the pit, I'd managed to make a friend among my fellow slaves. During the day, that boy and I occupied cages next to each other, and when we weren't sleeping, we talked.

"At night, they did what they did to both of us, but when daylight came, we found a sort of freedom describing our hopes for better lives to each other. Discussing how we were going to get the money to buy new lives, passage to other places..."

He sat for a moment, not saying anything. I gave him time.

"The slavers' rules for pit fighters and gladiators are simple. Fight until one of you is dead. If you stop before killing your man, or if you refuse to fight at all, they'll take both of you out of the ring and torture you to death, slowly. You learn these rules right before you walk into the pit for the first time, and the man with the electric prod repeats them to you every time you're put into the chute.

"The old owner contacted his son, and told him to bring my friend to the pit. I didn't know he'd done this until I ran through the chute again and found myself facing him. He couldn't fight. He was weak, small, slow. I could not save him — if I let him kill me, he would die in the next fight.

"So I killed him, so quickly he didn't even know I'd done it. He looked up at me, looked down at my blade through his belly, through his aorta, into his spine. Said, 'Oh!'

"I lowered his body to the ground, soaked my hands with his blood, and dragged my bloody fingers across my face. I felt his blood soaking into my skin, burning into my blood. His blood was the physical representation of my warpaint. It was my promise to my owners that they would pay for their evil, and that I would be the one to make them pay. That I would never give up, never lie down, never walk away, until slavery was dead — and every slaver with it. That until no man or woman had a hand on the chain around another human being's neck, no matter how small that chain, I would not stop.

"Warpaint," he told me, "is the fight you choose. It is the hill you promise to live long enough to take, no matter what it takes, no matter however long you need, no matter the price you pay. Once you put on warpaint, it never comes off."

I felt a chill run down my spine.

"So from now until you can kill me as often as I kill you, you and I are going to break each other in every way possible. Every day. My promise to Storm Rat was that I would watch your back. That implies that you're capable of watching your front. You're not. But you will be.

"And while you learn a thousand ways to kill me, you are going to find your warpaint. Once you wear warpaint, death has no hold over you."

Chapter 16

We caught the first of our programmed transmissions from the *Delegate One* off the Spybee stationed as we came out the origami point nearest Cantata. I filtered it out of the traffic to Elemost, another major point of civilization in settled space, and a good fifteen systems away from us. The *Delegate One* has requested emergency clearance for the purpose of distributing a vaccine to protect humans from vampires. Clearance has been denied.

I smiled — though it was a grim smile — and sent that exchange in coded form back to the *Delegate One*. It would be useful later. If there was a later.

But between my first lessons in fighting Herog, and all of us gorging ourselves on synthetic blood so we could minimize the risk we posed to humans, we'd reached Cantata.

This first time, we were going down to the surface without the welcoming party I was willing to bet would greet us on every world we visited thereafter.

We filed our docking permit at the lovely new Meileone Spindle Station, and donned our silks, velvets, or... pants...

brushed up on our nicknames to make sure we didn't make any embarrassing slips in front of strangers, sprayed ourselves with human scent so our prey wouldn't realize we weren't *their* prey, and dropped down to Meileone via the spindle gravdrop, which is a hideously touristy thing to do, but we *were* posing as tourists. Of a sort.

Tarko, Bluejay, and Wire didn't have to play a part. They'd never been to Cantata, or to Meileone, my home city. It's one of the largest cities in settled space. The tourist orientation board just off the gravdrop station noted the day's population as 457,384,521, with the last four digits changing every second.

I wondered what percentage of that population our future clients made up. The board didn't have the count split into Human and Minion of Evil.

My companions pointed at an exhibition paratenka game going on beneath the big sign, *Meileone Level 27, Birthplace of Paratenka*, so we wandered over to watch, and I resisted the urge to explain the game. I'd played once. Had been good enough to be ranked in junior intramurals. I might have made pro. God knows, I worked hard enough at it. But then life intruded, and Badger and I fled Meileone and the people we'd been.

I loved paratenka, though.

The game is ubiquitous on Cantata, and has spread to other settled worlds that permit the grav technology (a lot don't).

It's an exciting game to watch, and even more exciting to play. Headdropping through a downgrav and missing your rollout to the corresponding upgrav while trying to get the ball past your competitors is a quick trip to the medichamber — especially when you're playing semi-pro, where the gravities are set higher to speed up the game. Watching the game also let me focus on something besides the delicious smell of real blood — a smell I realized we had *not* perfected with our fuel.

My companions watched, picking sides, cheering blue or red. The teams were two I didn't know, both from a downlevel that hadn't even existed as habitable space when I'd lived there... but the players were good.

When the game finished — Red won — I joined in the act my crew was putting on. And it was an act. We were fishing for the sort of folks who might be hunting tourists.

Our striking appearances caught stares. So did the fact that we were stopping to look at, and comment on, *all* the tourist crap. We were the very definition of *fresh meat*.

Petty thieves eyed us, though, and between Wire, Herog, and Tarko, kept their hands in their pockets.

A few Sellers started toward us, but the act of really looking at our group apparently triggered their senses of self-preservation, and they veered off to solicit more mundane custom.

Hawkers, however, not having as much skin in the game as Sellers — literally or metaphorically — crowded around us, pitching everything from pheromone sprays to microdot meals to guide service to "many exciting locations" in Cantata.

And it was in this guise that we met our first target. He was tall and lean and gawky, young and homely. No one's idea of perfection, no one's vision of an immortal. And I was betting he was far down the hierarchy of master-slave relationships... but he was still a vampire.

This was where our game plan kicked in.

I looked at my crew and said, "I want to see the lower levels. You all want to hire him with me?"

HOLLY LISLE

They all gave excuses. Also part of the plan. They were going to split up and find their own special companions.

I hired the skinny young man to give me the grand tour — and I told him I wanted to see *his* favorite parts of Meileone, presented in the way he thought I would like most. I was hoping in this fashion to skip the games before he and I got down to business.

So my guide, who introduced himself as Yorg, and who looked like he couldn't believe his luck, led me toward the main gravdrops, giving me a well-practiced spiel on how to drop the first time without bumping into other people, how to maneuver through traffic, how to change lanes. He would, he told me, hold my hand.

I let him, and we dropped in the lane for the timid, new, and lost, while all around me citizens zipped through the drops like fish in fast water, dancing through beautiful maneuvers I remembered well and yearned to embrace again. Once you know how to use them, the gravdrops are like flying from the top of the world to the bottom and back. I missed them, the way I missed skies made of stone and strellitas, the way I missed the comfort of enclosed space, the way I missed a city that strove always to embed the newest technology within itself, that embraced progress, that forever pushed through the barriers of what humans were and did to what they could become and might do. Meileone was in my blood, and when I dared sneak back at all, it sang the lullabies of my childhood to me, and made me ache to stay.

As we dropped, Yorg talked, pointing out levels and telling me what was on them, enthusing about wonderful things we were going to see after we started at his very favorite place of all.

He was, I realized with a start, a very good guide — and

in the same instant I realized that he had been a guide before he became a Legend, and that what I was seeing in this stranger beside me was who he really was. Or at least, who he had been before someone recruited him to bring home meat.

I liked him.

And had to acknowledge that he would die because of me. Because of what he was, what he did, because of the part of him that was *not* this effervescent Meileone booster ardently pitching the high points of a city we both clearly loved.

I kept playing my part, asking questions, suggesting places I'd heard of that were supposed to be wonderful as possible stops, but my heart wasn't in it anymore.

One vampire in, and the face of my enemy broke my heart. He was no innocent, and he preyed on innocents, and had mistaken my delicate, teenage form and charming enthusiasm as signs of innocence.

But I could see who he had once been, and the human he had been would have been someone I would have sat down with over coffee, would have debated proposed additions to Meileone with, would have enjoyed going with to Banger matches or paratenka games.

I *liked* him — and vampire mind tricks no longer had any effect on me.

Dammit.

He stepped me off into a place new to me. "We're starting," he told me, "at Level Fifty-Two. This is the lowest inhabited level of Meileone."

"Are there lower levels that aren't inhabited?" Pure tourist question. The city digs down to feed itself stone and precious metals, from which it still manufactures much of its wealth. But if you don't ask, then you don't look like a tourist.

"Nearly a hundred," he told me — which was new. When I'd left, there'd been maybe fifty machine-only levels, and the lowest inhabited level had been Twenty-Nine. But that's Meileone. It grows. It breathes.

And with some difficulty, I reminded myself that if it was to continue growing and breathing, the Legends, including this one I liked, had to go.

But by their own hand, and of their own choice. They were going to sign papers, they were going to agree to terms, they were going to *choose* their fates.

Meanwhile, Yorg led me into Level Fifty-Two, Meileone's newest vision of "place where people live." Every level is different, built in a different time, with different technology, to different standards born of different esthetics.

Level Fifty-Two told me evil had taken deep root in my city.

"Welcome," he said, turning to face me and spreading his arms, "To Cruentus."

Cruentus embraced primitivism and regression, and in it, I saw the true face of my enemy. It had narrow streets made of rough, rounded stones, curved tightly to impede clear lines of sight. It was lit by what looked to me like gas lights — I'd seen them in some of the appallingly backward worlds I'd visited while finding belongings and people the wealthy and the powerful wished to reacquire. The level was built new to look old, battered, disturbing. The buildings were crooked, low, squeezed tightly together. In places they overhung the street, seeming almost ready to topple. This ratty, seedy, dark, ominous throwback to filth and poverty had no place in a city that stood at the pinnacle of innovation, of creativity, of progress.

The buildings were made to look like wood — and again, I drew my observations from experience of the real thing. Wood — a substance that can catch fire and burn, that can be knocked over by hard wind, that can be rotted by water. It has its place — it makes a lovely material for artists — but its place is not in the infrastructure of a city.

"Wood buildings?" I asked. "They're very good imitations... but not at all what I hoped for on Meileone. We have places like *this* back home."

"I doubt that," he murmured. Then, catching himself, he asked, "Where's home?"

And I considered a world I knew that *did* have places like this. "Up Yours," I said, and he started.

"I apologize for giving offense," he told me. "I had not intended to breach your privacy."

Which is one of very few reasons I have fond memories of that world. That name can be fun when you introduce it on the unprepared. "That's the name of my world," I told him. "Up Yours. It's an independent settlement world, taking no subsidies and no loans, building strictly on what it can produce itself. It told the settling organizations where they could stuff their help offers — and their attached strings. Hence the name. My world is making good progress, but it hasn't moved past wood buildings, or wind and fossil energy yet." This was all true. If he chose to check later, he would find my details held together.

He laughed faintly. "Oh. I see." Then he raised an eyebrow. "A creature as exquisite as you came from a world like that?"

I smiled and nodded slightly. "*From. Well away from.* I want adventure, technology, everything the universe can offer me. I don't want to wait until I'm ancient to see it. I don't, in fact, want to *get* ancient. I've heard technology exists that will let me be young almost forever — and that worlds like this one have it."

"You may well find what you're looking for here," he said, and set off down the winding street past the fake wood houses, the fake gas lamps, toward a real and growing smell of blood.

Ah.

My people, such as they were.

We stopped in front of yet another narrow, leaning, ugly building.

Cruentus Welcome Center, the sign above the door said. Behind the door, I could feel them waiting, could almost see them from the strength of the energy they exuded. They were not hiding what they were, and as we'd drawn nearer, Yorg had stopped being the charming guide, and had started radiating mind control at me in the form of soothing waves of sexual attraction. I trotted by his side, silent and obedient.

He opened the door and walked in, and I followed him.

He smiled at me, and then at about fifteen creatures far more powerful than he was. I sensed more in the back.

One of the men in the front room stood. "*Yorg*," he said in a voice that outwardly expressed admiration, but that under its words, pushed Yorg to move away from me and sit in a corner, "what a prize you've brought us this time."

I stood, wide-eyed, silent, looking only in front of me.

"Oh, you tried to mark her," the senior vampire in the room said. "How adorable. But she's far too lovely to belong to you — and there is nothing you can mark that I cannot claim."

He walked over and stared into my eyes. I kept the power within me contained, hidden, utterly silent. I leaked nothing but my little "I'm human" suggestion. I simply stood, blinking occasionally, but was otherwise still as a carved woman, while Yorg's creator walked around me, ran his fingers over my arms and down my cheek, tugged down my red silk blouse and untied the black velvet corset over it, so that my breasts were visible to everyone.

"She's simply perfect," the senior vampire said. "What's your name, my darling girl?" he asked me, and I said, "Velvet."

"Perfect," he murmured, and bent as if to suckle at my breast. But I could see his fangs.

"More perfect than you can imagine," I said so softly no human would have heard the words. Yet everyone in that room heard them clearly.

I willed him to prostrate himself at my feet, to bow and cringe and cower, to shake and tremble and piss himself, to whimper from the shame — and as I thought it and willed it, he did it.

And up my spine ran the little shiver of *yes*. The voice in me, the creature in me that was all the evil I could imagine, liked this. That creature hungered for displays like the one before me, yearned to make this vile bastard utterly abase himself in front of the lesser monsters he owned. These monsters that he had made. His slaves, all of them.

My own voice of evil whispered in my mind, *Now make his slaves kill him. Slowly.*

And it was still my voice. The horror in me was a true part of me, I realized, and it had always been in there, simply waiting for the power that would set it free to work its will. I could let it, I knew. I could become the god of all these monsters. I could make them grovel, could make them do whatever I wanted, and they would have no choice but to do it.

I could be the God of Evil.

Humanity would die. Vampires would go mindless. Settled space would blink out like a cinder in the vast universe. Something that had once been wondrous would crash into dead and dusty silence, wondrous no more. But it would blink out with me as its god.

Or I could do the job I'd come to do, remembering Yorg, and how he had once been a young man who had loved the city of Meileone the way I had loved it, and I could prevent more young men from following him into the path of certain death.

I looked around the room and said, "My name is Velvet. I am the face of Legend II. And I've been looking for you."

And then I stretched my arms, and made them wings, and stretched my smile, and gave my clients a good look at my fearfully pointed teeth.

Chapter 17

On our one-day visit to Cantata, we accomplished two things.

We made contact with five different groups of vampires, dominated and terrified them all, and gave them the details on how a select few of them might hope to survive the coming nightmare we were bringing down upon the rest of them by purchasing the Legend II nanovirus.

We emphasized four key points to our future clients.

One: Legend II created vampire masters — only vampire masters.

Two: The drinkers of the blood of Legend II vampires would be bound forever to their masters, and would obtain longevity, but would not become Legends.

Three: Clients would only be able to order Legend II on the single day we offered it, and would have to agree, in writing, to our terms before purchasing it.

And there was a fourth condition... our kicker. But how we came to that kicker had been a piece of magic for the five of us trying to save humanity.

And it had started with a prolonged argument over how much we were going to charge for each dose of Legend II.

I said the price had to be insanely high, because we were offering the thing to these damned monsters that they most desired in the universe, and they had to think it would be hard to get. Wire had agreed with me. Bluejay wanted to give Legend II away, on the theory that if it were free, all the vampires would automatically use it. Herog suggested we offer versions that claimed to have different, and increasing, strengths, so that all vampires, even the scruffy little bottom-level ones, would be able to get their hands on some.

Tarko however, had plenty to say. "Let's talk about value, and perceived value. What is the single most valuable substance in the universe to a human being?"

It was easy to tell which people were from natural worlds, and which from adapted worlds. "Oxygen," I said instantly, and in unison with Wire.

Tarko nodded. "Right. Because without it, you're dead in four minutes. How much does it cost?"

Wire shrugged. "Depends. Where it occurs naturally, it's free. Where you have to build generators to produce and filter it and shields to keep it in, and have to increase production in step with population, no matter what it costs, people will keep paying."

Tarko said, "We have to be in the business of selling oxygen to vampires. And as Wire has so nicely illustrated, value comes from both need and scarcity. Price is situational, and flexible. It can be based on the cost of creation plus delivery plus profit, or it can be based on creation plus delivery plus extortion — but price is simply a reflection of the value other people attach to what you're offering." He spread his arms wide, palms up. I guessed the span at about three meters. Tarko in his new form was imposing.

We waited.

"You don't see the clear path?" he asked when we didn't say anything.

We kept waiting. He saw something obvious, but I didn't. Apparently neither did anyone else.

Which is, I suppose, why he can make money fall out of the sky, and I'd been scrounging missing-spouse jobs just to prevent my ship from following that same path.

"You base your price on your objective, and then you create value to match your price."

I sat there hoping I wasn't the only one feeling stupid for not getting something he clearly thought was obvious.

"What's our objective with Legend II?" Tarko asked.

Ah. One I knew. "We want every vampire in the universe to take it and die."

"Right."

"For that to happen, where *must* we set the price?"

"Low," most of us said. Hell, maybe all of us. I missed seeing who else answered. I was just happy to be right twice in a row — even if I was having to give up my idea of charging a lot of money for each dose.

"Right," he said again. "But what does a low price suggest about the value of what you're selling?"

"That it's also low." That was Wire, who had been with me on the "price high" end of the argument.

"Right again. So how do you give high value to something with a low price?"

And I was out of the game again, and back to feeling like I was missing something. "If it's scarce, it has a high price, and they'll all want it, but only a few will be able to have it. If it's common, it has a low price, and there will be vampires who will not bother with it, because if it's priced low, it can't be valuable." I looked at Tarko and said, "I don't see how we can bridge that gap."

"With a story," he said. "A reason why. We have to have a story that explains a low price, and still convinces our future clients of scarcity. Because we want every fanged, bleeding bastard in settled space sending in his order the *instant* our offer goes live. With money he or she already had — not money he or she killed people to get."

"A story?"

"A story. Why would we have the most amazing transforming nanovirus in the universe and offer it to anyone? Why would we *share*, Cady? Because if we have this thing no one else has, it makes us gods. If we share, then we're sharing godhood. Once we have the answer to that question — and the answer can't be that we need the money, because for a vampire who will live forever and can force people to give him their money simply by playing with their minds, money is not an issue — we'll have the answer to the problem of price."

We *all* stared at him. A story?

He'd stood up and started pacing. "I've had to do this for years. And the thing is, it's a hell of a lot easier to get people on board if you tell them the truth."

"That we made Legend II as a trap to rid settled space of vampires," I growled. "They'll love that."

He paced, and I watched him. Then he stopped, and turned and grinned at me. "Yes. Something like that."

"You think we should tell them we want to kill them?" I asked it, but even as the words came out of my mouth, I knew I was missing it. That he was talking about something completely different.

Only he wasn't.

"You called them vermin," he said. "When you first

came to us, when you said you had a problem, before any of us realized that your problem was our problem too, you said you were being overrun by the vermin you were fighting."

I nodded.

"So this is the story. There are too damn many of them. Motley little rats, making more rats, encroaching on all the best places in settled space, ruining a good thing for the vampires who were there first."

We waited. So far, it was true, but it wasn't much of a story.

He started pacing again. "*We* are the Legend II vampires, the gods of vampires, and we have had enough. We want... something. Something. Got it. We want wide open spaces. We want room to breathe, to find our own worlds and run them alone, with our own handpicked groups of minions who *can't make other minions*, so we can be the immortal, eternal gods of our worlds with no threat of competition."

"But to do this, we need a few more vampires like us. Vampires who will wipe out all the rats on their own worlds. Clean them up, get rid of *all* the Legend I vampires. And because they'll be doing us and themselves a service, we're not looking to make a profit. So we'll sell Legend II at a price that will just cover our expenses. First come, first served — but they have to sign something that says they'll be a Master and accept the terms of being a Master by wiping out all the Legend I vampires in their worlds."

"Oh. Holy. Hell." I whispered.

That was why he could make money fall out of the sky, and why I'd been just barely making ends meet. He could do *that*.

I said, "That's *perfect*. With that story, all of them *have* to try to buy, since if they don't, they're just vermin waiting to be picked off by the one who becomes Master."

Bluejay tipped her head to one side, studying Tarko, and said, "They'll have their delivery made to the most private place they have, so they can be sure of opening it alone and using it alone. So some other vampire won't take it from them."

Wire laughed. "They'll lie to each other. Say they didn't get their orders in fast enough, that they're trying to figure out where to hide, how to get off-planet because they don't want to be around when the Master comes looking for them. Every one of them will stay put, will drop out of sight for just a while, and will wait for our package to arrive. They'll wait in private, and when they die, they'll die in private. Word won't spread, there will be no warnings that it's a trap."

Tarko smiled. "And while they're waiting, we'll have in writing the official name and delivery address of every vampire in settled space, and a signature stating that he agrees to kill thousands or tens of thousands of citizens in exchange for getting a discount on our fancy designer navovirus, *after* he turns himself into a worse version of the human-murdering monster he already is. And we'll have transaction records of payment proving he was serious."

Which is when I had my little flash. "We already knew we needed to get some of their blood," I said. "To prove that no innocents got caught up in this. We *must* have proof that anyone who purchases Legend II is a Legend already, that he is *already* a human-murdering monster. But now I know how to do it. I have that part of the story."

Tarko raised an eyebrow. "Tell me."

"Tell them no humans are permitted to become Masters over the Legends. That we are the masters. So they must include their fingertip blood scan with their signature to prove they are not food."

Tarko said, "The scan will have in it the nanoviral marker for Legend in it, clearly visible. And they *know* it will. They *know* they are providing proof that they are nanovampires... and they give consent for us to use that specific information. Lovely, lovely, lovely. If we survive this, Cady, I'll hire you in a heartbeat."

I grinned at him. "If we survive this, I'll happily hire you."

And, knowing neither of us would ever willingly work for anyone but ourselves, we both laughed.

SO THAT WAS the first thing we accomplished on Cantata. We had our meetings, we told our story, said we would distribute *one* package per world on small worlds, *one* package per major city to worlds with more than one city with a population of one hundred million, and for megacities like Meileone, one package per hundred million. So there would be four master vampires in Meileone. Maybe five, if the population went up fifty million between our visit and the day we sent out order forms. We told our future clients we would distribute the order forms through the datastream when, and only when, we had our supply ready.

The second thing we accomplished on Cantata required a trip up to the *Immortal Velvet*, and then a trip back down to the surface. This part was tricky, was against all sorts of conventions, laws, and rules, and if it were not for the fact that this was the only way we could start saving human lives right away, we wouldn't have done it.

We turned all the spray junk and sealed-container foods and drinks we'd purchased in our gaudy Legend II-tourist guises over to Wire, who laced them with aerosolized or liquid AntiLegend.

Then, in the dullest, plainest human forms we could assume, Herog and I went back to the landing level in Meileone, met with Hawkers pitching the products I already had handy, and asked to look at their wares. With our better, non-human reflexes, we swapped their real versions with our doctored ones.

And then we gravdropped back up the spindle, and we left Cantata.

We'd placed a dozen. Some tourist would buy at least one of the products we'd swapped out. Would use it either on Cantata, or in the spindle station. Would be in contact with other humans, who would catch our manufactured sneeze. And we only needed one — but we'd get more than one. AntiLegend — one hundred percent non-lethal, but only eighty percent contagious, would start working its way through settled space.

And no one would be able to link its sudden appearance to us.

"IN HERE," Herog said, "you are not the captain, and I am not the first mate. In here, I am your killer and you are my victim. Do you understand?"

Herog and I were in the physical training room where I'd practiced kicks and punches, where I'd run through paratenka drills, where I'd worked through the various Banger moves I remembered from my childhood on Cantata.

Until I met Herog, I thought my training routine was good.

Things change.

"Yah," I said.

He watched me, then shook his head. "No," he said. "You don't. You're too relaxed, not wary enough. Understand this now: I am going to hurt you until what I have done would kill you, were you human, or would kill you in your present form were I using an edged weapon. Then I will stop while you heal, and we will begin again. We are going to come in here every day, and I am going to hurt you every day, over and over again, until you learn how to stop me. And until you have found your warpaint."

Said that way, what he was talking about didn't sound like a training routine. Instinctively, my shoulders went back, my muscles tensed, and I backed away from him.

He nodded, shed his shipsuit, and stripped down to black work shorts.

"There's a place where you can do that behind the changing wall." I'd already changed. At his insistence, I wore an equally form-fitting top and shorts — his first lesson. Anything loose-fitting gives your enemy something to grab. We were both in our bare feet.

Being alone with him in the padded room made me nervous. But as he stretched and loosened up his muscles I realized he was focused on teaching me how to fight. He was working to help me.

I relaxed.

In the instant I did, he punched me in the head and sent me sailing across the room. I'd felt the bones of the left side of my skull crush from his punch. I felt my neck snap when I hit the opposite wall at a deadly angle.

White-hot pain screamed through my skull and my neck. I wasn't breathing. Below my neck, I felt nothing.

He stomped over to me, his face furious, and I discovered fury on a demon face is something you never want to have aimed at you. "What the hell happened?" he growled in his monster voice.

"You *hit* me." The pain was already subsiding, and I'd started breathing again.

"Before that, you idiot! You were alert. Watchful. Ready. Then all of a sudden you dropped your guard and disappeared."

"I thought about you being here to help me. To train me."

"*Training.*" He snarled. "All training is flawed, because you have to be careful not to do real damage to your opponent. So people in training pull punches, stop short of full-out attacks, and in their minds, train themselves to fail. Train themselves to die. Killers don't train. Killers kill. Every successful kill teaches them to be better killers the next time."

He growled down at me, *"I am not training you.* You'll heal from any damage I do to you short of cutting off your head, so I am going to *kill* you. You are going to have to stop me, and you can use any means at your disposal to do it. But if you try something that doesn't work, I will kill you again."

The picture got clearer. This was going to be horrible.

"I won't lose focus again."

"It only has to happen once. I killed you. Crushed your skull, broke your neck. If you were human, I'd be dragging your body away."

My spinal cord had regenerated. I could feel my hands and feet. I didn't move them though.

I tried to imagine how, unarmed, lying on my back, I

could kill him. He didn't know — yet — how long it would take me to heal. I was stronger and faster than a human, and I could do things a human couldn't. From lying flat, I pushed with my arms and kicked with my feet, launching myself in a trajectory over his head.

Had he been where I thought he'd be, I would have grabbed his head on the way over and snapped his neck. Or tried, anyway. I wasn't too sure my attack would work.

But he sidestepped my attack, straight-armed me into the wall, and crushed my throat with a punch, killing me again.

While I was healing from not being able to breathe or talk, he said, "That was better. It was surprising. But you telegraphed your intent with your eyes."

When my airway rebuilt itself and my voice came back, I said, "Could you please transform into your human shape. Between your horns and your claws and your teeth, I can't compete with you." I could hear the exasperation in my voice.

"No," he said. "You can't. And no. I won't. You are starting to learn that if you try to compete with a big, fast male on an equal footing, you're going to die. For real. Because you are up against monsters no different than you. If one of them gets the advantage of you and wants you dead, he will incapacitate you, then cut your head off. The first thing you have to remember is that you're a woman."

"I've never forgotten."

And now I could hear the exasperation in *his* voice. "Yes. You have. You have comparatively little upper body strength, you have less reach, you're slower, you weigh less. You want me to revert to my human form to remove what you perceive to be the advantages I have with horns, long claws, and pointed teeth — because you think by doing so, you'll have a chance against me. But I am a trained killer, and you are not. My built-in advantage is testosterone. And if you try to fight me, or the majority of males, strength to strength, you cannot win."

"Then how do I beat you?"

"Every strength carries its own weakness. My strength is testosterone. My weakness is testosterone. Your weakness is estrogen. But your strength is also estrogen. You have to learn to fight strength to weakness. First, acknowledge that the man attacking you — *in most cases* — does not wish to kill you. At least, not immediately."

"What does... oh. Never mind."

I stood back up. Warily. Ready to get away from him.

He nodded. "We're talking. I won't kill you while we're talking."

"All right."

"If you understand testosterone, you can use the window of opportunity it gives you to survive." He put his hands on both sides of my face and turned me so I was looking directly into his eyes. "Listen, now. Your objective is to survive. If you can run, you run. If you can win by eliciting the help of another male, you do that. But in here, you live inside the worst-case scenario. You have nowhere to run, and no help is coming. So you talk if you can, you delay, you deceive, and if you must, you kill. You *do not have to win* a fight to survive. What you have to do is *live*."

"I thought winning a fight helped," I said.

"Winning a fight is what men do. It's a monkey dance. Two men try to establish dominance over each other for access to females and territory in which to keep females. This is hard-wired into testosterone. There are steps. Men establish eye contact, make threats, posture, and initiate ritual attacks. Because you are a woman, you cannot actually fight a man."

"I have."

"No. You did not square off with a man and trade punches. That's a fight."

This was true. I hadn't ever done that.

"What did you do?"

"I've shot vampires with AntiLegend. Badger and I once defended ourselves from a vampire that attacked us. He'd been told to kill us."

"Right. At the end of every fight between two men lies dominance. Dominance is the objective. It's the point. At the end of every conflict between a man and a woman, however, lies the potential for sex — or for whatever the attacker has substituted for sex. Sometimes that's killing. Most of the time, it isn't. Because most of the time testosterone does not see estrogen as a threat. It sees estrogen as a goal."

I thought I saw an exception. "What about men who prefer men?"

He looked annoyed. His eyebrow arched upward. "Any *schron* ever attack you?"

I thought about it. "Not that I know of."

"Barring such a man being a contract killer hired to come after you, he won't. He cannot gain dominance by fighting you, and he doesn't want sex with you."

He walked away from me, turned, and said, "For men who fight men, the steps are critical. If a man doesn't go through the steps — eye contact, threatening, approaches and posturing, squaring off to face each other, and punching — it doesn't look like a fight to other males, and it doesn't look like a fight to the females who are their prospective mates. The man who attacks without following the steps gains no dominance from it."

I was studying him intently, sure I was right on the edge of grasping something about him that I needed to understand. It was important.

"You know this to be true," I said. "You used this yourself. It was how you survived."

"Yes." He stood watching me. "This was how I lived, and how all others died. My challengers thought they were in the arena to gain status. They were fighting for the cheers of the crowd, and they allowed the monkey brain to guide them. To lead them through all the steps — staring each other down, making threats, getting red in the face, thumping their chests, circling each other. I skipped the steps, went for the kill instantly and without warning. They all died."

He looked away. "It was also how I earned my name."

"Herog?"

He nodded. Still looking away from me, he said, "Pazagha, the language of most slavers — and the language most slaves learn — has thirty-seven words for death. There is *aga*, which is death with courage. There is *spuk*. That's cowardly death. *Mesu* is death of old age. *Gero* is the death of disease. And so on."

"And *herog*?"

"Inevitable death. Death by fate or predestination. A tree falls on you — that's *herog*. The earth opens up and swallows you. That's *herog*. The gods weary of you and crush you in a mountain-slide? *Herog*."

"And those men sent into the ring with you — you were the mountain-slide, the earth opening up, the tree crashing down upon them." I was feeling my way toward it. Toward the important thing. "When they walked into the pit or the arena with you, it was already understood that they would die. There was no other alternative. It was what it was."

"Yes. No honor or dishonor for them. No honor or dishonor for me."

"And when you escaped, you kept the name, and pursued the slavers who named you."

"Yes."

"*Because* they know you. Because they believe in *herog.*"

"Yes. Do you understand why I tell you this?"

It was there. Somewhere in the back of my mind, there was a connection between his name and what he was teaching me. But it eluded me. Fighting not for glory but for survival... but there was more. Something deeper.

I shook my head.

"You do not put on warpaint for vengeance. For glory. For power. You do not put on warpaint for the thing that is worth dying for.

"You put on warpaint only to preserve what matters most to you in all of existence. *You put on warpaint when you find the thing that is worth living for, because living is harder than dying. And warpaint is your promise to live.*

"When you make that promise, you too will be *herog.*"

WE CAME out of the origami point exactly where the previous Spybee and our flight plan promised we would be. We were heading toward Wellspring. We anticipated that news of our visit to Cantata would have preceded us. We anticipated that the nanovampires would now have confirmation that we were real and that Legend II was real. We anticipated building desire for our product spreading through the vampire-controlled channels of the datastream.

In those expectations, we were right.

What we did not expect was for our sensors to register a ship right at the periphery of our scan range.

Unlike us, it wasn't on a registered flight plan. Had no business being out there. And when we scanned it, it sped away in the direction opposite the one we needed to take if we were to stay on schedule. I worried about it for a moment, then realized it was either pirates or slavers, and shrugged it off. The pirates or slavers who took *us* on would die.

I ran the worms and found the doppler I'd recorded of my meeting with the Cruentus vampires — which Wire had worked into a demo hologram of our Legend II pitch, then pumped into the datastream, made to look like it had originated from an unsecured Cruentas sendstation — and discovered chatter about Legend II had gone crazy. Because I'd used the unsecured sendstation, along with the vampire chatter on the secure bands, there was human chatter on public human bands. Suddenly, people who hadn't suspected the existence of the nightmares hidden in plain sight were getting their first looks at the reality of blood-sucking murderers in their midst.

Humanity had not suspected the mind-controlling, memory-wiping nightmares in their midst — but they did now. And that, too, was according to plan.

Chapter 18

We were waiting on permits to go down to the surface of Wellspring. It was a big, rich, lush, open-atmosphere world with surface cities, oceans, trees, wildlife, and all the other things that made my skin crawl, and apparently they were having *weather* in their major city — a hurricane we could see from our top deck as we hung from the station above it.

Big, spirally clouds. Winds ripping buildings apart. Water climbing up out of the ocean where it belonged and racing across land, drowning people and wildlife with equal ferocity.

Weather. I'm not an admirer.

So while my crewmates watched the ponderous spiraling of the clouds from above, and the holos of the devastation going on beneath them, I decided to check up on a bit of private information-gathering I'd had working its way through the worms since Sky took off with the first *Delegate One*.

I didn't want to let the other four know about my search until I'd either had my suspicions confirmed or had been proven wrong, because all of them had personal connections to her. I didn't want to put myself in the position of an outsider casting aspersions on their friend or colleague.

So I went to my quarters, and stretched out on my bunk, hands behind my head, well away from excited discussions and gigantic infoscreen images of vile, twisty weather.

I called up com from the comfort of my bunk.

"Status regarding search on the actual identity of Sky-Tegosshu, using all biometric scans and narrative data from point of rescue."

Shipcom's response was instant. "Previous identity located and confirmed."

Which is significantly more final than the percentages-plus-"working-on-it" replies my searches usually elicit from the shipcom. "Actual identity of Sky-Tegosshu is Youko Skylander."

"Any relation to the Corrigans?"

"Associative only. Youko Skylander was a co-developer with Haskell Corrigan of the LECReNE Project — Life Extension and Cell Regeneration through Nanoviral Enhancement, code-named 'Angel.' This project was publicly funded through several special taxes, with the ostensible goal of offering thousand-year-plus lifespans with perfect auto-regenerating health to everyone via one simple, inexpensive nanoviral injection. This project was primarily funded by radical healthcare reformers, and fought vigorously by the Professional Society of Medix Programmers, the Medix lobbies, markers and providers of emergency supplies, and the Natural Health Alliance, which promotes unaugmented lifespans and recommends against the use of any medications or treatments for any conditions."

"I'm familiar with the NHA," I muttered. "Badg and I called them the Death Squad."

Com paused, waiting for whatever instruction I'd intended to include with my statement. Even the best AIs fail to recognize interjections and utterances presented as full sentences. Maybe I needed to consider a personality for the ship. But I hated ship personalities. I preferred the occasional annoyance of the ship misunderstanding my conversation.

I told it, "Continue."

"Memos located in storage in Haskell Corrigan's effects detail the private progress of the project, as well as noting the point ten years, three months, and eight days ago when Youko Skylander reported to Haskell Corrigan that their current direction with nanovampirism would lead to inevitable Darkout."

"She knew this was going to happen ten *years* ago?"

"Yes."

"Is that what she called it? Darkout?"

"Yes."

I remembered Bluejay saying Sky had come up with the name Darkout. Bluejay hadn't realized how long ago, though. "It really *was* her term," I said, and then realizing I'd just stalled com again, said, "Continue."

"When she reported her findings to Corrigan and proved them, he offered her the use of his facilities in the Corrigan compound — as well as free access to as many test subjects as she needed to overcome the problem. He would continue working on a way to create Legend. Her objective was to develop a way to make the nanovirus non-transferrable, so that when he had Legend, she would be able to make it safe. In the following three years, she developed twenty-three variants of her non-transference into human subjects, then either did live dissections on her subjects, or killed them and dissected them, or simply killed and disposed of them in batches of twenty, when her live-test results did not give her the outcomes she wanted. She sent regular coded reports to Corrigan, along with frequent requests for more funding, and she kept very good books. His copies of her reports show that she spent one hundred percent of the funds he sent her on research. Meanwhile, Corrigan struggled to build Legend, but diverted nearly half of the LECReNE funding to the purchase of slaves for her live tests and for equipment and other supplies to speed up her results.

"In total, but not including the slaves she murdered during the compound raid, she personally killed one thousand eight hundred thirty-seven men and women before being rescued by Herog and his men."

"Pause," I said.

I stood up. Couldn't lie still all of a sudden. I needed to be moving, needed to hit things, hurt someone. Find *her*. *Vivisection?* She'd *vivisected* people. Had murdered almost two thousand of them, sometimes in batches of twenty, after injecting them with her experimental compounds.

I wondered if perhaps I could drag Herog back to the physical training room so we could kill each other a few times, just to get the rage that boiled in me down to a controllable level.

But I hadn't heard everything yet.

"Continue," I said.

"Their correspondence demonstrates that from the beginning, the two of them were working together to create nanovampirism. Their memos to each other use an ancient phrase — "boondoggle" — to describe their funding from forced taxation to a project always intended to benefit only them and a few of their friends. From the beginning, they used Haskell Corrigan's reputation and past successes to obtain the funding for a project they never intended to deliver. As a side note, one hundred percent of LECReNE Fund directors are or were also members of the following two groups: Kartach Norgan 50 Club, which accepts members based on a minimum Kartach Norgan score of fifty, and current head of state on one of a number of low-population worlds. Their presence as heads of state demonstrates they received the Legend nanovirus in payment for diverting funds — they were able to use their vampiric powers to manipulate their way past tests and rules to take those heads-of-state seats."

And there was the Kartach Norgan again. I winced.

I said, "The funders were in on the lie from the beginning, then. Take money stolen from taxpayers, funnel it into research only the directors would benefit from, and win a ticket to becoming an evil god at the end. Corrigan paid them off by making them vampires."

"No solid evidence of this exists, but correlation suggests it is likely."

"Agreed," I said. "Anything else?"

"I have located the vivisection and dissection reports for you."

"Not now," I said. I paced in my quarters, took deep breaths. Corrigan's and Sky's work was about to end humanity, and had already been the cause of uncountable human deaths, horrific torture, mass enslavement, and probably nightmares even worse than those I'd personally witnessed. In light of all that, and the potential for all that, murdering nearly two thousand humans in three years had probably seemed to both of them like a matter of no importance.

"So why didn't Corrigan incorporate her research into his own to make the spread of the nanovirus self-limiting?"

"All of Youko Skylander's research, along with all the other private documents in the Corrigan compound, were destroyed by a compound insider when it became clear the Corrigan property was going to fall. Most likely, these documents were destroyed to preserve and protect other assets held by the family elsewhere, as well as to protect the reputations of individual family members."

I leaned against a bulkhead and closed my eyes. Little chunks of ugliness were falling around me, and I couldn't relax. Almost couldn't think.

"Right," I said. "Why didn't Sky... Skylander... abandon Tegosshu to go back to working with Corrigan?"

"Only speculative correlations are available in response to that question."

"Fine. Speculate away. Correlate. Just give me something to put in front of my people."

"Following the raid, Haskell Corrigan was linked to the slave deaths via connection to the rest of his family, and lost all public funding. Both he and his project disappeared entirely, to be revived only when he met Peter Crane at a convention of immortalists — people pursuing scientifically generated immortality. But he never appeared publicly again."

"So Youko Skylander couldn't find him."

"Speculative, but possible. Youko Skylander received her own laboratory on Tegosshu at approximately the same time she became intimately involved with Storm Rat."

Intimately involved? Who else knew about this?

Pacing, I banged the hell out of my shins on my locker. I swore.

"All right. Give me a timeline of events in the Haskell Corrigan — Youko Skylander nanovampire research project, from first documentable date to today. Bullet point it to ten words or fewer per entry, link every point to all available sources in footnotes, make one print copy for me here, store copies of this document and every related or speculatively related document in my locked private memory core. Distribute file copies to all my deadman-switch accounts. And store one copy in active memory for infoscreen display. I have to put this in front of my folks."

THEY WERE STILL on the bridge, still watching weather that looked to me like it had been invented by a vid producer to scare the skin off paying viewers. It looked simply too big and too horrible to be real.

I stared at it and thought, *A whole universe of worlds to live on, and they chose that world. CHOSE.*

I simply couldn't escape images of people making horrible choices, and then ending up with deadly conse-quences from those choices. But they did. All the damn time.

"Infoscreens, bring up Corrigan-Skylander report," I said.

Com put the report up on all the screens that had been displaying death and destruction. Now they were going to be displaying more of the same, in a different form.

My allies all turned to look at me, questions in their eyes.

"I have something bigger than a world-eating storm," I told them. And I read through my copy of the list displayed on the screen, bullet point by bullet point, and let them look at the documentation as I went.

The vivisection and dissection records were live record-ings, something com had not mentioned.

Each of them turned away from those quickly. Only Herog didn't look sick. He, instead, looked ready to kill. It was an expression I'd come to know well — cold, unblinking, patient.

"This is who Sky was," I said. "This is what she did. And at the point where I came in, I gave her both safe access to the vampires who had infiltrated Tegosshu, so that she could finally get her hands on Legend I, and a cover to bring out into the open research she had probably been pursuing as a sideline for the past seven years. And I gave her test subjects and the unpaid help of the most brilliant researchers Storm Rat could find."

"Cady," Herog said, "if you hadn't, settled space would die for sure. The only reason she was able to create the airborne versions of AntiLegend was that she'd been working on similar problems for years. Because of her, we have a chance to save humanity. I could as easily say that humankind would be in no danger of Darkout had I and my men not rescued the slaves in Corrigan's compound. Sky would have finished her research and gotten her version of Legend II to Corrigan before the Legend I virus spread out of control.

"But saying that would be saying that humans have a legitimate right to enslave each other, own each other, torture each other, vivisect each other, murder each other — and that those who fight against slavery can be blamed for the consequences of the evil actions of the slavers. Haskell Corrigan and Youko Skylander were working to create a new, eternal kind of slavery with masters who could never be killed and never die, and were planning to make at least themselves absolute rulers over both the bodies and the minds of their fellow human beings.

"The two of them are wholly responsible for the chain of events set in motion by their actions."

"I know that," I said. "I wasn't blaming myself. I was simply going to say that I think when we're done with what we're doing now, I want to be a part of hunting down and killing Youko Skylander. I want to finish what I started."

"Oh," Herog said.

"Meanwhile," I said, "we still have to deal with the consequences of what *they* started. Corrigan's dead, so no surprises will come from him. But Youko Skylander is alive, and is now the creature she fought so long and worked so hard to become.

"My question now is, *What will she do?*"

I took my seat in the captain's chair, and swiveled around to face the rest of them in the horseshoe of the bridge command station.

"Ideas?"

Tarko said, "I think she'll disappear and hope we succeed in cleaning up the mess she and Corrigan made. She'll gather a clean food supply and build a realm of subjects over whom she can play god."

Bluejay was shaking her head. "She'll wait until she's sure we've succeeded, then come after us. She'll want to be the only Legend II vampire in the universe."

Wire said, "She'll send us a little thank-you note for giving her the universe she dreamed of." His voice held in it a knife-edged rage I'd never heard there before.

Herog said nothing.

I looked to him.

He shook his head. "You asked the wrong question. When you ask the wrong question, every answer you get will be the wrong answer. What's the right question."

I thought hard, trying to figure out what Herog was getting at. But I couldn't see it. "I don't know."

"You asked what she *might* do. But we have no information on which to weigh the likelihood of any potential actions, because we cannot even guess the range of her potential actions. The question you must ask, instead, is 'What *can* she do?'" he said. "And the answer to that question — at least right now — is 'We don't know.' We find out what we can about her. We watch our backs. We prepare for the worst case as best we can.

"But mostly, we stay focused on the issue of Darkout, because if we fail at that, nothing else matters. If we get through this, *then* you can think about revenge."

WE'D JUST RETURNED from our visit to West Clarion on Wellspring, where the various vampire clusters we encountered had treated us like gods. Or entertainers. The humans were rebuilding the mess left behind by their hurricane, the vampires were eager to bribe us for special consideration in getting their doses of Legend II first.

We did not accept bribes. We presented our case, our goals, and our future product with fierce integrity.

And the Wellspring Legends went away impressed. Maddened, frustrated, cowed by our terrifying power. But impressed.

Integrity is not something you find among those who lust after power, so we stood apart. We showed them what they could become if they joined us. We showed them grace. Power. Incorruptibility.

It was all nonsense, but it was elegant, convincing nonsense.

And my leaked meeting with *my* group of West Clarion Legends, (leaked by me, of course) spread across the datastream in every imaginable form into every conceivable databand.

Humanity was waking up. The rumors of AntiLegend were causing pleas from human populations, and — because we had so carefully picked the planets the *Delegate One* would contact — its record of being turned away when it announced its cargo and its cause remained unbroken. Public human clamor for something that would protect them be damned — the vampires in charge of the worlds the *Delegate One* was contacting were not suicidal.

And yet, mysteriously, an infection was spreading from space station to space station and from world to world that was turning human blood into a deadly poison to vampires.

There were five reports of exploding people coming out of four worlds that had in common one space station and one connection through an origami point. The "exploding people" stories were *not* showing up in the human chatter, however. They were buried deep in the secure channels the Legends used.

The Legends were having no luck pinning down sources. They were clear that the victims had exploded while feeding on prey, in one case they'd managed to keep the prey alive to study, and had located an antiviral agent, but the prey had infected the food supply — they were pretty sure transmission was airborne, and were "concerned." But they reported successful containment, and that they were working on an unobtrusive test that would screen any new virus carriers before they could get planet-side.

I'd known they'd do whatever they had to do to protect themselves against us. I only hoped our virus would spread faster than their countermeasures.

The news was small but spreading, good, but too easy to mistake as great. We were playing for the survival of humanity, and we had to win everything, or we'd lost.

Wire, encouraged, wanted to make a short detour to a world marked *Low Risk Low Vampire* on Bluejay's vampire heat map to see if he could quickly locate and rescue an old lover.

I wanted to tell him we could do it.

But we had to win everything to win anything. To use the metaphor of playing pool, we had to make every shot perfectly; we had to run the table — and we had to do it on world after world, against enemies who were not idiots, with the potential of complications we couldn't see coming, knowing that not once could we slip up, not once could we give any hint that we were other than what we were pretending to be. We were exactly one handful of people against billions, and we did not have the luxury of being human. We had to be perfect.

I was the captain of my ship and the leader of the mission. My authority as captain was absolute and unquestionable — in space, where instant death lies on the other side of ten molecules' thickness of moleibond, and *careless* is a synonym for *dead*, only one person can command. The luxury of debate belongs to places where time is measured in minutes and hours, not nanoseconds. Further, I'd earned overall *mission* command because I was the only one among us who'd fought the monsters.

So.

I would not call for a vote. Both the decision and the responsibility for its outcome rested on my shoulders. Wire had someone in settled space he'd cared about. Had lost. We were close to where he'd lived when they were parted.

I tried to imagine it being Badger. And knew I could not

throw away our precious, irreplaceable time, not even had there been a chance I would find Badger on a nearby world.

It was human to want to find and save a loved one — part of what was best about humanity.

Until we knew humanity would survive, we did not have the luxury of being human.

I closed my eyes and rested my head in my hand.

We did not have the luxury of being human.

All five of us had taken the Kartach Norgan. All five of us had, by the standards valued by society, failed miserably.

Even as humans, we had shown ourselves to be monsters in our own right — or at least to be people who would be very skilled at becoming monsters, should the fancy take us.

The fact that we Kartach Norgan nightmares were all individualists who wanted nothing more than for the universe to leave us alone was what stood between us and our decisions not to become what we could have excelled at.

I opened com to every cabin and enclosure in the ship and said, "All crew to the command deck. Hurry."

When they arrived, I said, "We have a problem."

I said, "We have no room for error, for doubt, for fear, for second thoughts. We have one chance, and only one chance, to stop the wave of Darkout that is about to devour humanity. The five of us held up against the initial pain and pleasure of our new forms, and have so far remained steady to our course against the lures of the power we now wield."

I paced. The command deck is tight, but pacing steadies me. Helps me think. If I'm alone, I also talk out loud to myself, and wave my hands around when I'm talking.

Fortunately, my thoughts at the moment didn't need *that* much help.

"We are all of us still linked to our human pasts, and the

possibility exists that at some time during our mission, one or all of us will want to make allowance to pursue something personal from our pasts."

I thought of Bailey's Irish station, close to one of the big stopping points on our planned path, and of my friends there who were currently protected from monsters who wanted me dead by everyone's certainty that I already was, and pushed them out of my mind.

"Wire has asked if we could divert our course briefly so he could try to contact and rescue his sister from a world nearby, where he thinks she might be enslaved.

"He mentioned that we were doing well.

"I agree that our plan seems to be working. However, we cannot divert. We cannot relent in our attack."

"Don't ask to save friends, or relatives, or lovers, no matter how close we might be to where you think they are. No matter how dear they were to you. You cannot know if they survive. If they survive, you cannot know if they are still human. And neither you nor I wish to be placed in the position of killing someone you loved because that person has become a vampire since you last saw him. Or her.

"It would be easy to be moved by love or pity to do something stupid that could destroy this one fragile, pathetic chance we have to keep humanity alive."

"We do not dare divert from our mission for *any* purpose until we know we have succeeded."

I stopped pacing and stared down at my feet.

"Or until we know the mission has failed utterly, and that nothing we do can alter the outcome. If we're lucky and perfect, we can search for loved ones in three months. If we're not, well, there will be no place to search."

I looked up into their faces. "Five of us, my friends.

Against all of them, with their numbers growing every day. We. Must. Be. Perfect."

I exhaled slowly. "I'm sorry."

I wanted for any of them to speak. But I could see horror in their eyes — the realization that someone they had once loved might already have become the enemy.

Wire, Tarko, and Bluejay left. Not one said a word. Not one offered argument.

Herog stayed behind. "You were expecting an argument," he said.

"Yes."

"The idea of having to kill someone you once loved — or still love — is the worst thing in the world. The truth of it is worse yet. They won't hate you for telling them the truth."

"I had to face it first for myself — I hated myself for choosing the priorities I did."

"But you chose right."

"I know. But doing the right thing is not the easy thing. And frequently not the happy thing."

"Put the damn ship on auto for a while, and let's go kill each other. You'll feel better once we get that out of the way."

What does it say about me that I knew he was right?

Chapter 19

"**I**mmortal Velvet, I have you bound for Galatia Fairing. Captain, please bring up visual com."

That was odd. Visual com is available on all ships, but it's essentially useless. Weekend yachters and pleasure cruisers love it for chatting with their friends, but working ships and working crews — and professional stationmasters — ignore that sort of nonsense. With crew biometrics linked directly into com and instantly sendable with a single spoken word from ship to station or from ship to ship, visual ID is completely unnecessary.

Which suggested to me that the stationmaster might be something other than a professional.

I brought up vid, and found myself face to face with a man born to command, in full dress uniform, who was staring at me with an unnerving expression of lust and wonder.

"It *is* you," he whispered. "You're Velvet."

He smiled, and I caught the flash of fangs. "I caught the notice that your ship was coming here, and I switched rotations with an underling so I could be here to greet you personally. We are honored to have you here. All of us. We want..." He smiled and shook his head. "We're holding a masquerade in your honor. Please just come as yourselves. We'll have greeters in place for your arrival planetside, and the best quarters in our finest hotel have been reserved for you."

I was nonplussed.

I nodded, and he continued. "Please let me know what time will be convenient for you."

"We'll need about two hours," I said.

"Thank you," he said. "My goddess." He bowed and cut com, and I slammed a closed fist into the arm of my chair.

"Open private com, privacy shields up," I told the ship. And said, "Folks, weirdness has ensued. Meet me on deck."

When they arrived, I said, "The Legends of Galatia Fairing are throwing a party for us. We are here to let them know that we are offering magnificent immortality to a handful of them at the price of the slaughter of all the rest. They've clearly seen our leaked recordings of previous meetings, so they know that's why we're here. And *they've* set aside their best hotel rooms for us, and are putting together a fancy-dress shindig."

"It's a trap," Tarko said. Everyone else nodded.

"No shit." I laughed ruefully. "What we need to figure out before we get down there is, what *kind* of trap, and how do we counter it? We have two hours before we have to either attend their damn party, or cut and run. And we don't actually have the option of cutting and running. We have to be PERFECT. We are selling godhood, and gods don't run.

"Which means," I continued, "that we figure out how they think they can either kill us or blackmail us — in case they have a giant pit of fire or a team of master swordsmen standing by to cut off our heads — we figure out how to block their trap, we show up and walk unscathed and unflustered through whatever they think they're going to pull, and we leave every damned one of them determined to be the one monster who gets to be a bigger better monster, instead of one of the horde of monsters who end up dead."

"What do you need from us?" Herog asked.

"Research. They haven't had much time to prepare, we have access to their private channels. We need the right question and the right words to figure out what they're planning. And we have to look nice when we go down there — it's a fancy-dress party — so we don't have long."

We searched. Weapons, poisons, cages, shipments of quantities of any of the former to any site large enough to hold a lot of people.

And we found *nothing*.

We didn't even find places where information had gone missing.

With half an hour left to put on our best clothes, make sure we looked our most dramatic, and get ourselves planet-side, we had absolutely no clue what they were going to throw at us.

Bluejay asked, "Could it be a genuine party? Because they like us? Or admire us? Or..."

Herog, Tarko, and I all said, "No," at the same instant.

"So... trap," she said, and shrugged.

We stepped off the ship into the station, and two beautiful young women, neither with the slightest hint of Legend about her, said, "We're here to take you to the party, gracious ones." And they trotted ahead of us, blonde and brunette, delicately featured, scantily dressed. They smelled like the best meal I'd never had. They seemed bait-like to me. Stupidly trusting, meant to look tasty. They led us to an express spindle shuttle. A private one. The five of us, and the two young human women. Were they a test? Were we supposed to snack on them on the way down? Or were we supposed to avoid the temptation, proving we were of a higher order than the Legends with whom we would be meeting?

I was grateful we'd all drunk our synth blood to the point of discomfort before we left. It wasn't as much help as I might have wished, though.

We glided downward, our incredible speed imperceptible within the shuttle. We sat comfortably around a central console that offered visual and gaming entertainment, news from Galatia Fairing's main city — also named Galatia Fairing. And we had access to public datastreams from outlying regions.

And a whole menu of reconsta foods, the prices of each neatly listed and deductible automatically from our ship credit. Being what we were, we couldn't eat any of the reconsta.

I ignored the entertainment and information, and fought to ignore the sweet scent of tender young human, and chatted with my two guides. While I recognized that both of them had been marked by a Legend, and were therefore useless as information sources, my crew used the public datastreams, ostensibly to entertain themselves. They were surreptitiously continuing to search for anything that might give us a clue about the sort of trap planned for us.

When our guides ran out of banalities, I ended up looking out the window at views of the receding station, the approaching planet surface, and the vast lot of nothingness in between. Anything to distract myself. The trip took less than six minutes, and at the end of it, my crew signaled no luck in their searches. They all looked as strained as I felt. We had no information about what our hosts were up to.

We would, then, go in blind. But we would go in.

We were met by Galatia Fairing Port Authority security controllers on our arrival to the surface. *They* were not human, and they eyed our guides hungrily. "If you're here to access Galatia Fairing data, we have to stamp your hands," one of them said. Galatia Fairing guards its data ferociously through the use of tracking and monitoring chips it embeds in the palm of the visitor's hand. You cannot even reach a data level without the chip, and if you try to remove one or tamper with it in any way before it's deactivated by your exit scan, it will explode, blowing you into bits small enough to be cleaned out by the planetary air filters.

Nobody plays games with the palm chips.

But none of us needed one. I said, "We're here for personal reasons."

"We'd be delighted to arrange a tour of the data facilities," one said. "They're fascinating."

They're not in the least fascinating. They're deadly dull, with bad lighting, tasteless low-quality reconsta, and the bleak decor usually reserved for prisons and torture chambers. The information in them is spectacular, but the fine folks of Galatia Fairing have made sure paying customers will be as uncomfortable and unhappy as possible while getting it.

Which left me wondering if the trap had been tied in to the data facilities... or the palm chips.

Either way, we'd be sidestepping anything in that direction.

"We haven't time. This will be a short visit," I told him.

So we passed through untagged, and with our nubile young guides intact.

Galatia Fairing is, if you're avoiding the data centers, quite a lovely place. It's domed, free of wildlife, with an excellent controlled environment and no weather. The architecture is a bit fanciful for my tastes, trending toward spirals, cones, and arabesque-laced cubes. Transportation is accelerated pedestrian — powered walkways, null-grav foot gliders, and liftbelts.

I'll note that the data centers are utilitarian, and you walk your full weight via non-enhanced foot power, or they don't let you through the doors. These people have *no* sense of humor, lightheartedness, or whimsy where their data is concerned.

But if you're going to go to a party on Galatia Fairing, make sure you can float or fly.

Having been there before, I knew what to expect, and all of our costumes were fitted with null-grav field generators. We'd dance on air with the best of them.

We arrived fashionably late, to find a room full of loud talkers, all beautifully dressed in costumes from all eras. Many of them were already dancing on air to Debalkas. He's primarily a classicist who likes to use odd instruments in his compositions, like the stone piano, which was featured in the piece being played by the live orchestra.

This was all about ostentation, money, and power, then.

The dancers looked like Wire's locker brought to life and multiplied.

Some of the guests wore masks. More did not.

It took me just an instant to figure out why.

The barefaced guests were the Legends.

The masked ones were human slaves — or refreshments.

I kept my expression neutral. The presence of human slaves suggested that at some point, the party was going to turn into a bloodletting orgy, a slaughterfest of humanity for the amusement of their masters. The fact that we had arrived and been given no notice, no introduction, and no attention suggested further that we as visitors were to be put in our places and schooled in "how we do things here."

I thought not. If you intend to be the biggest badass in the universe, you do not walk into a vast chamber of a room where you are supposedly guests of honor and wait to be recognized while the party swirls around you. You command attention.

"Look at me."

I whispered the words, but put all the force of my thoughts behind them.

The silence was instant, shocking, brutal. Faces snapped in my direction as if moved by one hand, and all eyes focused on mine. In each face, I saw fear — and the fear was greater in the eyes of the Legends than in the eyes of the humans.

My command was more powerful, more all-encompassing than any slap to the face, any electric shock, any bloodthirsty roar. I owned them, and the Legends present, who radiated power and thus certainly held high positions within the Galatia Fairing hierarchy, were not accustomed to being owned.

"On the floor. Now."

Everyone dropped, tumbling from the air, landing hard. Every human slave. Every vampire Legend. Nor did they land on their feet. They went belly down, noses pressed to the floor, breath shivering out of them as if they were freezing. They trembled before me, a hundred powerful monsters and their quaking human retinues, and not a soul made a sound.

If you intend to be recognized as the biggest badass in the universe, it helps if you actually are.

Beside me, my own people had dropped to their knees, and were fighting the compulsion to go nose-down with the jellyfish.

"Up," I whispered, and my too-broadly targeted compulsion left them. We weren't vulnerable to anything Legends could throw at us, but we were somewhat vulnerable to each other.

I wondered idly how far beyond the walls of the chamber my command had traveled.

The Galatia Fairing vampires had gathered the cream of their Legend society in this room, and I had no doubt they were one of the most influential tribes of monsters in settled space. This city had once been home to Danniz Oe, a Master Legend subordinate only to Peter Crane and Haskell Corrigan — all three now dead by my hand.

These offspring of the original three had thought to intimidate us, to prove we were no match for so many of them. They had thought to make demands.

I said, "We are not commanded, we are not summoned, we are not compelled or compellable. We are not *you,* in other words. Who among you is chief Legend?"

Nobody twitched. Nobody moved. I realized they couldn't — that I still had them locked to the floor with the gravity of my mind.

You don't want to think of yourself as the sort of person who delights in perverse displays of power, but I have to admit that, after more than a year of fighting these bastards and losing ground with every battle, it felt wonderful to crush them to the ground and hold them there with a word and a thought.

You tell yourself, *I don't want power.*

When you have it, though, it's hard to not want.

"You may stand," I whispered.

They all stood. The music did not resume, nor did the conversation. Everyone stood still, staring at me, and I tasted their fear like a rich and filling meal.

I spoke in my normal voice. It carried nicely in the chamber. "You do not get special favors. The fact that you are currently the richest and most powerful vampires on Galatia Fairing means nothing to me. You will have to apply for the Legend II nanovirus at the same time and in the same way as everyone else, and you will be in competition with every other Legend on your world — no matter how insignificant, new, or weak — for the few packages I'm offering. Of those of you here, it is entirely possible that not one will survive the coming purge, because I will give Legend II to those whose applications I receive first, selected by my own algorithms to fit the number and distribution I have decided is optimum for Legend Masters."

I studied them. In a few eyes, I saw a canniness that suggested I had not yet sprung their trap.

Always give the enemy enough rope to hang himself.

"So have you anything to say?" I asked.

And Canny Eyes Vampire in the front row said, "We had hoped to offer you a view of the world we have created here for vampires. Our populations have not run so out of control as Legend mobs elsewhere, and we can certainly police the extras ourselves. And we do a good job of tending our human population. All of them are under complete control. None leave or arrive without our knowledge or consent. They are obedient slaves who worship us, as is the right and proper role for humans."

All right. This was what he considered his selling points — the things that he hoped would convince me these creeps were worth preserving.

I waited.

"We brought you slaves," he said when I said nothing. "As a token of our esteem, as a proof of our good will."

His eyes said he was lying.

So I gave a slight nod of acknowledgment, and waited to see what he and his friends had thought up as their trap.

They herded forward a dozen human men and women... all wearing the costumes of harem dancers and sword dancers. The proffered slaves were — to a one — exotic, sexy... and veiled. The veils were not quite right, though; as air moved them against the faces of each of the slaves moving toward us, I could see faint outlines of something else that outlined an oval shape around each nose and mouth.

The shape clicked in the back of my mind.

Our gifts were wearing droplet filters, I realized.

And I almost laughed.

The bastards had found themselves with a dozen humans infected with AntiLegend, and had thought to rid themselves of us with their little gift of appreciation.

Which — if you're already the most powerful Legends on a world, and you realize you're about to end up the prey to something bigger and meaner than you — does make sense. You aren't going to get Legend II if you kill the bearers. But neither will the other monster who might have, and who would have slaughtered you without a second thought.

I considered the choices of the lovely folks who were

providing our evening's entertainment, and I did smile. "Thank you so much," I said. "How very thoughtful."

I felt the surprise of my crew at my sides, though they gave no outward indication.

When I added, "Do you mind if I sample one here?" my host returned my smile with a genuine, happy one of his own.

"Please," he said, and bowed to me.

I took the wrist of one of the young women, and looked into her eyes. Her expression was yearning, hopeful.

Yes. I remembered the feeling when Peter Crane was getting ready to kill me. I wanted his bite at my throat. Wanted him with a yearning lust that I could still remember when I looked in her eyes.

I told her, "Just a little taste," and bit into her wrist, being careful to avoid arteries. I'd never bitten anyone before, but I had a good knowledge of anatomy, and where a hole would cause dangerous bleeding, versus where it would cause just a little. Having to patch yourself together just to survive to get to your Medix is an excellent teacher in how your body works.

The girl's blood tasted like the fake stuff we'd been drinking from the ship to exactly the same degree that low-grade, end-run reconsta tasted like grass-fed steak. The jolt of it damn near brought me to my knees. I needed to stop. I yearned to continue. Herog's hand on my shoulder was a warning. His whisper in my ear was a command.

"Stop."

I stopped, and managed to take a steadying breath without being obvious about it. "Lovely," I said.

"Perhaps your allies would like to sample some of the others," the host said.

"Maybe later," I told him. I saw him through a haze of

red. The taste of human blood filled me with an animal lust I could barely control, and honed my every sense, and sharpened my every emotion.

Foremost among my emotions, it honed my rage at these cowardly bastards who had thought to use trickery to murder my crew and me. "First, however, I'm going to share my new slave with you. You will take one tiny sip of her now to celebrate how well we're getting along."

And there it was. Raw, cold horror in his eyes. "I'm not worthy," he whispered.

"Sure you are." And I whispered, just to him, *"Drink. One sip."*

He did, and when he finished, I held him locked in front of me, stone-still, and stood looking at him.

"One thing we didn't mention, and perhaps should have," I said to everyone in the chamber, pitching my voice to carry all the way to the back of the huge room, "is that Legend II confers immunity to that vile toxin AntiLegend." I smiled at him, and then at all of them, and said, "For those few who get it, every human once again becomes... untainted. And simply delicious."

In front of me, Canny Eyes, victim of his own cleverness, started to swell.

"I drank from a human infected with AntiLegend — gives the blood a delightfully bright aftertaste. And you'll notice that my host drank from the same human, and from the same spot. You see that I'm fine. He, however—"

My host exploded at that moment, raining bits and pieces of himself all over the room.

The explosion scattered bits of him across the room, many of them so microscopically tiny they could be inhaled.

I picked up at the point where he'd interrupted my narration. "—went to pieces."

The human slaves who were natural carriers were all maskless. Breathing in those microscopic Antilegend viroids.

It took only seconds before one of the uninfected humans sneezed.

Seconds again before the next one did.

"Every Legend is this room will now take one sip of the blood of a sneezing, AntiLegend-infected human," I commanded the rest of the throng.

The humans stood frozen, sneezing. The vampires, knowing what would happen when they did it, but unable to resist my command, moved to the sneezing humans and, one by one, drank lightly from those who sneezed. And then they exploded.

The mess was battlefield horror, minus the battlefield. The doppler recorder in my right thighbone was capturing every moment in flawless three-dimensional detail.

My rage, my bloodlust, my triumphant fury, filled me.

As much as I was able to think, I thought our next leaked transmission into the datastream of a meeting between Legend II and Legend I vampires was going to be a big hit.

Chapter 20

The five of us, in blood-soaked fancy dress, wandered the streets of Galatia Fairing with our unmasked human cohort, spreading AntiLegend wherever we went.

I talked to my doppler chip, explaining what we were doing.

"This is punishment for the arrogant," I said as we walked. "Those of you Legends who think you want to take us on, consider the fate of the Legends of Galatia Fairing, who will — save one — be no more. We have claimed their humans as our own, and set them to our task, which is the destruction of the Legends on this world.

"Galatia Fairing would have had thirty Masters. But they sealed their fate with their treachery, and on them we visit the plague of a world filled with infected humans, and horrible, brutal death to Legends. All worlds must be ruled by Masters. But we will create only one Legend II Master here — if one can survive long enough to win our prize. All others will die.

"If you hope to become a Legend II Master, consider

the company you keep — because there were no doubt Legends on this world who would have joined our mission, who would have made fine Masters. Who would have ruled gloriously.

"Now all but one — the deadliest one — will survive."

Which of course wasn't exactly true. The infection rate for AntiLegend was 80%, more or less. There would be a few vampires in the city of Galatia Fairing who would survive — and any of them who sent in applications would get their dose of Legend II. If the Legends in the other cities and outposts of the world of Galatia Fairing stopped all travel to or from the main city, the vampires in those locations would remain untouched by today's exercise in demonstrating the principle that actions have consequences.

Our visit made one hell of an object lesson, though. Not a vampire in settled space would miss the importance of that image of the Galatia Fairing vampires in their fancy dress walking like so many sheep to their doom, knowing what faced them, but unable to save themselves. In that instant, I had shown them to be as weak before Legend II vampires as humans were weak before them.

My last act before leaving Galatia Fairing was to turn off the doppler recorder in my right thigh and do a blanket command, as far as I could send it, to the humans on the world who were in reach of my projected will.

The command of a Legend II vampire ought to supersede any commands given by Legend I vampires. So I freed as many of the slaves as I could, simply by focusing my will and shouting, *"Humans! Know your own minds, and be free!"*

THE SAME SYSTEM that was home to the now-Legend-depleted Galatia Fairing also held one other world worth visiting, and we had intended to go there. I told my crew that — considering events on Galatia Fairing — we could skip the visit to Haff. Our injection into the datastream of our visit with the Galatia Fairing elites needed to have a chance to get around.

So Bluejay and I sat down with her most current update of the map of vampire hotspots, and found an alternate world that would meet our criteria — short distance from origami point to target, evidence of heavy vampire population, and a world well-known throughout settled space.

Napoleon.

I detested Napoleon. It was a world ruled by a little man who styled himself after the eighteenth century Old Earth French dictator, and who'd convinced whole masses of Old Earth French and settled space francophiles to join him in creating "the world as it would have been had Napoleon won."

My problems with Napoleon — the world and its pretender — are many.

First, I look at history the way I look at evolution. Some things die out for a good reason, and should be left dead. I put dictatorships and velociraptors in the same category: leave them in the past, where they can serve as frightening object lessons for the present.

Second, Napoleon is not a megaworld — its population is only two or three billion, held back by the meager technological advances Napoleon allows (only technology invented by Frenchmen, Napoleonites, or people whom the God Emperor Napoleon deems "French by command" because he wants a specific technology for his own personal use.)

Third, I hate worlds that don't permit Standard. You have to hire a damn translator when you go there, and the translators all act like you're some sort of sub-human because you don't speak French.

I might as well confess right now that I look at languages the same way I look at history and biology. Standard won the linguistic evolutionary war. Best vocabulary, simplest construction. Any idiot can learn enough of it to communicate, but any genius has all the best words and concepts from thousands of other languages brought in and stored to create works of beauty and wonder — and if he can't find the words he needs, Standard accommodates him by letting him make his own words to test against need. Standard grows bigger every year.

I say, keep your historical languages for your own use if you want, but learn Standard so you can communicate in settled space. And so you can read Bashtyk Nokyd — best writer ever — in his original language.

But I digress. After the mess on Galatia Fairing, a trip to charming, backwards, dictator-run, weather-bedeviled Napoleon would be a brilliant change of pace. Galatia Fairing was one of settled space's great technological triumphs — but nobody loved it. Napoleon was the most popular tourist destination in the known universe. People needed to see from our data leaks that vampires were in control there, too.

Rumor was that the God Emperor Napoleon was being recruited by them, but that the Legends had satisfied themselves with merely controlling him from the background because his argument about not wanting to give up French food was so compelling.

There, I think they had a point.

Besides, we'd done something interesting and unexpected on Galatia Fairing, and I wanted to give that experiment a day or two in which to bear fruit.

So I filed our flight plan, and we went through the origami point, and I suffered the anguish of seeing Badger, and being almost able to reach him, and then having him ripped away from me again when we came out the other end, perfectly on time, exactly where we were expected...

...And we were under attack.

One ship. Paranoid captain that I am, I have all systems set to auto-protect in case of attack. Wire had augmented the ship's existing systems with some ferocious weapons, and before I or my crew had even shaken off the post-entry disorientation, the *Immortal Velvet* had scored a couple solid hits on our attacker, had locked down shields, and had sealed the compartment breach from the damage we'd taken.

I managed to scan and data-capture details of our attacker before it turned tail and fled.

We did not pursue, both because we were on a mission and could not allow ourselves the luxury of a drawn-out chase, and because we needed to take care of our injured.

Crew quarters, which are aft on the command deck level, had been specifically targeted. The target had been murderously specific, using exact knowledge of where my crew would be during and immediately following passage through the origami point. We'd been scanned by someone at some point, and only occupied quarters had been attacked

Two of my crew — Tarko and Bluejay — had been hit.

Both had managed to get themselves into their Medix units, which I credited to the powerful recuperative powers of the Legend II nanovirus. What had injured them would have killed them instantly had they still been in human form. Their injuries were so severe, however, that their medichambers had them in induced comas while making major repairs.

The kind of damage you have to do to a nanovampire to require that sort of repair effort is almost inconceivable.

The damage to the two rooms had been a straight slice, right at bunk level, starting exactly at the point of the first bunk and slicing into the space directly above where it was designed to be, transversely. The shot had been done by a steady Anabond-cutter stream, kept narrow and precise, done by someone who knew the layout of this particular ship, and whose sole intent had been to kill crew.

The cutter had been moving fast. My shields had gone up point-two seconds after the initial hit — point-one seconds after my ship had blasted the attackers with a combination of gravity shear sweep and 50 sticky pies that had just about coated the hull — and in that time that cutter had burned through 17.144 meters of my hull. Hell of a lot of power running through that thing to go through ten layers of moleibond for 17.144 meters in two tenths of a second.

Just about all the enemy ship's power had to have been shunted into their cutter. Which did mean they got the full benefit of my weapons, though, and that the majority of the ship's occupants had been pulped.

Both my cabins and their occupants had suffered through the massive pressure changes within their cabins. But it looked like only Bluejay had taken a direct hit from the moleibond cutter — her room was spattered with blood.

Tarko's wasn't.

Tarko had removed his bunk when he'd changed himself into the form he laughingly referred to MegaFreak. He'd been sleeping on the floor, where he'd upholstered the bed area of his room with Nul-Grav-Fom — the stuff they use in prisons so prisoners in body-lock for extended punishment won't develop pressure sores.

I have no intention of telling you how I know about Nul-Grav-Fom. Or body-lock. I'll just say that not all of my clients have been gems to work for, or honest about their intentions, and leave it at that.

Wire, Herog, and I cleaned up the mess, which included body parts. Tarko and Bluejay were both healing rapidly. They'd be better by the time we reached Napoleon. We'd get there in five hours. Wire and Herog came up to join me on the deck, to help me look over scans of the ship that had hit us. I pulled up the ship's recordings of the attack.

"That's a Colson StarStream," Wire said, studying our playback.

I shrugged. I was no yacht connoisseur.

He said, "The ship that was watching us from right at the periphery of our scan range back when we came through to the Wellspring system was a Colson StarStream."

"You sure?"

He snorted. "Bet my life on it. I've done adaptations on two. The *Immortal Velvet* and the other Monoceros sidewinders have dispersal bands, which is part of what makes it possible for them to make mid-course changes in hyperspace. Every other TFN ship in existence has fixed-plane dispersal fins, *except* for the Colson Starstream. The Colson StarStream has dispersal *coils*. Not bands, but flexible in the same fashion that bands are flexible. Guess why."

I felt my gut twist. "Because the Colson StarStream can make mid-course corrections in hyperspace?"

Wire tapped his nose and grinned. "Someone at Colson got hold of a Monoceros sidewinder without getting caught doing it, dissected it, reverse-engineered the tech to create a process that did not violate the locked-down Monoceros patents, and built a new source for sidewinders."

Shit. Shit, shit. With Crane officially missing and presumed dead — well *definitely* dead, but only my friends and I knew that at the moment — lawyers had Monoceros Starcraft Ltd. locked up, and the patents frozen while they and their many clients wrangled over who among a long list of claimants had any right to the billions of rucets in spoils.

I'd liked having sidewinders out of production, because it meant I knew how many other ships like mine were in existence — twenty-six — and that the number would only get fewer over time.

When you track people for a living, you'd like to have the odds in your favor as much as possible.

New sidewinders in manufacture meant that if we survived Darkout, I had to anticipate working harder to find people who didn't want to be found.

I set up a couple of worms to quietly gather information for me about who had purchased Colson Starstreams.

Wire went aft to do finish work on rebonding the hull.

And, because we were on track and the ship was capable of getting us to Napoleon without input from me, I started digging through my existing data gathering. I started with Fedara Contei, and discovered there were an enormous number of women in databases across settled space with one or the other of those names. But none with both of them.

At least not that the worms had yet unearthed. Annoying. But it takes a while for worms to burrow. I'd find her.

I moved on to reaction to our latest Legend II leak, and it was fair to say that all hell had broken loose on Galatia Fairing after we left. Humans infected with AntiLegend had banded together and were traveling to the other cities and settlements on the planet to spread the virus, but they were not meeting the resistance I would have anticipated. Something none of us had anticipated in any of our meetings or discussions had happened.

We'd anticipated a good number of emergency-departure-without-flight-plan exits from Galatia Fairing — as we were leaving, we'd talked about the demonstration of the lethality of the AntiLegend virus, and how vampires were going to see for the first time the speed and ease with which it spread among human populations. We'd been sure vampires would flee anyplace known to contain infected humans.

What we had not foreseen — ever, at any point in our work or planning, was the other reaction the damned Legends were having to our visit to Galatia Fairing.

They had gone to war against each other. They were hunting each other down, slaughtering each other, the powerful wiping out the weak with terrifying speed and ferocity.

This was something Legends had never done.

I sat there thinking about it, and realized it made perfect sense.

The more rivals any particular vampire could slaughter in advance of the release of Legend II, the better his odds of being the vampire who *got* Legend II, to become a unique, all-powerful Master. A master immune to AntiLegend.

And from the point of view of Legend vampires who'd already managed to rise to power, they had the opportunity to use that power to eliminate inferiors, rather than waiting for the luck of a draw that did not care who had won his way to power through skill, intelligence, and other superior qualities, and who had not.

The images leaking into the datastream from Galatia Fairing were stunning — taken by humans freed from vampiric mind-slavery, capturing monster-against-monster battles where every survivor of one fight immediately turned against another potential rival.

Those fleeing the world were as likely to be weak monsters who knew they had no chances of survival against their own kind as they were to be rich and powerful monsters avoiding a deadly human-borne disease.

I sat watching the filtered feeds from Galatia Fairing for a while, then remembered that Legends and humans across settled space had been following the leaked adventures of the crew of the *Immortal Velvet*.

I widened my search from Galatia Fairing to other big worlds.

It seemed no one had missed our message, or its import.

Humans on Cantata were reporting massacres as the rich, the famous, the adulated, and the beloved started slaughtering each other in the midst of work.

The comptroller of Meileone, the financial director, the director of tourism, and the director of mining each received an alert from their coms. They stopped in the middle of a meeting on future westward expansion of the mines to check the details of their alert — and the instant they finished watching it, grew fangs and talons and attacked each other in front of horrified human subordinates. *That* leaked recording was short, because the human doing the recording apparently realized once one survivor remained, witnesses would be unwelcome.

Humans watching a live concert in Cantata's Pinnacle City saw one fanged monster leap onto the stage from three rows back and rip the throat out of the group's lead singer. The rest of the band then grew their own fangs and talons and destroyed the attacker — but were then destroyed by their own manager, wielding a weapon with exploding ammunition.

As the Cantata humans watched, they discovered not just that they had deadly killers in their midst, but that the killers were people they had voted into office. Had paid to watch perform. Had loved. Had envied for their wealth, their connections, their ability to sway the masses with their words. They were discovering that they had admired, and obeyed, and loved monsters.

Humans on Rangell, as yet untouched by AntiLegend... and which had been one of the *Immortal Velvet's* next stops... were leaking images of and talking in terrified tones about the imposition of martial law, of house-to-house searches, of people they had known for years and had liked and trusted being dragged into the streets and slaughtered. About how these once-loved friends grew fangs and talons and fought for their lives against police and military forces who also had fangs and talons.

On some worlds, communication ceased, and the space stations that served them speculated that issues with vampires might be involved.

What had been the biggest and best-kept secret in settled space had turned into a human-directed, human-reported exposé of the disintegration of elites into blood-spattered animals hunting each other.

For the moment, the humans were untouched — because they were food, and *no one* was going to go around destroying food.

But I didn't hear humanity rejoicing, either.

The refrain was, "What happens when the survivors — the worst, deadliest, and most powerful vampires out there — don't have any more Legends to fight. And worse yet, what happens when these monsters get hold of Legend II?"

A ship-wide alert blatted through the *Immortal Velvet*, scaring the daylights out of me. Wire jumped. Herog didn't.

I'd been sitting, transfixed by the datastream for more than three hours, and had missed the visual on overhead of two official Napoleon government interceptors and a destroyer moving into range with targeting systems on and weapons readied against the *Immortal Velvet*.

The hail blasted the three of us.

"Battle deck now," I whispered. Both of them took off at a dead run for the fight deck hidden down, back, and midship, out of reach of shock, percussion, and Anabond weapons.

They were already gone when image transmission took over the central third of my forward infoscreen, and a snarling, uniformed man with a bloody face shouted something at me in a language I did not speak. French, no doubt.

The translation came right after, minus the shouting.

"Velvet, captain of the *Immortal Velvet*, you and Hellspawn crew are under arrest for Crimes Against Humanity, with warrant for your arrest or destruction"

The captain — clearly human, not vampire, because he was bleeding from a cut that was *not* healing as I watched — snarled something else into my screen as my people fled the forward command deck for the mid-ship battle deck.

The translation was not encouraging. "Destruction will suit me just fine."

Chapter 21

S o there I was. The face behind Legend II, with my ship neatly trackable to every stop on our itinerary, looking into the eyes of a human who wanted me dead, and who wanted to the depths of his angry soul to be the one who could take credit for killing me.

I was a known monster, now a famous one, and not just famous to the folks for whom my "be-a-bigger-monster" pitch had been intended.

Humans had seen me. Knew my face. Were not swayed by my fragile teenage beauty, my wide-eyed expression of innocence, my black-as-night, white-as-snow, red-as-blood fairytale presentation.

They'd seen what I could do, and they wanted no part of the universe I claimed to be remaking in my own image.

But we were headed toward Napoleon, which meant *I shouldn't have been dealing with humans*. My own kind should have been there to greet me, in whatever fashion they'd decided would work for them.

Three hours earlier, Napoleon had been a world firmly under the control of a powerful cabal of nanovampires—

overflowing with Legends in fancy dress and their enthralled human underlings.

Which just goes to show that things change. Not always to the favor of those of us who are fighting to save humanity.

"I see that," I told the captain on my screen, and heard the unseen translator rendering my comment to the caption. For an instant I stood there, eyeing the destroyer with its many big guns. It was a *big* destroyer, and apparently a concession by the Napoleonese Navy to the realities of war, because it was modern as all hell.

As were the two interceptors.

I ran through my contingency evasive maneuvers, and the coded phrases for each of them.

In general, I'm grateful for every special power vampires *don't* have, but right at that instant, I wished to the depths my soul could reach that for that one moment, mind control would work for me via sub-light transmission against the guy controlling the big guns.

The man facing me wasn't the official captain of the ship. He'd been—prior to whatever had given him the bloody face—a subordinate, and by my best guess, one pretty far down the chain of command.

I couldn't make out what he was from his uniform, though.

Every damn world that has an army—on big worlds, that can be *armies*—creates its own uniforms and rank designations, but in most places, the designers of military uniforms agree on just one set for each branch of the military. And most of the worlds in settled space aim for a sort of standardized vision of rank symbols in order to prevent ugly interworld incidents caused by stupid misunderstandings.

"No, sir, our sergeant did *not* know three slices of pie and a cookie on your man's left shoulder meant he was the

Grand Commander of the Fleet. We thought he was a pastry chef, so we housed him with the cooks."

Situations like that.

But Napoleon did not give a asteroid miner's cold iron damn about preventing confusion. Oh, no. Because it had recreated Napoleon's Grande Armée, with authentic period uniforms.

I remembered from previous visits—back in better days when Napoleonites had been happy to be rude to me instead of wanting to kill me—that recreating the Grande Armée had meant duplicating the ancient uniforms from fifteen or so nations who had joined in with the original Napoleon to help him conquer some place or other that ended up not working out—and all of those nations had provided their own uniforms. None of which matched.

And all of those uniforms had been from an era fond of velvet and gold and silver braid, with useless decorations of every imaginable kind pinned to all sorts of unlikely places.

What I noticed about the ugly, angry man threatening me was that he didn't have any gold braid or gold rope or stars or bars or ribbons of any sort. His uniform was plain. Light blue. Had two rows of buttons down the front.

I tried a stalling gambit, just to get a bit of information.

"I want to speak to your commander," I said.

Mumble, mumble, from the voice of the translator.

Red-faced snarling from the acting captain.

"I will bet you do, monster, since he was one of your sort."

"What happened to him?" I asked.

Mumble, mumble. Shout, shout.

"*You* did. All humanity knows about your kind because of you."

Probably not, I thought, but a lot more did than when we left Tegosshu. Overall, a very good thing.

But...shout, shout shout. He still had more to say.

"You will surrender now so we can try you, then execute you," the translator's voice said while the acting captain glared at me—a glare that lost half its effectiveness when he had to wipe blood out of his eye.

"Well, no," I told him. "I can't do that."

He apparently understood that without translation, because he screamed something, and several shocks ran through my ship.

So much for stalling.

"*Dangerous ballet*," I said to the ship, and the *Immortal Velvet* fluctuated gravity to compensate for that programmed maneuver, fired thrusters straight up, pushed us down to what I guessed to be about fifty meters, flipped us over, and shot us straight under the belly of the destroyer

"*Paratenka skinner run,*" I told the ship.

We bolted out from under cover, running a random-number-generated pattern of evasive maneuvers similar to those I'd used once I got the ball back in my paratenka-playing days.

The objective of that evasion program was to make it impossible for the enemy to line up aimed shots, and to give my ship's targeting system the pattern the enemy ships' self-targeting shots would follow.

My objective was to kill no humans—and if the humans were in charge on Napoleon, we weren't going to Napoleon.

But neither was I going to leave a trail of corpses belonging to the people I was fighting so hard to save behind me—if they gave me any other alternative at all.

I fled the main deck and hit the battle deck.

"We're locked off weapons," Herog said.

"I know," I said. "I'll bring them up. Right now we're evading two interceptors and a destroyer—and I think we still have an advantage. They have more weapons, but we have better weapons. Their crews are now human. Our reflexes are better, so if this goes bad, we'll be able to react about twice as quickly to their actions as they'll be able to act against ours. Right now, we're taking passive evasive action. *Velvet* is selectively targeting and destroying weapons fired against us, but not sending anything back at them."

I looked from Wire to Herog.

"As long as we can survive the situation, we do not touch those ships, and we do not kill or endanger any humans. Understood?"

Both nodded.

"Why?" a recently familiar, French-accented voice asked over com.

I froze. Ran back through my actions.

Got distracted going through data feeds. Right.

Took a hail on forward command, identified the acting captain as human. Right.

Tried to stall, failed, gave the computer evasive maneuvers, was evading my ass off to get away from two interceptors and a destroyer. Right.

During any of that, had I closed com?

No.

I had not closed com.

I. Had. Not. Closed. Com.

Sons of fatherless mothers of depravity, I had not closed com.

I buried my head in my hands.

We'd been perfect.

Perfect.

We'd played the perfect villains, the flawless dark gods of seduction, temptation, lust, power, perversity, and sin.

And I, Goddess of the Coming Hell, had just ordered my crew to leave the humans I was supposed to despise unscathed. I had given the command that we were to protect our attackers from our superior power.

I froze.

Herog didn't miss a beat. "Because, *lunch*," he snarled, sounding like a pirate-hunter crossed with the demon god of death, "if we kill you now, we can't drink you later."

Then *he* cut com.

I sagged against the battle console, forehead on forearms.

"Thanks." I was shaking. I had just about destroyed our cover, and with that, our one chance to stop Darkout. "You just saved all of humankind."

"No problem. You can sleep with me later."

I sat straight up, my spine went rigid, and my head snapped sideways like a high-speed turret. I stared at him, speechless.

Wire was watching him too, mouth agape.

Herog stared back at me, wincing. There was a long silence, finally broken when he cleared his throat. "I said that out loud?" Another long pause, during which none of us moved. Then, "I didn't say that," he said. "It was *him*. And I apologize on his behalf."

I didn't ask which *him*. Vampire alter-ego or human pants commander, I didn't imagine there was a lot of difference between them.

So much for my comforting fantasy of asexual cama-raderie between me and my second-in-command and body-guard. If he said it, he'd thought it. And no matter what else he might say, I now had to acknowledge there was a whole man in there.

But he was a whole man who had managed to shock me simply because he'd never let that part of himself show.

"Herog, you just saved us from my screw-up, my sloppiness, my complete failure to keep all aspects of what I had to do to protect our mission at the front of my mind."

I paused, considering our daily half-naked grappling in the physical training room—doing our damnedest to kill each other. In all the time he'd been running me through testosterone versus estrogen, he'd never let slip any sign that he included himself in 'testosterone.' He'd made it possible for me to focus on survival, because he had never let that unending physical combat be about anything but survival.

"This one slip aside, you've maintained an unbelievable degree of professionalism," I told him.

We stared into each other's eyes, unblinking. His gaze was as distant as the farthest galaxy in space. His expression, his body language, everything about him said, *Nothing meaningful happened.*

"Thank you," I added.

He nodded.

I went back to contemplating my near-destruction of everything.

One stupid slipup, and I was the one who'd made it. If the Napoleonites had leaked my orders when I thought no one else was listening into the datastream, only fools would have failed to question why the toughest vampires in the universe were bending over backwards to protect humans. The Legends were not fools.

They would distrust Legend II. They would stop killing each other to get it. Darkout would arrive on schedule.

Thanks to Herog, however, all three Napoleonite ships,

reassured that we were not secret friendlies, fired on us with everything they had. That was fun. We got bounced around the battle deck when a couple of percussions hit at the same time, and the combined force weakened our shields.

"Screw being clever," I yelled. "Ship! Straight line, full speed, nearest origami point, NOW!"

We kept shields up and concentrated aft, we destroyed every incoming shot we could, and we still took a lot of hits and a fair amount of internal damage. But the moleibond hull was intact, and we made it to the origami point still functional.

We jumped.

I was willing to bet at least the two interceptors jumped after us, even though they knew they'd be running hot into someone else's jurisdiction. I hoped with all my heart the destroyer followed us in, too.

What they didn't know was that they were going to go roaring out into some other part of settled space, into existing traffic, guns blazing—and the ship they claimed to be chasing would not be in front of them.

Napoleon was about to have a nasty interplanetary incident. The sort of incident that got worlds decommissioned.

Couldn't happen to a nicer bunch of folks.

WE MADE THREE FAST, rough point changes in hyperspace, and came out the other end at an origami point not on the maps. I marked it, and then Tarko and Bluejay—both fresh out of the Medixes and reset by them to their normal human appearances—and Herog, Wire, and I met in the dining hall for big glasses of body-temperature fresh fake blood.

I thought longingly of the Emergency Cookies tucked away in eleven of the twelve RexSurvyve kits on the ship.

They were untouched. I'd forgotten I wouldn't be able to eat them. Human food had no flavor to me.

I was thoroughly sick of fake blood.

I wanted a damn steak, and I wanted an Emergency Cookie.

Blood forever. The diet of Legends. I shuddered.

"Aside from using these disguises for one or two more datastream feeds," I said, "I think we're done as the *Immortal Velvet* team. Vampires know who we are, and want our product, but humans know who we are, and will do anything they can to keep us from delivering Legend II."

Tarko and Bluejay had missed both the attack from the unidentified ship that may have been following us, and the settled-space-wide vampire versus vampire fallout from our trip to Galatia Fairing.

So I caught them up on the events there, ending with the big surprise. The one I never saw coming.

I said, "We never figured for vampires wiping each other out to make sure they were the ones who got Legend II."

"We should have," Tarko said. "Looking backward, it's an obvious response."

I shook my head. "If the Galatia Fairing Legends hadn't brought AntiLegend-infected humans to their party, I would never have thought to make the claim that Legend II provides immunity against AntiLegend. And had there not been all those other humans present, no one would have seen how quickly AntiLegend spreads." I shrugged.

Wire said, "We got lucky."

Bluejay said, "How is it lucky? Now we can't go to all the worlds we'd planned on."

I said, "But now we don't *have* to. They're killing each other off. They're buying us time. They're slowing down Darkout, and they may put an end to the possibility entirely if they wipe enough of each other out now, and if the spread of AntiLegend continues."

Herog said, "You're missing both big problems."

We all turned to look at him.

He sat facing us, arms crossed on his chest, eyes closed. The impression he gave was not of inattention, however, but of deep thought, of intent focus.

"What are we missing?" Tarko asked.

"Locked-out low-tech worlds," he said. "Where AntiLegend is unlikely to go, because the worlds block legal travel. Most of these worlds are going to have Legend infestations, though, because the Legends can get around "legal" by controlling the mind of the person guarding passage. Some of them may have become Legend people farms by now."

"That's one," I said.

"Two: Legend I vampires who have clean food supplies and aren't pursuing Legend II. Who are tucked away where no one will look for them, and who can still make new vampires when this is done."

"All Legend I vampires are vulnerable to AntiLegend."

Wire was looking at Herog and nodding, though. "Remember that human populations only have an eighty-to-ninety-percent susceptibility to airborne AntiLegend, though, Cady. You didn't want to kill innocents in spreading the antivirus—and you were right in that. But here is where *my* point rears its ugly head. Innocents are still out there who can both serve as clean, safe food to Legends, and who can be converted into Legends themselves. And ten to twenty percent, spread across billions, is a lot of clean, available food for those vampires who figure out how to find it, lure it in, and weed it out from the lethal kind."

We'd had parts of that discussion before. I'd won my argument. But my argument meant cleanup was difficult rather than simple.

Bluejay said, "We may be able to track down solo Legends later, but they're not our problem now. Large numbers is the emergency we're fighting. And we can still work to decrease the number of existing Legend I vampires. We buy one of those other TFN ships—the sidewinders with coil dispersers Wire was so excited about."

"Dispersal coils," Wire corrected. "There's no such thing as a coil disperser."

Bluejay gave him a look. "*Dispersal coils,*" she snarled. "*THEN* we change our appearance—we make ourselves over into people who look human and who can go anywhere, and we start dropping in on no-tech worlds unannounced and spraying the populations with AntiLegend." She shrugged. "I'm not saying it won't be dangerous, but it's certainly simple enough. While we're waiting for the supply of Legend II to reach quantities necessary to target all Legend I vampires, it will give us something to do that will protect people who currently have no idea what's killing them."

"Perfect," I said. "We'll do that."

Chapter 22

"There are five classes of Colson StarStream for you to choose from," Wire said.

We were back in settled space, but far on the periphery, hanging out of sight of the station that serviced the wormhole. I'd made sure the station got an identification code completely unrelated to the *Immortal Velvet* when the Spybee tagged us coming through. It wasn't a good code, though—it didn't come from one of Storm Rat's deep covers. We were going to have to move again soon.

But we'd needed to be in traveled space to have access to current information via the datastream. We just needed to be out of sight when we caught up on recent events.

Tarko spent time figuring a money angle for buying a ship. Herog and Bluejay manned weaponry and shields, just in case we had to bolt again.

I'd used Bluejay's newest map update to plot a course between low-tech worlds that, if we beat back Darkout, would become likely sources of survival pockets for Legends.

And Wire had spent two hours crawling over every

sales brochure and tech-spec document he could worm out of the datastream. Now he sat across from me on the bridge, with what he'd found spread all over the infoscreens. "The coil-sidewinders are available in the basic two-back, the five-back, the ten-back, the twenty-back, and the fifty-back. The two-back berths two crew plus two passengers. It has in-hyperspace on-the-fly course recalc, but cannot find unknown origami points. It also has no space for a battle deck, very limited storage, and a maximum time-from-dock of one month."

"Won't work," I said. "There've been times when I've needed to be off the grid for more than a month. And it's too small, even if we slept tight. We need a place for hidden weapons. Finally, we need to be able to find unknown origami points and plot them into our map for re-use." We had the coordinates to two such points set into autonav, in case we had to run. We were alive because we'd been able to go where no one had gone before. For us, this feature was not a luxury.

He nodded. "The five-back berths two crew in separate quarters or four doubled up, and five passenger rooms in a configuration of double-double-single-single-single."

"That could work."

"No extrapolation of unknown origami points."

"Save us time," I said. "Which is the smallest ship they offer that will actually work for us?"

"How many of the extra weapons do you want?"

"All of them."

"Colson doesn't do holds and crawl spaces and dupli-cate-function rooms the way Monceros did. I'm pretty sure the Monoceros ships were purpose-built with smuggling in mind. If you want to keep all the weapons and stock levels from this monstrosity, and have everything hidden, you're looking at a squeeze into the twenty-back, or way too much ship with the fifty-back, which *requires* a minimum crew of four."

"So we go with the twenty-back," I said with a shrug. "And we squeeze."

"That's fine. But realize that the twenty-back goes for one-point-seven billion rucets from a dealer, and there's a waiting list."

"Did they make the freaking thing out of gold!" I yelped. "Even Tarko would have a hard time pulling together that amount of money in the time we have."

Wire nodded. "Colson did use some gold moleibond, actually. And a lot of rare woods and natural gemstones and a bunch of other fancy nonsense. There's no such thing as a base twenty. It's designed exclusively as a luxury ship."

I sighed. "What's the configuration of the ten-back?"

He flicked a finger and one of the schematics slid to center-screen and enlarged.

"Compared to this, it's small," I muttered, looking at the lumpy wireframes and peelback walkthrough. "Plain. The scoop hull is fat, and the shuttle placement makes it look like a hunchback. Meanwhile, the designers manage to make the TFN bulge look like the ship has a bad overbite."

"On the bright side, a dumpy, much smaller ten-back will blend much better at the dock than this thing."

"*This thing*," I snarled, "looks like sex in space. It's big and sleek and gorgeous and fast..."

"And it costs a fortune to keep running, and it's identified now with Legends everywhere. When this is over—"

"—*if* this is over—"

"—Peter Crane's attack on you is going to be part of your legal defense in getting criminal charges against you on Cantata dropped. As is your mother's attempt to kill you.

And when it comes out that Monoceros was directly linked to Legends, and that the near-death of humanity in settled space was made possible primarily because of these ships— one of which Velvet of Legend II fame owned—owning one is going to be an unhappy thing."

"The Peter Crane defense is designed to get me legal ownership of the *Corrigan's Blood,* and to allow me to resume my real identity."

"You want to be really identified with this ship? There will only ever be twenty-seven of them, and by process of elimination, someone curious and patient will be able to figure out where this one has been. It has a history. Better you claim it was stolen from you by vampires. Then maybe you can at least get replacement damages out of the deal."

He was right. I needed to dump the *Immortal Velvet/Corrigan's Blood.* I needed to shed it, and move to something that was mine because I bought it. Chose it. Not because it was the ship I got because the previous owner had tried to kill me.

I hated the idea of dumping something roomy and fully appointed for something that was less than half the size, and ugly.

But less than half the size and ugly was still three times bigger than the *Hope's Reward* had been, and Badger and I had managed to make a nice living and attract good clients with that ship.

"All right." I sighed. "I want the gravity shear. I want as much capacity for sticky-pies as you can give me. I want the big external Anabond cutter. And a retrofit to give me smuggling spaces. And a core war room. You can fit it in a closet if you have to, but I want voice and manual controls. Duplicate ship-wide system controls, absolute override on anything, and keyed to live biometrics for me only. Any of the rest of the secret stuff you can wedge in, I will gratefully take. Any public or extra quarters space you have to eliminate, I'll accept. *If* we survive this, the ship only has to carry me, any rescues I end up with, and any cargo I recover. But I have to survive the process of getting cargo—in whatever form it may take—back to my clients."

"I can do that."

TARKO and I met up in the solar. The view of the origami point was worth tracking only to make sure we didn't have something coming through at us, but otherwise was the definition of "why bother looking?" An origami point is the opposite of a black hole, which is so dense that light cannot escape its pull. An origami point is a place in space so thin, so nonexistent, that light has nothing to travel through. When a ship bends that fracture, that line of weakness, and pushes through it, the nothingness expands into a rippling sphere of light, ejecting a ship into the system. Origami points are fun to watch in busy systems. Out here, at a point I'd chosen for its lack of traffic...well, like I said. Why bother?

"Not much has come through since we got here," Tarko said, noting the direction of my gaze. "Counted two, but I haven't been watching the whole time."

"Ship's monitoring. If we have a problem, the alarm will go off. How are we looking, funds-wise?"

"Decent. How much are you planning to spend?"

"Well, not one-point-seven billion rucets."

He raised an eyebrow. "Had you *considered* spending that much?"

"Briefly."

293

"Don't."

"Why not?"

He made a frustrated face. "Purchases over five hundred million rucets, or local equivalents, are tagged and flagged for mandatory investigation by every agency linked into the interplanetary coalition database for the sharing of crime data and criminal profiles. You spend that much and every hostile pair of eyes in settled space will be digging into your background. Your finances. Your travels. For five Standard years, every rucet you spend will show up everyplace where anyone cares about catching criminals, along with your name, and a reminder that you—with your odd non-corporate job—once dropped a bundle of cash into a system without any history explaining how you got that cash."

"Good reason." That sort of probing would do nothing to help my previous well-earned reputation for discretion. I told him, "The ship I want is a Colson StarStream Ten-Back, no frills, no upgrade packages. Ugly and stripped, they run a hundred sixty million rucets, and there are two distributors who have them in stock."

Tarko nodded. "I'll act as buyer. I have a deep ID I use for expensive things—and if you're not going to make me spend one-point-seven billion rucets, I'll be happy to use that ID and get your ship for you. When we get through this—"

I noticed he didn't say *if*. Bluejay never said *if*. Wire never said *if*. Herog did. I did. But the other three?

I didn't understand their determination to only see the best outcome. They'd all been slaves. They'd all seen at least some of the worst things human beings could do to each other. They knew, as I knew, that the universe was not a safe and friendly place.

Yet they would not admit to *if*.

I found their response unnerving. It was as though, faced with the almost certain end of everything, they thought if they never admitted the worst could happen, it wouldn't.

The worst thing can always happen. If you don't acknowledge it, and fight it with everything you have in you, it will.

I said, "We need the ship right away."

He nodded. "We can't go in this ship to get it."

I started to ask why, then stopped myself before the stupid fell out of my mouth.

He grinned. "Right. We need to leave this someplace where it won't be found, and we need to purchase tickets on a passenger ship, and we need to get from here to the place where we can purchase tickets— You're shaking your head. Why are you shaking your head."

"We don't need to buy tickets. Or use any sort of commercial transportation. We just need to hide the *Immortal Velvet*, change our appearances, and use the *Delegate One*," I said. "It's just sitting there. Stocked with Anti-Legend, on a mission to save humanity, and a ship like that with a crew of humanitarian zealots on a mission to save the universe would be happy to take a guy like you on as a passenger, and drop you off where you can get your own ship before we go our own way, doing good."

Wire said, "It's not a sidewinder. It's a standard TFN."

"For one trip," I said, "we can get by with standard TFN."

Meanwhile, Tarko stared into my eyes, silent for a long time, an expression of puzzlement on his face. "Someday, I'd really like to get a good look inside that mind of yours."

"You wouldn't. Trust me. It's a dark and frightening place in here. But long practice at surviving through fear does give me an edge in finding the next hole to escape through."

"Good hole," he said.

I TOLD THE GATHERED CREW, "We're going to do a quick jump through to the *Delegate One*. We're going to take that as far as the Raythonade origami point. We're going to drop Tarko and Herog off at the Raythonade station, where Tarko will buy a stripped StarStream Ten-Back for upgrade and resale.

"Meanwhile, we make our token request to the Raythonade worlds to visit them to distribute AntiLegend. They'll turn us down, we'll be on record—for once not forged—as having made the attempt, and we'll go through an origami point without Spybees I previously located in the *Corr*—in the *Immortal Velvet*, and that will get us back to our hiding place. The new ship will already be there to meet us.

"We'll do a fast and dirty transfer of weapons and possessions to the new ship, and then we'll take the *Immortal Velvet* to a new hiding place, and keep it tucked away."

Bluejay said, "And then what?"

"Then we stop looking like vampires, and start looking like lunch, and we go to every horrible backworld nightmare we can find and start spraying AntiLegend-laced fake blood like there's no tomorrow. If we do it right, maybe there will be one."

It was a simple plan.

You want to watch out for those.

WE TOOK *Immortal Velvet* through three recalculations inside hyperspace, and by the end of it, I almost didn't come back.

In that third recalculation, I encountered Badger alone, with *me*, for the second time.

Our hands intertwined, our eyes gazed into each other's, and we were so close, we could have shared the same breath—but we could not hear, did not feel. We only saw.

If I held onto him right there, the small voice told me *—kept close to him right then, stayed with him, I could have him. Keep him. We would be together.* Where? *Somewhere.* How? *Somehow.*

In that moment that was not time, in that space that was not place, who I was and why I mattered and what I had yet to do fell away from me, all flesh and all reason discarded, and I readied myself to let go. We joined hands, our fingers interlocked, and I could not feel them, but I could see them intertwined with mine.

His face brightened and he held out his arms to welcome me, and he mouthed the word, *Come.*

In my head, another voice.

This is your life fighting your death, and you're doing everything you can to hold on to what's killing you.

This is your life. Fighting your death.

Your life. Your death.

Is. The reflection. Real?

No, I said, and backed away from Badger. Rejected his joyful smile. His yearning eyes. His promise that he still loved me—from beyond death, in the realm of shadows.

No, I said.

No, I shouted.

No! I screamed, and shook off my dance with destruction, and was the first to pull back my hand.

The magic of that connection, that tenuous link, shattered and he was whipped away from me like a dustmote in a gale.

Gone.

And gone.

And...gone.

I was on the bridge, and Herog was watching me.

"You're here?"

He said, "It was a difficult crossing."

"Give me your knife," I said. He always had one with him.

He unsheathed it, held it by the blade, passed it to me.

I had become both familiar with that knife, and good at pain overall. I jabbed the point into the muscle of my left arm, and blood spurted. I caught it in a puddle in my right hand, and even as the wound healed over, I smeared the blood from the bridge of my nose across my cheeks in long, defiant stripes.

Then I handed the blade back to Herog.

"I found my own warpaint: life itself, lived each moment, with the freedom and the right to preserve and defend myself and the people I love and care about in the moments I have them.

"It isn't life deferred until some better time or some better place. The cost of life deferred is Badger, whose love I never fully embraced because the time to enjoy it was not ideal. Life deferred is life unlived, life lost.

"In this moment, in whatever form it comes, lies the only opportunity I will ever have to act, to think, to love.

Only this moment, out of every moment I have ever lived, or will ever live, allows me to matter *now*.

"My warpaint is the love I have for my life, and I will fight to live so that I can make each minute I have matter *now*."

Herog watched me, and I saw a tear slip down his nose to vanish into his pointed beard.

"Yes," he said. "Yes. *That's* warpaint."

Tarko joined us on the bridge. Herog rose, saying, "We'll talk later." He left.

Tarko sat in the seat Herog had vacated. "Everything all right?"

I considered for a moment. What I had stepped away from, what I had stepped toward. I'd been through hellish point crossings, and at the end of it, I felt...good. "Yes," I said, and could heard the surprise in my own voice."

He gave me an odd look, and I realized I had my own blood smeared all over my face. "All right," he said. "I'm glad to hear it. Bluejay and Wire have everything set up in the solar for your final two datastream feeds. Come up as soon as you can, and we'll get this done."

"Now sounds good," I said.

I put the ship on auto, and kept it headed toward the *Delegate One*. I took the forward gravdrop up to the solar to create the last two acts of what I was coming to see as The Final Temptation of Hell.

Chapter 23

We did our last two presentations as the Legend II vampires. In one, I said that since Legends everywhere now saw what we were offering— and how it would open the universe to those few who got it —and since they knew what to expect, we were going to go home and make our batches of Legend II, and the *next* time they heard from us, it would be to announce that Legend II was ready, and they needed to be ready to order instantly, with their biometric scanner and purchase ID in hand, because quantities were *extremely* limited, and when we ran out, there would be no more.

I was uncomfortable saying the lines Tarko wrote out for me.

"You're right to be," he said. "In the systems where marketing is regulated, this is illegal marketing—and the fact that you don't like what you're doing is a good thing. You're presenting something as being of rare or limited quantity, when in fact everyone whose application reaches us will get one. There are trade commissions from one end of settled space to the other that could choose to investigate this promotion and could fine you every rucet you made, and triple or quadruple that amount in damages, and could lock you away forever based on the number of people you're conning."

"I think I'd throw up now, if I didn't have to eat first to do it."

"But," he said, holding up a hand, "one, you aren't *you*. Two, the you right now is going to disappear forever once this is over. Three, when humans discover what Legend II actually did, they're going to be unlikely to investigate the people who got it into the hands of the toughest vampires anywhere." He looked me in the eye and said, "Right?"

"Right," I said, and got over my queasiness.

In the second presentation—for which we all did complete wardrobe changes—all of us held up dummy injectors identical to the injectors we would be sending out. I said Legend II was ready, and the ordering process was starting immediately. I explained the two simple steps to order—which Tarko had worked out so carefully—and informed the future viewers that the purchase connection would open when my presentation ended.

"It's simple. If you're ready to be a Legend Master," I said, smiling, "use your biometric scanner to blood-sign the document agreeing that in exchange for Legend II and total domination over all humans and immunity to AntiLegend, you will hunt down and kill all Legend I vampires. Then say *Send Payment*. Your account will *only* be charged if you are one of the few whose applications are accepted. If you are, you'll receive delivery within hours. Be at the address you give us. Be ready to join me as a Master."

Once we finished recording, I fed the first of the two recordings into the datastream. Wire hauled all the equipment over to the *Delegate One*. We'd be coming back to the

Monoceros ship one last time, to strip it for salvage we could use on my new Ten-Back.

But I was done with the *Corrigan's Blood*. If we stopped Darkout, Storm Rat could send out salvage crews to "find" it and claim it, refit it, and keep it or sell it.

I would never step aboard it again.

Uncoupling the utterly ordinary *Delegate One* from the elegant, capable, beautiful *Blood*, still blazoned *Immortal Velvet*, I felt a sudden wave of relief. It was like being rid of a bad partner—in any sense of that word.

"HAIL, *DELEGATE ONE*," Raythonade Station called exactly two minutes after the ship had cleared the origami point.

"Hail, Raythonade Station," I returned. I was drinking vampire coffee. The *Delegate One's* personality, in an unnervingly familiar tone, had pulled me out of the short-but-painful crossing with a worried, "Sweetheart, drink this, it'll make you feel better, and you look so depressed. Would you like some chocolate? A cookie?"

God, I would have killed for a cookie. And the ability to enjoy it.

"Just the coffee," I'd muttered, and the ship had come back with, "If you're *sure*, dear," and I was deciding to tell Tarko *any personality but THAT one* when Raythonade hailed.

The ship shut up.

"I've checked, and you're the real *Delegate One*," the stationmaster said. "Do you have AntiLegend with you?"

"Of course," I told him. "No one has yet given us permission to distribute it."

"We will. When you dock, please come aboard—armed if you can—and spray the station."

I had to think about that for a moment. "There are legal ramifications—"

"I announced your arrival," he told me, "the instant I was sure you were the real *Delegate One*."

"Have there been fakes?"

"No. But you've been hard to find. We had a bad vampire problem here," he said. "We had no idea how bad, and as far as we can tell, most of them have now killed each other off, but no ships have arrived or left the station since the mess. So we need help. We have to make sure there are no surviving Legends. And the folks on the planets need help, too. No one is going to tell you folks you can't dock, or send down shuttles, or anything. You're heroes."

Everyone had returned to human physical forms—just not their own. Tarko was going in as the ship buyer, and already had his cover with deep ID in place. Herog too had a deep ID that would let him pilot Tarko's purchase.

Wire, Bluejay and I had the covers of ship's crew and captain of the *Delegate One*, and our covers weren't deep—but we weren't planning on getting deeply personal with anyone. We had names, and they'd check against real names on a minor dirt world that kept lousy records, if anyone wanted to look. To find out we were fakes would take a trip to the dirt world, and going through their lousy records, and comparing them against dead people from that world.

Someone could. Wasn't much reason why they *would*.

So Wire and Bluejay looked like their human selves. I had kept my comfortable size and shape, but had edited out my mother's genetic tampering with those three biological fathers. The blue-eyed, natural blonde black girl look is far too memorable.

So I was tall, shapely, dark-skinned, black-eyed, and with tightly curled black hair I'd cropped close to my skull. I liked the look. It wasn't me, but if my mother hadn't been a psychopath, it probably would have been me.

The three of us were wearing matching shipsuits—green with black arm patches on them that said *Delegate One.*

Each of us took a dispenser of AntiLegend with us. If we were what we appeared to be, I would have been terrified. Think of it…three unarmed humans on a purportedly unarmed ship—nothing that came from Storm Rat came without weapons, but the *Delegate One's* weapons were well-hidden—were walking into a place that had living vampires somewhere on it, and we were carrying in our hands the plague that would eradicate their kind from settled space if we could just manage to spread it around.

I expected we would be attacked by our enemies the instant we got off the ship.

So Wire, Bluejay, and I moved timidly out of the airlock, eyes darting everywhere looking for danger. To pass yourself off as human, you have to remember to act the part.

Bluejay spotted a man in a brown-and-gold shipsuit with shoulder chevrons crouched in a corner, weapons in hand, and at first I thought he intended to kill us. "Spray," he shouted. "Hurry!"

So apparently not.

I broke the top off the dispenser, and dropped it on the ground. The mist curled around us, and toward him. He got to his feet and raced to us, face pale and sweating. "Everyone in charge is dead," he said. "Far as I can tell, I'm the senior executive on the station. I've assumed temporary command until relieved by an officer of the company. I just want to make sure the officer is human. The others weren't."

Raytheon Station is corporate, which means the corporations are the government. Which means justice has a profit margin. You have to mind your manners and watch your back on corporate stations, and it's not a bad idea, I've discovered, to avoid signing back-loaded contracts on them.

"Do you have someplace safe that we can talk?"

He looked at me and laughed bitterly. "We're standing in the middle of it. Your mist cloud here is better than armor. But we need to spread it through the station." He eyed the three of us and our three dispensers. "We could do it faster if we split up."

Only morons split up.

"No!" all three of us said at the same time.

He looked a little startled, then nodded. "Don't blame you. Grab that thing," he nodded to the unit on the floor," and we'll do a run around the central hub. Once we've run the hub, we'll do ring three. Then ring five."

And the he paused. Sneezed. Looked at us.

"I have it?"

"Have what?"

"Angel Fever?"

I stared at him. Dammit, I almost laughed. "*Angel Fever?* Someone is actually calling it that?"

"It's what *everyone* calls it. You start sneezing. Sometimes you run a temperature. And then—you live, and they die. It's the magic disease that saves you."

All right. I could see the logic there. No magic involved —just a helluva lot of hard work. But the people on the receiving end never see the hard work. To them, it's all magic. "You have Angel Fever," I said.

I saw tears well in his eyes. Saw him blink them back. Swallow hard. "God, I wish you'd gotten here sooner." He sneezed again, and the expression on his face turned from tragic to fierce. "Come on. Double-time. We're saving everyone we can."

When he said run, he'd meant run. He was moving flat-out—and Raythonade Station is big. It's one of the hub-and-ring types—everything in circles, designed back before humans got good at creating real gravity, centrifugal force was the easiest way to fake gravity. The station had been moleibonded and modified with real gravity—but it maintained its archaic, annoying structure. We could have easily outrun him, but of course we didn't. We kept up, we huffed and puffed a bit, and we sprayed.

"AntiLegend coming through," he shouted as he ran. "AntiLegend coming through. Come out and breathe deep!"

Behind us, we heard some doors humming open. Some footsteps. Some doors humming closed.

We did not look back.

At the end of the run, we leaned against the walls, breathing hard. Well, he was breathing hard, and we were faking breathing hard, but the end result looked the same.

"What's the fastest way to distribute this planet-wide?" he asked us.

We looked at each other and shrugged. "You're the first place anywhere that has even given us permission to dock at the station. We've been stuck in our ship since we set out. We've never been able to get clearance for a planetary visit, so we've never had a chance to get this out there."

"But AntiLegend is already spreading."

I thought fast. "A few people found their way to us privately after we'd sent out our hail. After we'd been rejected. They wanted AntiLegend, so they docked with our ship, and when they came aboard, we sprayed them, then gave them dispensers to take with them. From there, people who were carriers traveled, and it spread that way. But it's slow."

"I thought it spread quickly."

"It spreads quickly when a carrier first catches it, especially if there are a lot of people around. The sneezes spread the droplets, and a whole crowd can become immunized in a few minutes. But once the carriers stop sneezing, AntiLegend stops spreading."

He was studying us. "So there's just the three of you, and your one ship, and all of settled space to immunize. Angel Fever needs fresh carriers to spread it where you can't go."

The three of us looked at each other. "Well...yes..."

"I don't know if you realize it," he said, "but Raytheon Station is the home office of FastIt."

"FastIt? Here?"

"Personal Next-Day Delivery To Your Door, Anywhere In Settled Space," he grinned, reciting the company's slogan.

I was fascinated. You see their ships everywhere. And their route guys. Brown and gold... I stared at the station-master with his brown-and-gold suit, and his two chevrons. It wasn't the suit they wear for deliveries, but there were similarities.

"You're a FastIt Guy." It explained his ability to run.

"Well, I was a sergeant in Raythonade Planetary Protective Forces. Opted out after my second enlistment and joined FastIt. I moved from a planetary route up to the home office a couple months ago. I'm in charge of routing." He frowned. "Actually, the top guys, and there were only three of them, killed each other. There were some second-tier officers, but I haven't seen any of them since the bloodbath, so they might have been bloodsuckers, too. But I'm thinking if we advertise that every one of our carriers has had Angel Fever, and every package we deliver now comes with a spray of AntiLegend for the recipient, we'll get human-only business, we'll be able to spread Angel Fever…"

"You'll have consent," I said.

"Yes. On an individual basis. Nobody has died from it that I know of—so our carriers should be able to distribute a spritz of AntiLegend at each stop."

"The antivirus was designed to be one hundred percent nonlethal. Well, to humans, anyway. It's only about eighty to ninety percent communicable, though."

"Some people can't catch it? I didn't know that."

"That was the design trade-off. It was either approximately fifteen percent of the population—averaged—were resistant to the viral package, or a small but nonzero percentage of people infected would die."

He nodded. "As long as our delivery guys can spray people knowing none of our customers are going to fall over dead, we can do this."

"You can?" I was floored. Having volunteers was something else none of us had anticipated.

You do a thing, and if it's something that matters, it gathers momentum, and the momentum changes it in ways you cannot imagine. Cannot foresee. It goes off in new directions, and suddenly they aren't your directions anymore.

Peter Crane and Haskell Corrigan discovered that when they created their version of immortality.

I was discovering it while putting an end to the gathered momentum of their mess.

"We're going to need a lot of AntiLegend," he said.

"We *have* a lot of AntiLegend," I said.

"Before the vampire wars against each other, we had over fourteen million route runners."

"We don't *have that* much AntiLegend," I said. And then I took a deep breath and added, "But the odds are pretty good you don't have that many route runners anymore, either. Package delivery would be an ideal job for someone looking for...um...easy, free lunch."

"Oh, hell." He closed his eyes and sighed. "Come back to the office with me, and we'll work out the logistics of delivery. I'll see if I can find out how many employees the company still has. And you can tell me how you three got involved in this. Vampires. AntiLegend. Monsters and insanity."

This *would* get awkward. But our would-be ally, whose name I realized I still did not know, would be able to spread AntiLegend fast enough and efficiently enough to immunize whole populations in just a couple days. It still left us with the pockets of immunity—the worlds that did not permit FastIt delivery, which were the same worlds we'd planned on visiting anyway.

But the tide was shifting in our favor. *Humanity* was shifting in our favor. It was a good feeling.

"Before we do go back to the office, though," I told him, "we need to get clearance for two passengers to debark here. They need to get to Colson Shipyards to buy a ship."

Chapter 24

Uejay, Wire, and I sat down at one end of a long table where two other FastIt employees were already waiting.

Our host said, "I just realized I haven't even introduced myself yet. I'm Will Amblin." Will sneezed again.

"Grace Falza," I said.

"Laola Hawntar," Bluejay said.

"Max Boling," Wire said.

Will nodded. "So very glad you're here. I'm...well, acting CEO of FastIt, until somebody human from one of the outlying offices shows up to relieve me. Next to me is Beza Wohl, who was in Accounting, and beside her is Dreyton Stathington, who was personal secretary to the OEO, now dead and we'll all give that a cheer and a beer. I'm in charge because I have a lot of experience in organizing and running large operations."

"From the military?" Bluejay asked.

"I was the supply coordinator for land units during wartime operations. I made sure things got where they needed to be, intact and on time, against superior firepower and with outnumbered forces. We won, and I had a part in that."

"All right, then." She nodded, looking pleased.

"Beza has all the financial access codes, and has been moving money and changing codes so that if there are any vampires still in the organizational chain of command, they won't be able to reach funds without our approval. And our approval is going to come at a price."

Wire said "The price being, *Prove you're not a vampire?*"

Will smiled. It was not a friendly smile.

I looked at the three of them. "How many people used to know how the top level of FastIt worked?"

"Twenty-seven," Dreyton said. Then shook his head. "I think. I can't be sure if there were more, but I wasn't supposed to know about them."

I raised an eyebrow.

Will said, "Dreyton is still recovering from having his mind played with. His bosses were controlling him somehow, and apparently made him forget.

I nodded. "Mind control."

All three FastIt survivors looked at me.

"I saw it in action up close. I'm still missing a few pieces of my past."

"Relates to how you got involved in what you're doing?" Will asked.

"Yes." I didn't elaborate, and he didn't pursue.

"Dreyton doesn't remember what his bosses did to him, but he has good memory of operations. Maybe not perfect. But good enough."

Beza said, "We're all three getting each other up to speed on what we know so that we have some redundancy built in. The passwords, routing numbers, and the code to access those are critical. But until everything settles and we're sure we don't have any more bloodsuckers in the chain of command, it's just the three of us."

"Shaky," I said.

"As long as the three of us can ride this out, there will still be a FastIt." Will sighed. "If our command structure is any indication, there are companies that are dead today because no one is left alive who knows how to access anything critical."

Dreyton nodded. "There's going to be chaos for a good long time after this. We're looking at probably the worst financial crisis in history."

Well, there was an ugly thought. Nanovampires had the charisma and power to force their way to the top of any business they desired. They didn't have to be capable...and in the places where they weren't capable, I hoped they'd kept human beings running the works while they raked off the profits.

But business was as appealing to people who hungered for power as it was for those who simply wanted to live a nice life and were willing to work hard to have it. And vampires were all about power.

There'd be some businesses out there that were still human-owned, and still intact.

They would be smaller, less profitable. Maybe family owned, or lacking the corporate structure that conferred power to whole boards of outsiders. Maybe they'd be outside Legends' interests because they were dirty work, or lacked prestige, or in some other way were considered to be appealing.

So some critical services both planetside and civiliza-tion-wide—which tended to be dirty, to lack prestige, and to be unappealing—would probably keep running.

But the good stuff of civilization was going to hit the dirt, and was going to be a long time standing back up.

I wondered how well Tarko had covered us in making sure our delivery of Legend II went off without a hitch. Had he planned on using FastIt to get the packages out?

Hell.

This was another direction none of us back on Tegosshu had foreseen.

Dreyton said, "I wish I could remember more. I'm pretty solid on how things run, but I'm certain I had access to much more than I remember."

I sympathized with Dreyton. I had some holes in my memory put there by vampires. The memories didn't come back with time. I suspected that might be a mercy.

Beza sneezed.

Will sneezed.

Dreyton looked at Will, and then at Beza, and chuckled. "Keep your germs to yourselves, would you?"

Will grinned at him. "I didn't want to tell either of you the great news until the three of us were here in private. But Grace and Laola and Max are the captain and crew of the *Delegate One*.

Neither Dreyton nor Beza looked like they had the slightest clue what he was talking about.

He said, "I caught news of this spaceship that was traveling from world to world, offering to inoculate human populations with AntiLegend."

Beza looked puzzled. The expression on Dreyton's face got a bit more focused.

"*Angel Fever*," Will said, looking like the kid with the biggest present.

That, they both got.

"Breathe deep. They sprayed the whole station before

we got here. By now, everyone has been exposed."

Beza looked at us, tears in her eyes. "Thank you," she said. "Thank you so much." She sneezed again.

Dreyton stood and walked behind Beza to stand between their chairs. He breathed deep. "I'm not sneezing," he said.

"You might not catch it. Twenty percent of the population, more or less, is going to be immune to the viral agent carrying the nanoviral payload," I told him. "So AntiLegend will never make it into their systems. You could be one of the fifteen or so people in any crowd of a hundred that won't catch it. But look at it this way—if eight out of every ten people around you will cause a vampire to explode if he drinks a single sip of their blood, and vampires have no way of telling which humans will kill them, and which won't, you'll be as safe from attack as any of them.

"Good. Good. But any vampires who survived the fighting—they'll inhale this AntiLegend and...explode? We can stop worrying about vampires on the station?" I caught the quaver in his voice when he said that, even though he'd tried hard to hide it. And I wished I could offer him the comfort he so clearly wanted.

I couldn't, though. "I wish it were that easy. The nanovampires have immune systems that have been designed to filter out and dispose of anything inhaled. The *only* way to get the toxin into their bloodstreams is in blood. They can drink it, get it via contact with mucous membranes, or it can be injected. Nothing airborne can touch them."

"Thank you," he said, and too fast for even my eyes to follow, grabbed both Will and Beza by the tops of their heads and twisted each in one full circle. The snapping of bones was ugly, and the vicious brutality of his attack, along with the surge of his power, shocked me. I froze for an instant. "That's tremendously comforting to know. Now that my food supply is contaminated, I'll have to go somewhere else. Pity the three of you are contaminated, too, or I'd take you with me. But your ship will make a spectacular vehicle for me. Certain to be welcome most where I'll find the best dining."

I unfroze, and told him, "*Don't move.*"

He locked into place. He didn't blink, he didn't twitch his eyes from side to side.

I stood. Bluejay stood. Wire stood.

"You are going to crouch beside Will, and bite him, and drink his blood from the wound in his throat," I told him. "And then you are going to do the same thing to Beza. Drink deep and die."

Beside me, Bluejay said, "*Stop. Don't drink.*"

Dreyton Stathington, nanovampire, caught between my command and Bluejay's, twitched toward and then away from the two people he'd just murdered.

I turned to Bluejay. "What do you think you're doing?"

"We can use him," Bluejay said. "He's the only one left who knows how to run FastIt. He can still distribute Anti-Legend for us, using Will's plan."

"He won't."

"For a guarantee to receive Legend II on delivery day, he will."

"And in the meantime? This station has been sprayed."

"In the meantime, we put him on daily maintenance. Two units of clean, AntiLegend-free blood, delivered to his office."

I looked at Bluejay with admiration. Another Kartach Norgan high-scorer came through in a big way.

"*Stand up,*" I told him. "*Face us.*"

Warpaint

He stood. He faced.

The expression on his face was beautiful—sheer horrified disbelief, hope, bewilderment.

"We're going to spare your life," I said. "If you do exactly as we command, you'll become a Legend II vampire. Do you understand?"

"Yes... No... I don't know," he said.

I relaxed my hold on him. I was annoyed. "What don't you know?"

"Who you are? How you did that?"

I sighed. Changed my face back to Velvet's face. Layers of brown skin peeled away, growing progressively lighter. "Recognize me now?" I asked.

He nodded.

I changed my face back to the Grace Falza face.

"You're behind *AntiLegend* as well as Legend II?"

I said, "We don't like Legend I vampires. They breed like rats, they have no sense of style, and they're everywhere. The Legend II vampires will hunt down and kill those that are close—but we want to make sure no little pockets of the pestilence remain."

I played on Bluejay's plan. "You're going to run FastIt. You're going to make sure every employee you have is inoculated with AntiLegend. You're going to pretend to be the best little human CEO this company ever had—no mind games with your employees, no human meals anywhere ever, no actions that could in any way reveal what you really are—and your carriers are going to spray every package recipient with AntiLegend when they deliver the package. Meanwhile, you're going to train new people into all the jobs necessary to keep FastIt going. And your new executives will all be human, because you are going to be the *only* vampire in FastIt. In exchange for that, you'll get two units of clean blood direct from us every day until you receive your Legend II."

"But I'll become a Legend II vampire?"

"Guaranteed," I told him. "Furthermore, your delivery of AntiLegend with all packages will fulfill your contractual obligation to hunt down Legend I vampires."

He stood there, staring at the three of us. "I can't believe you're here. I thought you were going back to make the Legend II."

"It's already done," I told him. "There aren't that many doses going out. We're tying up loose ends right now, privately. And we're monitoring the datastream. No one in the universe but you knows who we are or where we are, so if you decide to leak our little secret..."

"No," he said. "I want Legend II."

I believed him.

I looked over at Will, murdered, mangled—and in the seat beside him, Beza. Both dead, both now being treated as refuse. Rage filled me, and I wanted again to destroy Dreyton, right there, right then, where I could see him die. Will had been a good man, and I hated even the pretense of siding with the monster who'd murdered him.

"Take care of them," I told him. "As a human would. Funerals, benefits for their families, grief from you. They'll be the *last* murders by a vampire on this station. Is that clear?"

"My cover has to be perfect," he said.

"If you want clean blood every day and Legend II at the end, it does."

"You can count on me."

"We'll also get it in writing," I said. "Now. With your biometric signature."

He nodded.

That contract he signed privately. He signed for the deliveries of AntiLegend, too, and signed to distribute Anti-Legend without charge to all recipients of FastIt deliveries —those contracts he signed publicly, with citizens from the station, datastream reporters and curators, him, and us, all smiling as he announced what FastIt was going to do.

We'd established him as a hero, and that left me sick to my stomach. What was left of it in my current form, anyway.

We'd shown our faces in public.

We'd made a lot of noise, when what we'd hoped to do was to stay invisible.

It was messy, and if the fact that he'd signed his contract for Legend II on the same day ever came to light, people were going to notice.

But everything about our visit to Raythonade had been messy. We had created a link between us as the deliverers of AntiLegend and as the deliverers of Legend II that could come back to haunt us. Thanks to Bluejay, we hadn't ended up causing the total destruction of FastIt, and we now had one way to get AntiLegend out to most of the worlds and stations in settled space.

But we now had links to us that might somehow link back to Storm Rat, and Tegosshu, if Tarko had not been perfect in setting up the financing for the manufacture of both AntiLegend and Legend II.

And Dreyton Stathington was going to go down in history as a hero.

I intended to make sure he got his personal delivery of Legend II first. And maybe I'd figure out a way to have those same datastream reporters there to catch him as or right after he took it.

We were halfway back to the ship when I realized we

had no way to contact Tarko and Herog, and no way to know if Colson was still operating in the wake of the Legend war.

Without the StarStream Ten-Back, we couldn't do clean-up on the locked-down worlds. If they couldn't get the ship, Herog would contact us. But we were going to have to stay in dock until we got news.

And now we had the attention of the datastream reporters, which meant we needed to disappear as quickly as we could.

Back aboard the *Delegate One*, I gave Wire the message to encode to Storm Rat: Initial delivery of two hundred thousand AntiLegend dispensers to Raythonade Station and five other FastIt hubs, followed by one-hundred thousand units to each hub weekly, until further notice, plus delivery of two units of clean blood daily in special packages to a specific drop in Raythonade station.

And then we sat tight and waited to hear from Tarko and Herog.

You do a thing, and if it's something that matters, it gathers momentum, and the momentum changes it in ways you cannot imagine. Cannot foresee. It goes off in new directions, and suddenly they aren't your directions anymore.

Tarko had said his financing system would flex with any expenditures we made. This was going to be a monstrous expenditure.

But *if* his financing held, and *if* FastIt didn't fall apart before Dreyton could put it back together, and *if* there were enough carriers left to offer AntiLegend to every recipient, and *if* people agreed to be sprayed, we had in the press of a thumb against a biometric scanner used our enemy to help us achieve our goals, and that single agreement might have just won our war.

320

Chapter 25

"Tail 4YKN73-West hailing Delegate One."

Unlike the endless stream of other hails we'd received, all of which we'd turned away with a recorded message about the crew of the *Delegate One* working out our next stops in light of our sudden popularity, the shipcom green-lighted this transmission.

"This is *Delegate One*. Go ahead, *West*," I said.

"Just letting you know we got our ship. Thanks for waiting around to make sure we had a ride."

"Congratulations on the new boat. Good luck out there, *West*."

"Good luck to you, *Delegate One*. Sounds like you did good. *West* out."

And that was that. Enough of Colson had held together that Tarko and Herog had managed to purchase the Ten-Back.

Which meant we could move the weapons from the *Corrigan's Blood* to the new ship and go spread AntiLegend on locked-down worlds. The ethics of that had changed since our first debate—then, we'd been sure vampires would inhale the airborne virus and die, which had made spreading it genocide.

But they *didn't* catch the airborne version. So inoculating human populations, from whom vampires only caught AntiLegend when they attacked those humans, was not genocide.

Of course, exposing people who had not requested it to the nanovirus was an ethical issue. But so was the fact that if they were in the thrall of a vampire, they were both being held as slaves, and were incapable of giving consent, so the act of exposing them to something that would kill the one holding them captive was both ethical and legal. We'd had a big argument about this, trying to figure out what Books would have told us. Not being able to call back to Tegosshu to ask him directly was frustrating, but in the end, we were all sure we'd got it right.

The fight wasn't so desperate anymore, though. I knew countless Legends were still out there, hiding or waiting or in places where they still had easy access to humans with clean blood. I knew some of those Legends were still making new Legends, because that was what vermin did. The Legend War hadn't stopped Darkout. Maybe it had bought us a little time.

But people were going to be carrying AntiLegend door to door. We'd saved FastIt, and no matter what else fell apart, that one small fragment of functioning civilization would take the salvation of humanity into countless places we'd had no way to reach.

We'd multiplied ourselves a million times.

I could breathe again.

Meanwhile, however, we had a hard route ahead of us to get back to our hiding place and the *Blood*. While Herog would be able to enter the origami point with a specified destination and have the ship run a point recalculation inside hyperspace to take him straight to our hiding place, we in the *Delegate One* were now in the eye of reporters and people everywhere, we were going to have to make a public jump into a section of settled space we knew to be heavy in vampires—and because we were in a regular TFN ship, not a sidewinder, our route was public and fixed, and our course had been announced and channeled through public bands of the datastream and speculated on.

We needed an excuse to get off our announced route, to disappear into one of our Spybee-free origami points located by the *Blood*. We needed to make sure we'd shaken off any pursuers before we skipped back to our hiding place. We weren't the *West*, able to disappear. Any idiot would be able to follow our course from Spybee to Spybee, so we needed to find a way to get to a Spybee-free point without having everyone else follow us through.

No matter when we jumped, we were burning one of our private points to do it, because our route in would be recorded by the Spybee wherever we entered.

I still chafed at the necessity of our slow, clumsy exit from the public life we'd not intended, but I kept reminding myself we had our unlikely ally, and he was buying us time, and I managed to maintain my calm.

So we went to Havershand Dominion, which eons earlier had been one large world. Then something big and dense blew it apart on its way past. A number of the chunks had held atmosphere, and folks had bought up the chunks and chunklets, terraformed them when necessary, and built a wacky strip of independent domains smeared in a ribbon a quarter of the way around the orbit of the galaxy's sun.

And we took orders for AntiLegend, and set them up with FastIt delivery, and sprayed the station, and acted our parts. Meanwhile, Wire sent coded messages to Herog and Tarko that we would get there as soon as we could.

Havershand Dominion was three days in which we did not get any time alone. We got word from Herog that there were problems getting the first shipment to Raythonade—the automated delivery plant's drones had been incorrectly programmed, and because there had been no orders, no one had noticed. Folks back on Tegosshu were working out the fix.

We went to the Eastern Alliance, and sprayed their station, and handed out starter dispensers, and met FastIt carriers who were excited to be a part of what was coming together. The Eastern Alliance took five days.

Herog and Tarko were moving contents from the *Blood* to the new ship while they waited. But Wire was the one who knew how to install the weapon systems, and who could cut out moleibond panels and reconfigure the inside of the stripped-down Ten-Back to build temporary hiding places for our illegal modifications.

Until we got Wire to the new ship, our progress was as hung up as that first shipment of AntiLegend.

We went through the origami point to Creigh, fifth in a string of about a dozen private ships traveling together, some of them filled with news-gatherers and distributors, some with fans who wanted to be a part of history, some with young men who wanted to kill vampires.

I came out the other end shaken by the rough crossing, into chaos.

"—evasive action! Shields are up! Using programmed routines for evasive action! Shields are up! Using programmed routines for—"

Finding your ass in the middle of war on the other end of an origami point is a better wake-up than ship-

brewed coffee. Three *big* fighters were shooting at everything, and about half of everything was dead and floating
already.

Had we been in anything but one of Storm Rat's ships,
we would have been dead, too. But the *Delegate One* had
combat-grade shields, a full program of battle subroutines,
and ferocious weapons, and while it had not deployed
weapons the instant it was fired upon—we were, after all,
hard-set to peaceful interaction in order to maintain our
cover—it had so far avoided being hit.

I had vampires on my infoscreen, and they were grinning at me as I shook off the effects of hyperspace.

"This is the end of your mission, bitch," one said.

If I were them, looking to kill me, I would have had a
better line than that ready to go.

"Bet me?" I asked and told shipcom, "Origami jump to
NTK now, *baby steps* to *mad dog* on reentry."

Baby steps was peaceful mode—no weapons for any
reason. *Mad dog* was the code for "fire on all hostiles with
all weapons until they are destroyed or we run out of
weapons."

Delegate One did a beautiful drop-and-olly to get out of
the path of incoming fire, raced back into the origami point
on our preprogrammed path to our Spybee-free zone—

—And Badger was with me, beside me, not touchable,
but so close, so close, so close, and he ached for me as I
ached for him, both of us lost, apart from our otherselves
who were still content to have each other while the two of
us were held apart by worlds and the thin-but-unbroken
veils of the multiverse, by *if*, by whim, by *fate*—

—And we blasted back into reality and ollied and fired
gravity beams and sticky pies and boilers on the vampire
ships as they came through, but we were not alone. Another

ship fought beside us, one that had joined our ridiculous convoy just before the jump to Creigh.

Between us and the other armed ship, we wiped out the three fighters and their vampire crews almost instantly.

"*DELEGATE ONE,* we are friendly. *Eternal Flame* hails the *Delegate One.* We are friendly."

I opened com. "I'd already pretty much figured that out, *Eternal Flame,*" I said, "when you shot them instead of us."

I drank ship coffee and fake blood and shook off the lingering effects of jumping twice in thirty seconds real-time. A Colson StarStream Five-Back hung in space near us, now facing us instead of the three dead ships cluttered around the origami point.

"You don't have to stay on alert," the other ship said.

"Please forgive me, *Eternal Flame,* but we just jumped from an ambush where a lot of other folks got shredded, and I'm ragged after the second jump plus the fight—and I don't know what else might yet come popping out of that damn point, shooting in my direction. So we're going to sit here with our shields up and weapons ready. Because I really hate surprises."

"I hear that," the other ship said, but dropped its shields anyway, which from my perspective was monumentally stupid. The *Delegate One* had just proved it was armed, though we'd been pretending to be unarmed and peaceful. The captain of the other ship wasn't thinking...or at least wasn't thinking the way I would have thought in the same situation.

The coffee and all the extra stuff the ship put in it raced

through my bloodstream, pulling me out of my post-hyper-space darkness.

"Why did you follow us through?" I asked the other captain.

"Because we had guns, and we didn't think you did. I have to say it's good to know you weren't as stupid as you'd seemed. When you're dealing with Legends, never, ever give them any advantage they don't already have. They have enough of a head start as it is."

"Sounds like you have some experience."

"Unfortunately."

I laughed in spite of how I felt. "That one word defines everything about the damned Legends."

She laughed too. "It does."

"By the way," I told her, "I'm Grace Falza. How did you get involved with this mess?"

"I'm Seelie Long," she said. "Originally? A vampire hired me and my team a while back, then decided that rather than pay rucets for the very good job we did for him, he decided to kill us. He managed to kill two of us before my first hit him with liquid fire. My first and I were the only two survivors."

"Familiar story," I said. "Sounds a lot like mine."

"They seem to run to type," she said. "Anyway, the reason I was following you was to let you know to be care-ful. Well, more careful. What you're doing is important. I found out late what was going on, and had to race to catch up with you, but I have information you need. You were being set up back on Raythonade Station. You didn't know how much trouble you were in, but I can't even start to figure out how you didn't end up dead back there."

Raythonade? My gut twisted. Let her talk, my gut said. My brain listened. "What do you mean?"

Seelie said, "Dreyton Stathington was a vampire. One of the Legends. I know he was pretending he was going to help you, but he wouldn't have."

Oh, *shit*. How many people knew he was a vampire. Play dumb, I told myself. Play dumb, don't leak that you already knew this. "I don't understand," I said.

"He ended up in control of the entire station," she said. "And as far as we could tell, he would have been in control of the entire supply of AntiLegend except for what you have. He would never have shipped it out."

I couldn't tell her we had Dreyton Stathington by his pointy fangs, and he would do whatever we told him to do for just long enough for us to accomplish our goals.

So I said, "I don't think he's a vampire."

"He was," she said. "A while back, we ran into a guy who'd caught Angel Fever and decided to turn the serum in his blood into a weapon. He put it into darts—you probably have something like it. Anyway, it only kills vampires. And one dart of Angel Fever to the left thigh killed him almost instantly."

It took just an instant for the full meaning of that to roll over me.

"No," I whispered. "Dreyton Stathington was the only one left who could run FastIt."

She heard me. "The company has more than a million employees. There will be plenty of other people who can step in and run it."

"No." I buried my head in my hands, not really talking to her. "No. He had the passwords. Access to the money. He was the only one left who could move funds, who could send money for payroll, who had access to the top level of control. There's no one left who can release the money that will send AntiLegend to all the carriers, or keep interspace distribution running. We almost had it...almost had a clear path to halting Darkout..."

FastIt would have saved so many people. By "helping" us, Seelie Long had thrown us back into a desperate race against the implacable enemy of time, with a week lost to work that had all just been undone.

"We have to go," I said. "We have a lot to accomplish and not much time to do it in."

"Mind if we come with?" she asked, and smiled. "Romo and I would love to be involved in distributing Angel Fever."

"Sorry," I said. "I appreciate the backup and the offer, but we don't have time to train anyone else."

"If you were fooled by Dreyton Stathington, maybe we should train you," she said.

By way of reply, I took us through the origami point to another unmarked point, and from there through to our rendezvous with Herog, Tarko, and the *West*.

Badger was in the interstices of the universe, waiting. Watching. Holding out his hands to me.

I did not let myself look at him.

Chapter 26

Wire sent code back and forth to Tegosshu, and we got the news we'd dreaded.

The drones were working—which of course was news we wanted, since the drones were also our method of delivering payloads of Legend II—and they were delivering a steady stream of AntiLegend dispensers to Raythonade Station, spinning each delivery into moleibond bubbles away from the docks, where FastIt crews should have been on hand to cut out the moleibond and pack the bubble contents into FastIt ships for next-day delivery.

This was the bad news. Not one of those dispensers was going anywhere.

The FastIt company, like countless others following the Vampire War, had failed to make three code-checks in a row. Code checks were the way that banks and stockholders kept track of companies—the daily code check, validated by biometric backup, proved a senior officer of the company was present in corporate headquarters and capable of manually punching in the code. There was no way to auto-mate the process—to cheat—by intent of the creators of the system.

With failure to present a senior officer of the company to keep the doors open, FastIt had been locked down by centralized banking computers until a senior officer with the correct codes presented himself, or until the company's assets could be evaluated and broken out into separate, salable parts.

But FastIt had not died a pretty death.

The news of companies being locked down had spread everywhere, and FastIt employees, who had seen via datastream feeds what happened to rank-and-file employees during the first wave of business die-offs, knew exactly what would happen to them.

As non-executive employees, they would be treated as enemies of the stockholders. The instant FastIt's bank had a third code-check failure, it would notify Raythonade Station sporcs—space port controllers, the corporate-owned version of ground-based police or military units. The sporcs would show up with legal orders to forcibly remove non-executive employees from the premises, making sure those employees carried out nothing. The sporcs, whose contracts were owned by the station, and secondarily by the bank and stockholders who owned the station, would carry out their orders.

So when the FastIt employees heard the rumor that their new boss had been murdered, that he'd been a vampire, and that FastIt had missed its first code check the previous day, they'd not only cleared out their own personal belongings, which would have been forbidden had they waited for the arrival of the sporcs. They'd also looted every bit of company equipment they could run off with.

In twenty-four hours, all the FastIt trucks and ships

were gone, re-marked and repainted, with their tracking devices disabled. An equal number of new independent delivery vehicles were shipping loads of office furniture, supplies, networking hardware and software, and every-thing else that could be physically removed from FastIt, and delivering it to FastIt employees.

FastIt had highly skilled, well-trained employees who knew how to pack and move anything. From one end of settled space to the other, they'd gutted FastIt.

And even that could have worked for us, at least just once, if we'd set up deliveries to go to all the outlying FastIt hubs instead of to one central delivery point on a space station with a population of less than one hundred thousand.

The FastIt dockworkers took some of the AntiLegend. But not much. They weren't shipping anything at that point —they were simply taking things for personal use. So only one bubble-pack of AntiLegend was opened and stolen by employees. The rest—enough to turn a good part of settled space poisonous for vampires—was locked down and listed as a shareholder asset.

Just like that, our allies melted into nothingness.

We were on our own again. But we were worse off than before, because we'd lost a Standard week setting up Anti-Legend distribution that wasn't going to happen, and we'd demonstrated to our enemies their vulnerability to contami-nated food supplies, then had failed to successfully contam-inate their supplies.

Now the datastream was filled with reports of Legends stealing ships and kidnapping humans and slip-ping into space to hide out against the spread of AntiLegend...

...With streamed images of vampires rounding up

humans, blood-testing them, and killing any whose blood had AntiLegend in it.

...With a handful of escapees' stories of vampires using seduction and mind control to gain positions of power against humans in worlds where no AntiLegend had reached, and enslaving everyone.

We'd threatened, then failed to follow up on our threat with effective action, and as has been the case throughout history, those presented with genuine threats but given time to act had acted intelligently to save themselves and to improve their own positions.

They'd already had immense advantages over humans. Now they were using all of those advantages to eradicate the danger in their midst—with horrible loss of life, and the worsening of conditions for humanity in every place where humans lived.

Some of them—maybe even most of them—might decide they didn't need Legend II, either.

They could take their slaves and head beyond settled space with them, out past the periphery, into the far reaches.

Kept as slaves, and tended and bred as food by isolated vampires, little clusters of humanity might survive. But what sort of survival would that be?

THE *BLOOD* WAS COMING APART; the *West* was coming together.

But not fast enough. We were taking shortcuts, downwardly revising our list of essential weapons that had to be transferred, selecting based on what we could move fastest instead of on what we could use best.

Tarko, Bluejay, Wire, Herog and I were back on stims and blood cleansers—lighter doses, because our improved metabolisms were much better at handling toxins. And we skipped real sleep entirely.

Even so, five people working round the clock only gives you one hundred twenty hours a day, not the roughly two thousand we were getting when we had all of Storm Rat's people working on our problem.

And we weren't helped by the fact that neither Tarko nor Bluejay had any shipboard technical experience. You don't put life-or-death spaceship tech into the hands of folks who've never held a manual tripod moleibonder and say, "Have fun. Just don't do anything that will kill us."

So Tarko worked on keeping money channels open, on building out the production factories for Legend II and switching AntiLegend factories over to producing Legend II. There would perhaps come a time when humans could have AntiLegend in their bloodstream and it would protect them. Now? Now it was getting them murdered.

During one planning session, Tarko said, "I had to funnel more money into resources for the AutoBuilds, and I had to buy several mining operations that were about to go under, but Legend II will now be self-delivering."

And I said, "What are AutoBuilds?"

"Just another brand of self-designing factories," he said. "This brand is entirely robotic. As long as you can deliver an AutoBuild raw resources, it'll expand the factory to expand production. AutoBuilds are," and he sighed, "illegal in parts of settled space that favor human work forces. Places like Cantata," and here he nodded to me, "like them because nobody dies during mining operations, and in places where they can use the raw materials they mine as their own resources, they are hellishly efficient.

335

They can, however..." He stared off into space. "...Run amok."

Herog said, "Black marketeers like them."

"Black marketeers?" Bluejay looked puzzled.

"You've spent your whole life on worlds where most everything was legal," Herog told her. "You've missed black markets. Repressive governments like to make things illegal so they can create criminal underclasses. It allows them to restrict movement among people, to maintain large, oppressive police forces, to tax populations heavily for their 'protection,' and it gives government officials both tremendous power, and access to sources of immense wealth through graft."

I raised an eyebrow. "That's cynical."

"Prove me wrong," he said.

I shook my head. "Another time."

Tarko steered the conversation back to his problems. "I have the issue of the AutoBuilds running amok resolved. I have self-delivery resolved. What I don't have yet is a way to handle ordering problems."

I frowned. "Ordering problems?"

"We're pushing this through on a tight time frame—every Legend needs to take delivery on Legend II at about the same time, because otherwise there are going to be rumors of what Legend II really does—and rumors will breed survivors."

"We already know we cannot get them all," Wire said.

"We can get most of them."

And I asked again, "What do you mean by ordering problems?"

"There will be a subset of Legends who will not have the necessary funding to buy Legend II. Or who will have a glitch with their biometric scanner. Or who will not be able to automatically validate a delivery address because they're on a low-tech world. We need to be sure every single one of those monsters gets Legend II as well. I just haven't figured out how to do it yet."

No one said anything. Half the solution seemed obvious to me, though.

"Well, first you make sure they know they've won—that they're one of the few chosen to be a Legend II Master," I said. "Once you've told them that, they'll sit still for anything you want to do next."

Everyone looked at me, and Tarko murmured, "How seriously *did* you consider a life of crime?"

BLUEJAY'S skill sets had been built out from seduction, in her previous life as a slave, and statistical analysis in the self-education she pursued after her rescue. She had little technical skill, so she helped me physically move the database storage and the worm hardware over. Then she transferred and unpacked our personal belongings, and made the *West* more livable while we were installing weapons.

But it still took Herog, Wire, and me thirteen Standard days to get weapons installed and cross-wired between the main deck and the new thrown-together battle deck and to dummy up the ship exterior so we looked unarmed from the outside. That was in spite of us deciding to not bother hiding weapons inside. If settled space survived, we'd high-tail it back to Tegosshu and Storm Rat could put a full team on transforming my ship into a flawless imitation of an unarmed business transport.

If.

Until D-Day—Delivery Day for Legend II—since

vampires were murdering humans for being AntiLegend-positive, we changed our plans again, from inoculating low-tech worlds to clearing out as many Darkout Worlds as we could. After D-Day...well, we'd see if there was an after.

So as our first act aboard the functional *West*, I wormed the datastream for data on our Legend problem. Bluejay ran the analysis, and the news was bad. The number of vampires who'd slaughtered each other on their paths to obtaining Legend II was more than offset by the number of humans enslaved or slaughtered by Legends fighting to avoid contamination by AntiLegend.

Percentage-wise, there were more vampires than there had been before.

With everything we'd done so far, our situation was still worse than when we started.

Bluejay picked up the expanding ring of systems that had gone dark. We were up to forty certain, and a handful of 'trending toward.' She said, "One third of remaining systems show symptoms of nearing the fifteen-percent saturation mark. That's fewer than seven humans per vampire. That's not sustainable. And worlds that hit twenty percent of the population as Legends can go dark the same day. They *will* go dark within a few days."

Tarko said, "Latest date for D-Day?"

"The amount of Legend II you need to stop this accelerates past the tipping point in eight days by my worst-case scenario."

"Best case?"

"No," she said. "We use worst case, because using best case allows us the possibility to be too late. And frankly, if we could make D-Day tomorrow, I might be able to sleep again."

"But the Darkout worlds..." I said.

She stopped me. "The Darkout worlds are lost. We can burn the remains after we know there's a point."

And she was right.

"We still need to test the tech," Herog said. "Because if we can win this, our next step has to be to prevent re-infection."

So Bluejay marked out every world she was sure had gone dark, as well as those that looked like they were going to tip.

Tarko set the AutoBuilds to unlimited production, which he said was the thing that would cause them to overrun their programming and go rogue, and we set our route for the core of settled space, and for a system Bluejay said had fallen. It was on our path to Tarko's destination—an AutoBuild he'd had fit itself with some extras he said we'd need.

After one mid-point recalculation, just to be sure we hadn't picked up any distant tails, we slid out of the origami point next to Gathus Station.

Gathus Station had always been small, grimy, and uninspiring. Now, though, it was an unthinkable scene from the inside of insanity. The vampires trapped there when Darkout fell and starvation turned the entire population into mindless eaters had torn everything destructible apart in their search for blood. Shards of metal floated in the moleibond coating that formed the outer shell of the station. Dock ports had been forced open, though, resulting in rapid decompression and the spewing of most of the inside contents of the station into space.

All five of us were on the bridge, looking at the devastation illuminated by our navigation lights. I turned on all our external floods to get a better look, and immediately wished I hadn't. But we all had to see. We had to understand.

The denizens of the station, all converted to Legend I vampires, had been ejected into vacuum along with most of the ship contents.

Unlike the ship contents, the vampires had been vulnerable to decompression. A few had apparently attempted to hold their breath (something you learn never to do in Idiot Orientation—the training every passenger on every space flight since the dawn of time has received before the ship takes off) and had suffered explosive decompression.

Unlike humans dumped into space, however, the vampires who had exhaled didn't die after ninety seconds. Their hearts had kept beating, the nanovirus in their blood streams had removed the vapor forming there, and they'd kept exhaling until they'd hit a pressure equilibrium.

We breathed. We didn't need to breathe all that often. The Legend nanovirus was entirely capable of stripping carbon from oxygen and shunting the carbon into our unused gastrointestinal tracts, meanwhile scavenging O_2 out of our systems until it ran out of materials that could be broken down into O_2. We would digest ourselves if we went without oxygen long enough, and die eventually. But if radiation didn't cook us, we'd last a long time.

Haskell Corrigan had been a horrible man, but when he'd designed his Legends, he'd done an amazing job of making them tough.

And out there in the temperatureless vacuum of space, the nanovirus that had shaped human beings into Legends had not died...so the hosts had not died. The Legends were moving.

Arms and legs paddling, they were trying to move themselves toward our lights.

Because most of them had no way to change trajectory, they were flailing helplessly.

A few who were close to large bits of debris, however, were launching themselves toward us by grabbing the debris and pushing off of it in our direction.

They were essentially mindless, but movement attracted them. They would be dead eventually, when the nanovirus inside them could find nothing else to convert into oxygen. They'd no doubt be skeletal and potbellied when they finally died.

But in the meantime, if we dragged them into the ship and shot them full of human blood, they'd revert to monsters indistinguishable from people. If they found a way into or onto another ship coming in-system without being caught, they could do the same thing for themselves.

"How long do you think they can last out there?" Tarko asked.

I shrugged. "Sky could probably have told us. *Too* long, no matter how you look at it. If they're dead, they can't hurt anyone else."

Something thudded against our hull, and I was filled with the horror of remembrance. I heard claws scrabbling for purchase against the flawless moleibond skin of the ship.

Herog saw me shudder, and he glanced at Wire, and said, "Shuttle sprayer test time."

Wire grinned, "I wanted to fine-tune the delivery system—I didn't think I'd get a test like this with single targets."

Herog rose from his seat on the bridge. "I'll fire, you mix."

That worked for me. I'd already dealt with starving Legends close up. Neither Wire nor Herog had. They needed to know what they were up against, because if, if, *if* we fended off Darkout, we still had work to do.

So they went out, and they sprayed fake blood mist

around the monsters, and the monsters ingested, then exploded.

Our systems worked.

But I knew—we all knew—that what we were doing only had meaning if Legend II distribution worked.

BUT ALL THAT WORK, all that prep, and we didn't get to clean out a single Darkout site with our sprayers.

The message came in through the datastream as Herog and Wire were running down the last moving targets they could spot.

It came through in Clear, pumped into all bands.

"Kids, the candy store just filled up. Come and get it, sunshine dancers."

Those words, sent everywhere because Tegosshu couldn't be sure where we'd be, meant simply, *Production has surpassed our estimate for existing Legend I vampires by 33%. Time to distribute Legend II.*

Tarko had worked endlessly on programming distribution and forging a clear path for the money to follow, and on making sure every single order was accepted and delivered promptly.

He'd cloned production centers into dozens of unmarked origami points, and had programmed each to deploy and then stock local satellite distribution centers around every known point of human habitation—including Darkout worlds.

He'd dealt with large distributions before. No one, ever, had tried anything on this scale, though. Tarko said we were going to have to be available personally to handle problems.

He insisted that, no matter how well designed the system was, there would always be problems.

We could not handle the problems from Tegosshu—it had to be kept clean of any contact with anything related to our activities.

Instead, we went to one of the more than two thousand automated distribution centers Tarko had set up. He'd parked each of his AutoBuilds next to an uncharted origami point and accompanied it with a dormant Spybee that he would awaken with a pingball triggered from another Spybee he controlled. Tarko had been diverting and funneling funds stolen from slaver systems and known Legend-run governments into the AutoBuilds since the day we figured out our plan. I wondered how many slaver systems had gone bankrupt, and could not figure out where their money had gone while building his Legend II factories.

All of them, I hoped.

Until that moment, none of us had seen any of the immense machines Tarko was building. After this, none of us would see one again, because when the last call came through, each Autobuild would wait one hour, send its record of transactions back to Tarko's private Spybee, then self-destruct, taking its companion Spybee and its copy of its records with it.

But the AutoBuild was worth seeing.

Each starts out as a single three-meter AutoBuild cube. As with all AutoBuilds, the buyer selects actions he wants the unit to take, and programs exact details for the product he wants the unit to create. And he hooks the AutoBuild up to a funding source. The AutoBuild then designs itself to produce what is wanted in the most efficient manner possible.

Tarko's AutoBuild was the size of a city, an interconnected sphere of vacuum-grown crystals and metal cubes, tiny glass tunnels and heavy pipes, and as our search lights played over it, it glittered and gleamed, a filagreed moon of robust steel and copper and gold spun together with snowflake-crystals glittering like diamond and emeralds, rubies and sapphires. It's crystalline shapes of clear tubes and metallic spindles that could only exist in gravityless vacuum.

Only in one place did the structure make allowance for any human interaction, and that structure existed only on *this* Spybee.

A series of braced cubes poked out of one side, looking like an ugly stick poking out of a magical ball. At the bottom of that stick was a large cube made of three-meter cubes. At the bottom of *that* was a dock.

I brought the *West* in cautiously, on manual, attaching so gently to the dock that I could not even hear the connection. It was there, though—my maneuver showed green across the board.

Herog, the only one present capable of appreciating that artistry, said "Pretty."

And an automated voice blatted over my shipcom, "Identify, identify, code required now or self-destruct will initiate in one minute. Fifty-nine. Fifty-eight. Fifty-..."

"Tarko?" I said, "you didn't give me a code."

"You couldn't give it," he said, and told me, "Let me have com."

"Shipcom, give access to Tarko."

"Acknowledged," my ship said.

"...—Nine, forty-eight, forty-seven..."

.   .   .

"I BREATHED IN DARKNESS," Tarko said,
   Spun it out as light.
   Turned death to life,
   Brought day from murderous night,
   And captured pain,
   And spun it into pleasure.
   I've earned my life.
   I live it in full measure."

"SELF-DESTRUCT TERMINATED, MADO TARKO," the AutoBuild said. "You and your party may come aboard."

I glanced sidelong at Tarko Armbruster. "Not a password I'd choose in a situation where speed was of the essence."

He grinned. "It wasn't what it sounded like."

"It sounded like poetry."

He chuckled. "The poetry wasn't the code. The poetry was for dramatic effect. The code was simple voice recognition. We were clear the second I spoke the first word over com."

I raised an eyebrow. "You're a mystery."

"By intent. I've found it gets me laid."

Behind me, Bluejay burst out laughing. "So *that's* your secret."

But his face had turned serious.

"What comes next will be a tiny portion of this operation, but some of the most difficult, frustrating work you'll do in your life. And for it, we need to be the Gods of Legend II one final time."

I slid back into Velvet's pale skin, and watched my colleagues resuming their "beautiful monster" looks.

"Costumes, too?" Bluejay asked.

Tarko shrugged. "Why not?"

I looked out the infoscreen at the outline of the box the AutoBuild had created for us and said, "Because that thing is made of metal. It can be punctured by random space debris. Does it have gravity? Thermal controls? Atmosphere backups?"

Tarko gave me a look of frustrated annoyance. "It was thrown together at the last minute when I realized we were going to have to have manual input on D-Day. It's pressurized and has breathable air."

"Shipsuits," I told everyone. "And gravboots so you can walk in there instead of floating."

Chapter 27

We stood on the deck of the *West*, moments away from taking Legend II live, moments away from the moment that was either going to save humanity, or fail and leave Darkout to consume everything that mattered, and my heart raced.

When all of us were dressed, we went through the airlock into Tarko's com center.

It was...well, calling it *utilitarian* ignored the essence of utility—that a thing do what you needed it to do. Tarko's work station was five raised consoles and five seats bolted to the floor that had been designed to be used in gravity. Lacking gravity, they were going to have to be adapted by LDI (Least Dangerous Idiot) fixes before we could sit in them. These consoles and chairs were stuck in the center of a large metal box into which an atmosphere generation unit pumped air that included oxygen, and probably nitrogen, but that was laced with sulphur. The consoles had lighted buttons, but the room itself had no light, and no provision to add light.

"You forgot lights?" I muttered.

"I was focusing on the essentials."

"If you didn't think lights were essentials, I'm terrified to find out what else our temporary home here lacks. Reconsta units? Coffee?"

"We have screens, easy-to-use command buttons, and chairs."

This was going to be bad.

I told Herog, "You know where the emergency stores are. Grab a hundred-pack of stick-on flares, five sheets of half-meter peel-tape, and five disposer bags. Take Bluejay, and bring one of the coffeemakers and a blood synthesizer unit, too."

The two of them took off to get our fix-it supplies.

"Wire, can you tell this thing how to fix our air?"

"On it," he said.

Wire aimed his butt at one of the chairs, hooked his feet back around the anchored post, and Tarko clumped over to his side, grabbed the underside of the console to hold himself in place, and gave Wire specifications.

I scouted the location for additional problems.

There were several. The only exit was the dock link to the ship. The metal box had no windows, no external sensors, no way to warn us of incoming meteor swarms or space debris or anything else that might move through space. According to my shipsuit readout, the air being pumped in from the atmosphere generator was nitrox, a bit heavy on the ox, and along with trace sulphur, included hydrogen.

Which made me wonder if perhaps Tarko had been trying to kill us.

"Wire, make sure the damn atmo unit clears the hydrogen, too. We don't need that in here."

"Good god," he muttered. "Hydrogen *and* sulphur. On it."

Bluejay and Herog hurried back in and I divided the flares into five smaller bundles. We LDI'd the gravity and light issues by first ripping the underside covering off sheets of peel-tape, and sticking the tape to each chair seat. When we were ready to sit, we'd rip the top covering off to create sticky-chairs. Don't need gravity if your butt is stuck to the chair. Next we lifted the front right corner of the peel-tap and stuck one edge of a disposal bag to each seat that way, then dumped in a supply of flares and tightened the draw-string to a hand-width so most of them wouldn't float out. Each of us would have to adjust our own hand-widths, and Herog and Tarko would probably lose more flares to float-away than the rest of us. But with that, we solved our problems with both gravity and light.

Meanwhile, Wire and the AutoBuild's com muttered to each other.

Tarko looked at the consoles, at the sticky-grip seats, at the bags full of flares we'd tape to the chairs—flares that would glow for about six hours, gradually dimming until we added another.

"Interesting." He looked at me. "We're going to tape our asses to our seats?"

"It's quick and effective."

"Here's to efficiency."

Wire said, "Air's fixed. Sort of. I'm venting the hydrogen and sulphur outside. I figure as long as we don't have to breath it..." He shrugged.

"Works for me," I said.

"On that note, then," Tarko said, "let's get started. We're here to handle the part of this process that machines cannot do.

This method of problem-solving is ancient, it's slow, and it's flawed, and if I'd been able to come up with anything more acceptable in the time available, I would have. If I had been able to come up with extra help for us, I would have—but what we're doing here cannot ever be tracked back to Tegosshu, because every call in will became a permanent record leading from the call's origin to the place where the call was answered. If we brought in help from Storm Rat and the Tegosshuans, we'd be sticking an eternal sign to them saying, 'Yes, we were involved in the distribution of Legend II.' So the five of us must do the best we can do with just ourselves. What we're setting out to do will be difficult. It may in the end prove impossible. But we will do the best we can. It's important before we get started that you understand our objective. What is our objective?"

"To kill vampires," I said.

"Too vague. Our objective is to get one dose of Legend II to every single Legend in settled space, no matter what."

I didn't see how what he said was any different than what I'd said.

"Understand that you're going to have customers lying to you about having the money, about being Legends, about having broken biometric scanners—and you are going to listen to them lie, you are going to smile, and if they are Legends, you are going to get them their Legend II."

I asked, "If their biometric scanners are broken, how will we know if they're Legends?"

"From the first, we emphasized that the only way to get Legend II was to validate yourself as a Legend I vampire. If they're going to have a chance of winning the war of Legend II versus Legend I, they know they must prove what they are. But some of them will hope there is a way out of that. So they'll test you. But their biometric scanners *won't* be broken. They'll be lying, trying to get Legend II with out giving us their biodata. So you simply say, 'I can give you one minute to pull a replacement bioscanner from another room, but after that your Legend II will go to someone else. Legends will enter their biodata. Humans will cut the call."

He looked at each of us, one at a time, as if he were trying to burn the importance of his words into our minds with his glance.

"You are going to have customers on the backside of nowhere, hiding out in spaceships, in situations where they are not going to be able to take delivery of our product unless they work with us.

"And you are going to be dealing with some Legends who are simply too stupid to be breathing—but for the moment, they still are.

"Our job is to make sure every single Legend who tries to acquire Legend II succeeds, no matter how flawed his or her attempt."

He looked at all of us, unquestionably in charge of this station and his part of our plan. Massive again, hulking, fierce, he looked like the God of Chaos he'd done such a brilliant job pretending to be.

He said, "Understand that almost everything that goes on from the instant we leak our final message into the datastream will take care of itself without any intervention on our part. Delivery micro-drones are *already* inside drone-mothers set at target locations on each known world, satellite, and station in settled space."

He held up a metal ovoid, pointed at one end, as thin as a hair and half the length of my smallest fingernail. "This is a micro-drone. These micro-drones are self-propelling, collision-detecting, blood-sensing, auto-targeting, and each carries roughly a hundred thousand virons of Legend II. We all know that a single viron, if it reaches the Legend's bloodstream, will multiply and kill its target. But I didn't want to have to depend on one viron. I don't think I'd sleep, thinking about the doses where the viron didn't make it into the bloodstream, or was inactive. I can trust that with a hundred thousand virons, enough will get where they need to go."

We watched him, illuminated in red, yellow, green, and blue by the first round of flares. He didn't look at all nervous.

I was. I wanted to go to the physical training room on the *Blood*, turn the gravity to three, and fight bags and weights and distances until I collapsed.

He looked *comfortable*. Like this was something he'd done a million times, like the future of humanity didn't depend on it, like this was just another day of channeling money from one account to another, with nothing important riding on the outcome.

He said, "The micro-drones will carry almost all orders direct to buyers, will contact them via the comkey they feed into the system, will do a biometric scan to make sure the recipient is the customer who purchased Legend II, and then will locate the subject's most easily available artery, and will then inject the recipient with Legend II. But," he said, "we can have the following problems:

"The customer's method of payment may not work. Perhaps he has no money, perhaps he has a genuine issue with having his credit accepted, but it doesn't matter. If he cannot get his payment to work, you clear payment manually by pressing the *Payment Verified* button here. And you say, 'All fixed. It was just a little glitch. Your Legend II is on its way.'"

"How can that work?" Wire asked.

"We cheat. We use the customer's data, but take money

we've already received and credit that money into his account via a third party—so we are paying for the user's dose and delivery, but he's the one who will have signed the payment authorization."

Wire gave a low whistle.

"Remember, you have one job, and one job only here. You say 'yes' to every Legend, and you get Legend II into every vampire hand that wants it."

"Next, the customer may be outside our planned delivery area. This second issue is the reason we are *here*, on site, right next to an origami point and with our own datastream satellite that we'll hook into the system just before we send out our ordering instructions.

"If the customer is in a location that is not registering with the delivery system, you push the *Tone-Track* button. You don't call attention to the fact that you're doing this. Instead, you reassure him that he is one of the few selected to receive the Legend II nanovirus, and you will stay with him as long as it takes to work through his problem. Meanwhile, Tone-Track will map the path of the connection through the datastream—it's designed to look like random signal noise, and so to pass without setting off alarms no matter how secure our Legend's network. Your job is to keep him talking, follow whatever directions he offers for getting the package to where he says he is, and stay calm and polite even when you know he's lying to you."

"Why would a Legend lie about where he is, when telling the truth will get him the thing he wants most?" I asked.

"Because he's currently passing for human, and he wants to make sure his sheep continue to think he's what he says he is. It makes the game more fun for him. If no delivery comes to him in his location, to his name, no one can ever make the connection. He'll want to pick it up at his secondary location. He can play the game he likes best, but with more of the deck stacked in his favor."

"Sick bastard," Bluejay said.

"Universe is full of them," Tarko said. "And even if we wipe out nanovampires, all the other sorts of sick bastards will still be around to pick up the slack. Difference being, they won't be wiping out all intelligent life in settled space while they're being sick bastards."

"Finally, the customer might be a human lying about being a Legend. Most of these will not even reach you, but on the chance that some customers find ways to lock their connections long enough to speak to you, the orange button on your console will flash. Simply smile at your screen and press the button. The would-be customer will receive a notice that his Legend II is on the way." Tarko sighed. "It won't be, of course."

And with that, Wire took the datastream satellite live, and pumped transmission through the origami point, and our last call tore through the datastream across settled space, with Tarko's contact button appended to the very end of our message. His button and his error message would only show up when a transaction failed to go through. In it, he said, "You have been chosen to receive Legend II, but there is a problem with your order. Press the red button with a finger-tip, and when you feel the haptic response, wait for further instructions. We will make sure you receive Legend II. Please be patient—there are only five of us, and we antici-pate wait times as we ensure our chosen applicants receive their products."

He shook his shoulders and grinned. "Finally, to take a new customer, including the first one, you push the pink *Next* button. Let's go get 'em."

The calls didn't start the instant we sent out the message, though. We sat and fidgeted and panicked that something had gone wrong during a delay of eight minutes and twenty-seven seconds, unsure if anyone had received our message, unsure if anyone had listened. Our instructions took seven-minutes and forty-five seconds. We estimated the ordering process in the hands of someone who could follow instructions would take no more than thirty seconds.

The rest...that was waiting.

Then all five consoles lit up simultaneously, and all five of our clear infoscreens filled with the notice, *Calls Waiting*.

I *started* with seventy-eight, and found myself face to face with my first customer the instant I pressed the *Next* button. I discovered I could solve a payment issue in just under twenty seconds. It took me over a minute to process a Tone-Trace and send the micro-drone to the right location.

All the customers recognized me, and almost all were polite. Eager. Some wanted to chat, and I had to explain that I had a few more selectees waiting, and I wanted to get them started on their path to Mastery as quickly as I could.

My queue was piling up much faster than I could deal with respondents, though, and the pressure was getting to me. No one dropped—the wait message explained to each listener that because the selection was random, the person would not be chosen again if he dropped the connection and re-applied. That our few chosen were now picked, and those waiting had beaten astronomical odds.

But considering settled space harbored hundreds of billions of the damn nightmares, with the number rising by the second, the fact that I was five minutes in looking at only two thousand calls—with the number still rising of course, but not as fast as the population sign in Meileone, suggested that Tarko had built an efficient system.

The screen said, "Maryn Short." I pushed the *Next* button. Smiled at my customer, a surprisingly dumpy vampire wearing a gloomy expression. She brightened when she saw me. I said, "Hello, Maryn."

"Hello, Velvet. When I ordered, I was told I'd been chosen to receive Legend II, but I got a delivery-error message," she said.

My left hand moved just enough to press the Tone-Track button. "I'll make sure you get your delivery. Are you on a planet, station, ship, or other?"

"Planet," she said. She was lying. I'd already seen a lot of that. I recognized the texturized moleibond behind her as a Colson interior design detail. The *West* had the same texture pattern on the bridge bulkheads.

The fact that my customer was lying to me didn't matter. She was hooked to the datastream. So was I. No matter what she told me, my Tone-Track would follow our conversation from me to her, to her real location, and my little seed of death would race to embrace her. I'd have to give her instructions for getting it aboard her ship while pretending I didn't know she was on a ship—but I'd already had some practice with that.

Except the Tone-Track wasn't reporting back.

"I'm having a problem with our connection," I told her.

"I can't close the connection and try again," she said.

"No," I agreed, "you can't. You'll lose your acceptance. It will go to someone else."

"Couldn't you make an exception for me?"

"No," I told her. "Your odds the first time were, by our most recent calculations, five hundred thousand to one. If you break the connection, the next person behind you will receive notification that he or she has been chosen. Stay connected at all costs."

"You're right in wanting to kill all the Legends," she said. "They're breeding too fast, wiping out their food source."

"People," I corrected.

She didn't seem to notice. Instead, she told me, "But you're doing it wrong."

I raised an eyebrow. I was trying to figure out, with Tarko's controls-for-dummies console, how to initiate a trace to clear whatever had stopped my Tone-Track from reporting her location, and as far as I could tell, there was nothing I could do. My controls, such as they were, allowed me to open a connection, close one, make a payment for a customer, find the customer's actual location, and disconnect human calls. Tarko had not foreseen the need for more complexity.

My number of waiting calls was rising, and if I was being rational, I'd cut com, take the next call, and mark this one as a loss.

But Tarko had said, "However long it takes," and he and the other three were all taking calls, so I couldn't ask them. I stayed on the line. Cutting Maryn loose meant letting her live. I sent out another pulse, hoping it would get through.

"You want to get rid of the Legends," she told me. "But you're making the classic mistake of sending the cat after the mouse, and the wolf after the cat, and the dragon after the wolf. And what you never bothered to ask is, when this is done, how do you get rid of the dragons?"

Mice. Cats. Wolves. Dragons. There was nothing classic about that to me. I'd never heard of it before—but I could see how what she *thought* we were doing would look like just that scenario. "The dragons are sterile,

Maryn," I said. "They can't make little dragons—and over time, most will themselves be killed, so there will come a day when only the smartest and best of us are left." And I sighed.

"I don't understand what's going wrong," I told her. "I'm terribly sorry, but I've been trying to trace the problem through your connection so I could clear whatever was stopping your purchase." I stared down at my console, willing a solution to come to me."

"Oh, it's not going through because I'm blocking it," she said, and her voice changed.

I looked up to find Sky staring back at me.

She smiled at me, and her fangs gleamed. "You don't have to worry about finding me. I just found you."

My Tone-Track reported her location, but then went dead. My screen went dark, then showed me the number of calls still waiting. 3478. Sky had obtained the information she wanted, and then she'd cut com.

A connection away from you is a connection to you. No matter how clever you are about hiding it, someone else will, if given enough time, figure out how to trail the thread between the two of you back to you. Sky had made her purchase attempt not to get her dose of Legend II, but to connect to the center from which she thought we were sending it out. My Tone-Track couldn't get through because she'd blocked it while sending a similar pulse in my direction.

She'd been in a ship. Had been sitting right outside an origami point, waiting to get our coordinates so she could move through the point to us.

There is no real time involved in the move through hyperspace.

She had our location. She was either jumping, or had

jumped. And we were blind in an unarmored, unarmed metal box.

"Cut com!" I screamed. "Seal suits! Back to the ship! We have incoming!"

There was no time left.

Space is silent.

The AutoBuild hung in a vacuum, and beyond our little pocket of air, silence ruled.

The world blazed red-yellow-white as something ripped away the block wall and our atmosphere blazed and bled out into the silence and the dark in a tearing stream.

Sound was gone. Fire poured out of the atmosphere pump, which had not yet failed. It bled into space.

Fire and explosions seen and felt but not heard, floor falling away, world spinning, pieces and shards that slammed me and cut me and I exhaled and bled and did not hesitate or freeze but kept moving fighting clawing toward the ship hatch, blind, deaf, engulfed in fire.

A missile tore through me and my suit lost pressurization and my hair caught fire, my skin burned, and I knew fire could kill me, and the pain from the missile, the flames around the suit that no longer protected me, would have been too much, and Herog was right. Dying was easy.

I didn't want easy.

Herog had killed me a thousand times or more, and I'd discovered that pain is not death, and that movement is life. I kept moving, kept fighting toward the ship, for the hatch, for the corridor inside where light and armor and weapons lay, because I was not yet done, not yet dead, I had everything to live for.

First, I was going to kill Sky.

It was the mathematics of the mind, the simple equation.

You tried to kill me, and failed.

My turn.

I reached the airlock and palm-slapped the external biometric panel, it slid open, I flung myself inside. Tarko, Herog, and Wire had dragged themselves in ahead of me. They were burned, punctured, shredded, but alive. None of them had a hole the size of a man's head torn from side to side through their waist. I stripped out of the shreds of my shipsuit and flopped on the deck. Said, "Shipcom, load forty-five liters of blood onto an autopallet and send it to the war room now."

"Affirmative," the shipcom said.

We were all hurt enough that healing ourselves would push us toward starvation. We had to get fuel into us before that happened, or we'd lose our minds.

"Where's Bluejay," I asked.

"Pretty sure I saw her blown out the side in the first strike," Wire said, staring at the massive hole in me.

I glanced at the hole, too. It was awful. "She can be hurt worse than this and still be all right," I said. "She's a Legend. She doesn't even need to breathe. I didn't for a while. We'll find her, but first we have to kill Sky."

Herog went still. "Sky did this?"

"She tracked us back through the AutoBuild station's comlink."

A sticky pie hit the *West*, up on the bridge and shipcom said, "Navigation on bridge damaged twenty-five percent. Repairs initiated."

"She's still around," I said. "War room."

Tarko grabbed my arm as we started for Level Three and the war room, which was tucked into a converted guest suite, filled with shock dampers, and out of the way of obvious points of attack. "We need to find Bluejay," he growled. He was the size of a small moon, and angry.

"We will," I said. "But we can't find her if we're dead. We have to stop Sky first."

I rested a hand on his massive shoulder and said, "If she's still alive, she'll still be alive when we've killed Sky. We're tough, Tarko. Hellishly tough.

His massive hand still wrapped around my arm, and he stared into my eyes. I couldn't move.

"We can't save her until we've saved ourselves," I repeated, as a barrage of sticky pies hit the hull all along the starboard side.

Shipcom said, "Damage to air plant, sixty percent. Damage to gravity unit one, fifteen percent. Damage to sublight engine two, thirty-percent. Repairs on battle precedents. Air, then engines, then gravity, then navigation. Do you confirm?"

"Hold on air," I said. "Repair priority engines, then navigation, then gravity." And I looked into Tarko's eyes. "We have to fight now, Tarko."

He said nothing. But he nodded and released my arm.

Chapter 28

I made the tiny, crowded war room half a step ahead of Tarko, who led the autopallet loaded with blood by about five steps.

Herog and Wire were already there. My body was healing on its own, and because of the energy it was using to do this, I was having a hard time thinking. We were all four in the same condition, though I had less body mass to play with. I would, in other words, go crazy sooner. I grabbed liter bags and tossed them, the men caught them, and while the sticky pies started slamming against the port hull, we drank from the bags, threw the empties on the floor, and drank some more.

And my ability to think sharpened.

I asked Herog, "Where is Sky?"

He'd taken the targeting seat. "Drones are what's hitting us right now. We'll have to get through this swarm of them to get to her. I make her straight ahead, hanging out of range."

I watched Herog killing drones quickly and efficiently. There'd been maybe fifty or sixty when he started. Wire was pumping the big ammunition into our chutes—every hit was a kill, and Herog seemed never to miss.

It took him about eight minutes to wipe them out.

"Last drone," Herog said, pointing to the target he'd just acquired.

I took my own seat. Herog was to my right, Tarko off to my left.

I said, "I'll fly. Herog, shoot. You're much more accurate than I am. Tarko, run the life-form scans to let us know when she's dead. Wire, stay on ammo. Let's get rid of Sky, then get Bluejay quickly."

"Why's Sky attacking us now?" Wire muttered. "It seems premature."

Herog glanced over at him. "Because what we did either worked or it didn't—but either way, she knows this is the only arrow we had in our quiver. She had us all in one place in Tarko's call center, and it was both undefended and indefensible. She wouldn't have known than coming in, but she was ready to take advantage of it. Strategically, this was smart on her part."

Tarko said, "Let's make it the stupidest thing she ever did. Let me pump ammo. I want to kill her. I don't just want to watch her die."

"Wire, switch with Tarko," I said, and Wire said, "Sounds good to me."

Wire started running commands into the scanner, and making little noises at the back of his throat, "Cady? This is bad. Bad."

"New bad or same bad?" I asked.

"'Explains a lot' bad. This ship has the tail number of the ship that helped us out when we came through Creigh into the vampire attack."

"Seelie Long's ship?"

"That's the one."

For just a second, I wondered how Sky had found Seel-ie...and then it came together. Sky *was* Seelie.

Sky had shape-changed, just like us.

"So Sky helped us back on Creigh because we hadn't yet done the thing she wanted," Wire said.

"Don't know, don't care. She didn't help us all that much, though. She was the one who killed Dreyton."

I was taking us forward, accelerating cautiously. We hit big debris and little debris—it wouldn't hurt the moleibond hull, but the contents inside the ship, including us, were much more fragile.

"How do you want to run this?" I asked Herog.

"Do a barrage of sticky pies forward and aft to make sure we destroy both her sublight engines, then a slow over-flight with the gravity shear to pulp everyone inside.

"Everyone? There's more than one?"

Wire said, "Three alive and moving on your inset view now."

I saw the blips. They were spread out through the ship. One in back, one centered. One in front.

"Barrage of sticky pies first, Tarko."

"In the chutes now. You're good for a hundred shots."

Sky decided to run, but I already had momentum. I pushed the *West* faster as we broke out of the drone debris. Herog did the first set of sticky pies. The tail of the Five-Back in front of us lit up.

I overflew the ship, did an ollie-and-lift so that I approached her upside down, nose-to-nose, and fast. To avoid collision, she had to use her forward sublight engine to lift the nose of her ship. Mentally, I thanked Wire for the couple hours we spent looking over Colson ship specs—it helped to know how the enemy was put together.

She lifted—and Herog said, "*Very* pretty," and hammered the second barrage into the underbelly from nose to midship, which would knock out her forward sublight engine, her gravity, her air...and her reconsta, if anyone was worried about that over there. Apparently we also took out Sky's stabilizers, because the ship started into a nasty asymmetrical tail under nose roll that sent the ship's nose down and back about thirty degrees off midline. The ship continued to float forward while tumbling backward.

In there with the gravity dead, I figured that had to be a lot of fun.

We got a hail.

Herog glanced at me.

"Where are the people?" I asked Wire.

"They're scrambling toward the nose," Wire said. "Erratically."

"They would be," I said. "Looks like most of their systems are dead. Shipcom, take the hail, send to viewscreens if offered."

And there was Sky on our forward screen, with her human face on, looking somewhat the worse for wear. "I'm sorry," she said. "I'll make a deal with you. I'll get out of your way, leave you alone, leave Tegosshu alone—you won and I acknowledge that. It was a mistake to attack you."

"Hi, Youko," I said. "It was a mistake."

She was strapped into her captain's chair, so unlike the two men coming up behind her, she wasn't being tossed around by the ship's movement. But when I said her real name, she took on another whole level of stillness.

"Yeah, we found out who you really were."

"I have money. A lot of it. I can pay you."

Tarko started to laugh, and she stared at him. "Tarko?"

"We just sold at *least* a hundred billion doses of Legend

II and were paid mostly in asset-backed currencies. My personal bank is choking on real money. What else you got, you bitch?"

I turned to Herog. "I'm going to match pitch, yaw, roll and forward drift to keep us right above her so you can have a steady shot. Run the gravity shear on full power, full ship width, back to front, with a shear width of five micrometers. Pulp her shuttles, then get everything else. I want whoever finds the ship's moleibond shell to be able to wash it out with a high-pressure sprayer and start fresh."

"There has to be some sort of agreement we can reach— At least rescue my brother and my, um, friend before you kill me. They didn't have anything to do with this."

"Wire, can you tell a difference between humans and Legend II vampires via scan?"

He growled."Not sure. Let me see what I can come up with. If I change the settings a bit...yes. There. Got it."

"The men with her—are they humans or vampires?"

"Vampires."

"Thank you," I said. "Remember how you did that. We didn't get all the Legend I vampires, so humans are going to need a way to spot them from a distance. Put it into the datastream once we're finished here."

"I can do it now," he said.

"Works for me." I returned my attention to Youko. "So, you have no innocents to rescue on your ship. And, no. There isn't some sort of agreement we can reach. "

"We know *who you are*, Youko," Herog said. "We know *what you did.*"

He'd been setting the shear parameters as I matched the ship's motion. "We're steady," I told him. "Fire when ready."

Unlike the three men with me, I'd seen up close what a

gravity shear did. Its use wasn't something I took lightly. The gravity shear pushes immense gravities in one direction and pulls them in another along a plane or series of planes lined up horizontally. Think of it as a comb with teeth that pull down, and spaces between the teeth that pull up. Then imagine a comb that can be set to the width of a spaceship, with teeth that can be set to the thickness of a single molecule, with gravities so immense they can rip matter apart.

Herog started his pass, and our lights dimmed—the gravity shear at full power uses every bit of energy the ship can produce after subtracting out atmosphere, gravity, and shields. From our tucked-away, buffered, locked-down location in the war room, we couldn't hear the gravity shear on our end, but we could hear the sound of what it was doing coming from her ship. The gravity shear can't touch moleibond...but nothing else is immune. The sound of everything inside the ship being ripped apart, molecule from molecule, was a roar from hell.

"The mess when the three of them are ripped apart is going to be horrible, I said. We're going to want to turn info-screens off," I said.

And both Tarko and Herog said, "No we're not."

I knew what was coming. They didn't, but neither of them looked away. Right before the gravity shear destroyed the ship com, we witnessed her death and the deaths of her two associates.

Not even Legend II vampires could come back from that.

And when it was done and we knew that she would not share Legend II vampirism with anyone else, would not murder anyone else, would no longer be the poison in the universe she had been—and not incidentally, would never come after us again—I pulled out of my careful flight path and let what remained of the Colson Five-Back tumble into eternity.

"NOW WE GO GET BLUEJAY," I said. I handed the helm off to Herog, and went over to stand beside Tarko. After he'd witnessed Sky's death, he hadn't said anything. He was sitting there, slumped, frozen, staring at the infoscreen before him that showed remaining ammunition and chute paths to the weapons.

"Tarko?"

He made no reply, gave no indication that he'd heard me.

"Tarko," I said.

"I heard you."

"What is the nature of your relationship with Bluejay," I asked.

"Personal," he snarled.

"This is a situation where I need to know, because it affects the functioning of the ship and what we do next. Were...*are* the two of you lovers?"

"Yes," he said.

"We're going to find her," I told him.

"You can't promise that."

"I can't promise we'll find her alive, though we are durable creatures. She can survive losing limbs, having holes blown through her body, being dumped into vacuum, and from what we can tell, she can keep going for at *least* a week without oxygen."

"If she's alive, why hasn't she contacted me yet? Her suit has com."

Yes. That question had occurred to me, too.

"I can think of a couple of possibilities. First, the com in her shipsuit is nowhere near as durable as she is. It could have been damaged during the attack. Second, she sustained an injury bad enough that, when her body healed itself, put her into starvation mode. Starved and crazy, she won't be able to use her com. The worst case is possible, but I don't think the worst case is the most likely. I think odds strongly favor her being alive."

I took a deep breath to steady myself.

"In light of your relationship with Bluejay," I said, "I'd like to ask you to switch your infoscreen over to scanning, and scan in tandem with Wire. I'll run a third angle of scanning. That way, with the ship pinging for biomatter and the three of us looking for any visual clues, we'll find her faster."

He nodded slightly.

"Herog and Wire and I will take a Medix and blood and go down to get her," I added. "Just in case. We'll let you know when we've verified that everything is all right."

He glanced at me. "Yes," he said.

"We'll find her."

And his massive hands clenched tightly. "Yes. Thank you."

HEROG HAD CRUISED us back to the rapidly widening sphere of debris that marked the remains of the AutoBuild. "Can you figure the trajectory of the blow-out from the port wall, figuring port as facing the dock?"

"Roughly," he said. "Have to do a best-guess on that, then factor in the speed of expulsion and the scatter patterns of the debris, and we want to get her back in and fed and in oxygen again as quickly as we can. But we're done fighting Legends. We have time to find her."

Wire, Tarko, and I did grid searches along each of Herog's explosion paths, looking for anything vaguely human. I had no idea how much of her might be left. No idea what state she'd be in. The silence could mean a lot of things. I kept reminding myself of that while we searched.

I only knew that, at that moment, finding her was the most important thing we could be doing.

"You want to link into the datastream while we do this?" Wire asked at one point. "Follow up on the aftermath of the Legend II distribution?"

"No," I told him. "We took our shot, we made our stand, and either it worked or it didn't. Right now, nothing we hear will tell us if what we did was enough. Nothing will either prove we won, or prove we failed. We don't have anything left to take against the enemy, so all we could do by listening now would be to drive ourselves crazy. Which we'll do soon enough anyway. We fought our best fight. Now we've earned the right to take care of our friend."

Herog glanced over at me. "I'm glad you have your own face back," he said. "Those words belong to you. They fit you. Not *her*."

I glanced at my reflection in the infoscreen, and realized that when I'd healed up, I'd reverted to myself, rather than continuing as Velvet.

Good. I never wanted to be Velvet again.

We trawled an ever-widening cone, searching through a city's worth of debris for the one bit of debris that wasn't. The one that mattered.

We searched in silence for hours, going back to our marked center, crawling forward along Herog's next line, over, and over, and over.

Then we got a faint ping.

Tarko said, "Bio-matter. Reads as normal human body temperature, about the right size to be her—"

Off to port, I caught a minute blip with a core temperature that was still human. I exhaled a breath I hadn't even realized I'd been holding. "I confirm biomatter, core temperature perfect."

I sent out a hail to her to tell her we were coming.

Behind me, I heard Tarko sobbing.

I glanced at Herog. "Relief," he whispered.

We cut speed and angled trajectory so we could line her up with the cargo hatch.

I looked at Herog. "Get us as close as you can, then put us on auto. I'll go down to the hatch, grab a snagger. Wire, can you round up about ten units of fuel? We don't know how much healing she had to do—she might be a bit crazy. Herog, can you get the portable Medix, and then both of you meet me down there.

Tarko said, "I'm coming."

As one, Herog, Wire and I said, "No!"

Tarko said, "I was there when Storm Rat brought her— what was left of her—to Tegosshu. I was the one who helped her find the way back after what the slavers did to her. And she's always been there for me.

"I'm going to be there for her now.

"I'll be the one to bring her in, whether she's dangerous and starving, or crazy with fear that we wouldn't find her, or that we'd leave without her, or if she's dropped back into the mute depression she was when I met her. I'll get her, and I'll bring her back."

Herog waved us off with, "I'll be down as soon as I have us lined up and have momentum killed."

Tarko and Wire got supplies. I dropped down to the

hatch and located a snagger in storage. As tools go, it's pretty simple. Lightweight moleibond shaft that telescopes with the push of a button, with a large sticky pad at the end, and two small snakes, which are cables with robotic heads that will snake around whatever hits the sticky pad and attach to each other behind it.

Wire and Tarko arrived, and we waited until over com we heard Herog say, "I'm putting the ship on auto. I'll be right down. Wait for me."

As soon as Herog got there, we switched our suits to atmo, I told the ship to seal all hatches and depressurize the cargo hold, and Herog took the snagger, and Wire opened the hatch, and all four of us found ourselves face to face with Bluejay.

Only not.

I recoiled.

Tarko made a noise not recognizable as human.

Her suit was intact and had maintained her temperature as it was supposed to. The shaped-pressure helmet had kept the pieces of her head inside its field. But she'd been shot through the head and neck with shredder flanges, and while the nanovirus was still alive and had managed to attach the various pieces of her back together, her brain had been destroyed, and her life had gone irretrievably with it.

She was dead. Unfixably dead.

INTERIM. It's a funny word. It pretends to mean "in the time between."

It actually means "the tiny space in which one tries to remember how to breathe again."

We gave ourselves two Standard days before we

dropped ourselves back into settled space after pulling Tarko on board.

In the interim, we put Bluejay into a Medix so it could repair her remains. Tarko would never escape that first sight of her. But I wanted to be sure that horror wouldn't be his last memory of her.

In the interim, Tarko and Wire and Herog returned to their original forms. I'd been myself since just after the attack, but it was good to have the other monsters transformed into people again.

In the interim, we sat in the dayroom of the *West* and drank synth blood and stared at nothing, while we felt the weight of everything we had done and everything we had tried to do.

In our interim, we waited for some sort of balance. Some sort of truth that would make things right.

After two days, with Tarko still grieving, with the rest of us still raw, the four of us acknowledged that—if settled space still survived—we had to finish the job we'd started, and the longer we took getting back to it, the less success we'd have.

When Tarko asked everyone to come to his quarters, he greeted us with a nod. "Much of what has to be done is on me," he said. "I can work. It will be better than hanging in the middle of nothingness, with nothing but memories to occupy me."

When I'd been in his place, I'd spent a year hunting down and killing vampires, one at a time. I understood the need to *do* something.

Chapter 29

We inserted ourselves into hyperspace once more, and I pushed Badger away once more, and we came out the other end into a low-traffic cluster of worlds that were just opening up on the periphery.

They had lousy traffic monitoring, no militaries to speak of, and a latest-model Spybee with the broadest available spectrum of datastream feeds, placed less than a Standard year earlier by the Federated Alliance of Planets, a new planetary organization with great expectations of expansion.

I settled in with the worms, and started pulling in feeds.

"What are you seeing?" Wire asked.

"A mess, mostly. Across settled space, businesses have shut down because the people who had access to the verification codes and the money to keep them operating are gone. Whole worlds that depended on imports are reporting shipments not coming in, and are experiencing food shortages, riots, panics, hoarding, dictatorships and feudal thuggery springing up. Those places still connected to the datastream are trying to get the word out. A lot of places have gone silent.

"Beyond that, I'm picking up emergency hails from ships where confused humans have come out of what they're describing as trances to find themselves in space, with no memory of how they got there, and no idea how to get home."

"Not a happy position to find yourselves in."

"Could be worse. In the cases I'm checking, they report having a working ship, atmosphere, and plenty of food, and some have heard back from rescue vehicles, and are sitting tight."

"Big question," Herog said, "is what's coming to rescue them. If *we* figure they're AntiLegend-free, so will any vampires who didn't get themselves a little breeder herd before things got messy."

I nodded. "But humans with ships will figure the same thing. I hope. And go out after them armed."

I pulled in more. A lot more.

"Missing persons reports are unbelievable—at least from locations that still have working civil services to file them."

"They're from people searching for Legends who went splat," Wire said.

"Or searching for humans who were abducted by Legends," Herog said.

I'd counted on finding the missing persons reports on the Legends. A lot of Legends were simply going have vanished, leaving blood spatters in places where autobots weren't around to clean up, and no sign they'd ever existed in places where automated clean-up kept the world all shiny.

However, I'd forgotten about the potential large number of innocents who'd been snatched, and who might still be alive out there, and who needed to be found and saved.

I unhooked from the datastream and swiveled around to face my crew.

"Human survivors need to know whether they should be looking for their missing people with rescue supplies or with dart guns," I said. "Or maybe both."

"How many Legends bought Legend II?" Herog asked.

Tarko called up sales figures from shipcom, which had logged a running tally via pingballs from every AutoBuild, while our sale was going on, and during our fight with Sky.

"We had five hundred eighteen billion, two hundred twenty-three million, three hundred twenty-one thousand, six hundred four completed sales. By my best estimates, twenty-one percent of humanity received a dose of Legend II. We know we didn't get all the Legends, but we got most of them."

The silence on deck was stunned. I hadn't heard the numbers before. I had no idea how many had sold, or how many people proved they were Legend I vampires.

Tarko continued. "In spite of AntiLegend, in spite of vampires killing each other off, in spite of everything else we did, we'd already passed the tipping point and Darkout was falling. We had days—maybe less than days—before everything was gone forever."

"Oh, God," Wire whispered.

I had no words. I sat, staring at my hands, shivering on the inside against a reality I couldn't quite fathom.

More than one fifth of everyone had become a Legend.

More than one fifth of everyone was now dead.

And we hadn't even reached them all.

Some were still out there.

Some were still out there.

Some were still out there.

"*Cady!*"

I opened my eyes. I hadn't realized I'd closed them. I stared up at Herog, on his hands and knees over me staring down into my face. I didn't know I'd fallen.

"Are you all right?"

"I felt the pull of them," I said. "I fell into a memory, and suddenly it was real, and I could feel Corrigan and Crane drawing me to them all over again, making me want to let them murder me, making me yearn to feel them drinking me to death. I could see the bodies of tortured, slaughtered humans, stacked like cordwood in cold storage on their ships—decorations the Legends liked to look at. I was back in the middle of the worst of what they were, seeing one out of every five people *everywhere* as a monster...and they all wanted to be even worse, to be bigger, more deadly monsters, to own everyone." I stared up at him, willing him to see what he had never seen, to feel what he had never felt, to know what I had lived so he would understand.

He couldn't. His horrors were not my horrors.

"We stopped them," he said, resting his hand on my hair. "And we stopped their evil. Every single one of them signed on promising to murder others of their own kind in order to be able to enslave our kind." He sighed. "Well, not our kind. But humankind."

Unlike mine, his gut didn't knot when he thought of them. But he still knew what mattered.

And so did I. I needed to take hold of myself and move forward.

I took a deep breath and stood up. "Haven't had one of those in a while. Legend flashbacks are terrible," I said. "But they pass." I rolled my shoulders, shook out my wrists, bounced on the balls of my feet. They were things I'd done as a human, when my muscles tightened, when I was tense, when I'd worked out too hard.

As a Legend, they were meaningless—my muscles never hurt, never tightened, never worked against me. My automatic responses were, in this form, nothing but nervous tics.

"I'm over it. So. We'd intended to leak the database of Legend buyers later, once everything had settled down. But we hadn't anticipated people having to know whether their loved ones were humans in need of help, or nanovampires who were already dead, or who needed to be. So I say we figure out a way to leak all that data now."

Wire said, "That's doable. The sales records have to come from a plausible source, though. We can't just drop them into the stream from nowhere. In order to give them credibility, people have to be able to see a clear path from their origin to their appearance, and they have to understand why the records appeared when they did."

We all looked at each other.

"I hated Galatia Fairing," Herog said after a moment.

"Nasty place," Tarko agreed. "Though it *was* where we first managed to leak the existence of vampires into the public datastreams."

"My second bad encounter with vampires was on Galatia Fairing," I said. "It was when Badger and I discovered they could play with human minds."

Wire was thoughtful. "They had an entrenched vampire culture. We wrecked a lot of it, but the humans there would probably be thrilled to have the opportunity to leak vampire data."

Tarko and I were both shaking our heads at the same time. "You don't understand the place," Tarko told him. "Galatia Fairing lives by its data security. It is the religion of the data-keepers; it is the soul of that world. No matter what you tell them, if you mark it secure, it will stay secure."

"So have Velvet mark it for public distribution," Herog said.

And there it was. The simple solution. The clean solution. And the one that wouldn't harm the human survivors on Galatia Fairing who were trying to rebuild their cities and businesses and lives after shaking off their vampire masters.

Anyone can create a private distance account on Galatia Fairing, and can store any amount of data there. You need to have provable credit. Tarko could tap me into the extravagantly funded Legend II purchase account, which would not even twitch over the storage and public distribution fees. You need to have ID. Tarko, while he was not Storm Rat, had his own skills at ID generation—and Velvet wasn't an identity I had to live with.

You needed to pay upfront for the first year of storage— and again, the money was there to cover that.

Tarko built both credit and ID accounts for Velvet Storm Black and we forged a biometric print. I opened an account on Galatia Fairing. Streamed into my new account the identity, address, biometric print, credit line, and successful payment record for every single dose of Legend II, along with the identity and biometric print of every Legend who had been waiting on hold to speak to us when Youko Skylander blew up the AutoBuild.

I marked the account Public Access, Open and Clear distribution. And on a whim, Send Copies to Following Streams: All Police, All Space Port Authority, All Public Data Distribution, All Current Events Reporting.

In the data itself, I included my Galatia Fairing data storage account information. My Velvet Black passkey, my

Velvet Black biometric print, and just as a "what the hell," a holo of Velvet Black in full velvet-and-silk regalia. And a note.

FELLOW PASSENGERS THROUGH LIFE,

I'm not who they thought I was, I'm not what you think I am, and I figured you could use help cleaning up the mess.

Love, Velvet

IF YOU CAN'T BEAT them, and you can't join them—Badger once said to me—confuse the hell out of them.

THE NANOVAMPIRES WERE AS GONE as we could make them. The havoc of their passing was ripping apart everything that had been good and triumphant about humanity in settled space.

Progress requires freedom, skill, and intent, and in the growing corruption and thuggery engineered by those opportunistic humans who saw a way to gain power for themselves at the expense of others, progress had been thrown into a wall. Warlords grabbed weapons and territories, petty tyrants grabbed women and titles, the rule of law in many places became the rule of the law of the biggest stick.

Where datastream access still existed, or was still permitted, we began hearing the wails from those survivors who complained that at least the vampires had kept settled space running.

"Civilization is falling apart. It's the last problem they can't fix without us," I said.

The four of us were sitting at the captain's table in my quarters. The *West* was orbiting a world inhabited by nothing but starving nanovampires. Swarms of them, millions of them. Had we been even a few days slower, their existence would have been the existence of everyone, everywhere.

"People survive, but not understanding what they survived, vilify freedom and want to be slaves again."

"Screw that," Tarko said. "We can at the very least get the fix started. First, we need to show them what happened to the worlds where Darkout fell. Ignorance helps nothing here.

"Second, we need to give the survivors a stake in civilization. I need to find a way to get the people with skills out from under the people with clubs, put the skilled people in charge of reopening businesses, get people working, get industries back on their feet, put folks back in charge of their own lives. Where people control their own futures, they don't need or want the 'protection' of thugs."

The three of us looked at him. "You know some magic handwave that will get shareholders and banks to allow that to happen?" I asked.

Tarko patted the back of my hand. "Of course, darlin'. It's called asset-secured money, with which you buy from owners and shareholders both failed banks and the failed businesses that were supposed to protect the banks. Right now, I assure you, they will be glad to get anything back from the massive losses they've incurred. And thanks to certain investments I've been making for years, I have a lot of asset-secured money. And will turn as much of the significant payment we received from our recent sale of Legend

II into asset-backed funds, so when you get paid, *your* money will be worth something as well."

For an instant there, he seemed like himself.

So while Wire, Herog, and I ran shifts taking one of the shuttles down to the surface of the planet and operating the blood sprayer Wire had built—and while we recorded and narrated what we saw and did so we could leak the truth of what Darkout looked like to the survivors of settled space— Tarko bought failed banks and their holdings, and bought surviving shareholders out of failed companies.

Then he used the datastream to start recruiting surviving employees of dead businesses and offering them loans at low interest rates to buy their old places of employment and get the companies back on their feet.

He had a simple rule—he would only loan money to individuals who lived in areas with governments that had certified individual rights, and which were observing those rights.

Because the tyrants had not had enough time to establish themselves in previously free territories, people who saw their chance to live like human beings again stepped up and fought the encroaching tyrants to save themselves.

Tarko proved stunningly efficient. Within weeks, Tarko had acquired at least one primary bank on more than a hundred core worlds, and by doing so acquired title to major industries on more than a thousand worlds that had gone back to the banks when the officers of the business had failed to make their code checks. It was a fraction of settled space—but he was fighting to save the biggest and best of what had been. "I've used different IDs," he told me, "different types of backing securities, different terms of purchase. If it looks like one man is buying everything, suddenly nothing is for sale, and nothing gets fixed. If we can just keep some of the infrastructure working, we'll make it possible for the rest to come back over time. And we won't lose civilization, individual freedom, and space itself."

When I thought of one man controlling the majority of banks on large central worlds, the reason people in power were required to take the Kartach Norgan test reoccurred to me. I could understand why people would be wary.

But I didn't know how to fix worlds or economies, so I kept quiet.

He was watching my face though, and I'd clearly given away more than I thought. "It's not like that. I set these new owners up with five-year loans for companies sold at less than one one-hundredth of their base asset value. If the new owners can get them up and running and show a profit in that time, while making all their payments, they'll own these businesses free and clear in five years. If they can't, then they weren't competent enough to be in charge anyway, and the business will revert to me. And I'll find other owners more capable."

Meanwhile, Herog and Wire and I sprayed and recorded and data-leaked, and humans saw Darkout for the first time while still surviving. Most of the wailing about having had a better life under vampire rule ceased.

Not all. But most.

Time passed. Weeks. A month. Worlds are big, and we were trying our best to discover how tough it would be for small teams to rid Darkout worlds of their vampires so humans could return.

We were exhausted. Not physically—I wasn't sure the nanovirus that made us what we were would let us tire physically the way humans did.

But inside...

I'D CALLED THEM TOGETHER. We sat on the bridge, with the panorama of space above us and before us. I said, "We have done our best to put the pieces of settled space back together so that it doesn't need us. We haven't talked about this, but I've watched all of us doing the same thing.

"I have a...proposal...offer...for each of you, but before I make it, I want to be sure that we're now at the point where we can stop doing what we're doing."

I saw raised eyebrows. Tarko said, "You have something better you can suggest as a use for our time?"

I didn't want to lie. "Maybe. But first, are we done?"

Wire said, "The three of us could spray synth-blood on Darkout worlds for the next ten thousand years and not run out of vampires."

"Without food," I said, "They probably won't last that long. But is there any reason for the burden of all the Darkout worlds to rest on us?"

Wire shook his head. "I published my designs for the sprayer into the datastream a month ago. There have been some people who have refitted shuttles and set up services cleaning out satellites, resort moons, and home asteroids. The contraction in population has eliminated outward pressure to colonize, but people will get around to cleaning up the Darkout worlds sooner or later."

I nodded. "Tarko?"

"I set up everything I'm doing under capable managers. Most of them I knew before. Things might not run flawlessly without me, but they'll run."

I looked next to Herog. "There are still slavers," he said. "I am not done—but what I have pledged to do is no longer tied to...that." He flicked a hand in the direction of the planet around which the *West* orbited.

I said, "What I had to offer to humanity has also become unnecessary. So now the question changes. We are inarguably the four most powerful creatures in settled space. We have so far avoided contact with humans wherever possible, by choice and for the protection of the humans. We have kept ourselves apart, have lived on synthetic blood, have confined ourselves to the company of each other.

"But not one of us would choose the life we're living now for the rest of eternity. And yet, as we are now, what do we do with ourselves that does not remake us over time into the monsters we fought so hard to conquer?"

There was a long pause.

I waited, then said, "I've considered this. Endlessly. On Galatia Fairing, I tasted live human blood, and now that taste is in my mind. It calls to me. It is the taste this body was designed to live for, the liquid every cell of my body has been remade to crave. Haskell Corrigan was a brilliant man, and he used his brilliance to create creatures who would revel in the lives they lived. He made human blood a nectar. An elixir. A glorious siren song that now calls to me in my dreams, and leaves me waking up at the end of nightmares in which I have drunk deeply of the humans I have collected to sustain my hunger."

I stood and began to pace, first between my seated allies, and then along the deck's back run. "Through the worst of this, I became what I had to be to save everything that mattered to me. But now the price of what I became begins to come due, and I have no wish to continue as I am."

Herog came to his feet, his body tense. He was, I recognized, barely holding back an attack. "You're not killing yourself, Cady," he said. "That will not happen."

I looked at him and smiled. "You trained me too well, Herog. I found my warpaint, I burned it into my soul, and I am driven to live. I know what I have to live for."

I turned back to pacing, though, and my smile died. "But I cannot be who I need to be and still be this creature who can command with my voice, seduce with my presence, gather to me anyone I want without effort. I cannot be the person I must be if I can have it all simply by reaching out my hand and taking it."

I looked at them. My crew—but not mine. They were their own people, all of them, with futures they had set aside to save the one big future that was humanity.

"I have held power. Have commanded and been obeyed, have felt the thrill of controlling those who did not welcome my control. And you have, too."

They nodded.

"In the end, it comes back to the Kartach Norgan test. To the call of power, to the craving for it, and to whether we, who have power unlike anything anyone has ever known, will be able to walk among those who are no longer like us, and not abuse it."

I looked at them, waiting for one of them to say something.

No one spoke.

"I know myself," I said. "If I try to live among humans like this, sooner or later I will answer the call of blood. I will allow myself to be seduced, will allow myself to collect a handful of people who enjoy my companionship—and if I use what I can do to help them enjoy my companionship a little more than they would have of their own free will, surely that is for their own good—and I will make them my people, and will tell myself that neither they nor I are harmed by what I have done. And that will be a lie, and I will know when I tell it to myself that it is a lie. And that lie will make the next lie easier."

Tarko nodded. "When I decide to sleep for just a while, my dreams run in those lines. So most of the time I decide not to sleep."

Wire shrugged. "I've hungered for real blood. My body tells me I'm not getting everything I need. Or want."

Herog sat. Watching me. He said nothing, but he wasn't angry. Or offended. He was...waiting.

"We have power," I said. "We have immortality—or something close to it. We have become everything humanity has yearned for since first we discovered that we could die. But throughout history, the only people who had power but who did not abuse it have been those who, when they had done what they set out to do, relinquished their power and walked away."

I heard the silence settle around me. All of them, now, watched me pacing. I stopped. I turned to face them.

"Before I accepted the Legend II injection, I had already considered the power I would have and the history of those who had power and used it well, as well as the history of those who had power and abused it. I knew that if I survived, that if I did what I set out to do, this moment would come, when I would face a final test. Would I hold on to power, and allow myself to become the monster I had the potential to be? Or would I be strong enough to set power aside, and walk away from it. I thought if I were trapped inside the body of a nanovampire, I would eventually fail the test. So Wire put me in contact with a tech who was not one of Sky's chosen people, and who was therefore not working on Legend II. I had him secretly build for me a nanoviral switch. In theory, it turns off and eliminates from the body of the user all nanoviral augmentations."

They watched me. They waited.

"There are some problems."

"Of course," Tarko whispered.

"The switch is very limited in scope. It is not designed to undo the changes made by the nanovirus—so in the case of Legend II, it will not correct the anatomical changes made in the user's gastrointestinal system, or in the workings of our nervous systems, or our hearts and lungs. It is entirely possible that injecting the switch will be an instant death sentence.

"Second, it has not been tested. At all. Those upon whom it could have been tested were all out of reach in a locked wing on Tegosshu, and then they were dead."

"We have a whole planet still full of monsters below upon which to test it," Tarko said.

"We'd get to watch them die in new ways. That would be the result of the test. The tech who built it for me was very clear. He said, "If you take this, take it while you're standing above a Medix with your body angled over it so you'll fall inside, because every single function of your body that has been taken over by nanoviral augmentation is likely to stop cold the instant this circulates once through your bloodstream. Even if you land in the Medix instantly, there's a high chance you'll be so dead when you fall in that not even reju will save you. Remember, you can't reju a corpse."

I locked my hands together to keep from fidgeting, and locked my knees to stop myself from bouncing, or pacing, or any of the other things I did when I was too full of energy to stand still.

""We can't take it while already in the Medix, because the Medix will block the nanoviral switch from turning off. The best I've been able to figure is to strip down, open the

Medix door, stand on the edge leaning backward with the door propped against my leg, and drink, swallow, and fall. I've practiced that a few times. I'm pretty good at it, but it does hurt. The only way to find out if the switch works, though, is to try it. And we can't try it one at a time."

Tarko and Wire frowned at me. Tarko said, "Why not?"

Herog spoke. "Because the successful test leaves one human being in the presence of four vampires who are sick and tired of reconsta-blood."

I nodded.

"Oh," Wire said.

"I have thought this through a thousand different ways. Every single one of you has earned life however you choose to live it. You can't create new vampires, so you cannot become a plague like the one we just fought back. I will not attempt to push you to join me—to take the bad leap I'm going to take. However, I will also not allow any of you to talk me out of what I'm going to do.

"So if you want to live as you are now, this ship has two shuttles. I will fly you wherever you want to go, you can take the shuttles and leave, and I will understand. We will say our goodbyes, and you will go to whatever lives you choose to make for yourselves. You will go with my thanks for everything you did to help me. I would have fought alone— but you stood beside me, and it is only because you did this that humanity still exists.

"If you decide on the path that leaves you a Legend, know that you earned the right to live that life. All of settled space would be dead without you.

"If you decide to stay with me and make the attempt to become human again, we will take safeguards to ensure that only those who are human will be able to leave their rooms. And we will leave a message, should all of us die and the ship become our tomb, so that we can at least pass on the truth of who we were, and how we came to die.

"I've had a long time to think about this. I know my choice. I am going to either live human or die human."

I turned my back to them so they would not see the tears I was fighting to blink back.

"Take your time. Consider the consequences, consider destinations you would like, consider the life you want to live. You did something wonderful, and you *deserve* the best that life can give you. Every single one of you. Thank you so much for coming with me. For not leaving me to do this alone."

I turned, and all three of them were right behind me.

"There is no choice to make," Herog said. "I fought to save humanity. I will take any chance I can get to rejoin it."

The other two nodded.

Tarko said, "If we live, I'll make all of us an amazing dinner tomorrow. The best stuff on the ship."

Without a word, Herog went to my reconsta dispenser, and kept his back turned to us. When he came back an instant later, he carried four small glasses filled with synth blood.

He passed around the glasses, then raised his. "I've spent my life without a home, but I knew someday, when I knew what *home* was, I would find it. And now I know. Home is where we find what we most value held in highest regard. Home is our people, not our place. So I drink my last drink as a monster to the men and women who know that power is another form of slavery, and who have the courage to let go of its chains and walk away. To you, the men and women who make being human worthwhile."

AFTERLIGHT

Chapter 30

I woke with something changed.

I ached. I ached in every joint, in every muscle. I breathed in and my lungs burned.

I opened my eyes, and the world was dim and dull and fuzzed.

I stood, and had to fight with everything in me to move against the three gravities to which I'd set my quarters.

I dragged myself against the wall, fought for a deep breath, and turned the gravity down to one.

One. I couldn't remember the last time I'd set the gravity to Old Earth Standard.

Bunch of wimps on Old Earth, and now I felt like one of them.

I showered. It didn't help.

Dressed. Didn't help. I still felt like the universe had run over me wearing spiked shoes.

My stomach hurt.

That understates the issue impossibly. My stomach throbbed and burned like it was on fire, melting down.

I got on com, and said, "Folks, assemble on the bridge as soon as you can get there."

And then I opened the RexSurvyve kit in my quarters, and took out the Emergency Cookie.

Peeled back the wrapper.

And ate the damn thing, one slow, wonderful bite at a time.

Then I cried, but I did it where nobody could see me.

When I was done with my cookie, I dragged my ass to the front of the ship, reset the gravity there for one, and sat backwards on my seat so I'd have something comfortable to prop my arms and head on while I waited.

Nobody was there quickly. Herog was first, and he'd managed a shower and a change of clothes.

Tarko was next, still wearing what he'd fallen into his Medix in.

Wire was last, and looked like what he'd been through reju in had tried to eat him.

I wanted to dance. "We all made it," I said. "We all lived."

Wire said, "I'd like that in writing. And some proof." But he managed a grin.

I made the announcement I'd waited so long to make.

"We're going home."

IT WAS good to see Storm Rat again. Good to eat real food. Good to drink cold water and cherish the taste.

Good to work my lungs and my muscles until they burned.

Good to hurt, and then stop hurting.

Two days after we arrived, we held Bluejay's funeral.

Out of the Medix that had repaired her body—though it could not restore her life—she lay in a transparent molei-bond casket, eyes closed, still and pale. She looked empty— she looked like a stranger. Her friends filed past her casket one by one and slipped a little note into it, or whispered a promise that they would see her on the other side. Almost all of them whispered, "Now you're truly free."

When my turn came, I had no note to leave with her body. I no longer believed in the reflections of hyperspace, the promise of eternity beyond death. I whispered, "I'm sorry," to ears I knew did not hear me from some other, better place, and realized when I spoke, I was speaking those words to myself.

I was sorry. She and I had become friends during our ordeal, had fought an impossible battle, and she had not lived long enough to know that we had won. My life would be less with her gone.

Tarko went last.

He had been crying. His eyes were red, his body hunched.

He stood beside the casket, and lifted her hand, and held it. And he said,

"*YOU HID the truth of who you were*
  Behind a mended frame
  I saw the scars you hid from them
  I knew your secret name
  I had to fight to find the you
  No one else could ever see
  You were beautiful, beautiful,
  Beautiful to me.

. . .

I MADE you laugh at all the world
  But you wouldn't laugh at me
  You had conquered your own pain
  Your courage set me free
  You alone saw what I hid
  And yet you loved me, too
  And I was beautiful, beautiful
  Beautiful to you.

IF I COULD MAKE one change in us
  I'd put away that line
  That we were merely friends, I would
  Declare that you were mine
  I'll never have the chance to know
  How good we two could be...
  But you were wonderful, wonderful,
  Wonderful to me."

I COULDN'T LOOK at Tarko. Tears were streaming from my eyes. I wiped them surreptitiously with the back of one hand.

Nor was I alone. The toughest man I had ever known sat stiff and still beside me, blinking rapidly, with his eyes fixed straight ahead.

I don't think *anyone* had known about the two of them. Had even suspected.

Tarko had known love and had loved someone wonderful, and now he was alone. And I understood.

I STAYED on Tegosshu for a while, finding happiness in the place, and in being human.

Tarko hooked himself up to his financing network again, determined to get as much of settled space back on its feet as he could. Things were bad out there—but they were better because of him. He hurt. I knew how much he hurt. But he was better at it than I was. Reborn human, he spent his time with friends he thought he'd never see again. His home embraced his return, and his people gave him comfort and love.

Wire went back to fixing ships and creating new weapons for Storm Rat's special customers.

Herog led a few slaver raids, then said he was going to take some time away from it.

He kept close to the three of us who'd been together. He didn't say much. He was simply...there. He seemed to be waiting for something.

Tarko had taken a small percentage of the money we'd pulled in from all those Legends buying Legend II, and distributed it to everyone who remained on Tegosshu, and all of us (with somewhat larger shares for the four of us). He called it our "we saved humanity" bonus.

My share, after I paid Tarko for clear title to the *West*, came to forty million rucets. The rucet didn't have the buying power it had before the vampire collapse, but it would get stronger with Tarko backing it.

And me...?

I'd been living in a one-room on Tegosshu, furnished for free by Storm Rat. Wire and his crew were doing finish work on the *West*, hiding all the weapons we'd just thrown in there, giving me a better, well-hidden war room, putting in tougher, cooler-running sublight engines. I'd been invited to stay, to become Tegosshuan.

But I wasn't built to live on the ground. I was born to fly.

And before the *Corrigan's Blood* job, before Badger's death, I'd had a home of my own. The folks there had been the family I chose, and it was time for me to go back. Time to see who had survived. Time to clean up whatever remained.

Time for *me* to go home.

So the day came when I said my goodbyes to Storm Rat and Wire, to the friends I'd made on Tegosshu.

And I went looking for Herog.

HEROG FOUND ME FIRST, as I was rummaging through the RexSurvyve kits on the *West*, gathering up the remaining Emergency Cookies to take back to my quarters. I didn't know if the RexSurvyve company had made it, or if there were ever going to be any more Emergency Cookies.

I had ten. Maybe they were going to have to last me the rest of my life.

He cleared his throat and I looked up from kneeling over the last RexSurvyve kit.

"This is why I quit doing slaver runs," he said. "I knew one of these times, I was going to get back, and you were going to be gone."

"I love Storm Rat's place, and his people," I said. "But this isn't, and can't be, my home. I already have a home, back on Bailey's Irish Station, and the friends and family I made for myself there all still think I'm dead. If any of them made it, anyway. I need to go home now, to see if anyone is left, to mourn my own dead, and to pick up whatever is left of my life and begin to live it again."

Herog was silent for a long time, studying me, still and expressionless. Then he said, "It is who you are, and how you think and act, and how the people you love matter to you, that makes you the living definition of home to me," he said. "I don't know what we are to each other now. I don't know what we could be to each other. I have no experience with how I think of you. But I know I want to keep you close. And I want the time to find out what this means."

I had no words.

I had cookies, though.

Rule Number One of the Emergency Cookie is: Never share your Emergency Cookie, especially if there might never be any more of them.

But right there in the corridor, I pulled the tab and ripped the cover off one that turned out to be Chocolate Goldberry Creme. And split it in half. And handed the bigger half to him.

Because the Amendment to Rule Number One of the Emergency Cookie is: The man who just got you through hell and back...

...Who showed you how to find your warpaint, how to stay alive...

...Who is offering to stay close...

...Who has earned the only absolute trust you've ever given anyone...

He shares your cookie.

Herog took his half, and ate it solemnly. "Good cookie."

Good life.

If you loved this book...

Please leave a review

Like Cady? There's more...

Our Podcast: Alone in a Room with Invisible
People: My daughter Rebecca and I talk
about writing fiction & the fiction we write

Like Cady? There's more...

Settled Space

Hunting the Corrigan's Blood: A Cadence
Drake/ Settled Space Novel

Warpaint: A Cadence Drake/Settled Space
Novel

Like Cady? There's more...

Born From Fire: Tales from the Longview
Episode 1 (Free)

The Selling of Suzee Delight: Tales from the
Longview Episode 2

Like Cady? There's more...

The Philosopher Gambit: Tales from the
Longview Episode 3

Gunslinger Moon: Tales from the Longview
Episode 4

Like Cady? There's more...

Vipers Nest: Tales from the Longview Episode 5

The Owner's Tale: Tales from the Longview
Episode 6 (The Conclusion)

Like Cady? There's more...

The Longview Chronicles: The Complete Longview Saga:
Boxed Set

Some of my Fantasy Novels

Fire in the Mist: Arhel Book 1

Like Cady? There's more...

Bones of the Past: Arhel Book 2

Minerva Wakes

Like Cady? There's more...

Minerva Wakes

Afterword

So. Almost sixteen years ago (as I'm writing this) I finished the final draft of the first book in this series, *Hunting the Corrigan's Blood*, and sent it off to Baen, delighted to have finally received the green light to write science fiction (after years of writing fantasy), and to have another nine stories planned for a universe and character I loved. The book came out, hit a best-seller list (*Locus*), sold through its first printing... and the publisher refused to reprint.

As a result, I didn't get to write the second (or following) books. That story is in the afterword of the first book.

In this book, I'm doing the Dance of Joy over the fact that I now get to write the rest of the series.

In the mammoth gap between February of 1997, and December of 2012, I didn't forget Cady, or that I'd left her hanging in a bad place. **HTCB** was always the first book of an incomplete series to me, and the desire to write the next books never went away. Part of the immense lure of self-publishing was knowing that I'd be able to bring her back, and then keep her in print.

And it was getting Cady and her world back that finally

did make me decide to walk away from commercial publishing to publish myself.

What you have just read is the realization of a dream I never thought would come true. And taking on all the risks of publishing myself became worth it when I finished this book.

Thank you for buying. Thank you for reading.

It won't be fifteen years between this one and the next one.

Onward.

I'm writing each of these as stand-alone novels. I want readers to be able to pick up any one, start there, and then pick up others, also in any order, and never get lost.

I'm using as my model series like Lawrence Block's Matt Scudder books, or the late Robert Parker's Spenser novels.

So this isn't one big story that must be trudged through in order. Every story comes with a complete ending. I'll dangle a few teasers about the next book I'm writing for folks who want to pursue them in the order I write them. Just know that you don't have to.

And onward again.

I always *think* I know how a story is going to end.

I almost always discover that, in fact, I don't.

And the ending to this story took me three attempts to get right, and happened because while I was writing the first draft, while Cady and crew were in the middle of running from the Napoleonese, Herog — who was a mere cipher at the time, and had a completely different and meaningless name — uttered a remark that stopped me cold and made me reevaluate him... and in reevaluating him, also required me to rethink the entire novel.

And then rewrite the entire novel, top to bottom, in my revision.

And I'm glad I did.

Of course, I had to upend the physics of the universe, totally destroy what I'd planned for Book 3, and toss out much of what I had planned for the seven books after that.

So what was the line that upended a universe?

"No problem. You can sleep with me later."

Doesn't seem like something that would stop a world in its track, alter physics, or even make your French fries arrive in a slightly less salty condition, does it?

But that line came out of nowhere, and after I typed it, I stared at my fingers as if they'd been possessed by aliens. It made me laugh. And it was perfect.

It just needed someone who actually mattered to the story to support it.

So what followed was a massive replot.

Followed by a second, smaller replot after my editor read the book and noted that I'd failed to follow through on all the consequences of my whole-book rethink.

And the fallout from that?

Cady gets to go to home to Bailey's Irish station. And she gets to discover a conspiracy that has been destroying human lives for a very, very long time.

The conspiracy is what I'd planned (though for a later book), but how and why she finds it, and what it ends up meaning, is now entirely different.

And I have a tiny teaser to get you started on that on the next page.

Cheerfully,
    Holly Lisle
    December 12, 2012

The Wishbone Conspiracy

A Raw First-Draft Excerpt from
The Next Cadence Drake Novel

Important Note:
*Raw first-draft excerpts are subject to drastic change during
revision...*

The average career expectancy of a Trans-Fold Navigation
(TFN) hyperspace pilot is three hundred point crossings.

Commercial TFN pilots are limited to twenty crossings
per year, are required to prove that they've spent fifty
percent of their down time on R&R, and are compensated
like kings for their fifteen years of service.

Eighty-seven percent of all commercial TFN pilots die
during their three hundredth point crossing, on the flight
they know will be the last one they pilot.

I hate it, but I understand this. Once you've held the
stars in your hand, how could you let yourself be chained to
the ground?

I'm an indie TFN pilot, though, and not only am I not

compensated like kings, but nobody but Herog and I care about how much R&R I get... and I made my three hundredth point crossing, alone and unnoticed, about a year and a half ago, after piloting for fewer than ten years. It was my thirty-eighth of what would end up being something sunward of fifty crossings that year, in what was the second worst year of my life.

But what the commercial guys and I have in common is the experience of the point crossing itself. Like them, every time I went through a point crossing, I felt the pull of hyperspace, felt the lure of the overself and the otherselves, felt the futility seeing every choice I ever made unmade or done differently by other versions of me, so that in the end I believed that nothing I did mattered.

I got past that.

What I'm having a hard time getting past is Badger, who had been my best friend and on again, off again lover, my co-pilot, and my anchor (though not all at once) from the time since I was eight years old. Who was murdered two and a half years ago by my mother. And who now shows up in hyperspace every time I go through an origami point, and tries to get me to let go of myself, to give up, to release my hold on reality for whatever unproven thing lies beyond, and to go with him.

When the dead start holding your hand in hyperspace, you're dancing too close to the abyss.

I have to find a way to make him stop. To set him free.

To set myself free.

About the Author

I'm a commercial novelist who went indie.

Lots of reasons, all good but none easy. In July of 2011 I walked away from commercial publishing to pursue *My Career My Way,* and it's been interesting times ever since.

Now I'm back to writing the *Cadence Drake, Moon & Sun,* and *Longview* series, creating stand-alone fiction, building writing courses, and getting the chance to speak directly to the readers of both my fiction and nonfiction.

If you keep hoping I'll do a particular story, or book, or course, and I haven't yet — let me know.

Cheerfully,
Holly Lisle

P.S. To find out what's coming next, and let me know what you'd love to see next...

Get my email updates and know when there's something new in Settled Space:

https://hollyswritingclasses.com/fiction/settled-space-readers.html

Replies to emails come straight to me. I can't promise to

answer all of them, but I read them all, and answer when I can.

Find me here: HollyLisle.com
And here: HollysWritingClasses.com

Download Your Gifts

For WARPAINT, I updated the Minecraft space ships *Hope's Reward*, *Corrigan's Blood*, and *West*, and added the Bailey's Irish Space Station (still unfinished at the time of this writing because the map is something I use for writing, and I haven't had cause to fill in all the space yet). If you have Minecraft, you can download both maps with one click, along with the help file, and walk around through the latest versions of the various spaceships and space stations, as well as other things I'll add later.

Go to:
    https://hollyswritingclasses.com/free/settled-space-extras.html

Cheerfully,
    Holly

Also by Holly Lisle

Cadence Drake & Settled Space Stories

Hunting the Corrigan's Blood — A Cadence Drake Novel

Warpaint — A Cadence Drake Novel

Born from Fire: Tales from The Longview — Episode 1

The Selling of Suzee Delight: Tales from The Longview — Episode 2

The Philosopher Gambit: Tales from The Longview — Episode 3

Gunslinger Moon: Tales from The Longview — Episode 4

Vipers' Nest: Tales from the Longview — Episode 5

The Owner's Tale: Tales from the Longview — Episode 6

The Longview Chronicles: The Complete Longview Collection

My Other Novels

The Ruby Key: Moon & Sun I

The Silver Door: Moon & Sun II

The Emerald Sun: Moon & Sun III (in progress now)

Talyn: A Novel of Korre

Hawkspar: A Novel of Korre

Midnight Rain (reprinted as By Kate Aeon)

Last Girl Dancing (reprinted as By Kate Aeon)

I See You (reprinted as By Kate Aeon)

My Fiction Singles

Light Through Fog

Rewind

Strange Arrivals: Ten Tiny, Twisty Fantasy Tales

My Fiction in Collections

"*Light Through Fog,*" *The Mammoth Book of Paranormal Romance*

"*4EVR,*" *The Mammoth Book of Ghost Romance*

"*Last Thorsday Night,*" *The Mammoth Book of Time Travel*

"*Knight and the Enemy,*" *The Enchanter Reborn*

"*Armor-ella,*" *Chicks in Chainmail*

"*A Few Good Men,*" *Women at War*

My Nonfiction

Find these at HollysWritingClasses.com

FREE INTRO CLASS: How to Write Flash Fiction that Doesn't Suck

How to Write a Novel

How To Revise Your Novel

How To Write A Series

How To Think Sideways: Career Survival School for Writers

Create A Character Clinic

2019 Acknowledgments

My Terrific Bug Hunters

Rowan Wilson
Travis Nelson
Annette Grantham

Deepest thanks to my bug hunters for this edition, who hit a tight deadline and found a surprising number of remaining bugs.

Bugs being small and tricky, some probably still survive. Those are on me.

My Patreon Patrons

These are both current and former patrons who at any time supported me through my (now closed) Patreon, in top to bottom order from top donors to new folks. These folks have created a space in which I've been able to get back to writing new fiction, and I am grateful to every one.

Thomas Vetter
Julian Adorney
Karin Hernandez
Tuff Gartin
Nancy Nielsen-Brown
Holly Doyne
John Toppins
Cat Gerlach
Chris Muir
Kim Lambert
Rebecca Yeo
Eva Gorup
Rebecca Galardo
Dragonwing
Alexandra Swanson
Amy Fahrer
Ava Fairhall
Bonnie Burns
Charlotte Babb
Christine Embree
Claudia Wickstrom
Dan Allen
Elke Zimoch
Faith Nelson
Francine Seal
Jean Schara
Justin Colucci
madamebadger
Marya Miller
Meagan Smith
Misty DiFrancesco
Moley
Reetta Raitanen

Sarah Brewer
Ken Bristow
Susan Witts
Sylvie Granville
Wednesday McKenna
Amy Padgett
Becky Sasala
Beverly Paty
Brendan Fortune
Carolyn Stein
Dawn Morrison
Heather Wittman
Heiko Ludwig
Jane Lawson
Jennette Marie Powell
Joyce Sully
Juneta Key
Kirsten Bolda
Mary E. Merrell
Maureen Morley
Misti Pyles
Nicola Lane
Patricia Masserman
Paula C Meengs
Tammi Labrecque
Adelaida Saucedo
Doogie Glassford
Greg Miranda
Simon Sawyers
Zeyana Musthafa
Anders Bruce
Eric Bateman
Jess

Kari Wolfe

Nan Sampson

Barbara Lund

Benita Peters

Catherine Ellison

Eugenia George

Vanessa Wells

Jennifer Sakaida

Tim King

Gemma B

Rebecca Wade

Resa Edwards

Angelika Devlyn Erotica Author

Anna Bunce

Cassie Witt

Ernesto Montalve

Glenwood Bretz

Hope Terrell

Kristen Shields

Liza Olmsted

Teresa Horne

KM Nalle

Michelle Miles

Michelle Mulford

Alex G. Zarate

Amy Schaffer

Cathy Peper

Deb Evon

Elaine Milner

Erin O'Kelly

Susan Osthaus

Beverley Spindler

Linda George

Dori-Ann Granger

Hanna Tetens

Kyralae Bredi

Miriam Stark

Chris Langston

Alicia Mayo

Indy Indie

Stacey Anderson

Betty Widerski

Connie Cockrell

Irina Barnay

Kara

Peggy Elam

Stacie Arellano

Ewelina Sparks

Panos

Kathy Draxlbauer

Ruth Sard

Jason Anderson

Donna Mann

Laura Wilson-Anderson

Vorona

Anna K Payne

Felicia Fredlund

Denise M Johnson

Jalane Locke

Keenan Cole

LaShae Dorsey

Lynda Washington

Lizzie Merrill

Susanne

Tammy L Breitweiser

Thea van Diepen

Amber Hansford
C. L. Roth
Jack F Erikson
Keshia-Jade
Mary Wockenfuss
Pat Hauldren
Claire Smith
Jim Guererro
Kathleen Frost
Amelia Rolf
Ken Alger
Catherine Maguire

2012 Acknowledgments

For the book bug hunt against a painfully tight clock, I am deeply grateful to:

Douglas E. Glassford
Allie Vo
Craig York
Lisa P. Thierbach
Terry O'Carroll
Ann Beardsley
Thomas Vetter
Jennifer Wadsworth
Kelly Guerra
Peg Fisher
Marissa Kahn
Troy Larson
Greg Miranda
Maureen G. Tanafon
Deb Gallardo
Margaret Fisk

Those errors that *still* remain are all mine.

FOR HELP IN RENDERING VIOLENCE WELL, thanks to Rory Miller, whose books *FACING VIOLENCE: Preparing for the Unexpected*; *MEDITATIONS ON VIOLENCE: A Comparison of Martial Arts Training & Real World Violence*; and *DRILLS: Training for Sudden Violence* proved essential in both getting inside one character's head, and in figuring out what kind of training the other one needed.

FOR BEING THE VOICE OF REASON that kept me calm and focused when I overran my self-imposed deadline (the *last* of those, by the way), thanks and love and an Emergency Cookie to my amazing husband, Matt, who never loses sight of what actually matters.